FAMILIAR FACES

Best Contemporary
American
Short Stories

Also edited by Pat McNees:
(as Pat McNees Mancini)
and available from Fawcett Books:

CONTEMPORARY LATIN AMERICAN SHORT STORIES

FAMILIAR FACES

Best Contemporary American
Short Stories

Edited by
Pat McNees

Foreword by
Trent Batson

FAWCETT CREST ● NEW YORK

ISBN 0-449-24078-9

Printed in Canada

First Fawcett Crest Edition: August 1979
10   9   8   7   6   5   4   3

Contents

For my brother
Steve McNees
with thanks to
Steve Lopez

Foreword
by Trent Batson

The stories in this collection were selected, quite frankly, to provide a "good read." However, they also give us a picture of American life as only fiction can show it—a bit more structured than a good evening of gossip, more compelling (even distressing) than a sociological essay, but as familiar as the toast crumbs on the breakfast table. Most of the characters are easy to identify with, many of them underdogs who try to make reasonable adjustments to the tangles they get caught in. Taken as a whole, the stories provide a realistic glimpse of the American soul.

Because the stories were selected in this rather subjective manner, it's an unusual collection, more a book to cozy up with than to study. Not that it is out of place in the classroom, but it's perfect for the beach or the bus or the mellow half hour at bedtime. The stories are meant to be read together, not as a literary survey but for the impression they give of American culture, as conceived by some of the most productive and inventive fiction writers in America today.

At the heart of each story is a central conflict, a problem to be overcome or revealed. Remarkably, we are not angered or frustrated by the characters' problems (often society's) but encouraged, gladdened by their inventiveness and resolve in dealing with them. The mother in "The Sky Is Gray" displays the quietly heroic stature of proud mothers in difficult times; the bodega owner in "I Am Not Luis Beech-Nut" maintains wry hope in spite of a clearly

dead-end future. Our heart goes out to these characters
without our feeling unduly manipulated, without the con-
trived catharsis of four-hankie "soaps." The authors needn't
tug at our heartstrings by killing characters off or giving
them rare diseases—these characters face what all of us
face. Their poignancy for us lies in our close identification
with them; we know how they feel, we have all felt like that
at some time in our lives—or it's easy to think we might.
These are *our* stories. We are the familiar faces.

Many of the characters in this collection subscribe to the
tenet that a good sense of humor makes the unfairness of
life bearable, which is part of the reason the stories are such
fun to read. Listen to the self-mockery of the "ugliest
pilgrim" on her way to a faith healer:

> Lord! I am so ugly!
> Maybe the Preacher will claim he can't heal ugliness.
> And I'm going to spread my palms by my ears and show
> him—this is a crippled face! An infirmity! Would he do
> for a kidney or liver what he withholds from a face?

Smiling in the face of adversity (Daniel Boone grinning
down a bear)—there's a strikingly American sense of humor
at work in these stories, which often takes the form of irony
disguising pain. Harry Towns in "Back to Back" goes
through an old address book after his father dies:

> Halfway along, he came to his father's name and
> business number. He really went that time. For a
> period there, he didn't think he was ever going to stop
> [crying]. It was having to make that particular decision.
> What do you do, carry your dead father over into the
> new address book?

In trying to make the best of it, these characters often adopt
the American version of the stiff upper lip: if in doubt,
make a joke. Theirs is not the courage of Hemingway

heroes, but they don't give up, either. The contests they face are contests we all understand. The proportions in this fictional world are familiar proportions. Even Donald Barthelme's Saint Anthony gets mugged. (The *Times Literary Supplement* once noted the American pressure for a literature of extremes: American writers "desperately try to rise above society, as a Priest or Messiah, or stand outside it, as an expatriate or crank, or crouch beneath it, as a mock-criminal or pseudo-Negro.")

Only one story can be accused of having a happy ending in the Hollywood sense of the word, and naturally this one started a lively debate among a group of our friends who got together to talk about the stories: Is this happy ending untrue to life? We had grown up with the concept that happy endings mark the boundary between literary substance and fictional fluff. In the end we included the story because we realized that a) we all loved the ending, and b) our reasons for thinking the story first-rate were at least as good as our reasons for feeling ashamed that we loved it.

For me, it was hard to overcome the prejudice in favor of unhappy endings because my own predilection began at the dawn of my moral consciousness, the time I made the mistake of identifying with the bad guys in a western only to watch in shock as they were killed, one by one, at the end. That was the first time I had thought about good and bad, the first time I had a sense that appearances could be deceiving. After that, I knew that the only fiction that made you think had unhappy or ironic endings; such a long-standing prejudice dies hard.

Most of these stories are good for the kind of informal discussion we had over the story with the happy ending because they tend to combine straightforwardness of narration with a certain interpretive ambiguity of the type that arises so commonly in everyday life. It's easy to get a basic grasp on the stories—you aren't compelled to seek constantly for other levels of meaning—but beyond that simple understanding, questions come up which are easy to talk about because they are not points of literary allusion or interpretation that only the experts can address, but questions of life that we all have experience with. Has the piano player in "A Really Good Jazz Piano" done anything to disappoint the two Americans? Are Saint Anthony's temptations only the conveniences of modern life? How does Flannery O'Connor feel about Mrs. Turpin in "Revelation"? Should Una marry Boris, and is that part of "An Education"? Should the mother in "The Sky Is Gray" accept the food at the end? Should Sister Irene in the story by Oates be friendlier to Weinstein? Questions like these are so engrossing that we often forgot we weren't talking about mutual acquaintances; and in our group, at least, the "literati" had no advantage in the debate.

We have found ourselves puzzling over who the victims are in some of the stories and who the victimizers. We all take a certain pleasure in seeing the tables turned on people who consider themselves superior: the smug Mrs. Turpin gets hers in "Revelation," and the Chimeses in "An Education" also come to an unfortunate pass. But victimization is very much a question of the eye of the beholder. In a couple of stories, children who appear at first to be victims of powerlessness in the end appear better off than their elders. Stories that touch on black-white relationships are often less concerned with who the victims are than with how much communication there can be. (Has there been such a long history of distrust that only a severely truncated relationship is now possible?) At the end of "The Sky Is Gray," the white storekeeper realizes that the slightest suggestion of charity toward the two black characters would seem not kindness but condescension.

The style of the stories is in keeping with their proportions: It is direct, the diction is clean, the characterizations deft. The selection of the stories shows, I think, a real sense of what people will enjoy reading.

FAMILIAR FACES

DORIS BETTS

The Ugliest Pilgrim

I sit in the bus station, nipping chocolate peel off a Mounds candy bar with my teeth, then pasting the coconut filling to the roof of my mouth. The lump will dissolve there slowly and seep into me the way dew seeps into flowers.

I like to separate flavors that way. Always I lick the salt off cracker tops before taking my first bite.

Somebody sees me with my suitcase, paper sack, and a ticket in my lap. "You going someplace, Violet?"

Stupid. People in Spruce Pine are dumb and, since I look dumb, say dumb things to me. I turn up my face as if to count those dead flies piled under the light bulb. He walks away—a fat man, could be anybody. I stick out my tongue at his back; the candy oozes down. If I could stop swallowing, it would drip into my lung and I could breathe vanilla.

Whoever it was, he won't glance back. People in Spruce Pine don't like to look at me, full face.

A Greyhound bus pulls in, blows air; the driver stands by the door. He's black-headed, maybe part Cherokee, with heavy shoulders but a weak chest. He thinks well of himself—I can tell that. I open my notebook and copy his name off the metal plate so I can call him by it when he drives me home again. And next week, won't Mr. Wallace

Weatherman be surprised to see how well I'm looking!

I choose the front seat behind Mr. Weatherman, settle my bag with the hat in it, then open the lined composition book again. Maybe it's half full of writing. Even the empty pages toward the back have one repeated entry, high, printed off Mama's torn catechism: GLORIFY GOD AND ENJOY HIM FOREVER.

I finish Mr. Weatherman off in my book while he's running his motor and getting us onto the highway. His nose is too broad, his dark eyes too skimpy—nothing in his face I want—but the hair is nice. I write that down, "Black hair?" I'd want it to curl, though, and be soft as a baby's.

Two others are on the bus, a nigger soldier and an old woman whose jaw sticks out like a shelf. There grow, on the backs of her hands, more veins than skin. One fat blue vessel, curling from wrist to knuckle, would be good; so on one page I draw a sample hand and let blood wind across it like a river. I write at the bottom: "Praise God, it is started. May 29, 1969," and turn to a new sheet. The paper's lumpy and I flip back to the thick envelope stuck there with adhesive tape. I can't lose that.

We're driving now at the best speed Mr. Weatherman can make on these winding roads. On my side there is nothing out the bus window but granite rock, jagged and wet in patches. The old lady and the nigger can see red rhododendron on the slope of Roan Mountain. I'd like to own a tight dress that flower color, and breasts to go under it. I write in my notebook, very small, the word "breasts," and turn quickly to another page. AND ENJOY HIM FOREVER.

The soldier bends as if to tie his shoes, but instead zips open a canvas bag and sticks both hands inside. When finally he sits back, one hand is clenched around something hard. He catches me watching. He yawns and scratches his ribs, but the right fist sets very lightly on his knee, and when I turn he drinks something out of its cup and throws his head quickly back like a bird or a chicken. You'd think I could smell it, big as my nose is.

Across the aisle the old lady says, "You going far?" She shows me a set of tan, artificial teeth.

"Oklahoma."

"I never been there. I hear the trees give out." She pauses so I can ask politely where she's headed. "I'm going to Nashville," she finally says. "The country-music capital of the world. My son lives there and works in the cellophane plant."

I draw in my notebook a box and two arrows. I crisscross the box.

"He's got three children not old enough to be in school yet."

I sit very still, adding new boxes, drawing baseballs in some, looking busy for fear she might bring out their pictures from her big straw pocketbook. The funny thing is she's looking past my head, though there's nothing out that window but rock wall sliding by. I mumble, "It's hot in here."

Angrily she says, "I had eight children myself."

My pencil flies to get the boxes stacked, eight-deep, in a pyramid. "Hope you have a nice visit."

"It's not a visit. I maybe will move." She is hypnotized by the stone and the furry moss in its cracks. Her eyes used to be green. Maybe, when young, she was red-haired and Irish. If she'll stop talking, I want to think about trying green eyes with that Cherokee hair. Her lids droop; she looks drowsy. "I am right tired of children," she says and lays her head back on the white rag they button on these seats.

Now that her eyes are covered, I can study that face—china white, and worn thin as tissue so light comes between her bones and shines through her whole head. I picture the light going around and around her skull, like water spinning in a jar. If I could wait to be eighty, even my face might grind down and look softer. But I'm ready, in case the Preacher mentions that. Did Elisha make Naaman bear into old age his leprosy? Didn't Jesus heal the withered hand, even on Sunday, without waiting for the work week to start? And put back the ear of Malchus with a touch? As soon as Job had learned enough, did his boils fall away?

Lord, I have learned enough.

The old lady sleeps while we roll downhill and up again; then we turn so my side of the bus looks over the valley and its thickety woods where, as a girl, I pulled armloads of galax, fern, laurel, and hemlock to have some spending money. I spent it for magazines full of women with permanent waves. Behind us, the nigger shuffles a deck of cards and deals to himself by fives. Draw poker—I could beat him. My papa showed me, long winter days and nights snowed in on the mountain. He said poker would teach me arithmetic. It taught me there are four ways to make a royal flush and, with two players, it's an even chance one of them holds a pair on the deal. And when you try to draw from a pair to four of a kind, discard the kicker; it helps your odds.

The soldier deals smoothly, using his left hand only with his thumb on top. Papa was good at that. He looks up and sees my whole face with its scar, but he keeps his eyes level as if he has seen worse things; and his left hand drops cards evenly and in rhythm. Like a turtle, laying eggs.

I close my eyes and the riffle of his deck rests me to the next main stop where I write in my notebook: "Praise God for Johnson City, Tennessee, and all the state to come. I am on my way."

At Kingsport, Mr. Weatherman calls rest stop and I go straight through the terminal to the ladies' toilet and look hard at my face in the mirror. I must remember to start the Preacher on the scar first of all—the only thing about me that's even on both sides.

Lord! I am so ugly!

Maybe the Preacher will claim he can't heal ugliness. And I'm going to spread my palms by my ears and show him—this is a crippled face! An infirmity! Would he do for a kidney or liver what he withholds from a face? The Preacher once stuttered, I read someplace, and God bothered with that. Why not me? When the Preacher labors to heal the sick in his Tulsa auditorium, he asks us at home to lay our fingers on the television screen and pray for God's healing. He puts forth his own ten fingers and we match them, pad to pad, on that glass. I have tried that, Lord, and the Power was too filtered and thinned down for me.

I touch my hand now to this cold mirror glass, and cover all but my pimpled chin, or wide nose, or a single red-brown eye. And nothing's too bad by itself. But when they're put together?

I've seen the Preacher wrap his hot, blessed hands on a club foot and cry out "HEAL!" in his funny way that sounds like the word "Hell" broken into two pieces. Will he not cry out, too, when he sees this poor, clubbed face? I will be to him as Goliath was to David, a need so giant it will drive God to action.

I comb out my pine-needle hair. I think I would like blond curls and Irish eyes, and I want my mouth so large it will never be done with kissing.

The old lady comes in the toilet and catches me pinching my bent face. She jerks back once, looks sad, then pets me with her twiggy hand. "Listen, honey," she says, "I had looks once. It don't amount to much."

I push right past. Good people have nearly turned me against you, Lord. They open their mouths for the milk of human kindness and boiling oil spews out.

So I'm half running through the terminal and into the café, and I take the first stool and call down the counter, "Tuna-fish sandwich," quick. Living in the mountains, I eat fish every chance I get and wonder what the sea is like. Then I see I've sat down by the nigger soldier. I do not want to meet his gaze, since he's a wonder to me, too. We don't have many black men in the mountains. Mostly they live east in Carolina, on the flatland, and pick cotton and tobacco instead of apples. They seem to me like foreigners. He's absently shuffling cards the way some men twiddle thumbs. On the stool beyond him is a paratrooper, white, and they're talking about what a bitch the army is. Being sent to the same camp has made them friends already.

I roll a dill-pickle slice through my mouth—a wheel, a bitter wheel. Then I start on the sandwich and it's chicken by mistake when I've got chickens all over my back yard.

"Don't bother with the beer," says the black one. "I've got better on the bus." They come to some agreement and deal out cards on the counter.

It's just too much for me. I lean over behind the nigger's back and say to the paratrooper, "I wouldn't play with him." Neither one moves. "He's a mechanic." They look at each other, not at me. "It's a way to cheat on the deal."

The paratrooper sways backward on his stool and stares around out of eyes so blue that I want them, right away, and maybe his pale blond hair. I swallow a crusty half-chewed bite. "One-handed grip; the mechanic's grip. It's the middle finger. He can second-deal and bottom-deal. He can buckle the top card with his thumb and peep."

"I be damn," says the paratrooper.

The nigger spins around and bares his teeth at me, but it's half a grin. "Lady, you want to play?"

I slide my dishes back. "I get mad if I'm cheated."

"And mean when you're mad." He laughs a laugh so deep it makes me retaste that bittersweet chocolate off the candy bar. He offers the deck to cut, so I pull out the center and restack it three ways. A little air blows through his upper teeth. "I'm Grady Fliggins and they call me Flick."

The paratrooper reaches a hand down the counter to shake mine. "Monty Harrill. From near to Raleigh."

"And I'm Violet Karl. Spruce Pine. I'd rather play five-card stud."

By the time the bus rolls on, we've moved to its wider back seat playing serious cards with a fifty-cent ante. My money's sparse, but I'm good and the deck is clean. The old lady settles into my front seat, stiffer than plaster. Sometimes she throws back a hurt look.

Monty, the paratrooper, plays soft. But Flick's so good
he doesn't even need to cheat, though I watch him close.
He drops out quick when his cards are bad; he makes me
bid high to see what he's got; and the few times he bluffs,
I'm fooled. He's no talker. Monty, on the other hand, says
often, "Whose play is it?" till I know that's his clue phrase
for a pair. He lifts his cards close to his nose and gets quiet
when planning to bluff. And he'd rather use wild cards but
we won't. Ah, but he's pretty, though!

After we've swapped a little money, mostly the paratrooper's, Flick pours us a drink in some cups he stole in
Kingsport and asks, "Where'd you learn to play?"

I tell him about growing up on a mountain, high, with
Mama dead, and shuffling cards by a kerosene lamp with
my papa. When I passed fifteen, we'd drink together, too.
Applejack or a beer he made from potato peel.

"And where you headed now?" Monty's windburned in a
funny pattern, with pale goggle circles that start high on his
cheeks. Maybe it's something paratroopers wear.

"It's a pilgrimage." They lean back with their drinks.
"I'm going to see this preacher in Tulsa, the one that heals,
and I'm coming home pretty. Isn't that healing?" Their still
faces make me nervous. "I'll even trade if he says. . . . I'll
take somebody else's weak eyes or deaf ears. I could stand
limping a little."

The nigger shakes his black head, snickering.

"I tried to get to Charlotte when he was down there with
his eight-pole canvas cathedral tent that seats nearly fifteen
thousand people, but I didn't have money then. Now
what's so funny?" I think for a minute I am going to have to
take out my notebook, and unglue the envelope and read
them all the Scripture I have looked up on why I should be
healed. Monty looks sad for me, though, and that's worse.
"Let the Lord twist loose my foot or give me a cough, so
long as I'm healed of my looks while I'm still young
enough—" I stop and tip up my plastic cup. Young enough
for you, blue-eyed boy, and your brothers.

"Listen," says Flick in a high voice. "Let me go with you and be there for that swapping." He winks one speckled eye.

"I'll not take black skin, no offense." He's offended, though, and lurches across the moving bus and falls into a far seat. "Well, you as much as said you'd swap it off!" I call. "What's wrong if I don't want it any more than you?"

Monty slides closer. "You're not much to look at," he grants, sweeping me up and down till I nearly glow blue from his eyes. Shaking his head. "And what now? Thirty?"

"Twenty-eight. His drink and his cards, and I hurt Flick's feelings. I didn't mean that." I'm scared, too. Maybe, unlike Job, I haven't learned enough. Who ought to be expert in hurt feelings? Me, that's who.

"And you live by yourself?"

I start to say "No, there's men falling all over each other going in and out my door." He sees my face, don't he? It makes me call, "Flick? I'm sorry." Not one movement. "Yes. By myself." Five years now, since Papa had heart failure and fell off the high back porch and rolled downhill in the gravel till the hobblebushes stopped him. I found him past sunset, cut from the rocks but not much blood showing. And what there was, dark, and already jellied.

Monty looks at me carefully before making up his mind to say, "That preacher's a fake. You ever see a doctor agree to what he's done?"

"Might be." I'm smiling. I tongue out the last liquor in my cup. I've thought of all that, but it may be what I believe is stronger than him faking. That he'll be electrified by my trust, the way a magnet can get charged against its will. He might be a lunatic or a dope fiend, and it still not matter.

Monty says, "Flick, you plan to give us another drink?"

"No." He acts like he's going to sleep.

"I just wouldn't count on that preacher too much." Monty cleans his nails with a matchbook corner and sometimes gives me an uneasy look. "Things are mean and ugly in this world—I mean *act* ugly, do ugly, be ugly."

He's wrong. When I leave my house, I can walk for miles and everything's beautiful. Even the rattlesnakes have grace. I don't mind his worried looks, since I'm writing in my notebook how we met and my winnings—a good sign, to earn money on a trip. I like the way army barbers trim his hair. I wish I could touch it.

"Took one furlough in your mountains. Pretty country. Maybe hard to live in? Makes you feel little." He looks toward Flick and says softer, "Makes you feel like the night sky does. So many stars."

"Some of them big as daisies." It's easy to live in, though. Some mornings a deer and I scare up each other in the brush, and his heart stops, and mine stops. Everything stops till he plunges away. The next pulsebeat nearly knocks you down. "Monty, doesn't your hair get lighter in the summers? That might be a good color hair to ask for in Tulsa. Then I could turn colors like the leaves. Spell your last name for me."

He does, and says I sure am funny. Then he spells Grady Fliggins and I write that, too. He's curious about my book, so I flip through and offer to read him parts. Even with his eyes shut, Flick is listening. I read them about my papa's face, a chunky block face, not much different from the Preacher's square one. After Papa died, I wrote that to slow down how fast I was forgetting him. I tell Monty parts of my lists: that you can get yellow dye out of gopherwood and Noah built his ark from that, and maybe it stained the water. That a cow eating snakeroot might give poison milk. I pass him a pressed maypop flower I'm carrying to Tulsa, because the crown of thorns and the crucifixion nails grow in its center, and each piece of the bloom stands for one of the apostles.

"It's a mollypop vine," says Flick out of one corner of his mouth. "And it makes a green ball that pops when you step on it." He stretches. "Deal you some blackjack?"

For no reason, Monty says, "We oughtn't to let her go."

We play blackjack till supper stop and I write in my book, "Praise God for Knoxville and two new friends." I've not had many friends. At school in the valley, I sat in the back rows, reading, a hand spread on my face. I was smart, too; but if you let that show, you had to stand for the class and present different things.

When the driver cuts out the lights, the soldiers give me a whole seat, and a duffelbag for a pillow. I hear them whispering, first about women, then about me; but after a while I don't hear that anymore.

By the time we hit Nashville, the old lady makes the bus wait while she begs me to stop with her. "Harvey won't mind. He's a good boy." She will not even look at Monty and Flick. "You can wash and change clothes and catch a new bus tomorrow."

"I'm in a hurry. Thank you." I have picked a lot of galax to pay for this trip.

"A girl alone. A girl that maybe feels she's got to prove something?" The skin on her neck shivers. "Some people might take advantage."

Maybe when I ride home under my new face, that will be some risk. I shake my head, and as she gets off she whispers something to Mr. Weatherman about looking after me. It's wasted, though, because a new driver takes his place and he looks nearly as bad as I do—oily-faced and toad-shaped, with eyeballs a dingy color and streaked with blood. He's the flatlands driver, I guess, because he leans back and drops one warty hand on the wheel and we go so fast and steady you can hardly tell it.

Since Flick is the tops in cards and we're tired of that, it's Monty's turn to brag on his motorcycle. He talks all across Tennessee till I think I could ride one by hearsay alone, that my wrist knows by itself how far to roll the throttle in. It's a Norton and he rides it in Scrambles and Enduro events, in his leathers, with spare parts and tools glued all over him with black electrician's tape.

"So this bastard tells me, 'Zip up your jacket because when I run over you I want some traction.' "

Flick is playing solitaire. "You couldn't get me on one of them killing things."

"One day I'm coming through Spruce Pine, flat out, throw Violet up behind me! We're going to lean all the way through them mountains. Sliding the right foot and then sliding the left." Monty lays his head back on the seat beside me, rolls it, watches. "How you like that? Take you through creeks and ditches like you was on a skateboard. You can just holler and hang on."

Lots of women have, I bet.

"The Norton's got the best front forks of anybody. It'll nearly roll up a tree trunk and ride down the other side." He demonstrates on the seat back. I keep writing. These are new things, two-stroke and four-stroke, picking your line on a curve, Milwaukee iron. It will all come back to me in the winters, when I reread these pages.

Flick says he rode on a Harley once. "Turned over and got drug. No more."

They argue about what he should have done instead of turning over. Finally Monty drifts off to sleep, his head leaning at me slowly, so I look down on his crisp, light hair. I pat it as easy as a cat would, and it tickles my palm. I'd almost ask them in Tulsa to make me a man if I could have hair like his, and a beard, and feel so different in so many places.

He slides closer in his sleep. One eyebrow wrinkles against my shoulder. Looking our way, Flick smokes a cigarette, then reads some magazine he keeps rolled in his belt. Monty makes a deep noise against my arm as if, while he slept, his throat had cleared itself. I shift and his whole head is on my shoulder now. Its weight makes me breathe shallow.

I rest my eyes. If I should turn, his hair would barely touch my cheek, the scarred one, like a shoebrush. I do turn and it does. For miles he sleeps that way and I almost sleep. Once, when we take a long curve, he rolls against me, and one of his hands drifts up and then drops in my lap. Just there, where the creases are.

I would not want God's Power to turn me, after all, into a man. His breath is so warm. Everywhere, my skin is singing. Praise God for that.

When I get my first look at the Mississippi River, the pencil goes straight into my pocketbook. How much praise would that take?

"Is the sea like this?"

"Not except they're both water," Flick says. He's not mad anymore. "Tell you what, Vi-oh-LETTE. When Monty picks you up on his cycle" ("sickle," he calls it), "you ride down to the beaches—Cherry Grove, O.D., around there. Where they work the big nets in the fall and drag them up on the sand with trucks at each end, and men to their necks in the surf."

"You do that?"

"I know people that do. And afterward they strip and dress by this big fire on the beach."

And they make chowder while this cold wind is blowing! I know that much, without asking. In a big black pot that sits on that whipping fire. I think they might let me sit with them and stir the pot. It's funny how much, right now, I feel like praising all the good things I've never seen, in places I haven't been.

Everybody has to get off the bus and change in Memphis, and most of them wait a long time. I've taken the long way, coming here; but some of Mama's cousins live in Memphis and might rest me overnight. Monty says they plan to stay the night, too, and break the long trip.

"They know you're coming, Violet?" It's Flick says my name that way, in pieces, carefully: Vi-oh-LETTE. Monty is lazier: Viii-lut. They make me feel like more than one.

"I've never even met these cousins. But soon as I call up and tell them who I am and that I'm here . . ."

"We'll stay some hotel tonight and then ride on. Why don't you come with us?" Monty is carrying my scuffed bag. Flick swings the paper sack. "You know us better than them."

"Kin people," grunts Flick, "can be a bad surprise."

Monty is nodding his head. "Only cousin I had got drunk and drove this tractor over his baby brother. Did it on purpose, too." I see by his face that Monty has made this up, for my sake.

"Your cousins might not even live here anymore. I bet it's been years since you heard from a one."

"We're picking a cheap hotel, in case that's a worry."

I never thought they might have moved. "How cheap?"

When Flick says "Under five," I nod; and my things go right up on their shoulders as I follow them into a Memphis cab. The driver takes for granted I'm Monty's afflicted sister and names a hotel right off. He treats me with pity and good manners.

And the hotel he chooses is cheap, all right, where ratty salesmen with bad territories spend half the night drinking in their rooms. Plastic palm bushes and a worn rug the color of wet cigars. I get Room 210 and they're down the hall in the teens. They stand in my doorway and watch me drop both shoes and walk the bed in bare feet. When Monty opens my window, we can hear some kitchen underneath—a fan, clattering noise, a man's crackly voice singing about the California earthquake.

It scares me, suddenly, to know I can't remember how home sounds. Not one bird call, nor the water over rocks. There's so much you can't save by writing down.

"Smell that grease," says Flick, and shakes his head till his lips flutter. "I'm finding an ice machine. You, Vi-oh-LETTE, come on down in a while."

Monty's got a grin I'll remember if I never write a word.

He waves. "Flick and me going to get drunker than my old cousin and put wild things in your book. Going to draw dirty pictures. You come on down and get drunk enough to laugh."

But after a shower, damp in my clean slip, even this bed like a roll of fence wire feels good, and I fall asleep wondering if that rushing noise is a river wind, and how long I can keep it in my mind.

Monty and Flick edge into my dream. Just their voices first, from way downhill. Somewhere in a Shonny Haw thicket. "Just different," Monty is saying. "That's all. Different. Don't make some big thing out of it." He doesn't sound happy. "Nobody else," he says.

Is that Flick singing? No, because the song goes on while his voice says, "Just so . . ." and then some words I don't catch. "It don't hurt"? Or maybe, "You don't hurt"? I hear them climbing my tangled hill, breaking sticks and knocking the little stones loose. I'm trying to call to them which way the path is, but I can't make noise because the Preacher took my voice and put it in a black bag and carried it to a sick little boy in Iowa.

They find the path, anyway. And now they can see my house and me standing little by the steps. I know how it looks from where they are: the wood rained on till the siding's almost silver; and behind the house a wet-weather waterfall that's cut a stream bed downhill and grown pin cherry and bee balm on both sides. The high rock walls by the waterfall are mossy and slick, but I've scraped one place and hammered a mean-looking gray head that leans out of the hillside and stares down the path at whoever comes. I've been here so long by myself that I talk to it sometimes. Right now I'd say, "Look yonder. We've got company at last!" if my voice wasn't gone.

"You can't go by looks," Flick is saying as they climb. He ought to know. Ahead of them, warblers separate and fly out on two sides. Everything moves out of their path if I could just see it—tree frogs and mosquitoes. Maybe the worms drop deeper just before a footstep falls.

"Without the clothes, it's not a hell of a lot improved," says Monty, and I know suddenly they are inside the house with me, inside my very room, and my room today's in Memphis. "There's one thing, though," Monty says, standing over my bed. "Good looks in a woman is almost like a wall. She can use it to shut you outside. You never know what she's like, that's all." He's wearing a T-shirt and his dog tags jingle. "Most of the time I don't even miss knowing that."

And Flick says, disgusted, "I knew that much in grammar school. You sure are slow. It's not the face you screw." If I opened my eyes, I could see him now, behind Monty. He says, "After a while, you don't even notice faces. I always thought, in a crowd, my mother might not pick Daddy out."

"*My* mother could," says Monty. "He was always the one *started* the fight."

I stretch and open my eyes. It's a plain slip, cotton, that I sewed myself and makes me look too white and skinny as a sapling.

"She's waking up."

When I point, Monty hands me the blouse off the doorknob. Flick says they've carried me a soda pop, plus something to spruce it up. They sit stiffly on two hard chairs till I've buttoned on my skirt. I sip the drink, cold but peppery, and prop on the bed with the pillows. "I dreamed you both came where my house is, on the mountain, and it had rained so the waterfall was working. I felt real proud of that."

After two drinks we go down to the noisy restaurant with that smelly grease. And after that, to a picture show. Monty grins widely when the star comes on the screen. The spit on his teeth shines, even in the dark. Seeing what kind of woman he really likes, black-haired as a gypsy and with a

juicy mouth, I change all my plans. My eyes, too, must turn
up on the ends and when I bend down my breasts must fall
forward and push at each other. When the star does that in
the picture, the cowboy rubs his mustache low in the front
of her neck.

In the darkness, Monty takes my hand and holds it in his
swelling lap. To me it seems funny that my hand, brown
and crusty from hoeing and chopping, is harder than his. I
guess you don't get calluses rolling a motorcycle throttle.
He rubs his thumb up and down my middle finger. Oh, I
would like to ride fast behind him, spraddle-legged, with
my arms wrapped on his belt, and I would lay my face
between his sharp shoulder blades.

That night, when I've slept awhile, I hear something
brushing the rug in the hall. I slip to my door. It's very
dark. I press myself, face first, to the wood. There's breathing on the other side. I feel I get fatter, standing there, that
even my own small breasts might now be made to touch. I
round both shoulders to see. The movement jars the door
and it trembles slightly in its frame.

From the far side, by the hinges, somebody whispers,
"Vi-oh-LETTE?"

Now I stand very still. The wood feels cooler on my skin,
or else I have grown very warm. Oh, I could love anybody!
There is so much of me now, they could line up strangers in
the hall and let me hold each one better than he had ever
been held before!

Slowly I turn the knob, but Flick's breathing is gone. The
corridor's empty. I leave the latch off.

Late in the night, when the noise from the kitchen is
over, he comes into my room. I wake when he bumps on a
chair, swears, then scrabbles at the footboard.

"Viii-lut?"

I slide up in bed. I'm not ready, not now, but he's here. I
spread both arms wide. In the dark he can't tell.

He feels his way onto the bed and he touches my knee

and it changes. Stops being just my old knee, under his fingers. I feel the joint heat up and bubble. I push the sheet down.

He comes onto me, whispering something. I reach up to claim him.

One time he stops. He's surprised, I guess, finding he isn't the first. How can I tell him how bad that was? How long ago? The night when the twelfth grade was over and one of them climbed with me all the way home? And he asked. And I thought, *I'm entitled.* Won him a five-dollar bet. Didn't do nothing for me.

But this time I sing out and Monty says, "Shh," in my ear. And he starts over, slow, and makes me whimper one other time. Then he turns sideways to sleep and I try my face there, laid in the nest on his damp back. I reach out my tongue. He is salty and good.

Now there are two things too big for my notebook but praise God! And for the Mississippi, too!

There is no good reason for me to ride with them all the way to Fort Smith, but since Tulsa is not expecting me, we change my ticket. Monty pays the extra. We ride through the fertile plains. The last of May becomes June and the Arkansas sun is blazing. I am stunned by this heat. At home, night means blankets and even on hot afternoons it may rain and start the waterfall. I lie against my seat for miles without a word.

"What's wrong?" Monty keeps asking; but, under the heat, I am happy. Sleepy with happiness, a lizard on a rock. At every stop Monty's off the bus, bringing me more than I can eat or drink, buying me magazines and gum. I tell him and Flick to play two-handed cards, but mostly Flick lectures him in a low voice about something.

I try to stop thinking of Memphis and think back to Tulsa. I went to the Spruce Pine library to look up Tulsa in their encyclopedia. I thought sure it would tell about the

Preacher, and on what street he'd built his Hope and Glory Building for his soul crusades. Tulsa was listed in the *Americana*, Volume 27, Trance to Venial Sin. I got so tickled with that I forgot to write down the rest.

Now, in the hot sun, clogged up with trances and venial sins, I dream under the drone of their voices. For some reason I remember that old lady back in Nashville, moved in with Harvey and his wife and their three children. I hope she's happy. I picture her on Harvey's back porch, baked in the sun like me, in a rocker. Snapping beans.

I've left my pencil in the hotel and must borrow one from Flick to write in my book. I put in, slowly, "This is the day which the Lord hath made." But, before Monty, what kind of days was He sending me? I cross out the line. I have this wish to praise, instead of Him, the littlest things. Honeybees, and the wet slugs under their rocks. A gnat in some farmer's eye.

I give up and hand Flick his pencil. He slides toward the aisle and whispers, "You wish you'd stayed in your mountains?"

I shake my head and a piece of my no-color hair falls into the sunlight. Maybe it even shines.

He spits on the pencil point and prints something inside a gum wrapper. "Here's my address. You keep it. Never can tell."

So I tear the paper in half and give him back mine. He reads it a long time before tucking it away, but he won't send a letter till I do—I can tell that. Through all this, Monty stares out the window. Arkansas rolls out ahead of us like a rug.

Monty has not asked for my address, nor how far uphill I live from Spruce Pine, though he could ride his motorcycle up to me, strong as its engine is. For a long time he has been sitting quietly, lighting one cigarette off another. This winter, I've got to learn smoking. How to lift my hand up so every eye will follow it to my smooth cheek.

I put Flick's paper in my pocketbook and there, inside,

on a round mirror, my face is waiting in ambush for me. I see the curved scar, neat as ever, swoop from the edge of one nostril in rainbow shape across my cheek, then down toward the ear. For the first time in years, pain boils across my face as it did that day. I close my eyes under that red drowning, and see again Papa's ax head rise off its locust handle and come floating through the air, sideways, like a gliding crow. And it drops down into my face almost daintily, the edge turned just enough to slash loose a flap of skin the way you might slice straight down on the curve of a melon. My papa is yelling, but I am under a red rain and it bears me down. I am lifted and run with through the woodyard and into the barn. Now I am slumped on his chest and the whipped horse is throwing us down the mountainside, and my head is wrapped in something big as a wet quilt. The doctor groans when he winds it off and I faint while he lifts up my flesh like the flap of a pulpy envelope, and sews the white bone out of sight.

Dizzy from the movement of the bus, I snap shut my pocketbook.

Whenever I cry, the first drop quivers there, in the curving scar, and then runs crooked on that track to the ear. I cry straight-down on the other side.

I am glad this bus has a toilet. I go there to cool my eyes with wet paper, and spit up Monty's chocolate and cola.

When I come out, he's standing at the door with his fist up. "You all right, Viii-lut? You worried or something?"

I see he pities me. In my seat again, I plan the speech I will make at Fort Smith and the laugh I will give. "Honey, you're good," I'll say, laughing, "but the others were better." That ought to do it. I am quieter now than Monty is, practicing it in my mind.

It's dark when we hit Fort Smith. Everybody's face looks shadowed and different. Mine better. Monty's strange. We're saying goodbyes very fast. I start my speech twice and he misses it twice.

Then he bends over me and offers his own practiced line

that I see he's worked up all across Arkansas, "I plan to be right here, Violet, in this bus station. On Monday. All day. You get off your bus when it comes through. Hear me, Viii-lut? I'll watch for you?"

No. He won't watch. Nor I come. "My schedule won't take me this road going back. Bye, Flick. Lots of good luck to you both."

"Promise me. Like I'm promising."

"Good luck to you, Vi-oh-LETTE." Flick lets his hand fall on my head and it feels as good as anybody's hand.

Monty shoves money at me and I shove it back. "Promise," he says, his voice furious. He tries to kiss me in the hair and I jerk so hard my nose cracks his chin. We stare, blurry-eyed and hurting. He follows Flick down the aisle, calls back, "I'm coming here Monday. See you then, hear? And you get off this bus!"

"No! I won't!"

He yells it twice more. People are staring. He's out of the bus pounding on the steel wall by my seat. I'm not going to look. The seats fill up with strangers and we ride away, nobody talking to anyone else. My nose where I hit it is going to swell—the Preacher will have to throw that in for free. I look back, but he's gone.

The lights in the bus go out again. Outside they bloom thick by the streets, then thinner, then mostly gone as we pass into the countryside. Even in the dark, I can see Oklahoma's mountains are uglier than mine. Knobs and hills, mostly. The bus drives into rain which covers up everything. At home I like that washing sound. We go deeper into the downpour. Perhaps we are under the Arkansas River, after all. It seems I can feel its great weight move over me.

Before daylight, the rain tapers off and here the ground looks dry, even barren. Cattle graze across long fields. In the wind, wheat fields shiver. I can't eat anything all the way to Tulsa. It makes me homesick to see the land grow

brighter and flatter and balder. That old lady was right—the
trees do give out—and oil towers grow in their place. The
glare's in my eyes. I write in my notebook, "Praise God for
Tulsa; I am nearly there," but it takes a long time to get the
words down.

One day my papa told me how time got slow for him
when Mama died. How one week he waded through the
creek and it was water, and the next week cold molasses.
How he'd lay awake a year between sundown and sunup,
and in the morning I'd be a day older and he'd be three
hundred and sixty-five.

It works the other way, too. In no time at all, we're into
Tulsa without me knowing what we've passed. So many tall
buildings. Everybody's running. They rush into taxis
before I can get one to wait for me long enough to ask the
driver questions. But still I'm speeded to a hotel, and the
elevator yanks me to a room quicker than Elijah rode to
Heaven. The room's not bad. A Gideon Bible. Inside are
lots of dirty words somebody wrote. He must have been
feeling bad.

I bathe and dress, trembling from my own speed, and
pin on the hat which has traveled all the way from Spruce
Pine for this. I feel tired. I go out into the loud streets full of
fast cars. Hot metal everywhere. A taxi roars me across
town to the Preacher's church.

It looks like a big insurance office, though I can tell
where the chapel is by colored glass in the pointed
windows. Carved in an arch over the door are the words
"HOPE OF GLORY BUILDING." Right away, something in me
sinks. All this time I've been hearing it on TV as the Hope
and Glory Building. You wouldn't think one word could
make that much difference.

Inside the door, there's a list of offices and room num-
bers. I don't see the Preacher's name. Clerks send me
down long, tiled halls, past empty air-conditioned offices.
One tells me to go up two flights and ask the fat woman,

and the fat woman sends me down again. I'm carrying my notebook in a dry hand, feeling as brittle as the maypop flower.

At last I wait an hour to see some assistant—very close to the Preacher, I'm told. His waiting room is chilly, the leatherette chairs worn down to the mesh. I try to remember how much TB and cancer have passed through this very room and been jerked out of people the way Jesus tore out a demon and flung him into a herd of swine. I wonder what he felt like to the swine.

After a long time, the young man calls me into his plain office—wood desk, wood chairs. Shelves of booklets and colored folders. On one wall, a colored picture of Jesus with that fairy ring of light around His head. Across from that, one of His praying hands—rougher than Monty's, smoother than mine.

The young man wears glasses with no rims. In this glare, I am reflected on each lens, Vi-oh-LETTE and Viii-lut. On his desk is a box of postcards of the Hope and Glory Building. *Of* Glory. *Of* Glory.

I am afraid.

I feel behind me for the chair.

The man explains that he is presently in charge. The Preacher's speaking in Tallahassee, his show taped weeks ahead. I never thought of it as a show before. He waits.

I reach inside my notebook where, taped shut, is the thick envelope with everything written down. I knew I could never explain things right. When have I ever been able to tell what I really felt? But it's all in there—my name, my need. The words from the Bible which must argue for me. I did not sit there nights since Papa died, counting my money and studying God's Book, for nothing. Playing solitaire, then going back to search the next page and the next. Stepping outside to rest my eyes on His limitless sky, then back to the Book and the paper, building my case.

He starts to read, turns up his glitter-glass to me once to check how I look, then reads again. His chair must be hard, for he squirms in it, crosses his legs. When he has read every page, he lays the stack down, slowly takes off his glasses, folds them shining into a case. He leaves it open on his desk. Mica shines like that, in the rocks.

Then he looks at me, fully. Oh. He is plain. Almost homely. I nearly expected it. Maybe Samuel was born ugly, so who else would take him but God?

"My child," the man begins, though I'm older than he is, "I understand how you feel. And we will most certainly pray for your spirit. . . ."

I shut my eyes against those two flashing faces on his spectacles. "Never mind my spirit." I see he doesn't really understand. I see he will live a long life, and not marry.

"Our Heavenly Father has purpose in all things."

Stubbornly, "Ask Him to set it aside."

"We must all trust His will."

After all these years, isn't it God's turn to trust mine? Could He not risk a little beauty on me? Just when I'm ready to ask, the sober assistant recites, " 'Favor is deceitful and beauty is vain.' That's in Proverbs."

And I cry, " 'The crooked shall be made straight!' Isaiah said that!" He draws back, as if I had brought the Gideon Bible and struck him with its most disfigured pages. "Jesus healed an impediment in speech. See my impediment! Mud on a blind man's eyes was all He needed! Don't you remember?" But he's read all that. Everything I know on my side lies, written out, under his sweaty hand. Lord, don't let me whine. But I whine, "He healed the ten lepers and only one thanked. Well, I'll thank. I promise. All my life."

He clears his long knotty throat and drones like a bee, " 'By the sadness of the countenance the heart is made better.' Ecclesiastes. Seven. Three."

Oh, that's not fair! I skipped those parts, looking for

verses that suited me! And it's wrong, besides.

I get up to leave and he asks will I kneel with him? "Let us pray together for that inner beauty."

No, I will not. I go down that hollow hall and past the echoing rooms. Without his help I find the great auditorium, lit through colored glass, with its cross of white plastic and a pinker Jesus molded onto it. I go straight to the pulpit where the Preacher stands. There is nobody else to plead. I ask Jesus not to listen to everything He hears, but to me only.

Then I tell Him how it feels to be ugly, with nothing to look back at you but a deer or an owl. I read Him my paper, out loud, full of His own words.

"I have been praising you, Lord, but it gets harder every year." Maybe that sounds too strong. I try to ease up my tone before the Amens. Then the chapel is very quiet. For one minute I hear the whir of many wings, but it's only a fan inside an air vent.

I go into the streets of Tulsa, where even the shade from a building is hot. And as I walk to the hotel I'm repeating, over and over, "Praise God for Tulsa in spite of everything."

Maybe I say this aloud, since people are staring. But maybe that's only because they've never seen a girl cry crooked in their streets before.

Monday morning. I have not looked at my face since the pulpit prayer. Who can predict how He might act—with a lightning bolt? Or a melting so slow and tender it could not even be felt?

Now, on the bus, I can touch in my pocketbook the cold mirror glass. Though I cover its surface with prints, I never look down. We ride through the dust and I'm nervous. My pencil is flying: "Be ye therefore perfect as your Heavenly Father is perfect. Praise God for Oklahoma. For Wagoner and Sapulpa and Broken Arrow and every other name on these signs by the road."

Was that the wrong thing to tell Him? My threat that even praise can be withheld? Maybe He's angry. "Praise God for oil towers whether I like them or not." When we pass churches, I copy their names. Praise them all. I want to write, "Bless," but that's *His* job.

We cross the cool Arkansas River. As its damp rises into the bus and touches my face, something wavers there, in the very bottom of each pore; and I clap my rough hands to each cheek. Maybe He's started? How much can He do between here and Fort Smith? If He will?

For I know what will happen. Monty won't come. And I won't stop. That's an end to it.

No, Monty is there. Waiting right now. And I'll go into the bus station on tiptoe and stand behind him. He'll turn, with his blue eyes like lamps. *And he won't know me!* If I'm changed. So I will explain myself to him: how this gypsy hair and this juicy mouth is still Violet Karl. He'll say, "Won't old Flick be surprised?" He'll say, "Where is that place you live? Can I come there?"

But if, while I wait and he turns, he should know me by my old face . . . If he should say my name or show by recognition that my name's rising up now in his eyes like something through water . . . I'll be running by then. To the bus. Straight out that door to the Tennessee bus, saying, "Driver, don't let that man on!" It's a very short stop. We'll be pulling out quick. I don't think he'll follow, anyhow.

I don't even think he will come.

One hundred and thirty-one miles to Fort Smith. I wish I could eat.

I try to think up things to look forward to at home. Maybe the sourwoods are blooming early, and the bees have been laying-by my honey. If it's rained enough, my corn might be in tassel. Wouldn't it be something if God took His own sweet time, and I lived on that slope for years and years, getting prettier all the time? And nobody to know?

It takes nearly years and years to get to Fort Smith. My papa knew things about time. I comb out my hair, not looking once to see what color sheddings are caught in the teeth. There's no need feeling my cheek, since my finger expects that scar. I can feel it on me almost anywhere, by memory. I straighten my skirt and lick my lips till the spit runs out.

And they're waiting. Monty at one door of the terminal and Flick at another.

"Ten minutes," the driver says when the bus is parked, but I wait in my seat till Flick gets restless and walks to the cigarette machine. Then I slip through his entrance door and inside the station. Mirrors shine everywhere. On the vending machines and the weight machines and a full-length one by the phone booth. It's all I can do not to look. I pass the ticket window and there's Monty's back at the other door. My face remembers the shape of it. Seeing him there, how he's made, and the parts of him fitted, makes me forget how I look. And before I can stop, I call out his name.

Right away, turning, he yells to me "*Viii*-lut!"

So I know. I can look, then, in the wide mirror over a jukebox. Tired as I am and unfed, I look worse than I did when I started from home.

He's laughing and talking. "I been waiting here since daylight scared you wouldn't . . ." but by then I've run past the ugly girl in the glass and I race for the bus, for the road, for the mountain.

Behind me, he calls loudly, "Flick!"

I see that one step in my path like a floating dark blade, but I'm faster this time. I twist by him, into the flaming sun and the parking lot. How my breath hurts!

Monty's between me and my bus, but there's time. I circle the cabstand, running hard over the asphalt field, with a pain ticking in my side. He calls me. I plunge through the crowd like a deer through fetterbush. But he's running as hard as he can and he's faster than me. And, oh!

Praise God!

He's catching me!

ANN BEATTIE

Wanda's

When May's mother went to find her father, May was left
with her Aunt Wanda. She wasn't really an aunt; she was a
friend of her mother's who ran a boardinghouse. Wanda
called it a boardinghouse, but she rarely accepted boarders.
There was only one boarder, who had been there six years.
May had stayed there twice before. The first time was when
she was nine, and her mother left to find her father, Ray,
who had gone to the West Coast and had vacationed too
long in Laguna Beach. The second time was when her
mother was hung over and had to have "a little rest," and
she left May there for two days. The first time, she left her
for almost two weeks, and May was so happy when her
mother came back that she cried. "Where did you think
Laguna Beach was?" her mother said. "A hop, skip, and a
jump? Honey, Laguna Beach is practically across the
world."

The only thing interesting about Wanda's is her boarder,
Mrs. Wong. Mrs. Wong once gave May a little octagonal
box full of pastel paper circles that spread out into flowers
when they were dropped in water. Mrs. Wong let her drop
them in her fishbowl. The only fish in the fishbowl is made
of bright-orange plastic and is suspended in the middle of

the bowl by a sinker. There are many brightly colored things in Mrs. Wong's room, and May is allowed to touch all of them. On her door Mrs. Wong has a little heart-shaped piece of paper with "Ms. Wong" printed on it.

Wanda is in the kitchen, talking to May. "Eggs don't have many calories, but if you eat eggs the cholesterol kills you," Wanda says. "If you eat sauerkraut there's not many calories, but there's a lot of sodium, and that's bad for the heart. Tuna fish is full of mercury—what's that going to do to a person? Who can live on chicken? You know enough, there's nothing for you to eat."

Wanda takes a hair clip out of her pants pocket and clips back her bangs. She puts May's lunch in front of her—a bowl of tomato soup and a slice of lemon meringue pie. She puts a glass of milk next to the soup bowl.

"They say that after a certain age milk is no good for you—you might as well drink poison," she says. "Then you read somewhere else that Americans don't have enough milk in their diet. I don't know. You decide what you want to do about your milk, May."

Wanda sits down, lights a cigarette, and drops the match on the floor.

"Your dad really picks swell times to disappear. The hot months come, and men go mad. What do you think your dad's doing in Denver, honey?"

May shrugs, blows on her soup.

"How do you know, huh?" Wanda says. "I ask dumb questions. I'm not used to having kids around." She bends to pick up the match. The tops of her arms are very fat. There are little bumps all over them.

"I got married when I was fifteen," Wanda says. "Your mother got married when she was eighteen—she had three years on me—and what's she do but drive all around the country rounding up your dad? I was twenty-one the second time I got married, and that would have worked out fine if he hadn't died."

Wanda goes to the refrigerator and gets out the lemonade. She swirls the container. "Shaking bruises it," she says, making a joke. She pours some lemonade and tequila into a glass and takes a long drink.

"You think I talk to you too much?" Wanda says. "I listen to myself and it seems like I'm not really conversing with you—like I'm a teacher or something."

May shakes her head sideways.

"Yeah, well, you're polite. You're a nice kid. Don't get married until you're twenty-one. How old are you now?"

"Twelve," May says.

After lunch, May goes to the front porch and sits in the white rocker. She looks at her watch—a present from her father—and sees that one of the hands is straight up, the other straight down, between the Road-Runner's legs. It is twelve-thirty. In four and a half hours she and Wanda will eat again. At Wanda's they eat at nine, twelve, and five. Wanda worries that May isn't getting enough to eat. Actually, she is always full. She never feels like eating. Wanda eats almost constantly. She usually eats bananas and Bit-O-Honey candy bars, which she carries in her shirt pocket. The shirt belonged to her second husband, who drowned. May found out about him a few days ago. At night, Wanda always comes into her bedroom to tuck her in. Wanda calls it tucking in, but actually she only walks around the room and then sits at the foot of the bed and talks. One of the stories she told was about her second husband, Frank. He and Wanda were on vacation, and late at night they sneaked onto a fishing pier. Wanda was looking at the lights of a boat far in the distance when she heard a splash. Frank had jumped into the water. "I'm cooling off!" Frank hollered. They had been drinking, so Wanda just stood there laughing. Then Frank started swimming. He swam out of sight, and Wanda stood there at the end of the pier waiting for him to swim back. Finally she started calling his name. She called him by his full name. "Frank Marshall!" she screamed at the top of her lungs. Wanda is sure that Frank never meant to drown.

They had been very happy at dinner that night. He had bought her brandy after dinner, which he never did, because it was too expensive to drink anything but beer in restaurants.

May thinks that is very sad. She remembers the last time she saw her father. It was when her mother took the caps off her father's film containers and spit into them. He grabbed her mother's arm and pushed her out of the room. "The great artist!" her mother hollered, and her father's face went wild. He has a long, straight nose (May's is snubbed, like her mother's) and long, brown hair that he ties back with a rubber band when he rides his motorcycle. Her father is two years younger than her mother. They met in the park when he took a picture of her. He is a professional photographer.

May picks up the *National Enquirer* and begins to read an article about how Sophia Loren tried to save Richard Burton's marriage. In a picture, Sophia holds Carlo Ponti's hand and beams. Wanda subscribes to the *National Enquirer*. She cries over the stories about crippled children, and prays for them. She answers the ads offering little plants for a dollar. "I always get suckered in," she says. "I know they just die." She talks back to the articles and chastises Richard for ever leaving Liz, and Liz for ever having married Eddie, and Liz for running around with a used-car salesman, and all the doctors who think they have a cure for cancer.

After lunch, Wanda takes a nap and then a shower. Afterward, there is always bath powder all over the bathroom—even on the mirror. Then she drinks two shots of tequila in lemonade, and then she fixes dinner. Mrs. Wong comes back from the library punctually at four o'clock. May looks at Wanda's *National Enquirer*. She turns the page, and Paul Newman is swimming in water full of big chunks of ice.

Mrs. Wong's first name is Maria. Her name is written

neatly on her notebooks. "Imagine having a student living under my roof!" Wanda says. Wanda went to a junior college with May's mother but dropped out after the first semester. Wanda and May's mother have often talked about Mrs. Wong. From them May learned that Mrs. Wong married a Chinese man and then left him, and she has a fifteen-year-old son. On top of that, she is studying to be a social worker. "That ought to give her an opportunity to marry a Negro," May's mother said to Wanda. "The Chinese man wasn't far out enough, I guess."

Mrs. Wong is back early today. As she comes up the sidewalk, she gives May the peace sign. May gives the peace sign, too.

"Your mama didn't write, I take it," Mrs. Wong says. May shrugs.

"I write my son, and my husband rips up the letters," Mrs. Wong says. "At least when she does write you'll get it." Mrs. Wong sits down on the top step and takes off her sandals. She rubs her feet. "Get to the movies?" she asks.

"She always forgets."

"Remind her," Mrs. Wong says. "Honey, if you don't practice by asserting yourself with women, you'll never be able to assert yourself with men."

May wishes that Mrs. Wong were her mother. It would be nice if she could keep her father and have Mrs. Wong for a mother. But all the women he likes are thin and blond and young. That's one of the things her mother complains about. "Do you wish I strung *beads?*" her mother shouted at him once. May sometimes wishes that she could have been there when her parents first met. It was in the park, when her mother was riding a bicycle, and her father waved his arms for her to stop so he could take her picture. Her father has said that her mother was very beautiful that day—that he decided right then to marry her.

"How did you meet your husband?" May asks Mrs. Wong.

"I met him in an elevator."

"Did you go out with him for a long time before you got married?"

"For a year."

"That's a long time. My parents only went out together for two weeks."

"Time doesn't seem to be a factor," Mrs. Wong says with a sigh. She examines a blister on her big toe.

"Wanda says I shouldn't get married until I'm twenty-one."

"You shouldn't."

"I bet I'll never get married. Nobody has ever asked me out."

"They will," Mrs. Wong says. "Or you can ask them.

"Honey," Mrs. Wong says, "I wouldn't ever have a date now if I didn't ask them." She puts her sandals back on.

Wanda opens the screen door. "Would you like to have dinner with us?" she says to Mrs. Wong. "I could put in some extra chicken."

"Yes, I would. That's very nice of you, Mrs. Marshall."

"Chicken fricassee," Wanda says, and closes the door.

The tablecloth in the kitchen is covered with crumbs and cigarette ashes. The cloth is plastic, patterned with golden roosters. In the center is a large plastic hen (salt) and a plastic egg (pepper). The tequila bottle is lined up with the salt and pepper shakers.

At dinner, May watches Wanda serving the chicken. Will she put the spoon in the dish? She is waving the spoon; she looks as if she is conducting. She drops the spoon on the table.

"Ladies first," Wanda says.

Mrs. Wong takes over. She dishes up some chicken and hands the plate to May.

"Well," Wanda says, "here you are happy to be gone from your husband, and here I am miserable because my husband is gone, and May's mother is out chasing down her husband, who wants to run around the country taking pictures of hippies."

Wanda accepts a plate of chicken. She picks up her fork

and puts it in her chicken. "Did I tell you, Mrs. Wong, that my husband drowned?"

"Yes, you did," Mrs. Wong says. "I'm very sorry."

"What would a social worker say if some woman was unhappy because her husband drowned?"

"I really don't know," Mrs. Wong says.

"You might just say, 'Buck up,' or something." Wanda takes a bite of the chicken. "Excuse me, Mrs. Wong," she says with her mouth full. "I want you to enjoy your dinner."

"It's very good," Mrs. Wong says. "Thank you for including me."

"Hell," Wanda says, "we're all on the same sinking ship."

"What are you thinking?" Wanda says to May when she is in bed. "You don't talk much."

"What do I think about what?"

"About your mother off after your father, and all. You don't cry in here at night, do you?"

"No," May says.

Wanda swirls the liquor in her glass. She gets up and goes to the window.

"Hello, coleus," Wanda says. "Should I pinch you back?" She stares at the plant, picks up the glass from the windowsill, and returns to the bed.

"If you were sixteen, you could get a license," Wanda says. "Then when your ma went after your father you could chase after the two of them. A regular caravan."

Wanda lights another cigarette. "What do you know about your friend Mrs. Wong? She's no more talkative than you, which isn't saying much."

"We just talk about things," May says. "She's rooting an avocado she's going to give me. It'll be a tree."

"You talk about avocados? I thought that, being a social worker, she might do you some good."

Wanda drops her match on the floor. "I wish if you had anything you wanted to talk about that you would," she says.

"How come my mother hasn't written? She's been gone a week."

Wanda shrugs. "Ask me something I can answer," she says.

In the middle of the week a letter comes. "Dear May," it says, "I am hot as hell as I write this in a drugstore taking time out to have a Coke. Ray is nowhere to be found, so thank God you've still got me. I guess after another day of this I am going to cash it in and get back to you. Don't feel bad about this. After all, I did all the driving. Ha! Love, Mama."

Sitting on the porch after dinner, May rereads the letter. Her mother's letters are always brief. Her mother has signed "Mama" in big, block-printed letters to fill up the bottom of the page.

Mrs. Wong comes out of the house, prepared for rain. She has on jeans and a yellow rain parka. She is going back to the library to study, she says. She sits on the top step, next to May.

"See?" Mrs. Wong says. "I told you she'd write. My husband would have ripped up the letter."

"Can't you call your son?" May asks.

"He got the number changed."

"Couldn't you go over there?"

"I suppose. It depresses me. Dirty magazines all over the house. His father brings them back for them. Hamburger meat and filth."

"Do you have a picture of him?" May asks.

Mrs. Wong takes out her wallet and removes a photo in a plastic case. There is a picture of a Chinese man sitting on a boat. Next to him is a brown-haired boy, smiling. The Chinese man is also smiling. One of his eyes has been poked out of the picture.

"My husband used to jump rope in the kitchen," Mrs. Wong says. "I'm not kidding you. He said it was to tone his muscles. I'd be cooking breakfast and he'd be jumping and panting. Reverting to infancy."

May laughs.

"Wait till you get married," Mrs. Wong says.

Wanda opens the door and closes it again. She has been avoiding Mrs. Wong since their last discussion, two days ago. When Mrs. Wong was leaving for class, Wanda stood in front of the door and said, "Why go to school? They don't have answers. What's the answer to why my husband drowned himself in the ocean after a good dinner? There aren't any answers. That's what I've got against women's liberation. Nothing personal."

Wanda had been drinking. She held the bottle in one hand and the glass in the other.

"Why do you identify me with the women's movement, Mrs. Marshall?" Mrs. Wong had asked.

"You left a perfectly good husband and son, didn't you?"

"My husband stayed out all night, and my son didn't care if I was there or not."

"He didn't *care*? What's happening to men? They're all turning queer, from the politicians down to the delivery boy. I was ashamed to have the delivery boy in my house today. What's gone wrong?"

Wanda's conversations usually end by her asking a question and then just walking away. That was something that always annoyed May's father. Almost everything about Wanda annoyed him. May wishes she could like Wanda more, but she agrees with her father. Wanda is nice, but she isn't very exciting.

Now Wanda comes out and sits on the porch. She picks up the *National Enquirer*. "Another doctor, another cure," Wanda says, and she sighs.

May is not listening to Wanda. She is watching a black Cadillac with a white top coming up the street. The black Cadillac looks just like the one that belongs to her father's friends Gus and Sugar. There is a woman in the passenger seat. The car comes by slowly, but then speeds up. May sits forward in her rocking chair to look. The woman did not look like Sugar. May sits back.

"Men on the moon, no cure for cancer," Wanda says. "Men on the moon, and they do something to the ground beef now so it won't cook. You saw me put that meat in the pan tonight. It just wouldn't cook, would it?"

They rock in silence. In a few minutes, the car coasts by again. The window is down, and music is playing loudly. The car stops in front of Wanda's. May's father gets out. It's her father, in a pair of shorts. A camera bounces against his chest.

"What the hell is this?" Wanda hollers as May runs toward her father.

"What the hell are you doing here?" Wanda yells again.

May's father is smiling. He has a beer can in one hand, but he hugs May to him, even though he can't pick her up. Looking past his arm, May sees that the woman in the car is Sugar.

"You're not taking her *anywhere*!" Wanda says. "You've got no right to put me in this position."

"Aw, Wanda, you know the world always dumps on you," Ray says. "You know I've got the right to put you in this position."

"You're drunk," Wanda says. "What's going on? Who's that in the car?"

"It's awful, Wanda," Ray says. "Here I am, and I'm drunk, and I'm taking May away."

"Daddy—were you in Colorado?" May says. "Is that where you were?"

"Colorado? I don't have the money to go West, sweetheart. I was out at Gus and Sugar's beach place, except that Gus has split, and Sugar is here with me to pick you up."

"She's not going with you," Wanda says. Wanda looks mean.

"Oh, Wanda, are we going to have a big fight? Am I going to have to grab her and run?"

He grabs May, and before Wanda can move they are at

the car. The music is louder, the door is open, and May is in the car, crushing Sugar.

"Move over, Sugar," Ray says. "Lock the door. Lock the door!"

Sugar slides over behind the wheel. The door slams shut, the windows are rolled up, and as Wanda gets to the car May's father locks the door and makes a face at her.

"Poor Wanda!" he shouts through the glass. "Isn't this awful, Wanda?"

"Let her out! Give her to me!" Wanda shouts.

"Wanda," he says, "I'll give you this." He puckers his lips and blows a kiss, and Sugar, laughing, pulls away.

"Honey," Ray says to May, turning down the radio, "I don't know why I didn't have this idea sooner. I'm really sorry. I was talking to Sugar tonight, and I realized, My God, I can just go and get her. There's nothing Wanda can do."

"What about Mom, though?" May says. "I got a letter, and she's coming back from Colorado. She went to Denver."

"She didn't!"

"She did. She went looking for you."

"But I'm here," Ray says. "I'm here with my Sugar and my May. Honey, we've made our own peanut butter, and we're going to have peanut butter and apple butter, and a beer, too, if you want it, and go walking in the surf. We've got boots—you can have my boots—and at night we can walk through the surf."

May looks at Sugar. Sugar's face is set in a wide smile. Her hair is white. She has dyed her hair white. She is smiling.

Ray hugs May. "I want to know every single thing that's happened," he says.

"I've just been, I've just been sitting around Wanda's."

"I *figured* that's where you were. At first I assumed you were with your mother, but I remembered the other time, and then it hit me that you had to be there. I told Sugar that—didn't I, Sugar?"

Sugar nods. Her hair has blown across her face, almost obscuring her vision. The traffic light in front of them changes from yellow to red, and May falls back against her father as the car speeds up.

Sugar says that she wants to be called by her real name. Her name is Martha Joanna Leigh, but Martha is fine with her. Ray always calls her all three names, or else just Sugar. He loves to tease.

It's a little scary at Sugar's house. For one thing, the seabirds don't always see that the front wall is glass, and sometimes a bird flies right into it. Sugar's two cats creep around the house, and at night they jump onto May's bed or get into fights. May has been here for three days. She and Ray and Sugar swim every day, and at night they play Scrabble or walk on the beach or take a drive. Sugar is a vegetarian. Everything she cooks is called "three"-something. Tonight, they had three-bean loaf; the night before, they had mushrooms with three-green stuffing. Dinner is usually at ten o'clock, which is when May used to go to bed at Wanda's.

Tonight, Ray is playing Gus's zither. It sounds like the music they play in horror movies. Ray has taken a lot of photographs of Sugar, and they are tacked up all over the house—Sugar cooking, Sugar getting out of the shower, Sugar asleep, Sugar waving at the camera, Sugar angry about so many pictures being taken. "And if Gus comes back, loook out," Ray says, strumming the zither.

"What if he does come back?" Sugar says.

"Listen to this," Ray says. "I've written a song that's about something I really feel. John Lennon couldn't have been more honest. Listen, Sugar."

"Martha," Sugar says.

"Coors beer," Ray sings, "there's none here. You have to go West to drink the best—Coooors beeeer."

May and Sugar laugh. May is holding a ball of yarn that Sugar is winding into smaller balls. One of the cats, which is going to have kittens, is licking its paws, with its head against the pillow Sugar is sitting on. Sugar has a box of rags in the kitchen closet. Every day she shows the box to the cat. She has to hold the cat's head straight to make it look at the box. The cat has always had kittens on the rug in the bathroom.

"And tuh-night Johnny's guests are . . ." Ray is imitating Ed McMahon again. All day he has been announcing Johnny Carson, or talking about Johnny's guests. "Ed McMahon," he says, shaking his head. "Out there in Burbank, California, Ed has probably got a refrigerator full of Coors beer, and I've got to make do with Schlitz." Ray runs his fingers across the strings. "The hell with you, Ed. The hell with you." Ray closes the window above his head. "Wasn't there a talking horse named Ed?" He stretches out on the floor and crosses his feet, his arms behind his head. "What do you want to do?" he says.

"I'm fine," Sugar says. "You bored?"

"Yeah. I want Gus to show up and create a little action."

"He just might," Sugar says.

"Old Gus never can get it together. He's visiting his old mama way down in Macon, Georgia. He'll just be a rockin' and a talkin' with his poor old mother, and he won't be home for days and days."

"You're not making any sense, Ray."

"I'm Ed McMahon," Rays says, sitting up. "I'm standing out there with a mike in my hand, looking out on all those faces, and suddenly it looks like they're *sliding down on me.* Help!" Ray jumps up and waves his arms. "And I say to myself, 'Ed, what are you *doing* here, Ed?' "

"Let's go for a walk," Sugar says. "Do you want to take a walk?"

"I want to watch the damned Johnny Carson show. How come you don't have a television?"

Sugar pats the last ball of wool, drops it into the knitting basket. She looks at May. "We didn't have much for dinner. How about some cashew butter on toast, or some guacamole?"

"O.K.," May says. Sugar is very nice to her. It would be nice to have Sugar for a mother.

"Fix me some of that stuff, too," Ray says. He flips through a pile of records and picks one up, carefully removes it, his thumb in the center, another finger on the edge. He puts it on the record player and slowly lowers the needle to Rod Stewart, hoarsely singing "Mandolin Wind." "The way he sings 'No, no,' " Ray says, shaking his head.

In the kitchen, May takes a piece of toast out of the toaster, then takes out the other piece and puts it on her father's plate. Sugar pours each of them a glass of cranberry juice.

"You just love me, don't you, Sugar?" Ray says, and bites into his toast. "Because living with Gus is like living with a mummy—right?"

Sugar shrugs. She is smoking a cigarillo and drinking cranberry juice.

"I'm your Marvin Gardens," Ray says. "I'm your God-damned *Park Place.*"

Sugar exhales, looks at some fixed point on the wall across from her.

"Oh, *metaphor*," Ray says, and cups his hand, as though he can catch something. "Everything is like everything else. Ray is like Gus. Sugar's getting tired of Ray."

"What the hell are you talking about, Ray?" Sugar says.

"Your one cat is like your other cat," Ray says. "All is one. Om, om."

Sugar drains her glass. Sugar and Ray are both smiling. May smiles, to join them, but she doesn't understand them.

Ray begins his James Taylor imitation. "Ev-ery-body, have you hoid, she's gonna buy me a mockin' boid . . ." he sings.

Ray used to sing to May's mother. He called it serenading. He'd sit at the table, waiting for breakfast, singing and keeping the beat with his knife against the table. As May got older, she was a little embarrassed when she had friends over and Ray began serenading. Her father is very energetic; at home. he used to sprawl out on the floor to arm-wrestle with his friends. He told May that he had been a Marine. Later, her mother told her that that wasn't true—he wasn't even in the Army, because he had too many allergies.

"Let's take a walk," Ray says now, hitting the table so hard that the plates shake.

"Get your coat, May," Sugar says. "We're going for a walk."

Sugar puts on a tan poncho with unicorns on the front and stars on the back. May's clothes are at Wanda's, so she wears Sugar's raincoat, tied around her waist with a red Moroccan belt. "We look like we're auditioning for Fellini," Sugar says.

Ray opens the sliding door. The small patio is covered with sand. They walk down two steps to the beach. There's a quarter-moon, and the water is dark. There is a wide expanse of sand between the house and the water. Ray skips down the beach, away from them, becoming a blur in the darkness.

"Your father is in a bad mood because another publisher turned down his book of photographs," Sugar says.

"Oh," May says.

"That raincoat falling off you?" Sugar says, tugging on one shoulder. "You look like some Biblical figure."

It's windy. The wind blows the sand against May's legs. She stops to rub some of it away.

"Ray?" Sugar calls. "Hey, Ray!"

"Where is he?" May asks.

"If he didn't want to walk with us, I don't know why he asked us to come," Sugar says.

They are close to the water now. A light spray blows into May's face.

"Ray!" Sugar calls down the beach.

"Boo!" Ray screams, in back of them. Sugar and May jump. May screams.

"I was crouching. Didn't you see me?" Ray says.

"Very funny," Sugar says.

Ray hoists May onto his shoulders. She doesn't like being up there. He scared her.

"Your legs are as long as flagpoles," Ray says to May. "How old are you now?"

"Twelve."

"Twelve years old. I've been married to your mother for thirteen years."

Some rocks appear in front of them. It is where the private beach ends and the public beach begins. In the daytime they often walk here and sit on the rocks. Ray takes pictures, and Sugar and May jump over the incoming waves or just sit looking at the water. They usually have a good time. Right now, riding on Ray's shoulders, May wants to know how much longer they are going to stay at the beach house. Maybe her mother is already back. If Wanda told her mother about the Cadillac, her mother would know it was Sugar's, wouldn't she? Her mother used to say nasty things about Sugar and Gus. "*College* people," her mother called them. Sugar teaches crafts at a high school; Gus is a piano teacher. At the beach house, Sugar has taught May how to play scales on Gus's piano. It is a huge black piano that takes up almost a whole room. There is a picture on top of a Doberman, with a blue ribbon stuck to the side of the frame. Gus used to raise dogs. Three of them bit him in one month, and he quit.

"Racy you back," Ray says now, lowering May. But she is too tired to race. She and Sugar just keep walking when he runs off. They walk in silence most of the way back.

"Sugar," May says, "do you know how long we're going to be here?"

Sugar slows down. "I really don't know. No. Are you worried that your mother might be back?"

"She ought to be back by now."

Sugar's hair looks like snow in the moonlight. "Go to bed

when we get back and I'll talk to him," Sugar says.

When they get to the house, the light is on, so it's easier to see where they're walking. As Sugar pushes open the sliding door, May sees her father standing in front of Gus in the living room. Gus does not turn around when Sugar says, "Gus. Hello."

Everyone looks at him. "I'm tired as hell," Gus says. "Is there any beer?"

"I'll get you some," Sugar says. Almost in slow motion, she goes to the refrigerator.

Gus has been looking at Ray's pictures of Sugar, and suddenly he snatches one off the wall. "On my *wall*?" Gus says. "Who did that? Who hung them up?"

"Ray," Sugar says. She hands him the can of beer.

"Ray," Gus repeats. He shakes his head. He shakes the beer in the can lightly but doesn't drink it.

"May," Sugar says, "why don't you go upstairs and get ready for bed?"

"Go upstairs," Gus says. Gus's face is red, and he looks tired and wild.

May runs up the stairs and then sits down there and listens. No one is talking. Then she hears Gus say, "Do you intend to spend the night, Ray? Turn this into a little social occasion?"

"I would like to stay for a while to—" Ray begins.

Gus says something, but his voice is so low and angry that May can't make out the words.

Silence again.

"Gus—" Ray begins again.

"*What?*" Gus shouts. "What have you got to say to me, Ray? You don't have a damned thing to say to me. Will you get out of here now?"

Footsteps. May looks down and sees her father walk past the stairs. He does not look up. He did not see her. He has gone out the door, leaving her. In a minute she hears his motorcycle start and the noise the tires make riding through gravel. May runs downstairs to Sugar, who is picking up the pictures Gus has ripped off the walls.

"I'm going to take you home, May," Sugar says.

"I'm coming with you," Gus says. "If I let you go, you'll go after Ray."

"That's ridiculous," Sugar says.

"I'm going with you," Gus says.

"Let's go, then," Sugar says. May is the first one to the door.

Gus is barefoot. He stares at Sugar and walks as if he is drunk. He is still holding the can of beer.

Sugar gets into the driver's seat of the Cadillac. The key is in the ignition. She starts the car and then puts her head against the wheel and begins to cry.

"Get moving, will you?" Gus says. "Or move over." Gus gets out and walks around the car. "I knew you were going crazy when you dyed your hair," Gus says. "Shove over, will you?"

Sugar moves over. May is in the back seat, in one corner.

"For God's sake, stop crying," Gus says. "What am I doing to you?"

Gus drives slowly, then very fast. The radio is on, in a faint mumble. For half an hour they ride in silence, except for the sounds of the radio and Sugar blowing her nose.

"Your father's O.K.," Sugar says at last. "He was just upset, you know."

In the back seat, May nods, but Sugar does not see it.

At last the car slows, and May sits up and sees they are in the block where she lives. Ray's motorcycle is not in the driveway. All the lights are out in the house.

"It's empty," Sugar says. "Or else she's asleep in there. Do you want to knock on the door, May?"

"What do you mean, it's empty?" Gus says.

"She's in Colorado," Sugar says. "I thought she might be back."

May begins to cry. She tries to get out of the car, but she can't work the door handle.

"Come on," Gus says to her. "Come on, now. We can go back. I don't believe this."

May's legs are still sandy, and they itch. She rubs them, crying.

"You can take her back to Wanda's," Sugar says. "Is that O.K., May?"

"Wanda? Who's that?"

"Her mother's friend. It's not far from here. I'll show you."

"What am I even doing talking to you?" Gus says.

The radio drones. In another ten minutes they are at Wanda's.

"I suppose nobody's here, either," Gus says, looking at the dark house. He leans back and opens the door for May, who runs up the walk. "Please be here, Wanda," she whispers. She runs up to the door and knocks. No one answers. She knocks harder, and a light goes on in the hall. "Who is it?" Wanda calls.

"May," May says.

"May!" Wanda hollers. She fumbles with the door. The door opens, May hears the tires as Gus pulls the car away. She stands there in Sugar's raincoat, with the red belt hanging down the front.

"What did they do to you? What did they do?" Wanda says. Her eyes are swollen from sleep. Her hair has been clipped into rows of neat pin curls.

"You didn't even try to find me," May says.

"I called the house every hour!" Wanda says. "I called the police, and they wouldn't do anything—he was your father. I did too try to find you. Look, there's a letter from your mother. Tell me if you're all right. Your father is crazy. He'll never get you again after this, I know that. Are you all right, May? Talk to me." Wanda turns on the hall lamp. "Are you all right? You saw how he got you in the car. What could I do? The police told me there was nothing else I could do. Do you want your mother's letter? What have you got on?"

May takes the letter from Wanda and turns her back. She opens the envelope and reads: "Dear May, A last letter before I drive home. I looked up some friends of your father's here, and they asked me to stay for a couple of days to unwind, so here I am. At first I thought he might be in the closet—jump out at me for a joke! Tell Wanda that I've lost five pounds. Sweated it away, I guess. I've been thinking, honey, and when I come home I want us to get a dog. I think you should have a dog. There are some that hardly shed at all, and maybe some that just plain don't. It would be good to get a medium-size dog—maybe a terrier, or something like that. I meant to get you a dog years ago, but now I've been thinking that I should still do it. When I get back, first thing we'll go and get you a dog. Love, Mama."

It is the longest letter May has ever gotten from her mother. She stands in Wanda's hallway, amazed.

BRUCE JAY FRIEDMAN

Back to Back

"The thing I like about Harry Towns is that everything astonishes him."

An Italian writer friend he loved very much had been overheard making that remark and as far as Harry Towns was concerned it was the most attractive thing anyone had ever said about him. He wasn't sure it suited him exactly. Maybe it applied to the old him. But it did tickle him—the idea of a fellow past forty going around being astonished all the time. On occasion, he would use this description in conversation with friends. It did not slide neatly into the flow of talk. He had to shove it in, but he did, because he liked it so much. "Astonished" was probably too strong a word, but in truth, hardly a day passed that some turn of events did not catch him a little off guard. In football terms, it was called getting hit from the blind side. For example, one night, out of the blue, a girl he thought he knew pretty intimately came up with an extra marriage; she was clearly on record as having had one under her belt, but somehow the early union had slipped her mind. And for good measure, there was an eight-year-old kid in the picture, too, one who was stowed away somewhere in Maine with her first husband's parents. On another occasion, a long-time

friend of Towns's showed up unannounced at his apartment
with a twin brother, thin, pale, with a little less hair than
Towns's buddy, and a vague hint of mental institutions
around the eyes; but he was a twin brother, no question
about it. So out of nowhere, after ten years, there was not
one but two Vinnys and Harry Towns was supposed to
absorb the extra one and go about his business. Which he
did, except that he had to be thrown a little off stride. It was
that kind of thing. Little shockers, almost on a daily basis.

Late one night, the slender Eurasian woman who ran his
favorite bar turned to the "gypsies," an absolute rock-bottom
handful of stalwarts who closed the place regularly at four in
the morning (and after eight years of working a "straight"
job, nine-to-five, how he loved being one of them) and
suddenly, erratically, screamed out, "You're all shits,"
flinging her cash register through the window. What kind
of behavior was that? She was famed for handling difficult
situations with subtlety and finesse. Towns tried to grab on
to some gross piece of behavior that might have brought on
this outburst—the only one of which she had been guilty in
anyone's memory. All he could come up with was that one
of them had slumped over and fallen asleep with his head
on the table. A film dubber had done that, halfway through
his dinner. Is that why they were all shits? What's so shitty
about that?

If you walked the streets of the city, there was plenty to
be astonished about. He supposed that was true if you lived
in Taos, New Mexico, but he wasn't convinced of it. One
day Towns saw an elderly and distinguished-looking man
with homburg and cane hobble off briskly in pursuit of a
lovely young girl. She was about twenty feet ahead of him
and kept taking terrified looks over her shoulder at him.
About that brisk hobbling. It's a tough one to pull off, but
that's exactly what he was doing. She was stumbling along,
not handling her high heels too well. Even though she was
more or less running and he was doing his hobbling motion,
the gap between them wasn't getting any wider. It was a

crowded sunny lunchtime with plenty of secretaries floating around. Towns seemed to be the only one on the street
who was aware of this rope of urgency between the man
and the girl; he caught onto it, falling in step with them.
The girl twirled through traffic, caught her heel in a manhole cover, and fell, long legs gaping, flowered skirt above
her hips, black magnificent cunt screaming at the sky. The
man stopped, leaning on his cane, as though he did not
want to press his advantage. Towns stopped, too. She
seemed to take an awfully long time getting herself together. Not that there was any studied sensuality to her behavior. The confusion appeared to come out of those early
terrified looks over her shoulder. The girl was striking and
even aristocratic-looking, that movie kind of Via Veneto
aristocracy. Dominique Sanda, if you insist. But there was a
young-colt brand of clumsiness in the picture, too. She
started to run again and the man in the homburg resumed
his inevitable pursuit of her. The girl went through the
revolving door of a department store and, after a few beats,
the man followed her. That's when Towns decided to call it
a day. He could not testify to his source of information, but
he would have laid four to one they were going to wind up
in the lingerie department. They would get there by escala-
tor. What was Towns going to do up there with them? What
was he going to see? The manhole tableau was a tough act
to follow, so he decided to take it for what it was, a perfect
little erotic cameo that might just as well have been staged
for his benefit. It was a gift. He owned it and could play it
back any time he wanted to.

Now maybe events like that were a dime a dozen in Taos,
New Mexico. He doubted it. On the other hand, he had
never been there so he couldn't say.

If there were small daily shockers in his life, the broad
lines of Harry Towns's life had been clean and predictable.
He had a good strong body and a feeling that it was not
going to let him down. Thus far, knock wood, it hadn't. He

had always sensed that he would have a son and they would have baseball catches in a back yard somewhere. He had the son and they had plenty of catches. About ten years' worth. After a shaky start, he realized he had the knack of making money, not the kind that got you seaside palaces, but enough to keep everyone comfortable. Which he did. Early on in his marriage, he saw a separation coming; he wasn't sure when, but it was coming all right, and it came. He had read somewhere that when it came to the major decisions in life, all you had to do was listen to the deep currents that ran inside yourself, and they would tell you which way to go. He listened to his and they told him to get going. His wife must have been tuned in to some currents of her own. So they split up and there wasn't much commotion to it. He gave them both a slightly above-average grade on the way they had handled it. After all, take a look at the reason they had gotten married. It dated back to a time when, if you slept with a girl, it meant you had somehow "damaged" her and were obligated to snap her up for a lifetime. He had never told that to anyone, including his wife, but under oath, he would have to identify that as the reason he had gone down the aisle with her. (And it was some sleeping. Exactly twice, in a Plymouth, or at least half in and half out of one, with a door open. During the second session, her father had run outside in a bathrobe and caught them at it. His way of handling his daughter's getting laid was to put his hands on his hips, stick out his jaw and say, "I see that position is everything in life.") Towns had to be fair. There was at least one other reason he had gotten married. She was pretty. She'd had a screen test. The first time he spotted her, it almost tore his head off. He wasn't sure *what* he was, and at the time he'd felt it was a little on the miraculous side that he'd been able to get such an attractive girl interested in him. So he felt he had better marry her, because there was no telling what was coming. It might be his last shot at a pretty girl. That had all been a long time ago. He liked cocaine now—let's face it, he had a

modest habit going. On occasion, he had slept with two
girls at a time and he had gotten to the point where he
didn't think it was anything to raise the flag about. The first
time, it was really something, but after that, it was just a
matter of having an extra girl in there with you. Even if you
had twelve to work with, all you could really concentrate on
was one.

In any case, there had been some significant detours
along the way, but you couldn't say, overall, that there had
been any wild outrageous swerves to his life. Only when it
came to his father did he get handed a script that was
entirely different from the one he had had in mind.

For forty years, Towns's mother and father had lived in a
once-pleasant section of the city that, to use the polite
phrase, had "gone down." To get impolite about it, it meant
that the Spanish and black people had moved in and the
aging Jews, their sons and daughters long gone, had slipped
off to "safer" sections of the city. Whether any of this was
good or bad, and no matter how you sliced it, it was now a
place where old people got hit over the head after dark.
Young people did, too, but especially old people. Harry
Towns's father had plenty of bounce to his walk and had
been taking the subway to work for sixty years. Towns was
fond of saying that his father was "seventy-five, going on
fifty"; yet technically speaking, his parents were in the old
department and he didn't want to get a call one day saying
they had been hit over the head. Clearly, he wanted to get
them out of there. It was just that he was a little slow in
getting around to doing something about it. He sent them
on a couple of minor-league vacations to Puerto Rico. He
took them to at least one terrific restaurant a week and he
phoned them all the time, partly to make sure they hadn't
gotten killed. The one thing he didn't do was rent an
apartment for them, get it furnished, lay out a year's rent or
so, take them down to it, and say, "Here. Now you have to
move in. And the only possible reason to go back to the old
place is to get your clothes. And you don't even have to do

that." He was in some heavy tax trouble and he was not exactly setting the world on fire in the money department, but he could have pulled it off. How about the cocaine he bought? A year's worth of it—right there—could have handled six months' rent for a terrific one-bedroom apartment on lower Park Avenue. Which is what his father, in particular, had his eye on. From that location, he would be able to take one of his bouncy walks right over to work and bid a fond farewell to the subway. But Towns didn't do any of this for his folks and it was a failure he was going to have to carry on his back for a long time.

One day, Towns's mother received a death sentence and it all became academic. She wasn't budging and forget about a tour of the Continent before she went under. Maybe Towns would take one when he got *his* verdict; she just wanted to sit in a chair in her own apartment and be left alone. It was going to be one of those slow wasting jobs. She would handle it all by herself and give the signal when it was time to go to the hospital and get it over with. As she got weaker—and with this disease, ironically, you became physically bigger—Towns's father got more snap to him. It wasn't one of those arrangements in which you could say, metaphorically, that her strength was flowing into him. Or that he was stealing it from her. It's just that he had never handled things better. He had probably never handled things at all. It got into areas like holding her hand a lot even in the very late stages when she had turned into some kind of sea monster and the hands had become great dried-out claws. (He had seen something like what she resembled at California's Marineland, an ancient seal that could hardly move. It wasn't even much of an attraction for people; it just sat there, scaled and ancient, and about all you could say about it was that it was alive.) When they took her false teeth out so she wouldn't be able to swallow them, it gave her mouth a broken-fencepost look, with a tooth here and a tooth there, but Towns's father kissed her snaggled lips as though she were a fresh young girl on her way to a dance. He just didn't see any monster lying there. Harry Towns did, but his father didn't. When he was a boy, Towns remembered his father wearing pullovers all the time. He had been a little chilly all his life. The hospital released Towns's mother for a short time. The radiation made her yearn for cold air, so Towns's dad laid there next to her all night with great blasts of bedroom air-conditioning showering out on the two of them. He offered her the soothing cold while his own bones froze. Towns didn't know it at the time, but he was going to remember all of this as being quite beautiful. Real romance, not your movie bullshit. And it hadn't been that kind of marriage. For forty-five years, they had cut each other to ribbons; they had done everything but fight a duel with pistols. Yet he led her gently into death, courtly, loving, never letting go of her hand, in some kind of old-fashioned way that Towns didn't recognize as going on anymore. Maybe it had gone on in the Gay Nineties or some early time like that.

And Towns's father kept getting bouncier. That was the only flaw in the setup. He probably should have been getting wan and gray, but he got all this extra bounce instead. He couldn't help it. That's just the way he got. The only time he ever left Towns's mother was to go down to work. He would bounce off in the morning looking nattier than ever. He was the only fellow in the world Towns thought of as being natty. Maybe George Raft was another one. Towns remembered a time his father had been on an air-raid-warden softball team and gone after a fly ball in center field. He slipped, fell on his back, got to his feet with his ass all covered with mud—but damned if he didn't look as natty as ever. In fact, there was only one unnatty thing Towns could remember his father ever doing. It was when he took his son to swimming pools and they both got undressed in public locker rooms and his father tucked his undershirt between his legs so Towns couldn't see his cock. The maneuver was probably designed to damp down the sexiness of the moment, but actually it worked the other way, the tucked-in undershirt looking weirdly feminine on a hairy-chested guy and probably turning Towns on a little. His father definitely did not look natty during those moments.

It was a shame the old man (an expression that never quite fit) had to leave Towns's sick mother to go down to work. There was a Spanish record shop across the street that played Latin rhythm tunes full blast all day long and into the night. There was no way to get it across to the owners that a woman was dying of cancer about fifty feet away and two stories up and could they please keep the volume down a little. In their view, they were probably livening up the neighborhood a bit, giving it a badly needed shot in the arm. Possibly, on their native island, they kept the music up all the time, even during cancer. On two separate occasions, the apartment was robbed, once when his mother had dozed off. The second time, she sat there and watched them come in through the fire-escape window. They took the television set and a radio. The way Towns got the story, she merely waved a weary sea claw at them as if to say, "Take anything you want. I've got cancer." Oddly enough, they never got to Towns's father's strongbox which was in a bedroom bureau drawer and not that difficult to find if you were in the least bit industrious. All his life, Towns had wondered about the secrets that were in there; and also how much his father made a week. The news of the robberies just rolled off the shoulders of Towns's dad. It didn't take a bit of the bounce out of him. He comforted Towns's mother with a hug and then zipped inside to cook something she could get down.

A cynical interpretation of all this snap and bounciness might have been that Towns's dad was looking ahead. Towns was fond of saying his father had never been sick a day in his life. Actually, it wasn't quite true. He had had to spend a year strapped to a bench for his back and Towns remembered a long period in which his dad was involved with diathermy treatments. They didn't sound too serious,

but Towns was delighted when his father could say good-
bye to them. That was about the extent of it. He had every
one of his teeth and a smile that could mow down entire
crowds. Towns's dentist would stick an elbow in his ribs
and say, "How come you don't have teeth like your dad's?"
Tack on all that nattiness and bounce and you had a pretty
attractive guy on your hands. Maybe he was just giving the
old lady a handsome sendoff so he could ease his conscience
and clear the decks for a terrific second-time-around. Was
it possible he had someone picked out already? For years,
Towns's mother had been worried about a certain buyer
who had been with the firm for years and "worked close"
with Towns's dad. Except that Towns didn't buy any of this.
There were certain kinds of behavior you couldn't fake. You
couldn't hold that claw for hours and kiss that broken
mouth if you were looking ahead. You could do other
things, but you couldn't do those two. At least he didn't
think so. Besides, Towns was doing a bit of looking ahead
on his dad's behalf. He had put himself in charge of that
department. And that's about all he was in charge of. He
was almost doing a great many things. He almost went
down to the Spanish record shop and told them that they
had better lower the music or he would break every record
over their fucking heads. After the second robbery, he
called a homicide detective friend and said he wanted to
make a thorough cruise of the neighborhood and take a shot
at nailing the guys who'd come up through the fire escape.
He would go through every mug shot in the files to find the
sonsofbitches. Except that he didn't. He came very close to
getting his mother to switch doctors, using some friends to
put him in touch with a great cancer specialist who might
give her a wild shot at some extra life. He was Captain
Almost. Over and over, he asked his father if he needed any
money to which he would reply, "We've got plenty. You
just take care of yourself." One day Towns said the hell with
it and wrote out a check for two thousand dollars; this was
money he really needed, although, in truth, a third of it

would have gone over to coke. Mysteriously, he never got around to mailing it. There was only one department in which he demonstrated some follow-through. It's true he hadn't rented an apartment on lower Park Avenue for his parents and gotten them out of their old neighborhood, but that's a mistake he wasn't going to make again. He would wait a polite amount of time after his mother died and then he would make his move, set up the place, get his father down there to lower Park if he had to use a gun to get the job done. He sure as hell was getting at least one of them out. He would give up the coke for that. He would give up two fingers and a toe if he had to. He was going to put his father right there where he could bounce over to work and never have to ride a subway again. About ten blocks away from work would be perfect. Towns's father didn't want to retire. That business place of his was like a club; his cronies were down there. And the crisp ten-block walk to work would keep that snap in his walk. There was more to the script that Towns had written. His father could take broads up there with him. That buyer, if he liked, or anyone else he felt like hanging out with. Someone around forty-seven would be just right for him. Towns would scoop up a certain girl he had in mind and maybe they would all go out together. He didn't see that this showed any disrespect for his mother. What did one thing have to do with the other? Once his father was in the city, they would spend more time together, not every night, but maybe twice a week and Sundays for breakfast. He had had his father out with some friends and some of them said he fit right in with them. It was nice of them to say that. And even if he did not exactly fit in, at least he didn't put into play any outrageous old-guy things that embarrassed everybody. They would just have to accept him once in a while whether he fit in or not. Otherwise he would get some new friends.

That was the general drift of the script he had written for his father. But the key to it was the apartment. Right after they buried his mother, Towns called a real-estate agent and told her to start hunting around in that general lower Park vicinity. He used the same agent who'd gotten him his own apartment. He read her as being in her late thirties and not bad. Nothing there for him but maybe for his father. Towns's dad and the agent would prowl around, checking out apartments, and maybe get something going. He didn't have the faintest idea if his father's guns were still functional in that area, but he preferred to think they were. Maybe he would ask him. So Towns set the apartment hunt in motion and, after a few weeks, took his father to dinner at a steak house and hit him with it. "Let's face it, fun is fun, but you've got to get out of there, Dad."

"I know, Harry, and I will, believe me, but I just don't feel like it right now. I have to feel like it. Then I will." At that moment, Harry Towns noticed that his father had lost a little weight, perhaps a few more pounds than he had any business losing. He was one of those fellows who had been one weight all his adult life—and now he was a different one.

"I don't have any appetite," he said.

"But look how you're eating now," Towns told him. And, indeed, his father had cleaned up everything in front of him. Then Towns gave his father a small lecture. "Let's face it, Dad, you're a little depressed. You can't live with somebody that long and then lose them and not be. Maybe you ought to see somebody, for just an hour or two. I had that experience myself. Just one or two sessions and I got right back on the track." He didn't want to use the word "psychiatrist." But that's what he had in mind. He knew just the right fellow, too. Easy on the nerves and almost the same age as his father. He had expected to hear some grumbling, but his father surprised him by saying, "Maybe you have a point there." And then Towns's dad looked at him with some kind of wateriness in his eyes. It wasn't tears, or even the start of them, but some kind of deep and ancient watery comprehension. Then he cleaned off his plate and brought up the subject of bank books and insurance. Towns felt he was finally getting in on some of the secrets in the strongbox. He had about fifty grand in all and he wanted his son to know about it, "just in case anything happens."

"There ain't anything gonna happen," said Towns.

"Just in case. I want it split fifty-fifty, half for you and half for your brother."

"Give it all to him," said Towns.

"Never," said his father, with something close to anger. "Half and half, right down the middle. And it's nothing to sneeze at."

"I know that."

"I thought you were making fun of it."

"I wasn't," said Towns. "But will you get the goddamn apartment?"

"I will," he said, mopping up the last of the cheesecake. "But first I have to feel like it."

The appetite thing worried Towns. He was sure it connected to some kind of depression, because he ate so well when he was out with Towns. But he couldn't have breakfast with his father every morning. And no matter how much he loved him, he couldn't eat with him every goddamn night. What about lunches? Was he supposed to run over and have lunch with him, too? He finally teamed the old man up with the real-estate lady, and on a Saturday morning they checked out a few available apartments. On lower Park. That afternoon, the woman called Towns and said his father had gotten dizzy in one of the apartments and hit his head on the radiator. She said she had made him swear he was in good shape before she let him go home. She was all right. Towns got his father to go to the doctor—he admitted to getting dizzy once before on the subway and having to ask someone for a seat—and they ran some tests. They used the same doctor who hadn't performed

any particular miracles on his mother's claws. Towns had
meant to switch off to another one, but that's something
else he had not gotten around to. The tests zeroed in on his
prostate and Towns felt better immediately. He had a little
condition of his own and he knew it was no toothache, but
there was no way it could turn you into a Marineland
exhibition. The prostate had to go—and the fellow who
would take it out was named Doctor Merder. Towns and
his dad had a good laugh about that one. If you were a
surgeon with a name like that, you had better be good. So
they didn't worry a bit about him. The book on the doctor
was that he had never lost a prostate case. Towns's dad
checked into the hospital. He was concerned about how the
business, or "place" as he called it, would run in his
absence and he didn't relax until the boss called and told
him to take it easy, they would cover for him and everything would be just fine; just relax and get better. The boss
was around thirty years younger than he was, but Towns's
dad couldn't get over his taking the time to do a thing like
that. Once in the hospital, he went from natty to dignified.
Maybe he had always been dignified, even though he had
blown his one shot at being head of his own business, years
before. Using some fancy accounting techniques, his part-
ners had quickly cut him to ribbons and eased him out of
his share of the firm. This would have left most men for
dead; but Towns's dad had simply gone back to his old
factory job as second in command, dignified as ever. In the
hospital, the only thing he used the bed for was sleeping.
He sat in a flowered New England chair, neat as a pin,
reading the books Harry Towns brought him. His favorite
kind of book dealt with generals and statesmen, people like
Stettinius and Franklin Delano Roosevelt, and the goings-on
behind the scenes during World War II. Or at least Towns
assumed they were his favorites. Maybe they were his own
favorites, and all those years he had been pushing them on
his dad. Whenever Towns brought him a book, his father

felt obliged to "read it up," as if it would be "wasted" if he didn't. Like food. So whenever Towns showed up at the hospital with another one, he would hold up his hands and say, "Stop, for crissakes. How much can a guy read?"

Along with at least one volume about Secret-Service shenanigans in World War II, Towns would also bring a fistful of expensive Canary Island cigars. For most of his life, his father had smoked a cheaper brand, Admiration Joys when Towns was a boy, but in recent years Towns had promoted him to these higher-priced jobs. He complained that Towns was spoiling him. Sixty cents was too much to spend for a cigar. And there was no way to go back to the Joys. But he got a lot of pleasure out of the expensive ones. Towns had gotten the cigar habit from his father; he remembered a time when his father would greet a friend by stuffing a cigar in his handkerchief pocket and the friend would do the same for Towns's dad. It seemed like a fine ritual and Towns was sorry to see it go; there was probably a paper around proving it was all very phallic and homosexual. Now, when Towns showed up with the cigars, his father would say, "What the hell am I supposed to do with them?"

"Smoke 'em," said Towns.

"What if I don't feel like it?"

"Then just take a few puffs."

"All right, leave 'em over there."

And he would. He would take a few puffs of each one. So they wouldn't go to waste.

They kept taking more tests on Towns's dad; he didn't leave the room very often, but he did spend a little time with one other patient and he got a tremendous kick out of this fellow. He was trying to impeach the President and Towns's father couldn't get over that. If he had great admiration for people like Cordell Hull and Omar Bradley, his respect for the office of the President was absolutely overpowering. The idea of a guy running around trying to get the top executive impeached tickled the hell out of

Towns's dad. It was so outrageous. "You got to see this guy," he told Towns. "He's got a sign this big over his door, some kind of impeachment map. He's trying to get some signatures up. And he's important, too. I don't know what the hell he does, but he gives off an important impression. He says he wants to meet you."

"What's he want to meet me for?"

"I don't know. Maybe he heard you were important, too. Why don't you go over there and give him a tumble?"

Towns wasn't terribly interested in the impeachment man. He was more interested in the tests. But for his father's sake, he met the fellow in the lounge. He was a sparse-haired gentleman, a bit younger than his father, who talked a mile a minute and seemed to be carefully staying off the subject of impeachment. At the same time, he kept checking Towns's eyes as if he were looking for a go-ahead signal. Towns gave him a signal that said nothing doing. "What'd you think of him?" Towns's father asked as they walked back to the room.

"He's all right," said Towns.

"Well, I don't know what *you* think of him, but to me he's really something. Imagine a thing like that. Going around trying to im*peach* the President of the United States. And he's no bum. You can tell that by looking at him. I think he's got some dough." All the way back to his room, Towns's dad kept clucking his tongue about the fellow. He acted as though it was the most amazing thing he had ever come across in all his seventy-five years.

"Would you like to see that map he's got on the outside of his door?"

"I don't think so, Dad."

"I think you ought to take a look at it."

"Maybe I will, on the way out."

They decided to build up Towns's dad by giving him a couple of transfusions before the surgery. While this was going on, Towns ran into a nurse who came an inch short of

being one of the prettiest girls he knew in the city. He had
always meant to get around to her, but she lived with a
friend of his and he claimed that was one rule he would
never break. Or at least he'd try not to break it. She had a
private patient down the hall and said she knew about his
father and that a week before, he had stood outside his door
and asked her to come in and have a cookie. Towns wished
his father had been much more rascally than that. Why
didn't he just reach out and pinch her ass? On the other
hand, the cookie invitation wasn't much, but it was
something. Towns made her promise to go in and visit him
and sort of kid around with him and she said of course she
would, he didn't even have to ask. He had the feeling this
was the kind of girl his father would love to fool around with
in an old-guy way.

The transfusion gave Towns's father some fever, but they
went ahead and operated anyway. This puzzled Towns a
bit. Except that his father seemed to come out of the
surgery all right. He didn't appear to be connected up to
that many tubes, which struck Towns as a good sign. Towns
kept bringing him books about desert warfare, the defense
of Stalingrad, Operation Sea Lion, but he kept them over to
the side where his father couldn't see them and have to
worry about "reading them up." Before they got spoiled.
On the third day after the operation, he brought along a
real torpedo of a cigar, long, fragrant, aromatic, the best he
could find.

"What'd you bring that for?" asked his father, who was
down to one tube.

"Why do you think?"

"I ain't smoking it, Harry."

"The hell you're not."

The next day, his father looked a little weaker, but the
doctor said it was more or less normal to take a dip on the
way back from surgery. When they were alone, Towns's
father asked his son, "What the hell are you doing here?"

"I came to see you, Dad."

He turned his head away, waved his hand in disgust and said, "You ain't gonna do me any good." Then he turned back and chuckled and they started to talk about what was going on outside, but that cruel random slash had been there. Maybe you were allowed to be a little cruel right after surgery. Towns wasn't sure. It was only the second piece of bad behavior Towns could think of since he'd been born. The other had to do with Towns at around eight or nine, using the word "schmuck" about somebody; he didn't know what the word meant, but his father instantly lashed out and belted him halfway across the city. So that added up to two in more than forty years. "Schmuck" and "You ain't gonna do me any good." Not a bad score. The next morning, the doctor phoned and told Towns he had better come down, because his father's pulse had stopped. "What do you mean, stopped?" Towns asked.

"The nurse stepped out for a second and when she came back he had no pulse. She called a round-the-clock resuscitation team and they were down there like Johnny-on-the-spot. They do quite a job."

"How come the nurse stepped out?"

"They have to go to the bathroom."

"Is he gonna live?"

"It depends on how long his pulse stopped. We'll know that later."

Towns got down there fast. He met the doctor in the intensive-care unit. The doctor asked if he would like to see the team working on his dad and he said he would. He took Towns down the hall and displayed the huge resuscitation units the way a proud Soviet manager would show off his plant for a group of Chrysler execs. His father was hooked up to plenty of tubes now. He was like a part in a huge industrial city. The whole city of Pittsburgh. He was the part that took a jolting spasmodic leap every few seconds. Towns got as close as he could—what the hell, he'd seen everything now. He tried to spot something that wasn't covered up by gadgets. Something that looked like his father. He finally picked off a section from the wrist to the elbow that he recognized as being his father's arm. He was pretty sure of it. "There's no point in your staying around," the doctor said. "I know that," said Towns.

He went up to his father's room and got the cigar. Then he walked to the end of the hall and took a look at the impeachment map. It showed how much strength the fellow had across the country. He didn't have much. A couple of pins in Los Angeles, Wisconsin, New York, and out. On the way down, Towns stopped in at the snack bar and had some peach yogurt. It was the first time in his life he had ever tasted yogurt and it wasn't bad. It went down easy and it didn't taste the way he had imagined it would. He made a note to pick up a few cartons of it. The fruit kind. He went back to his apartment and fell asleep. The call came early in the evening. Towns had promised himself he would fix the exact time in his mind forever, but a week later, he couldn't tell you what time or even what month it had happened.

"That's it, huh?"

"I'm afraid so," said the doctor. "About five minutes ago. I'd like to get your permission to do a medical examination of your dad so that maybe we can find out something to help the next guy who comes in with the same condition."

"How come you operated on him with fever?"

"We tried to contact you on that to get your permission."

"You should've have tried harder."

"See," said the doctor, "that's just it. We talk to people when they're understandably upset and they say no to medical examinations. In Sweden, it's automatic."

"Work a little harder on what you know already."

"The next one could be your child. Or your children's children."

"Fuck you, doctor."

So that was it. The both of them. And for the moment, all Harry Towns had out of it was a new expression. Back to back. He had lost both his parents, back to back. He leaned on that one for about six months or so; especially if someone asked him why he was "low" or why he was late on a deadline. "Hey," he would say, "I lost both my parents, back to back." And he would be off the hook. He told his brother from Omaha to fly in as fast as possible and take care of everything, clean out his dad's apartment, settle the accounts, the works. He was better at that kind of thing. Maybe Towns would be good at it, too, but he didn't want to be. The only thing he could hardly wait to do was get in touch with the rabbi who had officiated over his mother's funeral. He was a fellow the chapel kept on tap in case you didn't have any particular rabbi of your own in mind. It was like getting an attorney from Legal Aid except that this one turned out to be a real find. He showed up in what Harry Towns liked to recall as a cloud of smoke, with a shiny black suit and a metaphysical tuft of hair sticking up on his head. He turned up two and a half minutes before the ceremony and asked Towns to sum up his mother. "What are you, nuts?" said Towns. "Trust me," said the rabbi, a homely fellow with an amazingly rocklike jaw that was totally out of sync with his otherwise wan Talmudic features. Towns took a shot. He told him they really shouldn't have limos taking his mother out to the grave, they ought to have New York taxis. Whenever she had a problem, she would simply jump inside one and have the driver ride around with the meter going while she talked to him until she felt better. Then she would pay the bill, slap on a big tip, and hop out. That was her kind of psychoanalysis. She couldn't cook and Towns didn't want anyone laying that word "housewife" on her. Not at the funeral. It was very important to get her right. This was almost as important to him as losing her. She was close to cabbies, bellhops, and busboys and she could brighten up a room just by walking into it. And damned if this faded little mysterious house rabbi didn't get her. In two and a half minutes. "Sparkle" was the key word. And it was his own. He kept shooting that word "sparkle" out over the mourners and it was as if he had known her all his life. Towns had never seen a performance quite like that.

After they had buried her in the Jersey Flats, the rabbi asked if anyone could give him a lift back to New York City. Everyone was staying at an aunt's house in Jersey, so no one could. With that, he hopped on the hearse. And then he disappeared; once again, it might just as well have been in a cloud of smoke. And he was only seventy-five bucks. So you can see why Towns was anxious to have him back for a repeat performance. It was enough to get Towns back to religion. Why not, if they had unsung guys like that around? Except that the minute he showed up at the chapel the second time, something was a little off. The rabbi looked barbered for one thing. And he was wearing flowing rabbinical robes. What happened to the black shiny suit that he had probably brought over from Poland? And he didn't get Towns's father at all. "Good, honest, hard-working man." "Lived only for his family." Shit like that. Right out of your basic funeral textbook. The very thing Towns wanted to head off. His diction was different, fancier. He could have been talking about anybody. And he seemed to be playing not to the audience but strictly to Towns. It occurred to Harry Towns that maybe there wasn't any way to get his father. Maybe that was it—honest, hard-working, et cetera. But for Christ's sake, he could have found something. "Sparkle" wasn't it—he had used that anyway—but how about that bounce in his walk. What about nattiness for a theme. The sharpness of his beard against Harry Towns's face when he was a kid. Anything. Cigar smoking. Handing them out and getting some back. His being an air-raid warden. An all-day fist fight he had with his brother. (When it was over, they didn't talk to each other for twenty-five

years.) Anything at all. Just so they didn't bury a statistic.
Maybe it was as simple as the old second-audition syndrome.
A performer would come and knock you on your ass the
first time. He would get called back and bomb. Show
people explained it by saying there was nothing on the line
the first time a performer auditioned. If you called him
back, it meant you were considering him for the part. In
that situation, nine out of ten performers choked. The rabbi
didn't choke. He was as smooth as silk. He probably felt he
was really cooking. But he sure did bomb.

Out they went to the Jersey Flats again, and after his
father was in the ground, alongside his mother, the rabbi
took Towns aside and said, "With your mother, I didn't even
know who you were." Who in the hell was he? A screenwriter? So that was it. The rabbi had caught his name
on a picture and felt he had to be classier. "I'm being
sponsored on a little trip to Israel," said the rabbi. "Is there
any chance you could meet me there so we could see it
together? It would be meaningful to both of us."

"I don't give a shit about Israel," said Towns. It wasn't
true. He did give a shit about Israel. When the chips were
down, he was still some kind of Jew. He was just sore as
hell at the rabbi for letting him down and not getting his
father right. And for not being that magical fellow with the
tuft of hair who had shown up in a cloud of smoke and
almost got him back to religion. After everyone had
climbed back into the limos, Towns went back to the grave
and dropped that big torpedo of a cigar inside. He was
aware of the crummy sentimentality involved—and he
knew he would probably tell it to a friend or two before the
week was over—as an anecdote—but he did it anyway. No
one was going to tell him whether to be sentimental or
not—not when he had just lost his mother and father. Back
to back.

He hung around the city while his brother cleaned things
up for him. He said he didn't want anything from the

apartment except an old-fashioned vest-pocket watch he remembered. And maybe his dad's ring, with the initials rubbed over with age so you couldn't really make them out. They got the finances straightened out in his brother's hotel room. The money coming to Towns was enough to cover his back tax bill to the government, almost to the penny. He hadn't slept easily for a year, wondering where he was going to get that kind of dough. And there were a handful of salary checks to be divided up. So he finally found out what his father's salary was. It was probably the last secret in the strongbox. He was sorry he found out. They had cut him down to nickels and dimes, probably because he was seventy-five. And here he was, settling his son's tax bill. Towns hugged his brother, saying, "Let's stay in touch. You're all I've got," and then his nephew came dancing out in one of his father's suits. Wearing a funny smile and looking very natty. Towns recalled a fellow he had once worked for who had come to the office wearing his father's best suit, one day after the old man had died. At the time, he wondered, what kind of a guy does that. Now, his brother said, "It fit him like a glove, so why not?" Towns couldn't answer that one. He just felt it shouldn't be going on. About a month later, he changed his mind and was glad the kid took the clothes.

Harry Towns planned on taking a long drive to someplace he hadn't been so he could be alone and sort things out, but he got whisked off to California on a job he felt he couldn't turn down. He told himself the work would be good for him. Just before he left, he ran into the cookie nurse at a singles place and asked her if she had ever gone in and fooled around with his father. She said she had but her eyes told him she hadn't. Cunt. No wonder he hadn't moved in on her. It wasn't that she was living with his friend. The guy wasn't that close a friend. It was this kind of behavior. She would tell you that she would go in and screw around with your father and then she wouldn't.

He polished off the California work in about a week; whenever it sagged a little, he would say, "Hey, listen, I just lost both my parents, back to back." It burned him up when people advanced the theory that his father died because he couldn't live without his wife. He heard a lot of that and he didn't buy any of it. Towns hadn't been married to anyone for fifty years the way his father had and it didn't look as if there was going to be time to squeeze someone in for half a century. But he just couldn't afford to think that if you loved someone very much and they died, you had to hop right into the grave with them. He preferred to think that you mourned for them and then went about your business.

He went on an erratic crying schedule. The first burst came at the Los Angeles airport, on the way for a quick stopover in Vegas. He was really smoking with the latenight check-in stewardess at the L. A. airport, a small girl with a huge chest and an angel's face. He almost had her talked into going to Vegas with him. One extra shove and she would have been on the seat next to him. He did it right in front of the Air West pilots, too, and they didn't appreciate it much. On the other hand, two hookers saw the whole thing and got a big kick out of it. Then he got on the plane and cried all the way to Caesar's Palace. The hookers saw that one, too, and must have wondered if he were crazy. He had just finished hustling a stewardess. He might just as well have been Cary Grant back there at the airport. What was he doing all that crying for? Back East, he gave himself the job of copying over his address book. Halfway along, he came to his father's name and business number. He really went that time. For a period there, he didn't think he was ever going to stop. It was having to make that particular decision. What do you do, carry your dead father over into the new address book? Or drop him from the rolls, no more father, no more phone number, and you pick up that extra space for some new piece of ass?

He never did get to take that drive. The one in which he was going to go to a strange place and sort things out. The awful part is that he never seemed to get any huge lessons out of the things that happened to him. He was brimming over with small nuggets of information he had gathered for his work. For example, when frisking a homicide suspect in a stabbing case, the first thing detectives check for is a dry-cleaning ticket. On the theory that the suspect is going to ship his bloodstained clothing right off to the cleaner's. When shot at, cops are taught to jump to their left since most gunmen are right-handed and will either fire wide of the mark or, at worst, nick your shoulder. He knew there was no such thing as a second wind in running. If you got one, it meant you had not been "red-lining it," that is, running full out. He kept his young son enthralled for hours with this kind of information. But he didn't own any real wisdom and this bothered him. Instead, he borrowed other people's. Never sleep with a woman who has more problems than you do. Nelson Algren. Don't look over your shoulder because someone might be gaining on you. Satchel Paige. People behave well only because they lack the character to behave poorly. La Rochefoucauld. Take short views, hope for the best, and trust in God. Some British guy. Stuff like that. Wasn't it time for him to be coming up with a few of his own? Pressed to the wall, he would probably produce this list:

1. Be very lucky.

2. Watch your ass.

Because if they could get your father's pulse to stop—considering the way he looked, the way he bounced along, his smile, and the fifteen years, minimum, that Harry Towns had scripted up for him—if they could keep him out of that paid-for apartment on lower Park, and on top of everything, get him to die back to back with Towns's mom, the two of them stowed underground in the Jersey Flats, why then all bets were off and anything was possible. Anything you could dream up. You name it. Any fucking thing in the world.

ERNEST J. GAINES

The Sky Is Gray

Go'n be coming in a few minutes. Coming round that bend down there full speed. And I'm go'n get out my handkerchief and wave it down, and we go'n get on it and go.

I keep on looking for it, but Mama don't look that way no more. She's looking down the road where we just come from. It's a long old road, and far 's you can see you don't see nothing but gravel. You got dry weeds on both sides, and you got trees on both sides, and fences on both sides, too. And you got cows in the pastures and they standing close together. And when we was coming out here to catch the bus I seen the smoke coming out of the cows's noses.

I look at my mama and I know what she's thinking. I been with Mama so much, just me and her, I know what she's thinking all the time. Right now it's home—Auntie and them. She's thinking if they got enough wood—if she left enough there to keep them warm till we get back. She's thinking if it go'n rain and if any of them go'n have to go out in the rain. She's thinking 'bout the hog—if he go'n get out, and if Ty and Val be able to get him back in. She always worry like that when she leaves the house. She don't worry too much if she leave me there with the smaller ones, 'cause she know I'm go'n look after them and look after

Auntie and everything else. I'm the oldest and she say I'm the man.

I look at my mama and I love my mama. She's wearing that black coat and that black hat and she's looking sad. I love my mama and I want put my arm round her and tell her. But I'm not supposed to do that. She say that's weakness and that's crybaby stuff, and she don't want no crybaby round her. She don't want you to be scared, either. 'Cause Ty's scared of ghosts and she's always whipping him. I'm scared of the dark, too, but I make 'tend I ain't. I make 'tend I ain't 'cause I'm the oldest, and I got to set a good sample for the rest. I can't ever be scared and I can't ever cry. And that's why I never said nothing 'bout my teeth. It's been hurting me and hurting me close to a month now, but I never said it. I didn't say it 'cause I didn't want act like a crybaby, and 'cause I know we didn't have enough money to go have it pulled. But, Lord, it been hurting me. And look like it wouldn't start till at night when you was trying to get yourself little sleep. Then soon 's you shut your eyes—ummmummmm, Lord, look like it go right down to your heartstring.

"Hurting, hanh?" Ty'd say.

I'd shake my head, but I wouldn't open my mouth for nothing. You open your mouth and let that wind in, and it almost kill you.

I'd just lay there and listen to them snore. Ty there, right 'side me, and Auntie and Val over by the fireplace. Val younger than me and Ty, and he sleeps with Auntie. Mama sleeps round the other side with Louis and Walker.

I'd just lay there and listen to them, and listen to that wind out there, and listen to that fire in the fireplace. Sometimes it'd stop long enough to let me get little rest. Sometimes it just hurt, hurt, hurt Lord, have mercy.

2

Auntie knowed it was hurting me. I didn't tell nobody but
Ty, 'cause we buddies and he ain't go'n tell nobody. But
some kind of way Auntie found out. When she asked me, I
told her no, nothing was wrong. But she knowed it all the
time. She told me to mash up a piece of aspirin and wrap it
in some cotton and jugg it down in that hole. I did it, but it
didn't do no good. It stopped for a little while, and started
right back again. Auntie wanted to tell Mama, but I told
her, "Uh-uh." 'Cause I knowed we didn't have any money,
and it just was go'n make her mad again. So Auntie told
Monsieur Bayonne, and Monsieur Bayonne came over to
the house and told me to kneel down 'side him on the
fireplace. He put his finger in his mouth and made the Sign
of the Cross on my jaw. The tip of Monsieur Bayonne's
finger is some hard, 'cause he's always playing on that
guitar. If we sit outside at night we can always hear Monsieur Bayonne playing on his guitar. Sometimes we leave
him out there playing on the guitar.

Monsieur Bayonne made the Sign of the Cross over and
over on my jaw, but that didn't do no good. Even when he
prayed and told me to pray some, too, that tooth still hurt
me.

"How you feeling?" he say.

"Same," I say.

He kept on praying and making the Sign of the Cross and
I kept on praying, too.

"Still hurting?" he say.

"Yes, sir."

Monsieur Bayonne mashed harder and harder on my
jaw. He mashed so hard he almost pushed me over on Ty.
But then he stopped.

"What kind of prayers you praying, boy?" he say.

"Baptist," I say.

"Well, I'll be—no wonder that tooth still kill him. I'm going one way and he pulling the other. Boy, don't you know any Catholic prayers?"

"I know 'Hail Mary,' " I say.

"Then you better start saying it."

"Yes, sir."

He started mashing on my jaw again, and I could hear him praying at the same time. And, sure enough, after while it stopped hurting me.

Me and Ty went outside where Monsieur Bayonne's two hounds was and we started playing with them. "Let's go hunting," Ty say. "All right," I say; and we went on back in the pasture. Soon the hounds got on a trail, and me and Ty followed them all 'cross the pasture and then back in the woods, too. And then they cornered this little old rabbit and killed him, and me and Ty made them get back, and we picked up the rabbit and started on back home. But my tooth had started hurting me again. It was hurting me plenty now, but I wouldn't tell Monsieur Bayonne. That night I didn't sleep a bit, and first thing in the morning Auntie told me to go back and let Monsieur Bayonne pray over me some more. Monsieur Bayonne was in his kitchen making coffee when I got there. Soon's he seen me he knowed what was wrong.

"All right, kneel down there 'side that stove," he say. "And this time make sure you pray Catholic. I don't know nothing 'bout the Baptist, and I don't want know nothing 'bout him."

3

Last night Mama say, "Tomorrow we going to town."

"It ain't hurting me no more," I say. "I can eat anything on it."

"Tomorrow we going to town," she say.

And after she finished eating, she got up and went to bed. She always go to bed early now. 'Fore Daddy went in the Army, she used to stay up late. All of us sitting out on the gallery or round the fire. But now, look like soon 's she finish eating she go to bed.

This morning when I woke up, her and Auntie was standing 'fore the fireplace. She say: "Enough to get there and get back. Dollar and a half to have it pulled. Twenty-five for me to go, twenty-five for him. Twenty-five for me to come back, twenty-five for him. Fifty cents left. Guess I get little piece of salt meat with that."

"Sure can use it," Auntie say. "White beans and no salt meat ain't white beans."

"I do the best I can," Mama say.

They was quiet after that, and I made 'tend I was still asleep.

"James, hit the floor," Auntie say.

I still made 'tend I was asleep. I didn't want them to know I was listening.

"All right," Auntie say, shaking me by the shoulder. "Come on. Today's the day."

I pushed the cover down to get out, and Ty grabbed it and pulled it back.

"You, too, Ty," Auntie say.

"I ain't getting no teef pulled," Ty say.

"Don't mean it ain't time to get up," Auntie say. "Hit it, Ty."

Ty got up grumbling.

"James, you hurry up and get in your clothes and eat your food," Auntie say. "What time y'all coming back?" she say to Mama.

"That 'leven o'clock bus," Mama say. "Got to get back in that field this evening."

"Get a move on you, James," Auntie say.

I went in the kitchen and washed my face, then I ate my breakfast. I was having bread and syrup. The bread was warm and hard and tasted good. And I tried to make it last a long time.

Ty came back there grumbling and mad at me.

"Got to get up," he say. "I ain't having no teefes pulled. What I got to be getting up for?"

Ty poured some syrup in his pan and got a piece of bread. He didn't wash his hands, neither his face, and I could see that white stuff in his eyes.

"You the one getting your teef pulled," he say. "What I got to get up for. I bet if I was getting a teef pulled, you wouldn't be getting up. Shucks; syrup again. I'm getting tired of this old syrup. Syrup, syrup, syrup. I'm go'n take with the sugar diabetes. I want me some bacon sometime."

"Go out in the field and work and you can have your bacon," Auntie say. She stood in the middle door looking at Ty. "You better be glad you got syrup. Some people ain't got that—hard 's time is."

"Shucks," Ty say. "How can I be strong."

"I don't know too much 'bout your strength," Auntie say; "but I know where you go'n be hot at, you keep that grumbling up. James, get a move on you; your mama waiting."

I ate my last piece of bread and went in the front room. Mama was standing 'fore the fireplace warming her hands. I put on my coat and my cap, and we left the house.

4

I look down there again, but it still ain't coming. I almost say, "It ain't coming yet," but I keep my mouth shut. 'Cause that's something else she don't like. She don't like for you to say something just for nothing. She can see it ain't coming, I can see it ain't coming, so why say it ain't coming. I don't say it, I turn and look at the river that's back of us. It's so cold the smoke's just raising up from the water. I see a bunch of pool-doos not too far out—just on the other side the lilies. I'm wondering if you can eat pool-doos. I ain't too sure, 'cause I ain't never ate none. But I done ate owls and blackbirds, and I done ate redbirds, too. I didn't want kill the redbirds, but she made me kill them. They had two of them back there. One in my trap, one in Ty's trap. Me and Ty was go'n play with them and let them go, but she made me kill them 'cause we needed food.

"I can't," I say. "I can't."

"Here," she say. "Take it."

"I can't," I say. "I can't. I can't kill him, Mama, please."

"Here," she say. "Take this fork, James."

"Please, Mama, I can't kill him," I say.

I could tell she was go'n hit me. I jerked back, but I didn't jerk back soon enough.

"Take it," she say.

I took it and reached in for him, but he kept on hopping to the back.

"I can't, Mama," I say. The water just kept on running down my face. "I can't," I say.

"Get him out of there," she say.

I reached in for him and he kept on hopping to the back. Then I reached in farther, and he pecked me on the hand.

"I can't, Mama," I say.

She slapped me again.

I reached in again, but he kept on hopping out my way. Then he hopped to one side and I reached there. The fork got him on the leg and I heard his leg pop. I pulled my hand out 'cause I had hurt him.

"Give it here," she say, and jerked the fork out my hand.

She reached in and got the little bird right in the neck. I heard the fork go in his neck, and I heard it go in the ground. She brought him out and helt him right in front of me.

"That's one," she say. She shook him off and gived me the fork. "Get the other one."

"I can't, Mama," I say. "I'll do anything, but don't make me do that."

She went to the corner of the fence and broke the biggest switch over there she could find. I knelt 'side the trap, crying.

"Get him out of there," she say.

"I can't, Mama."

She started hitting me 'cross the back. I went down on the ground, crying.

"Get him," she say.

"Octavia?" Auntie say.

'Cause she had come out of the house and she was standing by the tree looking at us.

"Get him out of there," Mama say.

"Octavia," Auntie say, "explain to him. Explain to him. Just don't beat him. Explain to him."

But she hit me and hit me and hit me.

I'm still young—I ain't no more than eight; but I know now; I know why I had to do it. (They was so little, though. They was so little. I 'member how I picked the feathers off them and cleaned them and helt them over the fire. Then we all ate them. Ain't had but a little bitty piece each, but we all had a little bitty piece, and everybody just looked at me 'cause they was so proud.) Suppose she had to go away? That's why I had to do it. Suppose she had to go away like Daddy went away? Then who was go'n look after us? They had to be somebody left to carry on. I didn't know it then, but I know it now. Auntie and Monsieur Bayonne talked to me and made me see.

5

Time I see it I get out my handkerchief and start waving. It's still 'way down there, but I keep waving anyhow. Then it come up and stop and me and Mama get on. Mama tell me go sit in the back while she pay. I do like she say, and the people look at me. When I pass the little sign that say "White" and "Colored," I start looking for a seat. I just see one of them back there, but I don't take it, 'cause I want my mama to sit down herself. She comes in the back and sit down, and I lean on the seat. They got seats in the front, but I know I can't sit there, 'cause I have to sit back of the sign. Anyhow, I don't want sit there if my mama go'n sit back here.

They got a lady sitting 'side my mama and she looks at me and smiles little bit. I smile back, but I don't open my mouth, 'cause the wind'll get in and make that tooth ache. The lady take out a pack of gum and reach me a slice, but I shake my head. The lady just can't understand why a little boy'll turn down gum, and she reach me a slice again. This time I point to my jaw. The lady understands and smiles little bit, and I smile little bit, but I don't open my mouth, though.

They got a girl sitting 'cross from me. She got on a red overcoat and her hair's plaited in one big plait. First, I make 'tend I don't see her over there, but then I start looking at her little bit. She make 'tend she don't see me, either, but I catch her looking that way. She got a cold, and every now and then she h'ist that little handkerchief to her nose. She ought to blow it, but she don't. Must think she's too much a lady or something.

Every time she h'ist that little handkerchief, the lady 'side her say something in her ear. She shakes her head and lays her hands in her lap again. Then I catch her kind of looking where I'm at. I smile at her little bit. But think she'll smile back? Uh-uh. She just turn up her little old nose and turn her head. Well, I show her both of us can turn us head. I turn mine too and look out at the river.

The river is gray. The sky is gray. They have pool-doos on the water. The water is wavy, and the pool-doos go up and down. The bus go round a turn, and you got plenty trees hiding the river. Then the bus go round another turn, and I can see the river again.

I look toward the front where all the white people sitting. Then I look at that little old gal again. I don't look right at her, 'cause I don't want all them people to know I love her. I just look at her little bit, like I'm looking out that window over there. But she knows I'm looking that way, and she kind of look at me, too. The lady sitting 'side her catch her this time, and she leans over and says something in her ear.

"I don't love him nothing," that little old gal says out loud.

Everybody back there hear her mouth, and all of them look at us and laugh.

"I don't love you, either," I say. "So you don't have to turn up your nose, Miss."

"You the one looking," she say.

"I wasn't looking at you," I say. "I was looking out that window, there."

"Out the window, my foot," she say. "I seen you. Everytime I turned round you was looking at me."

"You must of been looking yourself if you seen me all them times," I say.

"Shucks," she say, "I got me all kinds of boyfriends."

"I got girlfriends, too," I say.

"Well, I just don't want you getting your hopes up," she say.

I don't say no more to that little old gal 'cause I don't want have to bust her in the mouth. I lean on the seat where Mama sitting, and I don't even look that way no more. When we get to Bayonne, she jugg her little old tongue out at me. I make 'tend I'm go'n hit her, and she duck down 'side her mama. And all the people laugh at us again.

6

Me and Mama get off and start walking in town. Bayonne is a little bitty town. Baton Rouge is a hundred times bigger than Bayonne. I went to Baton Rouge once— me, Ty, Mama, and Daddy. But that was 'way back yonder 'fore Daddy went in the Army. I wonder when we go'n see him again. I wonder when. Look like he ain't ever coming back home. . . . Even the pavement all cracked in Bayonne. Got grass shooting right out the sidewalk. Got weeds in the ditch, too; just like they got at home.

It's some cold in Bayonne. Look like it's colder than it is home. The wind blows in my face, and I feel that stuff running down my nose. I sniff. Mama says use that handkerchief. I blow my nose and put it back.

We pass a school and I see them white children playing in the yard. Big old red school, and them children just running and playing. Then we pass a café, and I see a bunch of people in there eating. I wish I was in there 'cause I'm cold. Mama tells me keep my eyes in front where they belong.

We pass stores that's got dummies, and we pass another café, and then we pass a shoe shop, and that bald-head man in there fixing on a shoe. I look at him and I butt into that white lady, and Mama jerks me in front and tells me stay there.

We come up to the courthouse, and I see the flag waving there. This flag ain't like the one we got at school. This one here ain't got but a handful of stars. One at school got a big pile of stars—one for every state. We pass it and we turn and there it is—the dentist office. Me and Mama go in, and they got people sitting every- where you look. They even got a little boy in there younger than me.

Me and Mama sit on that bench, and a white lady come
in there and ask me what my name is. Mama tells her and
the white lady goes on back. Then I hear somebody
hollering in there. Soon's that little boy hear him hollering,
he starts hollering, too. His mama pats him and pats him,
trying to make him hush up, but he ain't thinking 'bout his
mama.

The man that was hollering in there comes out holding
his jaw. He is a big old man and he's wearing overalls and a
jumper.

"Got it, hanh?" another man asks him.

The man shakes his head—don't want open his mouth.

"Man, I thought they was killing you in there," the other
man says. "Hollering like a pig under a gate."

The man don't say nothing. He just heads for the door,
and the other man follows him.

"John Lee," the white lady says. "John Lee Williams."

The little boy juggs his head down in his mama's lap and
holler more now. His mama tells him go with the nurse,
but he ain't thinking 'bout his mama. His mama tells him
again, but he don't even hear her. His mama picks him up
and takes him in there, and even when the white lady shuts
the door I can still hear little old John Lee.

"I often wonder why the Lord let a child like that suffer,"
a lady says to my mama. The lady's sitting right in front of
us on another bench. She's got on a white dress and a black
sweater. She must be a nurse or something herself, I
reckon.

"Not us to question," a man says.

"Sometimes I don't know if we shouldn't," the lady says.

"I know definitely we shouldn't," the man says. The man
looks like a preacher. He's big and fat and he's got on a
black suit. He's got a gold chain, too.

"Why?" the lady says.

"Why anything?" the preacher says.

"Yes," the lady says. "Why anything?"

"Not us to question," the preacher says.

The lady looks at the preacher a little while and looks at Mama again.

"And look like it's the poor who suffers the most," she says. "I don't understand it."

"Best not to even try," the preacher says. "He works in mysterious ways—wonders to perform."

Right then little John Lee bust out hollering, and everybody turn they head to listen.

"He's not a good dentist," the lady says. "Dr. Robillard is much better. But more expensive. That's why most of the colored people come here. The white people go to Dr. Robillard. Y'all from Bayonne?"

"Down the river," my mama says. And that's all she go'n say, 'cause she don't talk much. But the lady keeps on looking at her, and so she says, "Near Morgan."

"I see," the lady says.

7

"That's the trouble with the black people in this country today," somebody else says. This one here's sitting on the same side me and Mama's sitting, and he is kind of sitting in front of that preacher. He looks like a teacher or somebody that goes to college. He's got on a suit, and he's got a book that he's been reading. "We don't question is exactly our problem," he says. "We should question and question and question—question everything."

The preacher just looks at him a long time. He done put a toothpick or something in his mouth, and he just keeps on turning it and turning it. You can see he don't like that boy with that book.

"Maybe you can explain what you mean," he says.

"I said what I meant," the boy says. "Question everything. Every stripe, every star, every word spoken. Everything."

"It 'pears to me that this young lady and I was talking 'bout God, young man," the preacher says.

"Question Him, too," the boy says.

"Wait," the preacher says. "Wait now."

"You heard me right," the boy says. "His existence as well as everything else. Everything."

The preacher just looks across the room at the boy. You can see he's getting madder and madder. But mad or no mad, the boy ain't thinking 'bout him. He looks at that preacher just 's hard 's the preacher looks at him.

"Is this what they coming to?" the preacher says. "Is this what we educating them for?"

"You're not educating me," the boy says. "I wash dishes at night so that I can go to school in the day. So even the words you spoke need questioning."

The preacher just looks at him and shakes his head.

"When I come in this room and seen you there with your book, I said to myself, 'There's an intelligent man.' How wrong a person can be."

"Show me one reason to believe in the existence of a God," the boy says.

"My heart tells me," the preacher says.

" 'My heart tells me,' " the boy says. " 'My heart tells me.' Sure, 'My heart tells me.' And as long as you listen to what your heart tells you, you will have only what the white man gives you and nothing more. Me, I don't listen to my heart. The purpose of the heart is to pump blood throughout the body, and nothing else."

"Who's your paw, boy?" the preacher says.

"Why?"

"Who is he?"

"He's dead."

"And your mom?"

"She's in Charity Hospital with pneumonia. Half killed herself, working for nothing."

"And 'cause he's dead and she's sick, you mad at the world?"

"I'm not mad at the world. I'm questioning the world. I'm questioning it with cold logic, sir. What do words like Freedom, Liberty, God, White, Colored mean? I want to know. That's why *you* are sending us to school, to read and to ask questions. And because we ask these questions, you call us mad. No sir, it is not us who are mad."

"You keep saying 'us'?"

" 'Us.' Yes—us. I'm not alone."

The preacher just shakes his head. Then he looks at everybody in the room—everybody. Some of the people look down at the floor, keep from looking at him. I kind of look 'way myself, but soon 's I know he done turn his head, I look that way again.

"I'm sorry for you," he says to the boy.

'Why?" the boy says. "Why not be sorry for yourself? Why are you so much better off than I am? Why aren't you sorry for these other people in here? Why not be sorry for the lady who had to drag her child into the dentist office? Why not be sorry for the lady sitting on that bench over there? Be sorry for them. Not for me. Some way or the other I'm going to make it."

"No, I'm sorry for you," the preacher says.

"Of course, of course," the boy says, nodding his head. "You're sorry for me because I rock that pillar you're leaning on."

"You can't ever rock the pillar I'm leaning on, young man. It's stronger than anything man can ever do."

"You believe in God because a man told you to believe in God," the boy says. "A white man told you to believe in God. And why? To keep you ignorant so he can keep his feet on your neck."

"So now we the ignorant?" the preacher says.

"Yes," the boy says. "Yes." And he opens his book again.

The preacher just looks at him sitting there. The boy done forgot all about him. Everybody else make 'tend they done forgot the squabble, too.

Then I see that preacher getting up real slow. Preacher's

a great big old man and he got to brace himself to get up. He comes over where the boy is sitting. He just stands there a little while looking down at him, but the boy don't raise his head.

"Get up, boy," preacher says.

The boy looks up at him, then he shuts his book real slow and stands up. Preacher just hauls back and hit him in the face. The boy falls back 'gainst the wall, but he straightens himself up and looks right back at that preacher.

"You forgot the other cheek," he says.

The preacher hauls back and hit him again on the other side. But this time the boy braces himself and don't fall.

"That hasn't changed a thing," he says.

The preacher just looks at the boy. The preacher's breathing real hard like he just run up a big hill. The boy sits down and opens his book again.

"I feel sorry for you," the preacher says. "I never felt so sorry for a man before."

The boy makes 'tend he don't even hear that preacher. He keeps on reading his book. The preacher goes back and gets his hat off the chair.

"Excuse me," he says to us. "I'll come back some other time. Y'all, please excuse me."

And he looks at the boy and goes out the room. The boy h'ist his hand up to his mouth one time to wipe 'way some blood. All the rest of the time he keeps on reading. And nobody else in there say a word.

8

Little John Lee and his mama come out the dentist office, and the nurse calls somebody else in. Then little bit later they come out, and the nurse calls another name. But fast 's she calls somebody in there, somebody else comes in the place where we sitting, and the room stays full.

The people coming in now, all of them wearing big coats. One of them says something 'bout sleeting, another one says he hope not. Another one says he think it ain't nothing but rain. 'Cause, he says, rain can get awful cold this time of year.

All round the room they talking. Some of them talking to people right by them, some of them talking to people clear 'cross the room, some of them talking to anybody'll listen. It's a little bitty room, no bigger than us kitchen, and I can see everybody in there. The little old room's full of smoke, 'cause you got two old men smoking pipes over by that side door. I think I feel my tooth thumping me some, and I hold my breath and wait. I wait and wait, but it don't thump me no more. Thank God for that.

I feel like going to sleep, and I lean back 'gainst the wall. But I'm scared to go to sleep. Scared 'cause the nurse might call my name and I won't hear her. And Mama might go to sleep, too, and she'll be mad if neither one of us heard the nurse.

I look up at Mama. I love my mama. I love my mama. And when cotton come I'm go'n get her a new coat. And I ain't go'n get a black one, either. I think I'm go'n get her a red one.

"They got some books over there," I say. "Want read one of them?"

Mama looks at the books, but she don't answer me.

"You got yourself a little man there," the lady says.

Mama don't say nothing to the lady, but she must've smiled, 'cause I seen the lady smiling back. The lady looks at me a little while, like she's feeling sorry for me.

"You sure got that preacher out here in a hurry," she says to that boy.

The boy looks up at her and looks in his book again. When I grow up I want to be just like him. I want clothes like that and I want keep a book with me, too.

"You really don't believe in God?" the lady says.

"No," he says.

"But why?" the lady says.

"Because the wind is pink," he says.

"What?" the lady says.

The boy don't answer her no more. He just reads in his book.

"Talking 'bout the wind is pink," the old lady says. She's sitting on the same bench with the boy and she's trying to look in his face. The boy makes 'tend the old lady ain't even there. He just keeps on reading. "Wind is pink," she says again. "Eh, Lord, what children go'n be saying next?"

The lady 'cross from us bust out laughing.

"That's a good one," she says. "The wind is pink. Yes sir, that's a good one."

"Don't you believe the wind is pink?" the boy says. He keeps his head down in the book.

"Course I believe it, honey," the lady says. "Course I do." She looks at us and winks her eye. "And what color is grass, honey?"

"Grass? Grass is black."

She bust out laughing again. The boy looks at her.

"Don't you believe grass is black?" he says.

The lady quits her laughing and looks at him. Everybody else looking at him, too. The place quiet, quiet.

"Grass is green, honey," the lady says. "It was green yesterday, it's green today, and it's go'n be green tomorrow."

"How do you know it's green?"

"I know because I know."

"You don't know it's green," the boy says. "You believe it's green because someone told you it was green. If someone had told you it was black you'd believe it was black."

"It's green," the lady says. "I know green when I see green."

"Prove it's green," the boy says.

"Sure, now," the lady says. "Don't tell me it's coming to that."

"It's coming to just that," the boy says. "Words mean nothing. One means no more than the other."

"That's what it all coming to?" that old lady says. That old lady got on a turban and she got on two sweaters. She got a green sweater under a black sweater. I can see the green sweater 'cause some of the bottoms on the other sweater's missing.

"Yes ma'am," the boy says. "Words mean nothing. Action is the only thing. Doing. That's the only thing."

"Other words, you want the Lord to come down here and show Himself to you?" she says.

"Exactly, ma'am," he says.

"You don't mean that, I'm sure?" she says.

"I do, ma'am," he says.

"Done, Jesus," the old lady says, shaking her head.

"I didn't go 'long with that preacher at first," the other lady says; "but now—I don't know. When a person say the grass is black, he's either a lunatic or something's wrong."

"Prove to me that it's green," the boy says.

"It's green because the people say it's green."

"Those same people say we're citizens of these United States," the boy says.

"I think I'm a citizen," the lady says.

"Citizens have certain rights," the boy says. "Name me one right that you have. One right, granted by the Constitution, that you can exercise in Bayonne."

The lady don't answer him. She just looks at him like she don't know what he's talking 'bout. I know I don't.

"Things changing," she says.

"Things are changing because some black men have begun to think with their brains and not their hearts," the boy says.

"You trying to say these people don't believe in God?"

"I'm sure some of them do. Maybe most of them do. But

they don't believe that God is going to touch these white people's hearts and change things tomorrow. Things change through action. By no other way."

Everybody sit quiet and look at the boy. Nobody says a thing. Then the lady 'cross the room from me and Mama just shakes her head.

"Let's hope that not all your generation feel the same way you do," she says.

"Think what you please, it doesn't matter," the boy says. "But it will be men who listen to their heads and not their hearts who will see that your children have a better chance than you had."

"Let's hope they ain't all like you, though," the old lady says. "Done forgot the heart absolutely."

"Yes ma'am, I hope they aren't all like me," the boy says. "Unfortunately, I was born too late to believe in your God. Let's hope that the ones who come after will have your faith—if not in your God, then in something else, something definitely that they can lean on. I haven't anything. For me, the wind is pink, the grass is black."

9

The nurse comes in the room where we all sitting and waiting and says the doctor won't take no more patients till one o'clock this evening. My mama jumps up off the bench and goes up to the white lady.

"Nurse, I have to go back in the field this evening," she says.

"The doctor is treating his last patient now," the nurse says. "One o'clock this evening."

"Can I at least speak to the doctor?" my mama asks.

"I'm his nurse," the lady says.

"My little boy's sick," my mama says. "Right now his tooth almost killing him."

The nurse looks at me. She's trying to make up her mind if to let me come in. I look at her real pitiful. The tooth ain't hurting me at all, but Mama say it is, so I make 'tend for her sake.

"This evening," the nurse says, and goes on back in the office.

"Don't feel 'jected, honey," the lady says to Mama. "I been round them a long time—they take you when they want to. If you was white, that's something else; but we the wrong color."

Mama don't say nothing to the lady, and me and her go outside and stand 'gainst the wall. It's cold out there. I can feel that wind going through my coat. Some of the other people come out of the room and go up the street. Me and Mama stand there a little while and we start walking. I don't know where we going. When we come to the other street we just stand there.

"You don't have to make water, do you?" Mama says.

"No, ma'am," I say.

We go on up the street. Walking real slow. I can tell Mama don't know where she's going. When we come to a store we stand there and look at the dummies. I look at a little boy wearing a brown overcoat. He's got on brown shoes, too. I look at my old shoes and look at his'n again. You wait till summer, I say.

Me and Mama walk away. We come up to another store and we stop and look at them dummies, too. Then we go on again. We pass a café where the white people in there eating. Mama tells me keep my eyes in front where they belong, but I can't help from seeing them people eat. My stomach starts to growling 'cause I'm hungry. When I see people eating, I get hungry; when I see a coat, I get cold.

A man whistles at my mama when we go by a filling station. She makes 'tend she don't even see him. I look back and I feel like hitting him in the mouth. If I was bigger, I say; if I was bigger, you'd see.

We keep on going. I'm getting colder and colder, but I

don't say nothing. I feel that stuff running down my nose and I sniff.

"That rag," Mama says.

I get it out and wipe my nose. I'm getting cold all over now—my face, my hands, my feet, everything. We pass another little café, but this'n for white people, too, and we can't go in there, either. So we just walk. I'm so cold now I'm 'bout ready to say it. If I knowed where we was going I wouldn't be so cold, but I don't know where we going. We go, we go, we go. We walk clean out of Bayonne. Then we cross the street and we come back. Same thing I seen when I got off the bus this morning. Same old trees, same old walk, same old weeds, same old cracked pave—same old everything.

I sniff again.

"That rag," Mama says.

I wipe my nose real fast and jugg that handkerchief back in my pocket 'fore my hand gets too cold. I raise my head and I can see David's hardware store. When we come up to it, we go in. I don't know why, but I'm glad.

It's warm in there. It's so warm in there you don't ever want to leave. I look for the heater, and I see it over by them barrels. Three white men standing round the heater talking in Creole. One of them comes over to see what my mama want.

"Got any axe handles?" she says.

Me, Mama and the white man start to the back, but Mama stops me when we come up to the heater. She and the white man go on. I hold my hands over the heater and look at them. They go all the way to the back, and I see the white man pointing to the axe handles 'gainst the wall. Mama takes one of them and shakes it like she's trying to figure how much it weighs. Then she rubs her hand over it from one end to the other end. She turns it over and looks at the other side, then she shakes it again, and shakes her head and puts it back. She gets another one and she does it

just like she did the first one, then she shakes her head.
Then she gets a brown one and do it that, too. But she don't
like this one, either. Then she gets another one, but 'fore
she shakes it or anything, she looks at me. Look like she's
trying to say something to me, but I don't know what it is.
All I know is I done got warm now and I'm feeling right
smart better. Mama shakes this axe handle just like she did
the others, and shakes her head and says something to the
white man. The white man just looks at his pile of axe
handles, and when Mama pass him to come to the front, the
white man just scratch his head and follows her. She tells
me come on and we go on out and start walking again.

We walk and walk, and no time at all I'm cold again.
Look like I'm colder now 'cause I can still remember how
good it was back there. My stomach growls and I suck it in
to keep Mama from hearing it. She's walking right 'side me,
and it growls so loud you can hear it a mile. But Mama don't
say a word.

10

When we come up to the courthouse, I look at the clock.
It's got quarter to twelve. Mean we got another hour and a
quarter to be out here in the cold. We go and stand 'side a
building. Something hits my cap and I look up at the sky.
Sleet's falling.

I look at Mama standing there. I want stand close 'side
her, but she don't like that. She say that's crybaby stuff.
She say you got to stand for yourself, by yourself.

"Let's go back to that office," she says.

We cross the street. When we get to the dentist office I
try to open the door, but I can't. I twist and twist, but I
can't. Mama pushes me to the side and she twist the knob,
but she can't open the door, either. She turns 'way from the

door. I look at her, but I don't move and I don't say nothing. I done seen her like this before and I'm scared of her.

"You hungry?" she says. She says it like she's mad at me, like I'm the cause of everything.

"No, ma'am," I say.

"You want eat and walk back, or you rather don't eat and ride?"

"I ain't hungry," I say.

I ain't just hungry, but I'm cold, too. I'm so hungry and cold I want to cry. And look like I'm getting colder and colder. My feet done got numb. I try to work my toes, but I don't even feel them. Look like I'm go'n die. Look like I'm go'n stand right here and freeze to death. I think 'bout home. I think 'bout Val and Auntie and Ty and Louis and Walker. It's 'bout twelve o'clock and I know they eating dinner now. I can hear Ty making jokes. He done forgot 'bout getting up early this morning and right now he's probably making jokes. Always trying to make somebody laugh. I wish I was right there listening to him. Give anything in the world if I was home round the fire.

"Come on," Mama says.

We start walking again. My feet so numb I can't hardly feel them. We turn the corner and go on back up the street. The clock on the courthouse starts hitting for twelve.

The sleet's coming down plenty now. They hit the pave and bounce like rice. Oh, Lord; oh, Lord, I pray. Don't let me die, don't let me die, don't let me die, Lord.

11

Now I know where we going. We going back of town where the colored people eat. I don't care if I don't eat. I been hungry before. I can stand it. But I can't stand the cold.

I can see we go'n have a long walk. It's 'bout a mile down

there. But I don't mind. I know when I get there I'm go'n
warm myself. I think I can hold out. My hands numb in my
pockets and my feet numb, too, but if I keep moving I can
hold out. Just don't stop no more, that's all.

The sky's gray. The sleet keeps on falling. Falling like
rain now—plenty, plenty. You can hear it hitting the pave.
You can see it bouncing. Sometimes it bounces two times
'fore it settles.

We keep on going. We don't say nothing. We just keep
on going, keep on going.

I wonder what Mama's thinking. I hope she ain't mad at
me. When summer come I'm go'n pick plenty cotton and
get her a coat. I'm go'n get her a red one.

I hope they'd make it summer all the time. I'd be glad if
it was summer all the time—but it ain't. We got to have
winter, too. Lord, I hate the winter. I guess everybody
hate the winter.

I don't sniff this time. I get out my handkerchief and
wipe my nose. My hands's so cold I can hardly hold the
handkerchief.

I think we getting close, but we ain't there yet. I wonder
where everybody is. Can't see a soul but us. Look like we
the only two people moving round today. Must be too cold
for the rest of the people to move round in.

I can hear my teeth. I hope they don't knock together too
hard and make that bad one hurt. Lord, that's all I need, for
that bad one to start off.

I hear a church bell somewhere. But today ain't Sunday.
They must be ringing for a funeral or something.

I wonder what they doing at home. They must be eating.
Monsieur Bayonne might be there with his guitar. One day
Ty played with Monsieur Bayonne's guitar and broke one of
the strings. Monsieur Bayonne was some mad with Ty. He
say Ty wasn't go'n ever 'mount to nothing. Ty can go just
like Monsieur Bayonne when he ain't there. Ty can make
everybody laugh when he starts to mocking Monsieur
Bayonne.

I used to like to be with Mama and Daddy. We used to be happy. But they took him in the Army. Now, nobody happy no more. . . . I be glad when Daddy comes home.

Monsieur Bayonne say it wasn't fair for them to take Daddy and give Mama nothing and give us nothing. Auntie say, "Shhh, Etienne. Don't let them hear you talk like that." Monsieur Bayonne say, "It's God truth. What they giving his children? They have to walk three and a half miles to school hot or cold. That's anything to give for a paw? She's got to work in the field rain or shine just to make ends meet. That's anything to give for a husband?" Auntie say, "Shhh, Etienne, shhh." "Yes, you right," Monsieur Bayonne say. "Best don't say it in front of them now. But one day they go'n find out. One day." "Yes, I suppose so," Auntie say. "Then what, Rose Mary?" Monsieur Bayonne say. "I don't know, Etienne," Auntie say. "All we can do is us job, and leave everything else in His hand . . ."

We getting closer, now. We getting closer. I can even see the railroad tracks.

We cross the tracks, and now I see the café. Just to get in there, I say. Just to get in there. Already I'm starting to feel little better.

12

We go in. Ahh, it's good. I look for the heater; there 'gainst the wall. One of them little brown ones. I just stand there and hold my hands over it. I can't open my hands too wide 'cause they almost froze.

Mama's standing right 'side me. She done unbuttoned her coat. Smoke rises out of the coat, and the coat smells like a wet dog.

I move to the side so Mama can have more room. She opens out her hands and rubs them together. I rub mine together, too, 'cause this keep them from hurting. If you let them warm too fast, they hurt you sure. But if you let them warm just little bit at a time, and you keep rubbing them, they be all right every time.

They got just two more people in the café. A lady back of the counter, and a man on this side the counter. They been watching us ever since we come in.

Mama gets out the handkerchief and count up the money. Both of us know how much money she's got there. Three dollars. No, she ain't got three dollars, 'cause she had to pay us way up here. She ain't got but two dollars and a half left. Dollar and a half to get my tooth pulled, and fifty cents for us to go back on, and fifty cents worth of salt meat.

She stirs the money round with her finger. Most of the money is change 'cause I can hear it rubbing together. She stirs it and stirs it. Then she looks at the door. It's still sleeting. I can hear it hitting 'gainst the wall like rice.

"I ain't hungry, Mama," I say.

"Got to pay them something for they heat," she says.

She takes a quarter out the handkerchief and ties the handkerchief up again. She looks over her shoulder at the people, but she still don't move. I hope she don't spend the money. I don't want her spending it on me. I'm hungry, I'm almost starving I'm so hungry, but I don't want her spending the money on me.

She flips the quarter over like she's thinking. She's must be thinking 'bout us walking back home. Lord, I sure don't want to walk home. If I thought it'd do any good to say something, I'd say it. But Mama makes up her own mind 'bout things.

She turns 'way from the heater right fast, like she better hurry up and spend the quarter 'fore she change her mind. I watch her go toward the counter. The man and the lady look at her, too. She tells the lady something and the lady walks away. The man keeps on looking at her. Her back's turned to the man, and she don't even know he's standing there.

The lady puts some cakes and a glass of milk on the counter. Then she pours up a cup of coffee and sets it 'side the other stuff. Mama pays her for the things and comes on back where I'm standing. She tells me sit down at the table 'gainst the wall.

The milk and cakes's for me; the coffee's for Mama. I eat slow and I look at her. She's looking outside at the sleet. She's looking real sad. I say to myself, I'm go'n make all this up one day. You see, one day, I'm go'n make all this up. I want say it now; I want tell her how I feel right now; but Mama don't like for us to talk like that.

"I can't eat all this," I say.

They ain't got but just three little old cakes there. I'm so hungry right now, the Lord knows I can eat a hundred times three, but I want my mama to have one.

Mama don't even look my way. She knows I'm hungry, she knows I want it. I let it stay there a little while, then I get it and eat it. I eat just on my front teeth, though, 'cause if cake touch that back tooth I know what'll happen. Thank God it ain't hurt me at all today.

After I finish eating I see the man go to the juke box. He drops a nickel in it, then he just stand there a little while looking at the record. Mama tells me keep my eyes in front where they belong. I turn my head like she say, but then I hear the man coming toward us.

"Dance, pretty?" he says.

Mama gets up to dance with him. But 'fore you know it, she done grabbed the little man in the collar and done heaved him 'side the wall. He hit the wall so hard he stop the juke box from playing.

"Some pimp," the lady back of the counter says. "Some pimp."

The little man jumps up off the floor and starts toward my mama. 'Fore you know it, Mama done sprung open the knife and she's waiting for him.

"Come on," she says. "Come on. I'll gut you from your neighbo to your throat. Come on."

I go up to the little man to hit him, but Mama makes me

come and stand 'side her. The little man looks at me and
Mama and goes on back to the counter.

"Some pimp," the lady back of the counter says. "Some
pimp." She starts laughing and pointing at the little man.

"Yes sir, you a pimp, all right. Yes sir-ree."

13

"Fasten that coat, let's go," Mama says.

"You don't have to leave," the lady says.

Mama don't answer the lady, and we right out in the cold
again. I'm warm right now—my hands, my ears, my
feet—but I know this ain't go'n to last too long. It done sleet
so much now you got ice everywhere you look.

We cross the railroad tracks, and soon's we do, I get cold.
That wind goes through this little old coat like it ain't even
there. I got on a shirt and a sweater under the coat, but that
wind don't pay them no mind. I look up and I can see we
got a long way to go. I wonder if we go'n make it 'fore I get
too cold.

We cross over to walk on the sidewalk. They got just one
sidewalk back here, and it's over there.

After we go just a little piece, I smell bread cooking. I
look, then I see a baker shop. When we get closer, I can
smell it more better. I shut my eyes and make 'tend I'm
eating. But I keep them shut too long and I butt up 'gainst a
telephone post. Mama grabs me and see if I'm hurt. I ain't
bleeding or nothing and she turns me loose.

I can feel I'm getting colder and colder, and I look up to
see how far we still got to go. Uptown is 'way up yonder. A
half mile more, I reckon. I try to think of something. They
say think and you won't get cold. I think of that poem,
"Annabel Lee." I ain't been to school in so long—this bad
weather—I reckon they done passed "Annabel Lee" by

now. But passed it or not, I'm sure Miss Walker go'n make me recite it when I get there. That woman don't never forget nothing. I ain't never seen nobody like that in my life.

I'm still getting cold. "Annabel Lee" or no "Annabel Lee," I'm still getting cold. But I can see we getting closer. We getting there gradually.

Soon's we turn the corner, I see a little old white lady up in front of us. She's the only lady on the street. She's all in black and she's a long black rag over her head.

"Stop," she says.

Me and Mama stop and look at her. She must be crazy to be out in all this bad weather. Ain't got but a few other people out there, and all of them's men.

"Y'all done ate?" she says.

"Just finish," Mama says.

"Y'all must be colt then?" she says.

"We headed for the dentist," Mama says. "We'll warm up when we get there."

"What dentist?" the old lady says. "Mr. Bassett?"

"Yes, ma'am," Mama says.

"Come on in," the old lady says. "I'll telephone him and tell him y'all coming."

Me and Mama follow the old lady in the store. It's a little bitty store, and it don't have much in there. The old lady takes off her head rag and folds it up.

"Helena?" somebody calls from the back.

"Yes, Alnest?" the old lady says.

"Did you see them?"

"They're here. Standing beside me."

"Good. Now you can stay inside."

The old lady looks at Mama. Mama's waiting to hear what she brought us in here for. I'm waiting for that, too.

"I saw y'all each time you went by," she says. "I came out to catch you, but you were gone."

"We went back of town," Mama says.

"Did you eat?"

"Yes, ma'am."

The old lady looks at Mama a long time, like she's thinking Mama might be just saying that. Mama looks right back at her. The old lady looks at me to see what I have to say. I don't say nothing. I sure ain't going 'gainst my mama.

"There's food in the kitchen," she says to Mama. "I've been keeping it warm."

Mama turns right around and starts for the door.

"Just a minute," the old lady says. Mama stops. "The boy'll have to work for it. It isn't free."

"We don't take no handout," Mama says.

"I'm not handing out anything," the old lady says. "I need my garbage moved to the front. Ernest has a bad cold and can't go out there."

"James'll move it for you," Mama says.

"Not unless you eat," the old lady says. "I'm old, but I have my pride, too, you know."

Mama can see she ain't go'n beat this old lady down, so she just shakes her head.

"All right," the old lady says. "Come into the kitchen."

She leads the way with that rag in her hand. The kitchen is a little bitty little old thing, too. The table and the stove just 'bout fill it up. They got a little room to the side. Somebody in there laying 'cross the bed—'cause I can see one of his feet. Must be the person she was talking to: Ernest or Alnest—something like that.

"Sit down," the old lady says to Mama. "Not you," she says to me. "You have to move the cans."

"Helena?" the man says in the other room.

"Yes, Alnest?" the old lady says.

"Are you going out there again?"

"I must show the boy where the garbage is, Alnest," the old lady says.

"Keep that shawl over your head," the old man says.

"You don't have to remind me, Alnest. Come, boy," the old lady says.

We go out in the yard. Little old back yard ain't no bigger

than the store or the kitchen. But it can sleet here just like it can sleet in any big back yard. And 'fore you know it, I'm trembling.

"There," the old lady says, pointing to the cans. I pick up one of the cans and set it right back down. The can's so light, I'm go'n see what's inside of it.

"Here," the old lady says. "Leave that can alone."

I look back at her standing there in the door. She's got that black rag wrapped round her shoulders, and she's pointing one of her little old fingers at me.

"Pick it up and carry it to the front," she says. I go by her with the can, and she's looking at me all the time. I'm sure the can's empty. I'm sure she could've carried it herself— maybe both of them at the same time. "Set it on the sidewalk by the door and come back for the other one," she says.

I go and come back, and Mama looks at me when I pass her. I get the other can and take it to the front. It don't feel a bit heavier than that first one. I tell myself I ain't go'n be nobody's fool, and I'm go'n look inside this can to see just what I been hauling. First, I look up the street, then down the street. Nobody coming. Then I look over my shoulder toward the door. That little old lady done slipped up there quiet 's mouse, watching me again. Look like she knowed what I was go'n do.

"Ehh, Lord," she says. "Children, children. Come in here, boy, and go wash your hands."

I follow her in the kitchen. She points toward the bathroom, and I go in there and wash up. Little bitty old bathroom, but it's clean, clean. I don't use any of her towels; I wipe my hands on my pants legs.

When I come back in the kitchen, the old lady done dished up the food. Rice, gravy, meat—and she even got some lettuce and tomato in a saucer. She even got a glass of milk and a piece of cake there, too. It looks so good, I almost start eating 'fore I say my blessing.

"Helena?" the old man says.

"Yes, Alnest?"

"Are they eating?"

"Yes," she says.

"Good," he says. "Now you'll stay inside."

The old lady goes in there where he is and I can hear them talking. I look at Mama. She's eating slow like she's thinking. I wonder what's the matter now. I reckon she's thinking 'bout home.

The old lady comes back in the kitchen.

"I talked to Dr. Bassett's nurse," she says. "Dr. Bassett will take you as soon as you get there."

"Thank you, ma'am," Mama says.

"Perfectly all right," the old lady says. "Which one is it?"

Mama nods toward me. The old lady looks at me real sad. I look sad, too.

"You're not afraid, are you?" she says.

"No, ma'am," I say.

"That's a good boy," the old lady says. "Nothing to be afraid of. Dr. Bassett will not hurt you."

When me and Mama get through eating, we thank the old lady again.

"Helena, are they leaving?" the old man says.

"Yes, Alnest."

"Tell them I say good-bye."

"They can hear you, Alnest."

"Good-bye both mother and son," the old man says. "And may God be with you."

Me and Mama tell the old man good-bye, and we follow the old lady in the front room. Mama opens the door to go out, but she stops and comes back in the store.

"You sell salt meat?" she says.

"Yes."

"Give me two bits worth."

"That isn't very much salt meat," the old lady says.

"That's all I have," Mama says.

The old lady goes back of the counter and cuts a big piece off the chunk. Then she wraps it up and puts it in a paper bag.

"Two bits," she says.

"That looks like awful lot of meat for a quarter," Mama says.

"Two bits," the old lady says. "I've been selling salt meat behind this counter twenty-five years. I think I know what I'm doing."

"You got a scale there," Mama says.

"What?" the old lady says.

"Weigh it," Mama says.

"What?" the old lady says. "Are you telling me how to run my business?"

"Thanks very much for the food," Mama says.

"Just a minute," the old lady says.

"James," Mama says to me. I move toward the door.

"Just one minute, I said," the old lady says.

Me and Mama stop again and look at her. The old lady takes the meat out of the bag and unwraps it and cuts 'bout half of it off. Then she wraps it up again and juggs it back in the bag and gives the bag to Mama. Mama lays the quarter on the counter.

"Your kindness will never be forgotten," she says. "James," she says to me.

We go out, and the old lady comes to the door to look at us. After we go a little piece I look back, and she's still there watching us.

The sleet's coming down heavy, heavy now, and I turn up my coat collar to keep my neck warm. My mama tells me turn it right back down.

"You not a bum," she says. "You a man."

PETER TAYLOR

A Wife of Nashville

The Lovells' old cook Sarah had quit to get married in the
spring, and they didn't have anybody else for a long
time—not for several months. It was during the Depression,
and when a servant quit, people in Nashville (and even
people out at Thornton, where the Lovells came from) tried
to see how long they could go before they got another. All
through the summer, there would be knocks on the
Lovells' front door or on the wooden porch floor, by the
steps. And when one of the children or their mother went
to the door, some Negro man or woman would be standing
there, smiling and holding out a piece of paper. A recom-
mendation it was supposed to be, but the illegible note
scribbled with a blunt lead pencil was something no white
person could have written if he had tried. If Helen Ruth,
the children's mother, went to the door, she always talked a
while to whoever it was, but she hardly ever even looked at
the note held out to her. She would give a piece of advice or
say to meet her around at the back door for a handout. If
one of the boys—there were three Lovell boys, and no
girls—went to the door, he always brought the note in to
Helen Ruth, unless John R., their father, was at home, sick
with his back ailment. Helen Ruth would shake her head

121

and say to tell whoever it was to go away! "Tell him to go
back home," she said once to the oldest boy, who was
standing in the sun-parlor doorway with a smudged scrap of
paper in his hand. "Tell him if he had any sense, he never
would have left the country."

"He's probably not from the country, Mother."

"They're all from the country," Helen Ruth said. "When
they knock on the porch floor like that, they're bound to be
from the country, and they're better off at home, where
somebody cares something about them. I don't care
anything about them any more than you do."

But one morning Helen Ruth hired a cheerful-looking
and rather plump, light-complexioned young Negro girl
named Jess McGehee, who had come knocking on the
front-porch floor just as the others had. Helen Ruth talked
to her at the front door for a while; then she told her to
come around to the kitchen, and they talked there for
nearly an hour. Jess stayed to fix lunch and supper, and
after she had been there a few days, the family didn't know
how they had ever got along without her.

In fact, Jess got on so well with the Lovells that Helen
Ruth even decided to let her come and live on the place, a
privilege she had never before allowed a servant of hers.
Together, she and Jess moved all of John R.'s junk— a grass
duck-hunting outfit, two mounted stags' heads, an outboard
motor, and so on—from the little room above the garage
into the attic of the house. John R. lent Jess the money for
the down payment on a "suit" of furniture, and Jess moved
in. "You would never know she was out there," Helen Ruth
told her friends. "There is never any rumpus. And her
room! It's as clean as yours or mine."

Jess worked for them for eight years. John R. got so one
of his favorite remarks was, "The honeymoon is over, but
this is the real thing this time." Then he would go on about
what he called Helen Ruth's "earlier affairs." The last one
before Jess was Sarah, who quit to get married and go to
Chicago at the age of sixty-eight. She had been with them

for six years and was famous for her pies and her banana dishes.

Before Sarah, there was Carrie. Carrie had been with them when the two younger boys were born, and it was she who had once tried to persuade Helen Ruth not to go to the hospital but to let her act as midwife. She had quit them after five years, to become an undertaker. And before Carrie there was Jane Blakemore, the very first of them all, whom John R. and Helen Ruth had brought with them from Thornton to Nashville when they married. She lasted less than three years; she quit soon after John R., Jr., was born, because, she said, the baby made her nervous.

"It's an honorable record," John R. would say. "Each of them was better than the one before, and each one stayed with us longer. It proves that experience is the best teacher."

Jess's eight years were the years when the boys were growing up; the boys were children when she came, and when she left them, the youngest, little Robbie, had learned to drive the car. In a sense, it was Jess who taught all three boys to drive. She didn't give them their first lessons, of course, because, like Helen Ruth, she had never sat at the wheel of an automobile in her life. She had not ridden in a car more than half a dozen times when she came to the Lovells, but just by chance, one day, she was in the car when John R. let John R., Jr., take the wheel. The car would jerk and lunge forward every time the boy shifted gears, and his father said, "Keep your mind on what you're doing."

"I am," John R., Jr., said, "but it just does that. What makes it do it?"

"Think!" John R. said. "Think! . . . *Think!*"

"I *am* thinking, but what makes it do it?"

Suddenly, Jess leaned forward from the back seat and said, "You letting the clutch out too fast, honey."

Both father and son were so surprised they could not help laughing. They laughed harder, of course, because what Jess said was true. And Jess laughed with them. When they had driven another block, they reached a boulevard stop, and in the process of putting on the brake John R., Jr., killed the engine and then flooded the motor. His father shouted, "Well, let it rest! We're just stuck here for about twenty minutes!"

Jess, who was seated with one arm around a big bag of groceries, began to laugh again. "Turn off the key," she said. "Press down on the starter a spell. Then torectly you turn on the key and she'll start."

John R. looked over his shoulder at her, not smiling, but not frowning, either. Presently, he gave the order, "Try it."

"Try what *Jess said?*" John R., Jr., asked.

"Try what Jess said."

The boy tried it, and in a moment he was racing the motor and grinning at his father. When they had got safely across the boulevard, John R. turned around to Jess again. He asked in a quiet, almost humble manner—the same manner he used when describing the pains in his back to Helen Ruth—where she had learned these things about an automobile. "Law," she said, "I learnt them listening to my brother-in-law that drives a truck talk. I don't reckon I really know'm, but I can say them."

John R. was so impressed by the incident that he did not make it one of his stories. He told Helen Ruth about it, of course, and he mentioned it sometimes to his close friends when they were discussing "the good things" about Negroes. With his sons, he used it as an example of how much you can learn by listening to other people talk, and after that day he would permit John R., Jr., to go for drives in the car without him provided Jess went along in his place. Later on, when the other boys got old enough to drive, there were periods when he turned their instruction over to Jess. Helen Ruth even talked of learning to drive, herself, with the aid of Jess.

But it never came to more than talk with Helen Ruth, though John R. encouraged her, saying he thought driving

was perhaps a serious strain on his back. She talked about it
for several months, but in the end she said that the time
had passed when she could learn new skills. When John R.
tried to encourage her in the idea, she would sometimes
look out one of the sun-parlor windows toward the street
and think of how much she had once wanted to learn to
drive. But that had been long ago, right after they were
married, in the days when John R. had owned a little Ford
coupé. John R. was on the road for the Standard Candy
Company then, and during most of the week she was alone
in their apartment at the old Vaux Hall. While he was away
John R. kept the coupé stored in a garage only two blocks
east, on Broad Street; in those days traveling men still used
the railroads, because Governor Peay hadn't yet paved
Tennessee's highways. At that time, John R. had not believed in women driving automobiles, and Helen Ruth had
felt that he must be right about it; she had even made fun
of women who went *whizzing* about town, blowing horns at
every intersection. Yet in her heart she had longed to drive
that coupé! Jane Blakemore was working for them then,
and one day Jane had put Helen Ruth's longings into
words. "Wouldn't it be dandy," she said, "if me and you
clomb in that car one of these weekdays and toured out to
Thornton to see all the folks—white and black?"

Without a moment's hesitation, however, Helen Ruth
gave the answer that she knew John R. would have given.
"Now, think what you're saying, Jane!" she said. "Wouldn't
we be a fool-looking pair pulling into the square at
Thornton? *Think* about it. What if we should have a flat tire
when we got out about as far as Nine Mile Hill? Who would
change it? *You* certainly couldn't! Jane Blakemore, I don't
think you use your head about anything!"

That was the way Helen Ruth had talked to Jane on more
occasions than one. She was a plain-spoken woman, and she
never spoke plainer to anyone than she did to Jane
Blakemore during the days when they were shut up
together in that apartment at the Vaux Hall. Since Jane was

from Thornton and knew how plain-spoken all Helen
Ruth's family were, she paid little attention to the way
Helen Ruth talked to her. She would smile, or else sneer,
and go on with her work of cooking and cleaning. Sometimes
she would rebel and speak just as plainly as Helen Ruth did.
When Helen Ruth decided to introduce butter plates to
their table, Jane said, "I ain't never heard tell of no butter
dishes."

Helen Ruth raised her eyebrow. "That's because you are
an ignoramus from Thornton, Tennessee," she said.

"I'm ignoramus enough to know ain't no need in nastying
up all them dishes for me to wash."

Helen Ruth had, however, made Jane Blakemore learn
to use butter plates and had made her keep the kitchen
scrubbed and the other rooms of the apartment dusted and
polished and in such perfect order that even John R. had
noticed it when he came on weekends. Sometimes he had
said, "You drive yourself too hard, Helen Ruth."

Jess McGehee was as eager and quick to learn new things
as Jane Blakemore had been unwilling and slow. She would
even put finger bowls on the breakfast table when there
was grapefruit. And how she did spoil the three boys about
their food! There were mornings when she cooked the
breakfast eggs differently for each one of them while John
R. sat and shook his head in disgust at the way she was
pampering his sons. John R.'s "condition" in his back kept
him at home a lot of the time during the eight years Jess
was with them. He had long since left off traveling for the
candy company; soon after the first baby came, he had
opened an insurance agency of his own.

When Jane Blakemore left them and Helen Ruth hired
Carrie (after fifteen or twenty interviews with other
applicants), she had had to warn Carrie that John R.'s hours
might be very irregular, because he was in business for
himself and wasn't able merely to punch a time clock and
quit when the day ended. "He's an onsurance man, ain't
he?" Carrie had asked and had showed by the light in her

eyes how favorably impressed she was. "I know about him," she had said. "He's a life-onsurance man, and that's the best kind to have."

At that moment, Helen Ruth thought perhaps she had made a mistake in Carrie. "I don't like my servant to discuss my husband's business," she said.

"No'm!" Carrie said with enthusiasm. "No, *ma'am!*" Helen Ruth was satisfied, but afterward she had often to tell herself that her first suspicion had been right. Carrie was nosy and prying and morbid—and she gossiped with other people's servants. Her curiosity and her gossiping were especially trying for Helen Ruth during her and John R.'s brief separation. They actually had separated for nearly two months right after Kenneth, the middle boy, was born. Helen Ruth had gone to her father's house at Thornton, taking the two babies and Carrie with her. The boys never knew about the trouble between their parents, of course, until Kenneth pried it out of his mother after they were all grown, and, at the time, people in Nashville and Thornton were not perfectly sure that it was a real separation. Helen Ruth had tried to tell herself that possibly Carrie didn't know it was a real separation. But she was never able to deny completely the significance of Carrie's behavior while they were at Thornton. Carrie's whole disposition had seemed to change the afternoon they left Nashville. Up until then, she had been a moody, shifty, rather loud-mouthed brown woman, full of darky compliments for white folks and of gratuitous promises of extra services she seldom rendered. But at Thornton she had put the old family servants to shame with her industriousness and her respectful, unassuming manner. "You don't find them like Carrie in Thornton any more," Helen Ruth's mother said. "The good ones all go to Nashville or Memphis." But Helen Ruth, sitting by an upstairs window one afternoon, saw her mother's cook and Carrie sauntering toward the back gate to meet a caller. She saw Carrie being introduced and then she recognized the caller as Jane Blakemore. Presently the

cook returned to the kitchen and Helen Ruth saw Carrie
and Jane enter the servants' house in the corner of the yard.
During the hour that they visited there, Helen Ruth sat
quietly by the window in the room with her two babies. It
seemed to her the most terrible hour of her separation from
John R. When Carrie and Jane reappeared on the stoop of
the servants' house and Carrie was walking with Jane to the
gate, there was no longer any doubt in Helen Ruth's mind
but that she would return to her husband, and return
without any complaints or stipulations. During that hour
she had tried to imagine exactly what things the black Jane
and the brown Carrie were talking about, or, rather, *how*
and in what terms they were talking about the things they
must be talking about. In her mind, she reviewed the sort
of difficulties she had had with Jane and the sort she had
with Carrie and tried to imagine what defense they would
make for themselves—Jane for her laziness and contrariness,
Carrie for her usual shiftiness and negligence. Would they
blame her for these failings of theirs? Or would they
blandly pass over their own failings and find fault with her
for things that she was not even aware of, or that she could
not help and could not begin to set right? Had she really
misused these women, either the black one or the brown
one? It seemed to her then that she had so little in life that
she was entitled to the satisfaction of keeping an orderly
house and to the luxury of efficient help. There was too
much else she had not had—an "else" nameless to her, yet
sorely missed—for her to be denied these small satisfactions.
As she sat alone with her two babies in the old nursery and
thought of the two servants gossiping about her, she
became an object of pity to herself. And presently John R.,
wherever he might be at that moment—in his office or at
the club or, more likely, on a hunting or fishing trip
somewhere—became an object of pity, too. And her two
babies, one in his crib and the other playing on the carpet
with a string of spools, were objects of pity. Even Carrie,

standing alone by the gate after Jane had gone, seemed a lone and pitiful figure.

A few days later, Helen Ruth and Carrie and the two baby boys returned to Nashville.

In Nashville, Carrie was herself again; everything was done in her old slipshod fashion. Except during that interval at Thornton, Carrie was never known to perform any task to Helen Ruth's complete satisfaction. Hardly a meal came to the table without the soup or the dessert or some important sauce having been forgotten; almost every week something important was left out of the laundry; during a general cleaning the upper sashes of two or three windows were invariably left unwashed. Yet never in her entire five years did Carrie answer back or admit an unwillingness to do the most menial or the most nonessential piece of work. In fact, one of her most exasperating pronouncements was, "You are exactly right," which was often followed by a lengthy description of how she would do the thing from then on, or an explanation of how it happened that she had forgotten to do it. Not only that, she would often undertake to explain to Helen Ruth Helen Ruth's reason for wanting it done. "You are exactly right and I know how you mean. You want them drapes shut at night so it can seem like we're living in a house out in the Belle Meade instead of this here Vox Hall flat, and some fool might be able to look in from the yard."

"Never mind the reasons, Carrie" was Helen Ruth's usual reply. But her answers were not always so gentle—not when Carrie suggested that she have the second baby at home with Carrie acting as midwife, not when Carrie spoke to her about having the third baby circumcised. And the day that Helen Ruth began packing her things to go to Thornton, she was certain that Carrie would speak out of turn with some personal advice. That would have been more than she could bear, and she was prepared to dismiss

Carrie from her service and make the trip alone. But neither then nor afterward did Carrie give any real evidence of understanding the reasons for the trip to Thornton.

In fact, it was not until long afterward, when Carrie had quit them to become an undertaker, that Helen Ruth felt that Carrie's gossip with other Nashville servants had, by accident, played a part in her separation from John R. She and John R. had talked of separation and divorce more than once during the first two years they were married, in the era of Jane Blakemore. It was not that any quarreling led to this talk but that each accused the other of being dissatisfied with their marriage. When John R. came in from traveling, on a weekend or in the middle of the week—he was sometimes gone only two or three days at a time—he would find Helen Ruth sitting alone in the living room, without a book or even a deck of cards to amuse herself with, dressed perhaps in something new her mother had sent her, waiting for him. She would rise from her chair to greet him, and he would smile in frank admiration of the tall, graceful figure and of the countenance whose features seemed always composed, and softened by her hair, which was beginning to be gray even at the time of their marriage. But he had not come home many times before Helen Ruth was greeting him with tears instead of smiles. At first, he had been touched, but soon he began to complain that she was unhappy. He asked her why she did not see something of other people while he was away—the wives of his business and hunting friends, or some of the other Thornton girls who were married and living in Nashville. She replied that she did see them occasionally but that she was not the sort of woman who enjoyed having a lot of women friends. Besides, she was perfectly happy with her present life; it was only that she believed that he must be unhappy and that he no longer enjoyed her company. She understood that he had to be away most of the week, but even when he was in town, she saw very little of him. When he was not at his office, he was fishing out on Duck River or was off to a

hunt up at Gallatin. And at night he either took her to
parties with those hunting people, with whom she had little
or nothing in common, or piled up on the bed after supper
and slept. All of this indicated that he was not happy being
married to her, she said, and so they talked a good deal
about separating.

After the first baby came, there was no such talk for a
long time—not until after the second baby. After the first
baby came, Helen Ruth felt that their marriage must be
made to last, regardless of hers or John R.'s happiness.
Besides, it was at that time that one of John R.'s hunting
friends—a rich man named Rufus Brantley—had secured
the insurance agency for him; and almost before John R.
opened his office, he had sold policies to other rich hunting
friends that he had. For a while, he was at home more than
he had ever been before. But soon, when his business was
established, he began to attend more and more meets and
trials, all over Tennessee and Alabama and Kentucky. He
even acquired a few dogs and a horse of his own. With his
friends he began to go on trips to distant parts of the
country. It seemed that when he was not deer hunting in
the State of Maine, he was deep-sea fishing in the Gulf.
Helen Ruth did sometimes go with him to the local horse
shows, but one night, at the Spring Horse Show, she had
told Mrs. Brantley that she had a new machine, and Mrs.
Brantley had thought she meant an automobile instead of a
sewing machine. That, somehow, had been the last straw.
She would never go out with "people like the Brantleys"
after that. She was pregnant again before the first baby was
a year old, and this soon became her excuse for going
nowhere in the evening. The women she did visit with very
occasionally in the daytime were those she had known as
girls in Thornton, women whose husbands were bank
tellers and office managers and were barely acquainted
with John R. Lovell.

After the second baby came, Helen Ruth saw these
women more frequently. She began to feel a restlessness

that she could not explain in herself. There were days when she could not stay at home. With Carrie and the two babies, she would traipse about town, on foot or by streetcar, to points she had not visited since she was a little girl and was in Nashville with her parents to attend the State Fair or the Centennial. She went to the Capitol, to Centennial Park and the Parthenon, even out to the Glendale Zoo. Once, with Nancy Tolliver and Lucy Parkes, two of her old Thornton friends, she made an excursion to Cousin Mamie Lovell's farm, which was several miles beyond the town of Franklin. They went by the electric interurban to Franklin, and from there they took a taxi to the farm. Cousin Mamie's husband had been a second cousin of John R.'s father, and it was a connection the Thornton Lovells had once been very proud to claim. But for a generation this branch of the family had been in decline. Major Lovell had been a prominent lawyer in Franklin and had been in politics, but when he died, he left his family "almost penniless." His boys had not gone to college; since the farm was supposed to have been exhausted, they did not try to farm it but clerked in stores in Franklin. There was said to be a prosperous son-in-law in St. Louis, but the daughter was dead and Cousin Mamie was reported to have once called her son-in-law a parvenu to his face. Helen Ruth and her friends made the excursion because they wanted to see the house, which was one of the finest old places in the country and full of antiques.

But Cousin Mamie didn't even let them inside the house. It was a hot summer day, and she had all the blinds closed and the whole L-shaped house shut up tight, so that it would be bearable at night. She received them on the long ell porch. Later, they moved their chairs out under a tree in the yard, where Cousin Mamie's cook brought them a pitcher of iced tea. While they were chatting under the tree that afternoon, they covered all the usual topics that are dealt with when talking to an old lady one doesn't know very well—the old times and the new times, mutual friends and family connections, country living and city living, and always, of course, the lot of woman as it relates to each topic.

"Where are you and John R. living?" Cousin Mamie asked Helen Ruth.

"We're still at the Vaux Hall, Cousin Mamie."

"I'd suppose the trains would be pretty bad for noise there, that close to the depot."

"They're pretty bad in the summer."

"I'd suppose you had a place out from town, seeing how often John R.'s name's in the paper with the hound and hunt set."

"That's John R.'s life," Helen Ruth said, "not mine."

"He runs with a fine pack, I must say," said Cousin Mamie.

Nancy Tolliver and Lucy Parkes nodded and smiled. Lucy said, "The swells of Nashville, Miss Mamie."

But Cousin Mamie said, "There was a day when they weren't the swells. Forty years ago, people like Major Lovell didn't know people like the Brantleys. I think the Brantleys quarried limestone, to begin with. I guess it don't matter, though, for when I was a girl in upper East Tennessee, people said the Lovells started as land speculators hereabouts and at Memphis. But I don't blame you for not wanting to fool with Brantleys, Helen Ruth."

"John R. and I each live our own life, Cousin Mamie."

"Helen Ruth is a woman with a mind of her own, Miss Mamie," Nancy Tolliver said. "It's too bad more marriages can't be like theirs, each living their own life. Everyone admires it as a real achievement."

And Lucy Parkes said, "Because a woman's husband hunts is no reason for her to hunt, any more than because a man's wife sews is any reason for him to sew."

"Indeed not," Cousin Mamie said, actually paying little attention to what Lucy and Nancy were saying. Presently, she continued her own train of thought. "Names like Brantley and Partee and Hines didn't mean a thing in this state even thirty years ago."

What Lucy and Nancy said about her marriage that day left Helen Ruth in a sort of daze and at the same time made her see her situation more clearly. She had never discussed her marriage with anybody, and hearing it described so matter-of-factly by these two women made her understand for the first time what a special sort of marriage it was and how unhappy she was in it. At the time, John R. was away on a fishing trip to Tellico Plains. She did not see him again before she took the babies and Carrie to Thornton. She sent a note to his office saying that she would return when he decided to devote his time to his wife and children instead of to his hounds and horses. While she was at Thornton her letters from John R. made no mention of her note. He wrote about his business, about his hounds and horses, about the weather, and he always urged her to hurry home as soon as she had seen everybody and had a good visit. Meanwhile, he had a room at the Hermitage Club.

When Helen Ruth returned to Nashville, their life went on as before. A year later, the third boy, Robbie, was born, and John R. bought a large bungalow on Sixteenth Avenue, not too far from the Tarbox School, where they planned to send the boys. Carrie was with them for three years after the separation, and though her work did not improve, Helen Ruth found herself making excuses for her. She began to attribute Carrie's garrulity to "a certain sort of bashfulness, or the Negro equivalent to bashfulness." And with the three small boys, and the yard to keep, too, there was so much more for Carrie to do than there had been before! Despite the excuses she made for her, Helen Ruth could see that Carrie was plainly getting worse about everything and that she now seemed to take pleasure in lying about the smallest, most unimportant things. But Helen Ruth found it harder to confront Carrie with her lies or to reprimand her in any way.

During the last months before Carrie quit, she would talk sometimes about the night work she did for a Negro undertaker. To make Helen Ruth smile, she would report things she had heard about the mourners. Her job, Carrie always said, was to sweep the parlors after the funeral and to fold up the chairs. It was only when she finally gave notice to Helen Ruth that she told her what she professed was the truth. She explained that during all those months she had been learning to embalm. "Before you get a certificate," she said, "you has to handle a bad accident, a sickness, a case of old age, a drowning, a burning, and a half-grown child or less. I been waiting on the child till last night, but now I'll be getting my certificate."

Helen Ruth would not even let Carrie go to the basement to get her hat and coat. "You send somebody for them," she said. "But *you*, you get off these premises, Carrie!" She was sincerely outraged by what Carrie had told her, and when she looked at Carrie's hands she was filled with new horror. Yet something kept her from saying all the things that one normally said to a worthless, lying servant who had been guilty of one final outrage. "*Leave,* Carrie!" she said, consciously restraining herself. "Leave this place!" Carrie went out the kitchen door and down the driveway to the street, bareheaded, coatless, and wearing her kitchen slippers.

After Carrie, there was old Sarah, who stayed with them for six years and then quit them to get married and go to Chicago. Sarah was too old to do heavy work even when she first came, and before she had been there a week, John R. had been asked to help move the sideboard and to bring the ladder up from the basement. He said it seemed that every minute he was in the house, he was lifting or moving something that was too much for Sarah. Helen Ruth replied that perhaps she should hire a Negro man to help in the house and look after the yard. But John R. said no, he was only joking, he thought Sarah far and away the best cook they had ever had, and besides business conditions didn't look too good and it was no time to be taking on more help. But he would always add he did not understand why Helen Ruth babied Sarah so. "From the first moment old Sarah set foot in this house, Helen Ruth has babied her," he would say to people in Helen Ruth's presence.

Sarah could neither read nor write. Even so, it took her only a short while to learn all Helen Ruth's special recipes and how to cook everything the way the Lovells liked it. For two weeks, Helen Ruth stayed in the kitchen with Sarah, reading to her from *How We Cook in Tennessee* and giving detailed instructions for every meal. It was during that time that her great sympathy for Sarah developed. Sarah was completely unashamed of her illiteracy, and it was this that first impressed Helen Ruth. She admired Sarah for having no false pride and for showing no resentment of her mistress's impatience. She observed Sarah's kindness with the children. And she learned from Sarah about Sarah's religious convictions and about her long, unhappy marriage to a Negro named Morse Wilkins, who had finally left her and gone up North.

While Sarah was working for them, John R. and Helen Ruth lived the life that Helen Ruth had heard her friends describe to John R.'s Cousin Mamie. It was not until after Sarah had come that Helen Ruth, recalling the afternoon at Cousin Mamie's, identified Lucy Parkes's words about a wife's sewing and a husband's hunting as the very answer she had once given to some of Carrie's impertinent prying. That afternoon, the remark had certainly sounded familiar, but she had been too concerned with her own decision to leave her husband to concentrate upon anything so trivial. And after their reconciliation, she tried not to dwell on things that had led her to leave John R. Their reconciliation, whatever it meant to John R., meant to her the acceptance of certain mysteries—the mystery of his love of hunting, of his choice of friends, of his desire to maintain a family and home of which he saw so little, of his attachment to her, and of her own devotion to him. Her babies were now growing into little boys. She felt that there was much to be thankful for, not the least of which was a servant as fond of her and of her children as Sarah was. Sarah's affection for the three little boys often reminded Helen Ruth how lonely Sarah's life must be.

One day, when she had watched Sarah carefully wrapping up little Robbie in his winter play clothes before he went out to play in the snow, she said, "You love children so much, Sarah, didn't you ever have any of your own?"

Sarah, who was a yellow-skinned woman with face and arms covered with brown freckles, turned her gray eyes and fixed them solemnly on Helen Ruth. "Why, I had the cutest little baby you ever did see," she said, "and Morse went and killed it."

"Morse *killed* your baby?"

"He rolled over on it in his drunk sleep and smothered it in the bed."

After that, Helen Ruth would never even listen to Sarah when she talked about Morse, and she began to feel a hatred toward any and all of the men who came to take Sarah home at night. Generally, these men were the one subject Sarah did not discuss with Helen Ruth, and their presence in Sarah's life was the only serious complaint Helen Ruth made against her. They would come sometimes as early as four in the afternoon and wait on the back porch for Sarah to get through. She knew that Sarah was usually feeding one of them out of her kitchen, and she knew that Sarah was living with first one and then another of them, but when she told John R. she was going to put her foot down on it, he forbade her to do so. And so through nearly six years she tolerated this weakness of Sarah's. But one morning in the late spring Sarah told her that Morse Wilkins had returned from up North and that she had taken him back as her husband. Helen Ruth could not find anything to say for a moment, but after studying the large diamond on her engagement ring for awhile she said, "My servant's private life is her own affair, but I give you fair warning now, Sarah, I want to see no more of your men friends—Morse or *any other*—on this place again."

From that time, she saw no more men on the place until Morse himself came, in a drunken rage, in the middle of a summer's day. Helen Ruth had been expecting something of the sort to happen. Sarah had been late to work several times during the preceding three weeks. She had come one morning with a dark bruise on her cheek and said she had fallen getting off the streetcar. Twice, Helen Ruth had found Sarah on her knees, praying, in the kitchen. The day Helen Ruth heard the racket at the back-porch door, she knew at once that it was Morse. She got up from her sewing machine and went directly to the kitchen. Sarah was on the back porch, and Morse was outside the screen door of the porch, which was hooked on the inside. He was a little man, shriveled up, bald-headed, not more than five feet tall, and of a complexion very much like Sarah's. Over his white shirt he wore a dark sleeveless sweater. "You come on home," he was saying as he shook the screen door.

Helen Ruth stepped to the kitchen door. "Is that her?" Morse asked Sarah, motioning his head toward Helen Ruth.

When Sarah turned her face around, her complexion seemed several shades lighter than Morse's. "I got to go," she said to Helen Ruth.

"No, Sarah, *he's* got to go. But *you* don't."

"He's gonna leave me again."

"That's the best thing that could happen to you, Sarah."

Sarah said nothing, and Morse began shaking the door again.

"Is he drunk, Sarah?" Helen Ruth asked.

"He's so drunk I don't know how he find his way here."

Helen Ruth went out onto the porch. "Now, you get off this place, and quick about it," she said to Morse.

He shook the screen door again. "You didn't make me

come here, Mrs. Lovellel, and you can't make me leave, Mrs. Lovellel."

"I can't make you leave," Helen Ruth said at once, "but there's a bluecoat down on the corner who can."

Suddenly Sarah dropped to her knees and began praying. Her lips moved silently, and gradually she let her forehead come to rest on the top of the rickety vegetable bin. Morse looked at her through the screen, putting his face right against the wire. "Sarah," he said, "you come on home. You better come on now if you think I be there."

Sarah got up off her knees.

"I'm going to phone the police," Helen Ruth said, pretending to move toward the kitchen.

Morse left the door and staggered backward toward the driveway. "Come on, Sarah," he shouted.

"I got to go," Sarah said.

"I won't let you go, Sarah!"

"She can't make you stay!" Morse shouted. "You better come on if you coming!"

"It will be the worst thing you ever did in your life, Sarah," said Helen Ruth. "And if you go with him, you can't ever come back here. He'll kill you someday, too—the way he did your baby."

Sarah was on her knees again, and Morse was out of sight but still shouting as he went down the driveway. Suddenly, Sarah was on her feet. She ran into the kitchen and on through the house to the front porch.

Helen Ruth followed, calling her back. She found Sarah on the front porch waving to Morse, who was halfway down the block, running in a zigzag down the middle of the street, still shouting at the top of his voice. Sarah cried out to him, "Morse! Morse!"

"Sarah!" Helen Ruth said.

"Morse!" Sarah cried again, and then she began mumbling words that Helen Ruth could not quite understand at the time. Afterward, going over it in her mind, Helen Ruth realized that what Sarah had been mumbling was, "If I don't see you no more on this earth, Morse, I'll see you in Glory."

Sarah was with the Lovells for four more months, and then one night she called up on the telephone and asked John R., Jr., to tell his mother that she was going to get married to a man named Racecar and they were leaving for Chicago in the morning.

Jess McGehee came to them during the Depression. Even before Sarah left the Lovells, John R. had had to give up all of his "activities" and devote his entire time to selling insurance. Rufus Brantley had shot himself through the head while cleaning a gun at his hunting lodge, and most of John R.'s other hunting friends had suffered the same financial reverses that John R. had. The changes in the Lovells' life had come so swiftly that Helen Ruth did not realize for awhile what the changes meant in her relationship with John R. It seemed as though she woke up one day and discovered that she was not married to the same man. She found herself spending all her evenings playing Russian bank with a man who had no interest in anything but his home, his wife, and his three boys. Every night, he would give a brief summary of the things that had happened at his office or on his calls, and then he would ask her and the boys for an account of everything they had done that day. He took an interest in the house and the yard, and he and the boys made a lily pool in the back yard, and singlehanded he screened in the entire front porch. Sometimes he took the whole family to Thornton for a weekend, and he and Helen Ruth never missed the family reunions there in September.

In a sense, these were the happiest years of their married life. John R.'s business got worse and worse, of course, but since part of their savings was in the bank at Thornton that did not fail, they never had any serious money worries. Regardless of their savings, however, John R.'s loss of

income and his having to give up his friends and his hunting
wrought very real, if only temporary, changes in him.
There were occasions when he would sit quietly and listen
to his family's talk without correcting them or pointing out
how foolish they were. He gave up saying "Think!" to the
boys, and instead would say, "Now, let's see if we can't
reason this thing out." He could never bring himself to ask
for any sympathy from Helen Ruth for his various losses,
but as it was during this time that he suffered so from the
ailment in his back (he and Helen Ruth slept with boards
under their mattress for ten years), the sympathy he got for
his physical pain was more than sufficient. All in all, it was a
happy period in their life, and in addition to their general
family happiness they had Jess.

Jess not only cooked and cleaned, she planned the meals,
did the marketing, and washed everything, from handkerchiefs
and socks to heavy woolen blankets. When the boys began
to go to dances, she even learned to launder their dress
shirts. There was nothing she would not do for the boys or
for John R. or for Helen Ruth. The way she idealized the
family became the basis for most of the "Negro jokes" told
by the Lovells during those years. In her room she had a
picture of the family, in a group beside the lily pool, taken
with her own box Brownie; she had tacked it and also a
picture of each of them on the wall above her washstand. In
her scrapbook she had pasted every old snapshot and pho-
tograph that Helen Ruth would part with, as well as old
newspaper pictures of John R. on horseback or with a
record-breaking fish he had caught. She had even begged
from Helen Ruth an extra copy of the newspaper notice of
their wedding.

Jess talked to the family a good deal at mealtime, but
only when they had addressed her first and had shown that
they wanted her to talk. Her remarks were mostly about
things that related to the Lovells. She told a sad story about
a "very loving white couple" from Brownsville, her home
town, who had been drowned in each other's arms when

their car rolled off the end of a river ferry. The point of the story was that those two people were the same, fine, loving sort of couple that John R. and Helen Ruth were. All three of the boys made good grades in school, and every month Jess would copy their grades in her scrapbook, which she periodically passed around for the family to appreciate. When Kenneth began to write stories and articles for his high-school paper, she would always borrow the paper overnight; soon it came out that she was copying everything he wrote onto the big yellow pages of her scrapbook.

After three or four years, John R. began to say that he thought Jess would be with them always and that they would see the day when the boys' children would call her "Mammy." Helen Ruth said that she would like to agree with him about that, but actually she worried, because Jess seemed to have no life of her own, which wasn't at all natural. John R. agreed that they should make her take a holiday now and then. Every summer, they would pack Jess off to Brownsville for a week's visit with her kinfolks, but she was always back in her room over the garage within two or three days; she said that her people fought and quarreled so much that she didn't care for them. Outside her life with the Lovells, she had only one friend. Her interest was the movies, and her friend was "the Mary who works for Mrs. Dunbar." Jess and Mary went to the movies together as often as three or four times a week, and on Sunday afternoons Mary came to see Jess or Jess went to see Mary, who lived over the Dunbars' garage. Jess always took along her scrapbook and her most recent movie magazines. She and Mary swapped movie magazines, and it was apparent from Jess's talk on Monday mornings that they also swapped eulogies of their white families.

Sometimes Helen Ruth would see Mrs. Dunbar downtown or at a P.T.A. meeting; they would discuss their cooks and smile over the reports that each had received of the other's family. "I understand that your boys are all growing into very handsome men," Mrs. Dunbar said once, and she

told Helen Ruth that Jess was currently comparing one of
the boys—Mrs. Dunbar didn't know which one—to Neil
Hamilton, and that she was comparing Helen Ruth to Irene
Rich, and John R. to Edmund Lowe. As the boys got older,
they began to resent the amount of authority over them—
though it was small—that Jess had been allowed by their
parents and were embarrassed if anyone said Jess had
taught them to drive the car. When John R., Jr., began at
the university, he made his mother promise not to let Jess
know what grades he received, and none of the boys would
let Jess take snapshots of them any more. Their mother
tried to comfort Jess by saying that the boys were only
going through a phase and that it would pass in time. One
day, she even said this in the presence of Robbie, who
promptly reported it to the older boys, and it ended with
John R., Jr.'s, complaining to his father that their mother
ought not to make fun of them to Jess. His father laughed at
him but later told Helen Ruth that he thought she was
making a mistake, that the boys were getting big enough to
think about their manly dignity, and that she would have to
take that into consideration.

She didn't make the same mistake again, but although
Jess never gave any real sign of her feelings being hurt,
Helen Ruth was always conscious of how the boys were
growing away from their good-natured servant. By the time
Robbie was sixteen, they had long since ceased to have any
personal conversation with Jess, and nothing would have
induced Robbie to submit to taking drives with her but the
knowledge that his father would not allow him to use the
car on dates until he had had months of driving practice.
Once, when Robbie and Jess returned from a drive, Jess
reported, with a grin, that not a word had passed between
them during the entire hour and a half. Helen Ruth only
shook her head sadly. The next day she bought Jess a new
bedside radio.

The radio was the subject of much banter among the boys
and their father. John R. said Helen Ruth had chosen the

period of hard times and the Depression to become more generous with her servant than she had ever been before in her life. They recalled other presents she had given Jess recently, and from that time on they teased her regularly about how she spoiled Jess. John R. said that if Jess had had his back trouble, Helen Ruth would have retired her at double pay and nursed her with twice the care that he received. The boys teased her by saying that at Christmas time she reversed the custom of shopping for the servant at the ten-cent stores and for the family at the department stores.

Yet as long as Jess was with them, they all agreed that she was the best help they had ever had. In fact, even afterward, during the war years, when John R.'s business prospered again and his back trouble left him entirely and the boys were lucky enough to be stationed near home and, later, continue their education at government expense, even then John R. and the boys would say that the years when Jess was with them were the happiest time of their life and that Jess was the best servant Helen Ruth had ever had. They said that, and then there would be a silence, during which they were probably thinking about the summer morning just before the war when Jess received a telephone call.

When the telephone rang that morning, Helen Ruth and John R. and the boys had just sat down to breakfast. As was usual in the summertime, they were eating at the big drop-leaf table in the sun parlor. Jess had set the coffee urn by Helen Ruth's place and was starting from the room when the telephone rang. Helen Ruth, supposing the call was for a member of the family, and seeing that Jess lingered in the doorway, said for her to answer it there in the sun parlor instead of running to the telephone in the back hall.

Jess answered it, announcing whose residence it was in a voice so like Helen Ruth's that it made the boys grin. For a moment, everyone at the table kept silent. They waited for

Jess's eyes to single out one of them. John R., Jr., and Kenneth even put down their grapefruit spoons. But the moment Jess picked up the instrument, she fixed her eyes on the potted fern on the window seat across the room. At once her nostrils began to twitch, her lower lip fell down, and it seemed only an act of will that she was twice able to say, "Yes, ma'am," in answer to the small, unreal, metallic voice.

When she had replaced the telephone on its cradle, she turned quickly away and started into the dining room. But Helen Ruth stopped her. "Jess," she asked, her voice full of courtesy, "was the call for you?"

Jess stopped, and they all watched her hands go up to her face. Without turning around, she leaned against the door jamb and began sobbing aloud. Helen Ruth sprang up from the table, saying, "Jess, honey, what *is* the matter?" John R. and the boys stood up, too.

"It was a telegram for me—from Brownsville."

Helen Ruth took her in her arms. "Is someone dead?"

Between sobs, Jess answered, "My little brother—our baby brother—the only one of 'em I cared for." Then her sobs became more violent.

Helen Ruth motioned for John R. to move the morning paper from the big wicker chair, and she led Jess in that direction. But Jess would not sit down, and she could not be pulled away from Helen Ruth. She held fast to her, and Helen Ruth continued to pat her gently on the back and to try to console her with gentle words. Finally, she said, "Jess, you must go to Brownsville. Maybe there's been some mistake. Maybe he's not dead. But you must go, anyway."

Presently, Jess did sit in the chair, and dried her eyes on Helen Ruth's napkin. The boys shook their heads sympathetically and John R. said she certainly must go to Brownsville. She agreed, and said she believed there was a bus at ten that she would try to catch. Helen Ruth patted her hand, telling her to go along to her room when she felt like it, and said that *she* would finish getting breakfast.

"I want to go by to see Mary first," Jess said, "so I better make haste." She stood up, forcing a grateful smile. Then she burst into tears again and threw her arms about Helen Ruth, mumbling, "Oh, God! Oh, God!" The three boys and their father saw tears come into Helen Ruth's eyes, and through her tears Helen Ruth saw a change come over their faces. It was not exactly a change of expression. It couldn't be that, she felt, because it was exactly the same on each of the four faces. It hardly seemed possible that so similar a change could reflect four men's individual feelings. She concluded that her own emotion, and probably the actual tears in her eyes, had made her imagine the change, and when Jess now pulled away and hurried off to her room, Helen Ruth's tears had dried and she could see no evidence of the change she had imagined in her husband's and her sons' faces.

While Jess was in her room preparing to leave, they finished breakfast. Then Helen Ruth began clearing the table, putting the dishes on the teacart. She had said little while they were eating, but in her mind she was all the while going over something that she knew she must tell her family. As she absent-mindedly stacked the dishes, her lips moved silently over the simple words she would use in telling them. She knew that they were watching her, and when Robbie offered to take Jess to the bus station, she knew that the change she had seen in all their faces had been an expression of sympathy for *her* as well as of an eagerness to put this whole episode behind them. "I'll take Jess to her bus," he said.

But Helen Ruth answered, in the casual tone she had been preparing to use, that she thought it probably wouldn't be the thing to do.

"Why, what do you mean, Helen Ruth?" John R. asked her.

"It was very touching, Mother," Kenneth said in his new, manly voice, "the way she clung to you." He, too, wanted to express sympathy, but he also seemed to want to distract his mother from answering his father's question.

At that moment, Jess passed under the sun-parlor windows, walking down the driveway, carrying two large suitcases. Helen Ruth watched her until she reached the sidewalk. Then, very quietly, she told her family that Jess McGehee had no baby brother and had never had one. "Jess and Mary are leaving for California. They think they're going to find themselves jobs out there."

"You knew that right along?" John R. asked.

"I knew it right along."

"Did she know you did, Helen Ruth?" he asked. His voice had in it the sternness he used when questioning the boys about something.

"No, John R., she did not. I didn't learn it from her."

"Well, I don't believe it's so," he said. "Why, I don't believe that for a minute. Her carrying on was too real."

"They're going to California. They've already got their two tickets. Mrs. Dunbar got wind of it somehow, by accident, from Mrs. Lon Thompson's cook, and she called me on Monday. They've saved their money and they're going."

"And you let Jess get away with all that crying stuff just now?" John R. said.

Helen Ruth put her hands on the handlebar of the teacart. She pushed the cart a little way over the tile floor but stopped when he repeated his question. It wasn't to answer his question that she stopped, however. "Oh, my dears!" she said, addressing her whole family. Then it was a long time before she said anything more. John R. and the three boys remained seated at the table, and while Helen Ruth gazed past them and toward the front window of the sun parlor, they sat silent and still, as though they were in a picture. What could she say to them, she kept asking herself. And each time she asked the question, she received for answer some different memory of seemingly unrelated things out of the past twenty years of her life. These things presented themselves as answers to her question, and each of them seemed satisfactory to her. But how little sense it would make to her husband and her grown sons, she reflected, if she should suddenly begin telling them about the long hours she had spent waiting in that apartment at the Vaux Hall while John R. was on the road for the Standard Candy Company, and in the same breath should tell them about how plainly she used to talk to Jane Blakemore and how Jane pretended that the baby made her nervous and went back to Thornton. Or suppose she should abruptly remind John R. of how ill at ease the wives of his hunting friends used to make her feel and how she had later driven Sarah's worthless husband out of the yard, threatening to call a bluecoat. What if she should suddenly say that because a woman's husband hunts, there is no reason for *her* to hunt, any more than because a man's wife sews, there is reason for him to sew. She felt that she would be willing to say anything at all, no matter how cruel or absurd it was, if it would make them understand that everything that happened in life only demonstrated in some way the lonesomeness that people felt. She was ready to tell them about sitting in the old nursery at Thornton and waiting for Carrie and Jane Blakemore to come out of the cabin in the yard. If it would make them see what she had been so long in learning to see, she would even talk at last about the "so much else" that had been missing from her life and that she had not been able to name, and about the foolish mysteries she had so nobly accepted upon her reconciliation with John R. To her, these things were all one now; they were her loneliness, the loneliness from which everybody, knowingly or unknowingly, suffered. But she knew that her husband and her sons did not recognize her loneliness or Jess McGehee's or their own. She turned her eyes from the window to look at their faces around the table, and it was strange to see that they were still thinking in the most personal and particular terms of how they had been deceived by a servant, the ignorant granddaughter of an ignorant slave, a Negro woman from Brownsville who was crazy about the movies and who would soon be riding a bus, mile after mile, on her way to Hollywood, where she might find the friendly faces of the real Neil Hamilton and the real Irene Rich. It was with effort that Helen Ruth thought again of Jess McGehee's departure and the problem of offering an explanation to her family. At last, she said patiently, "My dears, don't you see how it was for Jess? How else can they tell us anything when there is such a gulf?" After a moment she said, "How can I make you understand this?"

Her husband and her three sons sat staring at her, their big hands, all so alike, resting on the breakfast table, their faces stamped with identical expressions, not of wonder but of incredulity. Helen Ruth was still holding firmly to the handle of the teacart. She pushed it slowly and carefully over the doorsill and into the dining room, dark and cool as an underground cavern, and spotlessly clean, the way Jess McGehee had left it.

ROSELLEN BROWN

I Am Not Luis Beech-Nut

How long it take you to go all around the world? A day and a half something like that? A day and a half I get up, drink this Bustelo down with grit in the bottom, dirt, and I tell Adela get another sleeve for the coffee, this little flannel for the cup, this one is stinking by now and have a hole. I'm looking at the Bustelo bag, the yellow always look so old and faded, and in my mind I got to learn these things, it's true it say "TOSTADO Y ENVASADO POR BUSTELO COFFEE ROASTING CO. (Div. of Beech-Nut, Inc.)" Son of a bitch. "Tostado y Molido Para El Gusto Hispano"—y el Profit Americano. Like me. Their little fertilizer, manure, what you call it, for their flower gardens, beauty roses. Little shit, this Luis, and all day long George Street, Leon Street, going by the store so fast you think I'm selling the plague in here two for a dollar.

No, I was saying what I do while the world going round, and I could go with it—if I was Luis Beech-Nut. I drink this shit down, wipe my mouth, push my mustache out flat, scatter the crumbs for the birds, buckle up my belt that I keep loose for breakfast, and goodby, seven days a week. The girls, some of them are up, Enery go on sleeping, she'll be sleeping when the last day of the great world come, and

I go on. Adela come later, all the help she bring me. Whatever a woman is good for might be between the sheets she wash—Adela will do, I'm not a man who force a woman to be *una puta*, you know—but this one of mine, she is mostly a maker of girl children to embarrass me. Not one boy in that lot, just all these babies with those little bottoms that are always cloved like the devil's feet. I checked each time I had one of them alone the first time, put my hands in the diaper, hoping for a mistake, something to get hold of, but the only sticks in this family, Jesús, are this one of mine and the one that prop the kitchen window open in the summer!

And then after making herself round with kids in front before, and behind after, she is a first-class maker of mistakes at the store. The adding machine is like some mystery, it could be a rocket ship, she stand there with her fingers on the controls, they could be her feet in shoes, not graceful, and smile her little smile looking so scared, and drive away the customers right into the arms of Anthony and his thieves' market up there. So I tell her to scrub the counter while I go up to the money, eleven cents for one can of tomato sauce—tell me what can you do with one can?—and she polish and shine, that metal edge on the counter is like a mirror, till she deserve a genie popping out of it, and say: Lady, what your wish? I don't know about her but my wish is two dozen ladies coming in to do the whole week's shopping one after another, they say No More Supermarkets, Never, with their big squeaky carts parked over there in the corner. Asking, for staples first, economy size, and then all the stupid little things that last sucker, *coño*, had to go and order. What for? Capers? How many capers you think I sell in a week? Chili yes, *cumino*, but what is this other stuff here. This lemon-pepper, marjoram, coriander? This was never any Gristedes, not even the old days. No wonder that old Jew sold out.

So. This morning. I have seen the old McTave lady who buy Alka-Seltzer so often she going to take off her roof some morning and never stop, fly out to sea. Seventy-three

cents, plus tax on the Alka-Seltzer. Fontaine over there
come get himself an electric-green toothbrush. He brush in
the dark? Then from across the intersection, long distance,
that slut, that nigger girl who hustle for the *tecato*, what she
come for? Adela watch me with her eyes little when she
twitch her ass at me, but it's O.K., I don't like women that
are built like tweezers. I swear to the Virgin Mary, she
heap up a little pile and give me her business dimple: one
box kitchen matches, one small can Hormel corned beef
hash, pantyhose on sale, cloud-mist, two for $1.07, and a
pack of gum. The matches go for his habit, the stockings go
for hers, the dog eat the corned beef, I bet you, and they all
split the gum. What else I got to do here but think?

I rearranged everything on the shelves twice already,
I'm trying ways to get your eye when you walk in—if
nobody's around I pretend to come in the door and what hit
me? Campbell's Pork and Beans. O.K., now what would go
good with it to put by its right hand? You got to strain
yourself to do this, what they call good retailing practices.
Bread and butter pickles. I try that for a day. The label's
getting this dust that stick, damp dust, I'm afraid to go see
what the basement doing to me, but I can't dust it off and I
can't wash it. At the door when I'm pretending to come on
in smiling, pocket full of change and no holes in it, and the
cod stink and the whole place have such dust flying in on
the light it could be a barnyard back home with a cockfight
going on.

I don't know. Eight years' work at Cappy's Market, two
months here, my Grand Opening banners are still out there
looking like a lord's funeral, and that Jew that bought me all
that coriander went to where? Palm Springs? Palm Beach?
Someplace warm, a little closer to my Bayamón, no
seven-day-a-week nightmares, and gave it all to Luis
instead, and after my last breakfast of steamed shit they
going to bury me under the concrete out back if things
don't shake out better soon. I can add, my machine can add

if my wife stay off it, but all I get to add is OUTGOING, cash, credit. Everything else is *subtracción*.

I take a candle home. Adela will say shame but she be the first to help me light it. The candles are selling better because what's her name, that Hortensia, old Negri, down George corner of Smith, dropped dead a couple weeks ago with a goiter as big as that mailman's pouch out there. So her Botánica is shut up behind a ripped old black shade. How could she die, and screaming, they said, like a saint sent to hell by mistake, with all the herbs and candles and little sacks of cures right there? Well, she died sure as she lived, sitting there in that old couch popping springs, telling people how to change Jesus's mind or get their mans back, his wandering ass back in their bed, if you'll pardon me. She brought luck with the horses, luck with the *boleta*. Tony Aguilar said it was rat-shit but she did him a good turn, he won three hundred dollars the day before her goiter choked her. Luck with women who couldn't bear—not so much luck with the ones who bore stones they didn't want to carry, I can promise you that—but she died.

And I got her business. The nearest spirit woman now, it make you think, is a bus ride, thirty-five cents, or that blind woman up State Street who only do bad spells, death, or make sworn enemies disappear. And the nearest *bodega* that gots candles is a good solid walk. Nobody want to go a block rain or shine these days, you notice? We getting like the suburbs, only with rats and no parking. Anthony's little shelf shits but he don't need that business, when he sell one out, say St. Michael, it stay out till the person who need it fall down dead or go broke. Can they sue him for lousy inventory? So there's the PEACEFUL HOME candle, and the MONEY DRAWING that has to say (ALLEGED) in small letters we all so honest now, while Beech-Nut take all the money away in a wheelbarrow anyhow. SAFE CROSS-ING sell in going-home season, the 7 AFRICAN POWERS so-so, the WORK candle, all the saints, and the black ones

with no words and a cat hissing with his back arched way
up.

Maybe somebody gots one burning for me. Hey that's a
good idea. Trying to get me on the welfares. Two packs of
cigarettes. Adela sell them and what can she mess up? She
forget the matches. The blond bitch come on back in and
ask for them making these little lips to tell us she's pissed
off for the ten extra steps. I hold out a handful and she take
two. The cat bring a mouse up the cellar stairs and drop it
splat right in front of the bread rack. Stiff already. Some
kid, Widdoes his name is, come over from the Projects, and
I hate it but I tell him go home and tell your mama no, no
more credit, not till I get that page full of hot dog dinners
paid back here. Enough. It's enough this place eat up my
bank account, do they mean to pull my hairs out one by
one?

I went home last night, my Enery, my first best daughter
I had when I was nineteen and had the best still in me, she
is waiting to ask a question. What, dear? I got a problem,
from school. What, you got in some trouble? No. She is
almost blond, bless her, we call her Blanqui, I don't know
where she get that but she always like a movie starlet with
that wavy hair that give off lights like a three-way bulb. No,
I mean some homework, I don't know what to do with it.
She bring her notebook that's fat with doodlings of girls with
all their noses pointed up. It say on the blue line:

LIST 5 REASONS BEHIND MAN'S DESIRE TO
ESCAP THIS WORLD

This is for what class?

She don't remember that, only she going to have to
answer it somehow. I say, what you think, Dolly? My name
for this beautiful girl. Blanqui, you can do this.

Well, love? Maybe sometimes love goes wrong? She is
thinking of her soldier who took her little silver ring off to
Vietnam and she worry will they let him wear it? They took
all his hair away, maybe they get his ring too. She going to
get married when he come back (if, I say, but never to her)

and he get his army pay and then her sweet cherry she been saving, and her babysitting bank account too, and don't laugh, one of these days I wake up and see it bigger than mine. All those half-babies of hers get to wait a little longer where it's warm inside her while the other half run away from flying bullets.

Yes, I say. Love.

And there's always war.

War. Sure, war.

She bite her finger-knuckle thinking. Maybe they're afraid to die. I tell her write that. That's good. They can't escape but they want to if they could. She print it out slowly and carefully. Her writing go both ways, left, right, and straight up. That's three. Sickness, that's not the same as dying. Sí. Write it. Pain and sickness, you could say. Sometime it take forever just to die.

Now she is out of griefs. Imagine that, to be seventeen. Enery, *mi vida*, I say, and I take her hands. Enery, think hard.

She make big eyes at me, looking into mine. Little stranger who already outgrew all the Spanish she ever want to know, who is so smart in the dress department, and polished fingernails, and pants. *Muchacha*, money. You ever heard of money? *El dinero?* What make the whole world go around? And is killing your father? (I don't say that. Why make her wounds for me to bleed from?) She looking a little disappointed—oh that—but she still need one more or she get a bad grade, so she write in MONY and smile and slam her book closed, gone already halfway down the stairs to meet her friends. I watch them from the window going around to the church to play or up to Livingston, Fulton, the stores to spend her baby-sitting money? To go put her little nose, that don't turn up like her pictures, right against the dusty window at the *joyería*, she make eyes at this ring, fifty-eight carats or fifty-eight facets or what, she want her boy to buy her so bad she pay half herself. Why? I'm smart now. So they can get married and be in hock already on their wedding night to a man who hack up stones and sell the chips and dust? Then to the furniture man? Then everything, and sure to be a baby hatching by the time the sun come up. I don't want her eyes wet but once in a while I see a bullet keeping him there forever, a nice boy, decent, but so she remember the best of him, what they planned, not what the whole world gots planned for them.

Three times I left Adela or she left me, one time she had a good cut across her eye that left a scar, once a slash I won't say where, with a Gem, the usual thing. The first time Enery was just walking, then a couple more times, don't ask me why I went, why I came back like a tomcat bleeding between the legs. I feel like I grow up since then, or I don't care about some things as much as others no more. I mind my business. I only want to say, I wish my Enery could stay just like she is this minute, no matter what she doing: bending over to tie her shoe that's in style right up to the second, this year lacing shoes, like they always going out hiking, last year platforms, they up on the third floor just walking down the block, laughing, her teeth so perfect and white like baby teeth, and her skirt pulling up in back over these strong legs Adela never had with her tree-stumps. Looking like a girl who can go home to a comfortable bed and no sisters in it, no men, no tears in it, not real tears she bleed from her womb, or her little breasts like milk. No standing on line at the prison door with packages, no running to the hospital, Jesús, no doing foul things standing up in the stair wells like her father done. *Mi Blanquita*, who give me one more reason not to close the gates to this beat-down store for the last time and run someplace before the creditors come up behind me with blackjacks.

But. One more thing to tell about Rojas Spanish Favorites. It should have been born a pool hall. The one robbery don't matter much, it was only an insult because I knew this *maricón* who come bouncing in here with his finger poking in his pocket like a hard-on, he called it a *gun*. "Hey, spic, I got a *gun* here. No tricks." Was he on the late show? O.K., you know what he went home with, back down to Baltic Street where he live with his mama? Eleven dollars, one check I wasn't so sure was worth a piss against the wall, two unopen packages, one dimes, one pennies—see, I let him take it all out of the money box himself. He'd of killed me if I gave him that and say that's all. He had to come *see*. So he shovel it into his pocket, he still fierce, his cheeks going, his eyes bugged, and he can't smile or laugh at the little turds I get to call my profit. His profit now! Can't spare a smile. I can't even make change, man—these big executive bastards, whatever they are, they come in on the way home from the subway with their tens, their twenties for a pack of Larks, a quart of milk and I get wiped out, no change, I got to let them go. Right out of the net up to Anthony's or do without milk. So this bandit, he can't let up and laugh because we both getting the same pitchfork shook at both of us, he just go clomp, clomp, out, no more gun, and slam the door I keep propped open to be inviting. The bells jangle and I laugh till these giant tears come out and wash the scared shitless sweat right off my face. And you know what I'm thinking—just the luck, Luis, you could get your head blown off for eleven bucks too. For eleven cents.

But what I start to say. The only real trouble I had in here besides cream going bad and the offers on the box top expiring before some kid get his hands on them, and me drying up like 120 pounds of salt cod?—it was a time about a week ago some *chulo*, this pimp, come walking in here. Yeah, I'm remembering when I used to look at shoes like that, and suits—good I didn't see his car, the pain used to get me in the groin like a bite with all the teeth closed, when I was younger. As soon as I saw him I knew he had big trouble in his fist. He was a wop who tried some Spanish on me. But I didn't like that, I shook it off and asked him in English what he want. I felt, I tell you, like a whore some customer was trying to kiss, you know? Just close the door behind you and get the fucking over with. What you want, *amigo?* Some fruit juice, what you got? Tomato, prune, orange, orange-grapefruit, some of it's in the refrigerator, nice and cool. And, let's see, maybe a small bottle of grape. Right. Welch's. The best. Got any pineapple? All out. Sorry. Just sold the last can. (Adela took it home yesterday to drink herself. I got to watch that.) So he take this midget grapefruit juice and look all around, slow. Oh, and spaghetti-o's. For lunch, he tell me. What, he going to open the can with his teeth?

So this dago pimp talk a little. About how much noise and dirt the bus make, where does it go? George Street, this is a major thoroughfare? I laugh. Yeah, everybody go by so fast they can't stop themself. But they wave when they go by. No really. *Sí*, really. You want a good burial plot? I'm trying to discourage him, get him to not notice me. More, nonsense, this bubble-gum talk. I want to ask him what's the point. I mean, he don't want to buy me out. He walk around on the balls of his fifty-buck shoes while little Luz Pacheco buy a dime worth of candy penny by penny, thinking hard. I wasn't so sure I'd live long enough to hear what he want. Finally. I could guess. A little trouble with Anthony up there, the bodega where everything hot except for the grocery business. He didn't say that but it's clear. Something he wasn't doing that they wanted. Did I ever put a little money down on a number? *Ay*, who doesn't? What would I think of using this place for, you know, a drop? I could use a little business, no? And maybe a little consideration, one kind or another? Something nice to keep the warm juices flowing? This was a man not much bigger than me but broad in the shoulders, broad maybe only with a shoulder holster, how do you know? What do I see? Blood, of course—Anthony's, mine, Adela in the middle of some cross fire, the traffic ticket cops dropping their books and coming in with their guns out. Also I see myself wearing some shirts I like, maybe, not this worn-out dishrag because I won't keep more than rent and lights and school clothes for the kids out, all the rest of nothing stay in inventory. I want to go home and go to sleep, that's all. I'm young but not that young. People I know go around wishing they could make this kind of connections and I'm just standing here. But it's not the dirty part that scaring me, breaking the law, I mean we a people who gots our own law, the law down Court Street don't do much for me, give it all to the men with their feet up on their shiny desk. The part that scare me is all the rest. This connection put your clean face right up against an asshole that never get wiped. You know? Like you get involved you disappear down this long tunnel, who know where you come out, or how. And you can't call nobody for help, who you call?

See, I never was strong about much, just hung on. I just say this, I say so much already. All my life I got this little problem with women. With myself, I mean. I can get it up, no trouble, I always can, first thing, long before I see the bull's-eye in front of me, but only once. Can't hit a double, you could say, a triple, go all the bases, a grand slam. One time at a time. O.K.? No complaints. Well, this is it, the store. My one time. This is it for the rest of my life, and I admitted the first week when I totaled up it's a lousy lay, too—numb. Nothing. Is this what I been saving all these years for? Going without? But you never want it to stop, do you, anyway? You don't want to be all done with it and no more coming.

So I told him O.K. Fine. We get the guarantees straightened out, I say no hot goods in here, I don't want nobody's ripped-off televisions, no drugs, nothing like that. Sure, *amigo*. He pat my back. I'm not wearing his kind of sharkskin. We shake hands. Whose guarantees? These *chulos*, they can move around, go where they want, get out when the wind change, and here I am with my banners and my light bill and yesterday's potato salad. Luis Beech-Nut, he could sweep these bastards out with his broom, throw the cat at them, call the cops, say no blood on my floor, you listening, unless it's yours.

But I got to say maybe they'll be some new faces in here with their quarters, new friends, new half-dollars with some new president on them. Maybe I should have asked for time to think but I got this feeling they don't do that kind of business. Pay now, think later. Well, I don't got to make it gangster paradise in here, I can keep the place alive like Anthony never did, still selling two-year-old Ivory Snow that look like a car came in his window and ran over the box. If he don't come down here and kill me first.

So here I am. A couple more sales, they saying it take time, all the time take time. I'm taking my pail and go put suds in the water, wash down the sidewalk, the least I can do. Otherwise it all pile up out there and I see enough dust inside all day. George Street, you and your hurry, you looked so good to me when I came to see this place. Back and forth like the ocean tides, all these well-dressed people who look like they eat good, smoke a lot, drink a six-pack every night, and this corner is a little pebble sticking up in the tide. How was I supposed to know nothing stop here? Nothing except the cars for the stop sign, not even a mailbox, a trash can, nothing. I got a sign out there that say NO PARKING, M–F, 7–11, 4⅝–7. Big shit. Listen to Luis, goddamn. Goddamn, I'm cutting the price of milk today. Two cents, running a risk. *Mira!* Will you come in now?

DONALD BARTHELME

The Temptation of
St. Anthony

Yes, the saint was underrated quite a bit, then, mostly by
people who didn't like things that were ineffable. I think
that's quite understandable—that kind of thing can be
extremely irritating, to some people. After all, everything
is hard enough without having to deal with something that
is not tangible and clear. The higher orders of abstraction
are just a nuisance, to some people, although to others, of
course, they are quite interesting. I would say that on the
whole, people who didn't like this kind of idea, or who
refused to think about it, were in the majority. And some
were actually angry at the idea of sainthood—not at the
saint himself, whom everyone liked, more or less, except
for a few, but about the idea he represented, especially
since it was not in a book or somewhere, but actually
present, in the community. Of course some people went
around saying that he "thought he was better than everybody else," and you had to take these people aside and tell
them that they had misperceived the problem, that it
wasn't a matter of simple conceit with which we are all
familiar, but rather something pure and mystical, from the
realm of the extraordinary, as it were; unearthly. But a lot
of people don't like things that are unearthly, the things of

this earth are good enough for them, and they don't mind telling you so. "If he'd just go out and get a job, like everybody else, then he could be saintly all day long, if he wanted to"—that was a common theme. There is a sort of hatred going around for people who have lifted their sights above the common run. Probably it has always been this way.

For this reason, in any case, people were always trying to see the inside of the saint's apartment, to find out if strange practices were being practiced there, or if you could discern, from the arrangement of the furniture and so on, if any had been, lately. They would ring the bell and pretend to be in the wrong apartment, these people, but St. Anthony would let them come in anyhow, even though he knew very well what they were thinking. They would stand around, perhaps a husband-and-wife team, and stare at the rug, which was ordinary beige wall-to-wall carpet from Kaufman's, and then at the coffee table and so on, they would sort of slide into the kitchen to see what he had been eating, if anything. They were always surprised to see that he ate more or less normal foods, perhaps a little heavy on the fried foods. I guess they expected roots and grasses. And of course there was a big unhealthy interest in the bedroom, the door to which was usually kept closed. People seemed to think he should, in pursuit of whatever higher goals he had in mind, sleep on the floor; when they discovered there was an ordinary bed in there, with a brown bedspread, they were slightly shocked. By now St. Anthony had made a cup of coffee for them, and told them to sit down and take the weight off their feet, and asked them about their work and if they had any children and so forth: they went away thinking, He's just like anybody else. That was, I think, the way he wanted to present himself, at that time.

Later, after it was all over, he moved back out to the desert.

I didn't have any particular opinion as to what was the right thing to think about him. Sometimes you have to take the long way round to get to a sound consensus, and of course you have to keep the ordinary motors of life running in the meantime. So, in that long year that saw the emergence of his will as one of its major landmarks, in our city, I did whatever I could to help things along, to direct the stream of life experience at him in ways he could handle. I wasn't a disciple, that would be putting it far too strongly; I was sort of like a friend. And there were things I could do. For example, this town is pretty goodsized, more than a hundred thousand, and in any such town—maybe more so than in the really small ones, where everyone is scratching to survive—you run into people with nothing much to do who don't mind causing a little trouble, if that would be diverting, for someone who is unusual in any way. So the example that Elaine and I set, in more or less just treating him like any one of our other friends, probably helped to normalize things, and very likely protected him, in a sense, from some of the unwelcome attentions he might otherwise have received. As men in society seem to feel that the problem is to get all opinions squared away with all other opinions, or at least in recognizable congruence with the main opinion, as if the world were a jury room that no one could leave until everybody agreed (and keeping in mind the ever-present threat of a mistrial), so the men, and the women too, of the city (which I won't name to spare possible embarrassment to those of the participants who still live here) tried to think about St. Anthony, and by extension saintliness, in the approved ways of their time and condition.

The first thing to do, then, was to prove that he was a fake. Strange as it may sound in retrospect, that was the original general opinion, because who could believe that the reverse was the case? Because it wasn't easy, in the midst of all the other things you had to think about, to imagine the marvelous. I don't mean that he went around doing tricks or anything like that. It was just a certain— ineffable is the only word I can think of, and I have never understood exactly what it means, but you get a kind of feeling from it, and that's what you got, too, from the saint, on good days. (He had his ups and downs.) Anyhow, it was pretty savage, in the beginning, the way the local people went around trying to get something on him. I don't mean to impugn the honesty of these doubters; doubt is real enough in most circumstances. Especially so, perhaps, in cases where what is at issue is some principle of action: if you believe something, then you logically have to act accordingly. If you decided that St. Anthony actually was a saint, then you would have to act a certain way toward him, pay attention to him, be reverent and attentive, pay hom- age, perhaps change your life a bit. So doubt is maybe a reaction to a strong claim on your attention, one that has implications for your life-style, for change. And you absolutely, in many cases, *don't want* to do this. A number of great plays have demonstrated this dilemma, on the stage.

St. Anthony's major temptation, in terms of his living here, was perhaps this: ordinary life.

Not that he proclaimed himself a saint in so many words. But his actions, as the proverb says, spoke louder. There was the ineffableness I've already mentioned, and there were certain things that he did. He was mugged, for exam- ple. That doesn't happen too often here, but it happened to him. It was at night, somebody jumped on him from behind, grabbed him around the neck and began going through his pockets. The man only got a few dollars, and then he threw St. Anthony down on the sidewalk (he put one leg in front of the saint's legs and shoved him) and then began to run away. St. Anthony called after him, held up his hand, and said, "Don't you want the watch?" It was a good watch, a Bulova. The man was thunderstruck. He actually came back and took the watch off St. Anthony's wrist. He didn't know what to think. He hesitated for a minute and then asked St. Anthony if he had bus fare home. The saint said it didn't matter, it wasn't far, he could walk. Then the mugger ran away again. I know somebody who saw it (and of course did nothing to help, as is common in such cases). Opinion was divided as to whether St. Anthony was saintly, or simpleminded. I myself thought it was kind of dumb of him. But St. Anthony explained to me that somebody had given him the watch in the first place, and he only wore it so as not to hurt that person's feelings. He never looked at it, he said. He didn't care what time it was.

Parenthetically. In the desert, where he is now, it's very cold at night. He won't light a fire. People leave things for him, outside the hut. We took out some blankets but I don't know he if uses them. People bring him the strangest things, electric coffee pots (even though there's no electricity out there), comic books, even bottles of whiskey. St. Anthony gives everything away as fast as he can. I have seen him, however, looking curiously at a transistor radio. He told me that in his youth, in Memphis (that's not Memphis, Tennessee, but the Memphis in Egypt, the ruined city) he was very fond of music. Elaine and I talked about giving him a flute or a clarinet. We thought that might be all right, because performing music, for the greater honor and glory of God, is an old tradition, some of our best music came about that way. The whole body of sacred music. We asked him about it. He said no, it was very kind of us but it would be a distraction from contemplation and so forth. But sometimes, when we drive out to see him, maybe with some other people, we all sing hymns. He appears to enjoy that. That appears to be acceptable.

A funny thing was that, toward the end, the only thing he'd say, the only word was . . . "Or." I couldn't understand what he was thinking of. That was when he was still living in town.

The famous temptations, that so much has been written about, didn't occur all that often while he was living amongst us, in our city. Once or twice. I wasn't ever actually present during a temptation but I heard about it. Mrs. Eaton, who lived upstairs from him, had actually drilled a hole in the floor, so that she could watch him! I thought that was fairly despicable, and I told her so. Well, she said, there wasn't much excitement in her life. She's fifty-eight and both her boys are in the Navy. Also some of the wood shavings and whatnot must have dropped on the saint's floor when she drilled the hole. She bought a brace-and-bit specially at the hardware store, she told me. "I'm shameless," she said. God knows that's true. But the saint must have known she was up there with her fifty-eight-year-old eye glued to the hole. Anyhow, she claims to have seen a temptation. I asked her what form it took. Well, it wasn't very interesting, she said. Something about advertising. There was this man in the business suit talking to the saint. He said he'd "throw the account your way" if the saint would something something. The only other thing she heard was a mention of "annual billings in the range of five to six mil." The saint said no, very politely, and the man left, with cordialities on both sides. I asked her what she'd been expecting and she looked at me with a gleam in her eye and said: "Guess." I suppose she meant women. I myself was curious, I admit it, about the fabulous naked beauties he is supposed to have been tempted with, and all of that. It's hard not to let your imagination become salacious, in this context. It's funny that we never seem to get enough of sexual things, even though Elaine and I have been very happily married for nine years and have a very good relationship, in bed and out of it. There never seems to be enough sex in a person's life, unless you're exhausted and worn out, I suppose—that is a curiosity, that God made us that way, that I have never understood. Not that I don't enjoy it, in the abstract.

After he had returned to the desert, we dropped by one day to see if he was home. The door of his hut was covered with an old piece of sheepskin. A lot of ants and vermin were crawling over the surface of the sheepskin. When you go through the door of the hut you have to move very fast. It's one of the most unpleasant things about going to see St. Anthony. We knocked on the sheepskin, which is stiff as a board. Nobody answered. We could hear some scuffling around inside the hut. Whispering. It seemed to me that there was more than one voice. We knocked on the sheepskin again; again nobody answered. We got back into the Pontiac and drove back to town.

Of course he's more mature now. Taking things a little easier, probably.

I don't care if he put his hand on her leg or did not put his hand on her leg.

Everyone felt we had done something wrong, really wrong, but by that time it was too late to make up for it.

Somebody got the bright idea of trying out Camilla on him. There are some crude people in this town. Camilla is well known. She's very aristocratic, in a way, if "aristocratic" means that you don't give a damn what kind of damn foolishness, or even evil, you lend yourself to. Her folks had too much money, that was part of it, and she was too beautiful—she was beautiful, it's the only word—that was the other part. Some of her friends put her up to it. She went over to his place wearing those very short pants they wore for a while, and all of that. She has beautiful breasts. She's very intelligent, went to the Sorbonne and studied some kind of philosophy called "structure" with somebody named Levy who is supposed to be very famous. When she came back there was nobody she could talk about it to. She smokes a lot of dope, it's well known. But in a way, she is not uncompassionate. She was interested in the saint for his own personality, as well as his being an anomaly, in our local context. The long and short of it is that she claimed he tried to make advances to her, put his hand on her leg and all that. I don't know if she was lying or not. She could have been. She could have been telling the truth. It's hard to say. Anyhow a great hue was raised about it and her father said he was going to press charges, although in the event, he did not. She stopped talking about it, the next day. Probably something happened but I don't necessarily think it was what she said it was. She became a VISTA volunteer later and went to work in the inner city of Detroit.

Anyhow, a lot of people talked about it. Well, what if he *had* put his hand on her leg, some people said—what was so wrong about that? They were both unmarried adult human beings, after all. Sexuality is as important as saintliness, and maybe as beautiful, in the sight of God, or else why was it part of the Divine plan? You always have these conflicts of ideas between people who think one thing and people who think another. I don't give a damn if he put his hand on her leg or did not put his hand on her leg. (I would prefer, of course, that he had not.) I thought it was kind of a cheap incident and not really worth talking about, especially in the larger context of the ineffable. There really was something to that. In the world of mundanity in which he found himself, he *shone*. It was unmistakable, even to children.

Of course they were going to run him out of town, by subtle pressures, after a while. There is a lot of anticlericalism around, still. We visit him, in the desert, anyhow, once or twice a month. We missed our visits last month because we were in Florida.

He told me that, in his old age, he regarded the temptations as "entertainment."

FLANNERY O'CONNOR

Revelation

The doctor's waiting room, which was very small, was almost full when the Turpins entered and Mrs. Turpin, who was very large, made it look even smaller by her presence. She stood looming at the head of the magazine table set in the center of it, a living demonstration that the room was inadequate and ridiculous. Her little bright black eyes took in all the patients as she sized up the seating situation. There was one vacant chair and a place on the sofa occupied by a blond child in a dirty blue romper who should have been told to move over and make room for the lady. He was five or six, but Mrs. Turpin saw at once that no one was going to tell him to move over. He was slumped down in the seat, his arms idle at his sides and his eyes idle in his head; his nose ran unchecked.

Mrs. Turpin put a firm hand on Claud's shoulder and said in a voice that included anyone who wanted to listen, "Claud, you sit in that chair there," and gave him a push down into the vacant one. Claud was florid and bald and sturdy, somewhat shorter than Mrs. Turpin, but he sat down as if he were accustomed to doing what she told him to.

Mrs. Turpin remained standing. The only man in the room besides Claud was a lean stringy old fellow with a rusty hand spread out on each knee, whose eyes were closed as if he were asleep or dead or pretending to be so as not to get up and offer her his seat. Her gaze settled agreeably on a well-dressed gray-haired lady whose eyes met hers and whose expression said: if that child belonged to me, he would have some manners and move over—there's plenty of room there for you and him too.

Claud looked up with a sigh and made as if to rise.

"Sit down," Mrs. Turpin said. "You know you're not supposed to stand on that leg. He has an ulcer on his leg," she explained.

Claude lifted his foot onto the magazine table and rolled his trouser leg up to reveal a purple swelling on a plump marble-white calf.

"My!" the pleasant lady said. "How did you do that?"

"A cow kicked him," Mrs. Turpin said.

"Goodness!" said the lady.

Claud rolled his trouser leg down.

"Maybe the little boy would move over," the lady suggested, but the child did not stir.

"Somebody will be leaving in a minute," Mrs. Turpin said. She could not understand why a doctor—with as much money as they made charging five dollars a day to just stick their head in the hospital door and look at you—couldn't afford a decent-sized waiting room. This one was hardly bigger than a garage. The table was cluttered with limp-looking magazines and at one end of it there was a big green glass ash tray full of cigarette butts and cotton wads with little blood spots on them. If she had had anything to do with the running of the place, that would have been emptied every so often. There were no chairs against the wall at the head of the room. It had a rectangular-shaped panel in it that permitted a view of the office where the nurse came and went and the secretary listened to the radio. A plastic fern in a gold pot sat in the opening and trailed its fronds down almost to the floor. The radio was softly playing gospel music.

Just then the inner door opened and a nurse with the highest stack of yellow hair Mrs. Turpin had ever seen put her face in the crack and called for the next patient. The woman sitting beside Claud grasped the two arms of her chair and hoisted herself up; she pulled her dress free from her legs and lumbered through the door where the nurse had disappeared.

Mrs. Turpin eased into the vacant chair, which held her tight as a corset. "I wish I could reduce," she said, and rolled her eyes and gave a comic sigh.

"Oh, *you* aren't fat," the stylish lady said.

"Ooooo I am too," Mrs. Turpin said. "Claud he eats all he wants to and never weighs over one hundred and seventy-five pounds, but me I just look at something good to eat and I gain some weight," and her stomach and shoulders shook with laughter. "You can eat all you want to, can't you, Claud?" she asked, turning to him.

Claud only grinned.

"Well, as long as you have such a good disposition," the stylish lady said, "I don't think it makes a bit of difference what size you are. You just can't beat a good disposition."

Next to her was a fat girl of eighteen or nineteen, scowling into a thick blue book which Mrs. Turpin saw was entitled *Human Development*. The girl raised her head and directed her scowl at Mrs. Turpin as if she did not like her looks. She appeared annoyed that anyone should speak while she tried to read. The poor girl's face was blue with acne and Mrs. Turpin thought how pitiful it was to have a face like that at that age. She gave the girl a friendly smile but the girl only scowled the harder. Mrs. Turpin herself was fat but she had always had good skin, and, though she was forty-seven years old, there was not a wrinkle in her face except around her eyes from laughing too much.

Next to the ugly girl was the child, still in exactly the

same position, and next to him was a thin leathery old
woman in a cotton print dress. She and Claud had three
sacks of chicken feed in their pump house that was in the
same print. She had seen from the first that the child
belonged with the old woman. She could tell by the way
they sat—kind of vacant and white-trashy, as if they would
sit there until Doomsday if nobody called and told them to
get up. And at right angles but next to the well-dressed
pleasant lady was a lank-faced woman who was certainly the
child's mother. She had on a yellow sweat shirt and
wine-colored slacks, both gritty-looking, and the rims of
her lips were stained with snuff. Her dirty yellow hair was
tied behind with a little piece of red paper ribbon. Worse
than niggers any day, Mrs. Turpin thought.

The gospel hymn playing was, "When I looked up and
He looked down," and Mrs. Turpin, who knew it, supplied
the last line mentally, "And wona these days I know I'll
we-eara crown."

Without appearing to, Mrs. Turpin always noticed
people's feet. The well-dressed lady had on red and gray
suede shoes to match her dress. Mrs. Turpin had on her
good black patent leather pumps. The ugly girl had on Girl
Scout shoes and heavy socks. The old woman had on tennis
shoes and the white-trashy mother had on what appeared to
be bedroom slippers, black straw with gold braid threaded
through them—exactly what you would have expected her
to have on.

Sometimes at night when she couldn't go to sleep, Mrs.
Turpin would occupy herself with the question of who she
would have chosen to be if she couldn't have been herself.
If Jesus had said to her before he made her, "There's only
two places available for you. You can either be a nigger or
white-trash," what would she have said? "Please, Jesus,
please," she would have said, "just let me wait until there's
another place available," and he would have said, "No, you
have to go right now and I have only those two places so
make up your mind." She would have wiggled and squirmed

and begged and pleaded but it would have been no use and finally she would have said, "All right, make me a nigger then—but that don't mean a trashy one." And he would have made her a neat clean respectable Negro woman, herself but black.

Next to the child's mother was a red-headed youngish woman, reading one of the magazines and working a piece of chewing gum, hell for leather, as Claud would say. Mrs. Turpin could not see the woman's feet. She was not white-trash, just common. Sometimes Mrs. Turpin occupied herself at night naming the classes of people. On the bottom of the heap were most colored people, not the kind she would have been if she had been one, but most of them; then next to them—not above, just away from—were the white-trash; then above them were the home-owners, and above them the home-and-land owners, to which she and Claud belonged. Above she and Claud were people with a lot of money and much bigger houses and much more land. But here the complexity of it would begin to bear in on her, for some of the people with a lot of money were common and ought to be below she and Claud and some of the people who had good blood had lost their money and had to rent and then there were colored people who owned their homes and land as well. There was a colored dentist in town who had two red Lincolns and a swimming pool and a farm with registered white-face cattle on it. Usually by the time she had fallen asleep all the classes of people were moiling and roiling around in her head, and she would dream they were all crammed in together in a box car, being ridden off to be put in a gas oven.

"That's a beautiful clock," she said and nodded to her right. It was a big wall clock, the face encased in a brass sunburst.

"Yes, it's very pretty," the stylish lady said agreeably. "And right on the dot too," she added, glancing at her watch.

The ugly girl beside her cast an eye upward at the clock,

smirked, then looked directly at Mrs. Turpin and smirked
again. Then she returned her eyes to her book. She was
obviously the lady's daughter because, although they didn't
look anything alike as to disposition, they both had the
same shape of face and the same blue eyes. On the lady
they sparkled pleasantly but in the girl's seared face they
appeared alternately to smolder and to blaze.

What if Jesus had said, "All right, you can be white-trash
or a nigger or ugly"!

Mrs. Turpin felt an awful pity for the girl, though she
thought it was one thing to be ugly and another to act ugly.

The woman with the snuff-stained lips turned around in
her chair and looked up at the clock. Then she turned back
and appeared to look a little to the side of Mrs. Turpin.
There was a cast in one of her eyes. "You want to know
wher you can get you one of themther clocks?" she asked in
a loud voice.

"No, I already have a nice clock," Mrs. Turpin said.
Once somebody like her got a leg in the conversation, she
would be all over it.

"You can get you one with green stamps," the woman
said. "That's most likely wher he got hisn. Save you up
enough, you can get you most anythang. I got me some
joo'ry."

Ought to have got you a wash rag and some soap, Mrs.
Turpin thought.

"I get contour sheets with mine," the pleasant lady said.

The daughter slammed her book shut. She looked
straight in front of her, directly through Mrs. Turpin and on
through the yellow curtain and the plate glass window
which made the wall behind her. The girl's eyes seemed lit
all of a sudden with a peculiar light, an unnatural light like
night road signs give. Mrs. Turpin turned her head to see if
there was anything going on outside that she should see,
but she could not see anything. Figures passing cast only a
pale shadow through the curtain. There was no reason the
girl should single her out for her ugly looks.

"Miss Finley," the nurse said, cracking the door. The gum-chewing woman got up and passed in front of her and Claud and went into the office. She had on red high-heeled shoes.

Directly across the table, the ugly girl's eyes were fixed on Mrs. Turpin as if she had some very special reason for disliking her.

"This is wonderful weather, isn't it?" the girl's mother said.

"It's good weather for cotton if you can get the niggers to pick it," Mrs. Turpin said, "but niggers don't want to pick cotton any more. You can't get the white folks to pick it and now you can't get the niggers—because they got to be right up there with the white folks."

"They gonna *try* anyways," the white-trash woman said, leaning forward.

"Do you have one of the cotton-picking machines?" the pleasant lady asked.

"No," Mrs. Turpin said, "they leave half the cotton in the field. We don't have much cotton anyway. If you want to make it farming now, you have to have a little of everything. We got a couple of acres of cotton and a few hogs and chickens and just enough white-face that Claud can look after them himself."

"One thang I don't want," the white-trash woman said, wiping her mouth with the back of her hand. "Hogs. Nasty stinking things, a-gruntin and a-rootin all over the place."

Mrs. Turpin gave her the merest edge of her attention. "Our hogs are not dirty and they don't stink," she said. "They're cleaner than some children I've seen. Their feet never touch the ground. We have a pig-parlor—that's where you raise them on concrete," she explained to the pleasant lady, "and Claud scoots them down with the hose every afternoon and washes off the floor." Cleaner by far than that child right there, she thought. Poor nasty little thing. He had not moved except to put the thumb of his dirty hand into his mouth.

The woman turned her face away from Mrs. Turpin. "I know I wouldn't scoot down no hog with no hose," she said to the wall.

You wouldn't have no hog to scoot down, Mrs. Turpin said to herself.

"A-gruntin and a-rootin and a-groanin," the woman muttered.

"We got a little of everything," Mrs. Turpin said to the pleasant lady. "It's no use in having more than you can handle yourself with help like it is. We found enough niggers to pick our cotton this year but Claud he has to go after them and take them home again in the evening. They can't walk that half a mile. No they can't. I tell you," she said and laughed merrily, "I sure am tired of buttering up niggers, but you got to love em if you want em to work for you. When they come in the morning, I run out and I say, 'Hi yawl this morning?' and when Claud drives them off to the field I just wave to beat the band and they just wave back." And she waved her hand rapidly to illustrate.

"Like you read out of the same book," the lady said, showing she understood perfectly.

"Child, yes," Mrs. Turpin said. "And when they come in from the field, I run out with a bucket of icewater. That's the way it's going to be from now on," she said. "You may as well face it."

"One thang I know," the white-trash woman said. "Two thangs I ain't going to do: love no niggers or scoot down no hog with no hose." And she let out a bark of contempt.

The look that Mrs. Turpin and the pleasant lady exchanged indicated they both understood that you had to *have* certain things before you could *know* certain things. But every time Mrs. Turpin exchanged a look with the lady, she was aware that the ugly girl's peculiar eyes were still on her, and she had trouble bringing her attention back to the conversation.

"When you got something," she said, "you got to look after it." And when you ain't got a thing but breath and britches, she added to herself, you can afford to come to town every morning and just sit on the Court House coping and spit.

A grotesque revolving shadow passed across the curtain behind her and was thrown palely on the opposite wall. Then a bicycle clattered down against the outside of the building. The door opened and a colored boy glided in with a tray from the drugstore. It had two large red and white paper cups on it with tops on them. He was a tall, very black boy in discolored white pants and a green nylon shirt. He was chewing gum slowly, as if to music. He set the tray down in the office opening next to the fern and stuck his head through to look for the secretary. She was not in there. He rested his arms on the ledge and waited, his narrow bottom stuck out, swaying to the left and right. He raised a hand over his head and scratched the base of his skull.

"You see that button there, boy?" Mrs. Turpin said. "You can punch that and she'll come. She's probably in the back somewhere."

"Is that right?" the boy said agreeably, as if he had never seen the button before. He leaned to the right and put his finger on it. "She sometime out," he said and twisted around to face his audience, his elbows behind him on the counter. The nurse appeared and he twisted back again. She handed him a dollar and he rooted in his pocket and made the change and counted it out to her. She gave him fifteen cents for a tip and he went out with the empty tray. The heavy door swung to slowly and closed at length with the sound of suction. For a moment no one spoke.

"They ought to send all them niggers back to Africa," the white-trash woman said. "That's wher they come from in the first place."

"Oh, I couldn't do without my good colored friends," the pleasant lady said.

"There's a heap of things worse than a nigger," Mrs.

Turpin agreed. "It's all kinds of them just like it's all kinds of us."

"Yes, and it takes all kinds to make the world go round," the lady said in her musical voice.

As she said it, the raw-complexioned girl snapped her teeth together. Her lower lip turned downwards and inside out, revealing the pale pink inside of her mouth. After a second it rolled back up. It was the ugliest face Mrs. Turpin had ever seen anyone make and for a moment she was certain that the girl had made it at her. She was looking at her as if she had known and disliked her all her life—all of Mrs. Turpin's life, it seemed too, not just all the girl's life. Why, girl, I don't even know you, Mrs. Turpin said silently.

She forced her attention back to the discussion. "It wouldn't be practical to send them back to Africa," she said. "They wouldn't want to go. They got it too good here."

"Wouldn't be what they wanted—if I had anythang to do with it," the woman said.

"It wouldn't be a way in the world you could get all the niggers back over there," Mrs. Turpin said. "They'd be hiding out and lying down and turning sick on you and wailing and hollering and raring and pitching. It wouldn't be a way in the world to get them over there."

"They got over here," the trashy woman said. "Get back like they got over."

"It wasn't so many of them then," Mrs. Turpin explained.

The woman looked at Mrs. Turpin as if here was an idiot indeed but Mrs. Turpin was not bothered by the look, considering where it came from.

"Nooo," she said, "they're going to stay here where they can go to New York and marry white folks and improve their color. That's what they all want to do, every one of them, improve their color."

"You know what comes of that, don't you?" Claud asked.

"No, Claud, what?" Mrs. Turpin said.

Claud's eyes twinkled. "White-faced niggers," he said with never a smile.

Everybody in the office laughed except the white-trash and the ugly girl. The girl gripped the book in her lap with white fingers. The trashy woman looked around her from face to face as if she thought they were all idiots. The old woman in the feed sack dress continued to gaze expressionless across the floor at the high-top shoes of the man opposite her, the one who had been pretending to be asleep when the Turpins came in. He was laughing heartily, his hands still spread out on his knees. The child had fallen to the side and was lying now almost face down in the old woman's lap.

While they recovered from their laughter, the nasal chorus on the radio kept the room from silence.

> *"You go to blank blank*
> *And I'll go to mine*
> *But we'll all blank along*
> *To-geth-ther,*
> *And all along the blank*
> *We'll hep eachother out*
> *Smile-ling in any kind of*
> *Weath-ther!"*

Mrs. Turpin didn't catch every word but she caught enough to agree with the spirit of the song and it turned her thoughts sober. To help anybody out that needed it was her philosophy of life. She never spared herself when she found somebody in need, whether they were white or black, trash or decent. And of all she had to be thankful for, she was most thankful that this was so. If Jesus had said, "You can be high society and have all the money you want and be thin and svelte-like, but you can't be a good woman with it," she would have had to say, "Well don't make me that then. Make me a good woman and it don't matter what else, how fat or how ugly or how poor!" Her heart rose. He had not made her a nigger or white-trash or ugly! He had made her herself and given her a little of everything. Jesus, thank you! she said. Thank you thank you thank you! Whenever she counted her blessings she felt as buoyant as if she weighed one hundred and twenty-five pounds instead of one hundred and eighty.

"What's wrong with your little boy?" the pleasant lady asked the white-trashy woman.

"He has an ulcer," the woman said proudly. "He ain't give me a minute's peace since he was born. Him and her are just alike," she said, nodding at the old woman, who was running her leathery fingers through the child's pale hair. "Look like I can't get nothing down them two but Co' Cola and candy."

That's all you try to get down em, Mrs. Turpin said to herself. Too lazy to light the fire. There was nothing you could tell her about people like them that she didn't know already . And it was not just that they didn't have anything. Because if you gave them everything, in two weeks it would all be broken or filthy or they would have chopped it up for lightwood. She knew all this from her own experience. Help them you must, but help them you couldn't.

All at once the ugly girl turned her lips inside out again. Her eyes fixed like two drills on Mrs. Turpin. This time there was no mistaking that there was something urgent behind them.

Girl, Mrs. Turpin exclaimed silently, I haven't done a thing to you! The girl might be confusing her with somebody else. There was no need to sit by and let herself be intimidated. "You must be in college," she said boldly, looking directly at the girl. "I see you reading a book there."

The girl continued to stare and pointedly did not answer.

Her mother blushed at this rudeness. "The lady asked you a question, Mary Grace," she said under her breath.

"I have ears," Mary Grace said.

The poor mother blushed again. "Mary Grace goes to Wellesley College," she explained. She twisted one of the buttons on her dress. "In Massachusetts," she added with a grimace. "And in the summer she just keeps right on studying. Just reads all the time, a real book worm. She's done real well at Wellesley; she's taking English and Math and History and Psychology and Social Studies," she rattled on, "and I think it's too much. I think she ought to get out and have fun."

The girl looked as if she would like to hurl them all through the plate glass window.

"Way up north," Mrs. Turpin murmured and thought, well, it hasn't done much for her manners.

"I'd almost rather to have him sick," the white-trash woman said, wrenching the attention back to herself. "He's so mean when he ain't. Look like some children just take natural to meanness. It's some gets bad when they get sick but he was the opposite. Took sick and turned good. He don't give me no trouble now. It's me waitin to see the doctor," she said.

If I was going to send anybody back to Africa, Mrs. Turpin thought, it would be your kind, woman. "Yes, indeed," she said aloud, but looking up at the ceiling, "it's a heap of things worse than a nigger." And dirtier than a hog, she added to herself.

"I think people with bad dispositions are more to be pitied than anyone on earth," the pleasant lady said in a voice that was decidedly thin.

"I thank the Lord he has blessed me with a good one," Mrs. Turpin said. "The day has never dawned that I couldn't find something to laugh at."

"Not since she married me anyways," Claud said with a comical straight face.

Everybody laughed except the girl and the white-trash.

Mrs. Turpin's stomach shook. "He's such a caution," she said, "that I can't help but laugh at him."

The girl made a loud ugly noise through her teeth.

Her mother's mouth grew thin and tight. "I think the worst thing in the world," she said, "is an ungrateful person. To have everything and not appreciate it. I know a

girl," she said, "who has parents who would give her anything, a little brother who loves her dearly, who is getting a
good education, who wears the best clothes, but who can
never say a kind word to anyone, who never smiles, who
just criticizes and complains all day long."

"Is she too old to paddle?" Claud asked.

The girl's face was almost purple.

"Yes," the lady said, "I'm afraid there's nothing to do but
leave her to her folly. Some day she'll wake up and it'll be
too late."

"It never hurt anyone to smile," Mrs. Turpin said. "It
just makes you feel better all over."

"Of course," the lady said sadly, "but there are just some
people you can't tell anything to. They can't take criticism."

"If it's one thing I am," Mrs. Turpin said with feeling,
"it's grateful. When I think who all I could have been
besides myself and what all I got, a little of everything, and
a good disposition besides, I just feel like shouting, 'Thank
you, Jesus, for making everything the way it is!' It could
have been different!" For one thing, somebody else could
have got Claud. At the thought of this, she was flooded with
gratitude and a terrible pang of joy ran through her. "Oh
thank you, Jesus, Jesus, thank you!" she cried aloud.

The book struck her directly over her left eye. It struck
almost at the same instant that she realized the girl was
about to hurl it. Before she could utter a sound, the raw
face came crashing across the table toward her, howling.
The girl's fingers sank like clamps into the soft flesh of her
neck. She heard the mother cry out and Claud shout,
"Whoa!" There was an instant when she was certain that she
was about to be in an earthquake.

All at once her vision narrowed and she saw everything
as if it were happening in a small room far away, or as if she
were looking at it through the wrong end of a telescope.
Claud's face crumpled and fell out of sight. The nurse ran
in, then out, then in again. Then the gangling figure of the
doctor rushed out of the inner door. Magazines flew this

way and that as the table turned over. The girl fell with a thud and Mrs. Turpin's vision suddenly reversed itself and she saw everything large instead of small. The eyes of the white-trashy woman were staring hugely at the floor. There the girl, held down on one side by the nurse and on the other by her mother, was wrenching and turning in their grasp. The doctor was kneeling astride her, trying to hold her arm down. He managed after a second to sink a long needle into it.

Mrs. Turpin felt entirely hollow except for her heart which swung from side to side as if it were agitated in a great empty drum of flesh.

"Somebody that's not busy call for the ambulance," the doctor said in the off-hand voice young doctors adopt for terrible occasions.

Mrs. Turpin could not have moved a finger. The old man who had been sitting next to her skipped nimbly into the office and made the call, for the secretary still seemed to be gone.

"Claud!" Mrs. Turpin called.

He was not in his chair. She knew she must jump up and find him but she felt like some one trying to catch a train in a dream, when everything moves in slow motion and the faster you try to run the slower you go.

"Here I am," a suffocated voice, very unlike Claud's, said.

He was doubled up in the corner on the floor, pale as paper, holding his leg. She wanted to get up and go to him but she could not move. Instead, her gaze was drawn slowly downward to the churning face on the floor, which she could see over the doctor's shoulder.

The girl's eyes stopped rolling and focused on her. They seemed a much lighter blue than before, as if a door that had been tightly closed behind them was now open to admit light and air.

Mrs. Turpin's head cleared and her power of motion returned. She leaned forward until she was looking directly into the fierce brilliant eyes. There was no doubt in her mind that the girl did know her, knew her in some intense and personal way, beyond time and place and condition. "What you got to say to me?" she asked hoarsely and held her breath, waiting, as for a revelation.

The girl raised her head. Her gaze locked with Mrs. Turpin's. "Go back to hell where you came from, you old wart hog," she whispered. Her voice was low but clear. Her eyes burned for a moment as if she saw with pleasure that her message had struck its target.

Mrs. Turpin sank back in her chair.

After a moment the girl's eyes closed and she turned her head wearily to the side.

The doctor rose and handed the nurse the empty syringe. He leaned over and put both hands for a moment on the mother's shoulders, which were shaking. She was sitting on the floor, her lips pressed together, holding Mary Grace's hand in her lap. The girl's fingers were gripped like a baby's around her thumb. "Go to the hospital," he said. "I'll call and make the arrangements."

"Now let's see that neck," he said in a jovial voice to Mrs. Turpin. He began to inspect her neck with his first two fingers. Two little moon-shaped lines like pink fish bones were indented over her windpipe. There was the beginning of an angry red swelling above her eye. His fingers passed over this also.

"Lea' me be," she said thickly and shook him off. "See about Claud. She kicked him."

"I'll see about him in a minute," he said and felt her pulse. He was a thin gray-haired man, given to pleasantries. "Go home and have yourself a vacation the rest of the day," he said and patted her on the shoulder.

Quit your pattin me, Mrs. Turpin growled to herself.

"And put an ice pack over that eye," he said. Then he went and squatted down beside Claud and looked at his leg. After a moment he pulled him up and Claud limped after him into the office.

Until the ambulance came, the only sounds in the room were the tremulous moans of the girl's mother, who continued to sit on the floor. The white-trash woman did not take her eyes off the girl. Mrs. Turpin looked straight ahead at nothing. Presently the ambulance drew up, a long dark shadow, behind the curtain. The attendants came in and set the stretcher down beside the girl and lifted her expertly onto it and carried her out. The nurse helped the mother gather up her things. The shadow of the ambulance moved silently away and the nurse came back in the office.

"That ther girl is going to be a lunatic, ain't she?" the white-trash woman asked the nurse, but the nurse kept on to the back and never answered her.

"Yes, she's going to be a lunatic," the white-trash woman said to the rest of them.

"Po' critter," the old woman murmured. The child's face was still in her lap. His eyes looked idly out over her knees. He had not moved during the disturbance except to draw one leg up under him.

"I thank Gawd," the white-trash woman said fervently, "I ain't a lunatic."

Claud came limping out and the Turpins went home.

As their pick-up truck turned into their own dirt road and made the crest of the hill, Mrs. Turpin gripped the window ledge and looked out suspiciously. The land sloped gracefully down through a field dotted with lavender weeds and at the start of the rise their small yellow frame house, with its little flower beds spread out around it like a fancy apron, sat primly in its accustomed place between two giant hickory trees. She would not have been startled to see a burnt wound between two blackened chimneys.

Neither of them felt like eating so they put on their house clothes and lowered the shade in the bedroom and lay down, Claud with his leg on a pillow and herself with a damp washcloth over her eye. The instant she was flat on her back, the image of a razor-backed hog with warts on its face and horns coming out behind its ears snorted into her head. She moaned, a low quiet moan.

"I am not," she said tearfully. "a wart hog. From hell." But the denial had no force. The girl's eyes and her words, even the tone of her voice, low but clear, directed only to her, brooked no repudiation. She had been singled out for the message, though there was trash in the room to whom it might justly have been applied. The full force of this fact struck her only now. There was a woman there who was neglecting her own child but she had been overlooked. The message had been given to Ruby Turpin, a respectable, hard-working, church-going woman. The tears dried. Her eyes began to burn instead with wrath.

She rose on her elbow and the washcloth fell into her hand. Claud was lying on his back, snoring. She wanted to tell him what the girl had said. At the same time, she did not wish to put the image of herself as a wart hog from hell into his mind.

"Hey, Claud," she muttered and pushed his shoulder.

Claud opened one pale baby blue eye.

She looked into it warily. He did not think about anything. He just went his way.

"Wha, whasit?" he said and closed the eye again.

"Nothing," she said. "Does your leg pain you?"

"Hurts like hell," Claud said.

"It'll quit terreckly," she said and lay back down. In a moment Claud was snoring again. For the rest of the afternoon they lay there. Claud slept. She scowled at the ceiling. Occasionally she raised her fist and made a small stabbing motion over her chest as if she was defending her innocence to invisible guests who were like the comforters of Job, reasonable-seeming but wrong.

About five-thirty Claud stirred. "Got to go after those niggers," he sighed, not moving.

She was looking straight up as if there were unintelligible handwriting on the ceiling. The protuberance over her eye had turned a greenish-blue. "Listen here," she said.

"What?"

"Kiss me."

Claud leaned over and kissed her loudly on the mouth. He pinched her side and their hands interlocked. Her expression of ferocious concentration did not change. Claud got up, groaning and growling, and limped off. She continued to study the ceiling.

She did not get up until she heard the pick-up truck coming back with the Negroes. Then she rose and thrust her feet in her brown oxfords, which she did not bother to lace, and stumped out onto the back porch and got her red plastic bucket. She emptied a tray of ice cubes into it and filled it half full of water and went out into the back yard. Every afternoon after Claud brought the hands in, one of the boys helped him put out hay and the rest waited in the back of the truck until he was ready to take them home. The truck was parked in the shade under one of the hickory trees.

"Hi yawl this evening?" Mrs. Turpin asked grimly, appearing with the bucket and the dipper. There were three women and a boy in the truck.

"Us doin nicely," the older woman said. "Hi you doin?" and her gaze stuck immediately on the dark lump on Mrs. Turpin's forehead. "You done fell down, ain't you?" she asked in a solicitous voice. The old woman was dark and almost toothless. She had on an old felt hat of Claud's set back on her head. The other two women were younger and lighter and they both had new bright green sunhats. One of them had hers on her head; the other had taken hers off and the boy was grinning beneath it.

Mrs. Turpin set the bucket down on the floor of the truck. "Yawl hep yourselves," she said. She looked around to make sure Claud had gone. "No, I didn't fall down," she said, folding her arms. "It was something worse than that."

"Ain't nothing bad happen to you!" the old woman said. She said it as if they all knew that Mrs. Turpin was protected in some special way by Divine Providence. "You just had you a little fall."

"We were in town at the doctor's office for where the cow kicked Mr. Turpin," Mrs. Turpin said in a flat tone that indicated they could leave off their foolishness. "And there was this girl there. A big fat girl with her face all broke out. I could look at that girl and tell she was peculiar but I couldn't tell how. And me and her mama was just talking and going along and all of a sudden WHAM! She throws this big book she was reading at me and . . ."

"Naw!" the old woman cried out.

"And then she jumps over the table and commences to choke me."

"Naw!" they all exclaimed, "naw!"

"Hi come she do that?" the old woman asked. "What ail her?"

Mrs. Turpin only glared in front of her.

"Somethin ail her," the old woman said.

"They carried her off in an ambulance," Mrs. Turpin continued, "but before she went she was rolling on the floor and they were trying to hold her down to give her a shot and she said something to me." She paused. "You know what she said to me?"

"What she say?" they asked.

"She said," Mrs. Turpin began, and stopped, her face very dark and heavy. The sun was getting whiter and whiter, blanching the sky overhead so that the leaves of the hickory tree were black in the face of it. She could not bring forth the words. "Something real ugly," she muttered.

"She sho shouldn't said nothin ugly to you," the old woman said. "You so sweet. You the sweetest lady I know."

"She pretty too," the one with the hat on said.

"And stout," the other one said. "I never knowed no sweeter white lady."

"That's the truth befo' Jesus," the old woman said. "Amen! You des as sweet and pretty as you can be."

Mrs. Turpin knew exactly how much Negro flattery was

worth and it added to her rage. "She said," she began again and finished this time with a fierce rush of breath, "that I was an old wart hog from hell."

There was an astounded silence.

"Where she at?" the youngest woman cried in a piercing voice.

"Lemme see her. I'll kill her!"

"I'll kill her with you!" the other one cried.

"She b'long in the sylum," the old woman said emphatically. "You the sweetest white lady I know."

"She pretty too," the other two said. "Stout as she can be and sweet. Jesus satisfied with her!"

"Deed he is," the old woman declared.

Idiots! Mrs. Turpin growled to herself. You could never say anything intelligent to a nigger. You could talk at them but not with them. "Yawl ain't drunk your water," she said shortly. "Leave the bucket in the truck when you're finished with it. I got more to do than just stand around and pass the time of day," and she moved off and into the house.

She stood for a moment in the middle of the kitchen. The dark protuberance over her eye looked like a miniature tornado cloud which might any moment sweep across the horizon of her brow. Her lower lip protruded dangerously. She squared her massive shoulders. Then she marched into the front of the house and out the side door and started down the road to the pig parlor. She had the look of a woman going single-handed, weaponless, into battle.

The sun was a deep yellow now like a harvest moon and was riding westward very fast over the far tree line as if it meant to reach the hogs before she did. The road was rutted and she kicked several good-sized stones out of her path as she strode along. The pig parlor was on a little knoll at the end of a lane that ran off from the side of the barn. It was a square of concrete as large as a small room, with a board fence about four feet high around it. The concrete floor sloped slightly so that the hog wash could drain off into a trench where it was carried to the field for fertilizer. Claud was standing on the outside, on the edge of the concrete, hanging onto the top board, hosing down the floor inside. The hose was connected to the faucet of a water trough nearby.

Mrs. Turpin climbed up beside him and glowered down at the hogs inside. There were seven long-snouted bristly shoats in it—tan with liver-colored spots—and an old sow a few weeks off from farrowing. She was lying on her side grunting. The shoats were running about shaking themselves like idiot children, their little slit pig eyes searching the floor for anything left. She had read that pigs were the most intelligent animal. She doubted it. They were supposed to be smarter than dogs. There had even been a pig astronaut. He had performed his assignment perfectly but died of a heart attack afterwards because they left him in his electric suit, sitting upright throughout his examination when naturally a hog should be on all fours.

A-gruntin and a-rootin and a-groanin.

"Gimme that hose," she said, yanking it away from Claud. "Go on and carry them niggers home and then get off that leg."

"You look like you might have swallowed a mad dog," Claud observed, but he got down and limped off. He paid no attention to her humors.

Until he was out of earshot, Mrs. Turpin stood on the side of the pen, holding the hose and pointing the stream of water at the hind quarters of any shoat that looked as if it might try to lie down. When he had had time to get over the hill, she turned her head slightly and her wrathful eyes scanned the path. He was nowhere in sight. She turned back again and seemed to gather herself up. Her shoulders rose and she drew in her breath.

"What do you send me a message like that for?" she said in a low fierce voice, barely above a whisper but with the force of a shout in its concentrated fury. "How am I a hog and me both? How am I saved and from hell too?" Her free fist was knotted and with the other she gripped the hose, blindly pointing the stream of water in and out of the eye of the old sow whose outraged squeal she did not hear.

The pig parlor commanded a view of the back pasture where their twenty beef cows were gathered around the hay-bales Claud and the boy had put out. The freshly cut pasture sloped down to the highway. Across it was their cotton field and beyond that a dark green dusty wood which they owned as well. The sun was behind the wood, very red, looking over the paling of trees like a farmer inspecting his own hogs.

"Why me?" she rumbled. "It's no trash around here, black or white, that I haven't given to. And break my back to the bone every day working. And do for the church."

She appeared to be the right size woman to command the arena before her. "How am I a hog?" she demanded. "Exactctly how am I like them?" and she jabbed the stream of water at the shoats. "There was plenty of trash there. It didn't have to be me.

"If you like trash better, go get yourself some trash then," she railed. "You could have made me trash. Or a nigger. If trash is what you wanted why didn't you make me trash?" She shook her fist with the hose in it and a watery snake appeared momentarily in the air. "I could quit working and take it easy and be filthy," she growled. "Lounge about the sidewalks all day drinking root beer. Dip snuff and spit in every puddle and have it all over my face. I could be nasty.

"Or you could have made me a nigger. It's too late for me to be a nigger," she said with deep sarcasm, "but I could act like one. Lay down in the middle of the road and stop traffic. Roll on the ground."

In the deepening light everything was taking on a mysterious hue. The pasture was growing a peculiar glassy green and the streak of highway had turned lavender. She braced herself for a final assault and this time her voice rolled out over the pasture. "Go on," she yelled, "call me a hog! Call me a hog again. From hell. Call me a wart hog from hell. Put that bottom rail on top. There'll still be a top and bottom!"

A garbled echo returned to her.

A final surge of fury shook her and she roared, "Who do you think you are?"

The color of everything, field and crimson sky, burned for a moment with a transparent intensity. The question carried over the pasture and across the highway and the cotton field and returned to her clearly like an answer from beyond the wood.

She opened her mouth but no sound came out of it.

A tiny truck, Claud's, appeared on the highway, heading rapidly out of sight. Its gears scraped thinly. It looked like a child's toy. At any moment a bigger truck might smash into it and scatter Claud's and the niggers' brains all over the road.

Mrs. Turpin stood there, her gaze fixed on the highway, all her muscles rigid, until in five or six minutes the truck reappeared, returning. She waited until it had had time to turn into their own road. Then like a monumental statue coming to life, she bent her head slowly and gazed, as if through the very heart of mystery, down into the pig parlor at the hogs. They had settled all in one corner around the old sow who was grunting softly. A red glow suffused them. They appeared to pant with a secret of life.

Until the sun slipped finally behind the tree line, Mrs. Turpin remained there with her gaze bent to them as if she were absorbing some abysmal life-giving knowledge. At last she lifted her head. There was only a purple streak in the sky, cutting through a field of crimson and leading, like an extension of the highway, into the descending dusk. She raised her hands from the side of the pen in a gesture hieratic and profound. A visionary light settled in her eyes. She saw the streak as a vast swinging bridge extending upward from the earth through a field of living fire. Upon it a vast horde of souls were rumbling toward heaven. There were whole companies of white-trash, clean for the first time in their lives, and bands of black niggers in white robes, and battalions of freaks and lunatics shouting and clapping and leaping like frogs. And bringing up the end of the procession was a tribe of people whom she recognized at once as those who, like herself and Claud, had always had a little of everything and the God-given wit to use it right. She leaned forward to observe them closer. They were marching behind the others with great dignity, accountable as they had always been for good order and common sense and respectable behavior. They alone were on key. Yet she could see by their shocked and altered faces that even their virtues were being burned away. She lowered her hands and gripped the rail of the hog pen, her eyes small but fixed unblinkingly on what lay ahead. In a moment the vision faded but she remained where she was, immobile.

At length she got down and turned off the faucet and made her slow way on the darkening path to the house. In the woods around her the invisible cricket choruses had struck up, but what she heard were the voices of the souls climbing upward into the starry field and shouting hallelujah.

JOYCE CAROL OATES

In the Region of Ice

Sister Irene was a tall, deft woman in her early thirties. What one could see of her face made a striking impression—serious, hard gray eyes, a long slender nose, a face waxen with thought. Seen at the right time, from the right angle, she was almost handsome. In her past teaching positions she had drawn a little upon the fact of her being young and brilliant and also a nun, but she was beginning to grow out of that.

This was a new university and an entirely new world. She had heard—of course it was true—that the Jesuit administration of this school had hired her at the last moment to save money and to head off the appointment of a man of dubious religious commitment. She had prayed for the necessary energy to get her through this first semester. She had no trouble with teaching itself; once she stood before a classroom she felt herself capable of anything. It was the world immediately outside the classroom that confused and alarmed her, though she let none of this show—the cynicism of her colleagues, the indifference of many of the students, and, above all, the looks she got that told her nothing much would be expected of her because she was a nun. This took energy, strength. At times she had the idea that she was on trial and that the excuses she made to herself about her discomfort were only the common excuses made by guilty people. But in front of a class she had no time to worry about herself or the conflicts in her mind. She became, once and for all, a figure existing only for the benefit of others, an instrument by which facts were communicated.

About two weeks after the semester began, Sister Irene noticed a new student in her class. He was slight and fairhaired, and his face was blank, but not blank by accident, blank on purpose, suppressed and restricted into a dumbness that looked hysterical. She was prepared for him before he raised his hand, and when she saw his arm jerk, as if he had at last lost control of it, she nodded to him without hesitation.

"Sister, how can this be reconciled with Shakespeare's vision in *Hamlet?* How can these opposing views be in the same mind?"

Students glanced at him, mildly surprised. He did not belong in the class, and this was mysterious, but his manner was urgent and blind.

"There is no need to reconcile opposing views," Sister Irene said, leaning forward against the podium. "In one play Shakespeare suggests one vision, in another play another; the plays are not simultaneous creations, and even if they were, we never demand a logical—"

"We must demand a logical consistency," the young man said. "The idea of education is itself predicated upon consistency, order, sanity—"

He had interrupted her, and she hardened her face against him—for his sake, not her own, since she did not really care. But he noticed nothing. "Please see me after class," she said.

After class the young man hurried up to her.

"Sister Irene, I hope you didn't mind my visiting today. I'd heard some things, interesting things," he said. He stared at her, and something in her face allowed him to smile. "I . . . could we talk in your office? Do you have time?"

They walked down to her office. Sister Irene sat at her desk, and the young man sat facing her; for a moment they were self-conscious and silent.

"Well, I suppose you know—I'm a Jew," he said.

Sister Irene stared at him. "Yes?" she said.

"What am I doing at a Catholic university, huh?" He grinned. "That's what you want to know."

She made a vague movement of her head to show that she had no thoughts on this, nothing at all, but he seemed not to catch it. He was sitting on the edge of the straightbacked chair. She saw that he was young but did not really look young. There were harsh lines on either side of his mouth, as if he had misused that youthful mouth somehow. His skin was almost as pale as hers, his eyes were dark and not quite in focus. He looked at her and through her and around her, as his voice surrounded them both. His voice was a little shrill at times.

"Listen, I did the right thing today—visiting your class! God, what a lucky accident it was; some jerk mentioned you, said you were a good teacher—I thought, what a laugh! These people know about good teachers here? But yes, listen, yes, I'm not kidding—you are good. I mean that."

Sister Irene frowned. "I don't quite understand what all this means."

He smiled and waved aside her formality, as if he knew better. "Listen, I got my B.A. at Columbia, then I came back here to this crappy city. I mean, I did it on purpose, I wanted to come back. I wanted to. I have my reasons for doing things. I'm on a three-thousand-dollar fellowship," he said, and waited for that to impress her. "You know, I could have gone almost anywhere with that fellowship, and I came back here—my home's in the city—and enrolled here. This was last year. This is my second year. I'm working on a thesis, I mean I was, my master's thesis—but the hell with that. What I want to ask you is this: Can I enroll in your class, is it too late? We have to get special permission if we're late."

Sister Irene felt something nudging her, some uneasiness in him that was pleading with her not to be offended by his abrupt, familiar manner. He seemed to be promising another self, a better self, as if his fair, childish, almost cherubic face were doing tricks to distract her from what his words said.

"Are you in English studies?" she asked.

"I was in history. Listen," he said, and his mouth did something odd, drawing itself down into a smile that made the lines about it deepen like knives, "listen, they kicked me out."

He sat back, watching her. He crossed his legs. He took out a package of cigarettes and offered her one. Sister Irene shook her head, staring at his hands. They were small and stubby and might have belonged to a ten-year-old, and the nails were a strange near-violet color. It took him awhile to extract a cigarette.

"Yeah, kicked me out. What do you think of that?"

"I don't understand."

"My master's thesis was coming along beautifully, and then this bastard—I mean, excuse me, this professor, I won't pollute your office with his name—he started making criticisms, he said some things were unacceptable, he—" The boy leaned forward and hunched his narrow shoulders in a parody of secrecy. "We had an argument. I told him some frank things, things only a broad-minded person could hear about himself. That takes courage, right? He didn't have it! He kicked me out of the master's program, so now I'm coming into English. Literature is greater than history; European history is one big pile of garbage. Sky-high. Filth and rotting corpses, right? Aristotle says that poetry is higher than history; he's right; in your class today I suddenly realized that this is my field, Shakespeare, only Shakespeare is—"

Sister Irene guessed that he was going to say that only Shakespeare was equal to him, and she caught the moment of recognition and hesitation, the half-raised arm, the keen, frowning forehead, the narrowed eyes; then he thought better of it and did not end the sentence. "The students in your class are mainly negligible, I can tell you that. You're new here, and I've been here a year—I would have finished my studies last year but my father got sick, he was hospitalized, I couldn't take exams and it was a mess—but I'll make it through English in one year or drop dead. I can do it, I can do anything. I'll take six courses at once—" He broke off, breathless. Sister Irene tried to smile. "All right then, it's settled? You'll let me in? Have I missed anything so far?"

He had no idea of the rudeness of his question. Sister Irene, feeling suddenly exhausted, said, "I'll give you a syllabus of the course."

"Fine! Wonderful!"

He got to his feet eagerly. He looked through the schedule, muttering to himself, making favorable noises. It struck Sister Irene that she was making a mistake to let him in. There were these moments when one had to make an intelligent decision. . . . But she was sympathetic with him, yes. She was sympathetic with something about him.

She found out his name the next day: Allen Weinstein.

After this she came to her Shakespeare class with a sense of excitement. It became clear to her at once that Weinstein was the most intelligent student in the class. Until he had enrolled, she had not understood what was lacking, a mind that could appreciate her own. Within a week his jagged, protean mind had alienated the other students, and though he sat in the center of the class, he seemed totally alone, encased by a miniature world of his own. When he spoke of the "frenetic humanism of the High Renaissance," Sister Irene dreaded the raised eyebrows and mocking smiles of the other students, who no longer bothered to look at Weinstein. She wanted to defend him, but she never did, because there was something rude and dismal about his knowledge; he used it like a weapon, talking passionately of Nietzsche and Goethe and Freud until Sister Irene would be forced to close discussion.

In meditation, alone, she often thought of him. When she tried to talk about him to a young nun, Sister Carlotta, everything sounded gross. "But no, he's an excellent student," she insisted. "I'm very grateful to have him in class. It's just that . . . he thinks ideas are real." Sister Carlotta, who loved literature also, had been forced to teach grade-school arithmetic for the last four years. That might have been why she said, a little sharply, "You don't think ideas are real?"

Sister Irene acquiesced with a smile, but of course she did not think so: only reality is real.

When Weinstein did not show up for class on the day the first paper was due, Sister Irene's heart sank, and the sensation was somehow a familiar one. She began her lecture and kept waiting for the door to open and for him to hurry noisily back to his seat, grinning an apology toward her—but nothing happened.

If she had been deceived by him, she made herself think angrily, it was as a teacher and not as a woman. He had promised her nothing.

Weinstein appeared the next day near the steps of the liberal arts building. She heard someone running behind her, a breathless exclamation: "Sister Irene!" She turned and saw him, panting and grinning in embarrassment. He wore a dark-blue suit with a necktie, and he looked, despite his childish face, like a little old man; there was something oddly precarious and fragile about him. "Sister Irene, I owe you an apology, right?" He raised his eyebrows and smiled a sad, forlorn, yet irritatingly conspiratorial smile. "The first paper—not in on time, and I know what your rules are. . . . You won't accept late papers, I know—that's good discipline, I'll do that when I teach too. But, unavoidably, I was unable to come to school yesterday. There are many—

many—" He gulped for breath, and Sister Irene had the startling sense of seeing the real Weinstein stare out at her, a terrified prisoner behind the confident voice. "There are many complications in family life. Perhaps you are unaware—I mean—"

She did not like him, but she felt this sympathy, something tugging and nagging at her the way her parents had competed for her love so many years before. They had been whining, weak people, and out of their wet need for affection, the girl she had been (her name was Yvonne) had emerged stronger than either of them, contemptuous of tears because she had seen so many. But Weinstein was different; he was not simply weak—perhaps he was not weak at all—but his strength was confused and hysterical. She felt her customary rigidity as a teacher begin to falter. "You may turn your paper in today if you have it," she said, frowning.

Weinstein's mouth jerked into an incredulous grin. "Wonderful! Marvelous!" he said. "You are very understanding. Sister Irene, I must say. I must say . . . I didn't expect, really . . ." He was fumbling in a shabby old briefcase for the paper. Sister Irene waited. She was prepared for another of his excuses, certain that he did not have the paper, when he suddenly straightened up and handed her something. "Here! I took the liberty of writing thirty pages instead of just fifteen," he said. He was obviously quite excited; his cheeks were mottled pink and white. "You may disagree violently with my interpretation—I expect you to, in fact I'm counting on it—but let me warn you, I have the exact proof, right here in the play itself!" He was thumping at a book, his voice growing louder and shriller. Sister Irene, startled, wanted to put her hand over his mouth and soothe him.

"Look," he said breathlessly, "may I talk with you? I have a class now I hate, I loathe, I can't bear to sit through! Can I talk with you instead?"

Because she was nervous, she stared at the title page of

the paper: " 'Erotic Melodies in *Romeo and Juliet*' by Allen Weinstein, Jr."

"All right?" he said. "Can we walk around here? Is it all right? I've been anxious to talk with you about some things you said in class."

She was reluctant, but he seemed not to notice. They walked slowly along the shaded campus paths. Weinstein did all the talking, of course, and Sister Irene recognized nothing in his cascade of words that she had mentioned in class. "The humanist must be committed to the totality of life," he said passionately. "This is the failing one finds everywhere in the academic world! I found it in New York and I found it here and I'm no ingénu, I don't go around with my mouth hanging open—I'm experienced, look, I've been to Europe, I've lived in Rome! I went everywhere in Europe except Germany, I don't talk about Germany . . . Sister Irene, think of the significant men in the last century, the men who've changed the world! Jews, right? Marx, Freud, Einstein! Not that I believe Marx, Marx is a madman . . . and Freud, no, my sympathies are with spiritual humanism. I believe that the Jewish race is the exclusive . . . the exclusive, what's the word, the exclusive means by which humanism will be extended. . . . Humanism begins by excluding the Jew, and now," he said with a high, surprised laugh, "the Jew will perfect it. After the Nazis, only the Jew is authorized to understand humanism, its limitations and its possibilities. So, I say that the humanist is committed to life in its totality and not just to his profession! The religious person is totally religious, he is his religion! What else? I recognize in you a humanist and a religious person—"

But he did not seem to be talking to her or even looking at her.

"Here, read this," he said. "I wrote it last night." It was a long free-verse poem, typed on a typewriter whose ribbon was worn out.

"There's this trouble with my father, a wonderful man, a

lovely man, but his health—his strength is fading, do you see? What must it be to him to see his son growing up? I mean, I'm a man now, he's getting old, weak, his health is bad—it's hell, right? I sympathize with him. I'd do anything for him, I'd cut open my veins, anything for a father—right? That's why I wasn't in school yesterday," he said, and his voice dropped for the last sentence, as if he had been dragged back to earth by a fact.

Sister Irene tried to read the poem, then pretended to read it. A jumble of words dealing with "life" and "death" and "darkness" and "love." "What do you think?" Weinstein said nervously, trying to read it over her shoulder and crowding against her.

"It's very . . . passionate," Sister Irene said.

This was the right comment; he took the poem back from her in silence, his face flushed with excitement. "Here, at this school, I have few people to talk with. I haven't shown anyone else that poem." He looked at her with his dark, intense eyes, and Sister Irene felt them focus upon her. She was terrified at what he was trying to do—he was trying to force her into a human relationship.

"Thank you for your paper," she said, turning away.

When he came the next day, ten minutes late, he was haughty and disdainful. He had nothing to say and sat with his arms folded. Sister Irene took back with her to the convent a feeling of betrayal and confusion. She had been hurt. It was absurd, and yet— She spent too much time thinking about him, as if he were somehow a kind of crystallization of her own loneliness; but she had no right to think so much of him. She did not want to think of him or of her loneliness. But Weinstein did so much more than think of his predicament: he embodied it, he acted it out, and that was perhaps why he fascinated her. It was as if he were doing a dance for her, a dance of shame and agony and delight, and so long as he did it, she was safe. She felt embarrassment for him, but also anxiety; she wanted to protect him. When the dean of the graduate school

questioned her about Weinstein's work, she insisted that
he was an "excellent" student, though she knew the dean
had not wanted to hear that.

She prayed for guidance, she spent hours on her devotions,
she was closer to her vocation than she had been for some
years. Life at the convent became tinged with unreality, a
misty distortion that took its tone from the glowering skies
of the city at night, identical smokestacks ranged against the
clouds and giving to the sky the excrement of the populated
and successful earth. This city was not her city, this world
was not her world. She felt no pride in knowing this, it was
a fact. The little convent was not like an island in the center
of this noisy world, but rather a kind of hole or crevice the
world did not bother with, something of no interest. The
convent's rhythm of life had nothing to do with the world's
rhythm, it did not violate or alarm it in any way. Sister
Irene tried to draw together the fragments of her life and
synthesize them somehow in her vocation as a nun: she was
a nun, she was recognized as a nun and had given herself
happily to that life, she had a name, a place, she had
dedicated her superior intelligence to the Church, she
worked without pay and without expecting gratitude, she
had given up pride, she did not think of herself but only of
her work and her vocation, she did not think of anything
external to these, she saturated herself daily in the knowledge that she was involved in the mystery of Christianity.

A daily terror attended this knowledge, however, for she
sensed herself being drawn by that student, that Jewish
boy, into a relationship she was not ready for. She wanted
to cry out in fear that she was being forced into the role of a
Christian, and what did that mean? What could her studies
tell her? What could the other nuns tell her? She was alone,
no one could help; he was making her into a Christian, and
to her that was a mystery, a thing of terror, something
others slipped on the way they slipped on their clothes,
casually and thoughtlessly, but to her a magnificent and
terrifying wonder.

For days she carried Weinstein's paper, marked A, around with her; he did not come to class. One day she checked with the graduate office and was told that Weinstein had called in to say his father was ill and that he would not be able to attend classes for a while. "He's strange, I remember him," the secretary said. "He missed all his exams last spring and made a lot of trouble. He was in and out of here every day."

So there was no more of Weinstein for a while, and Sister Irene stopped expecting him to hurry into class. Then, one morning, she found a letter from him in her mailbox.

He had printed it in black ink, very carefully, as if he had not trusted handwriting. The return address was in bold letters that, like his voice, tried to grab onto her: Birchcrest Manor. Somewhere north of the city. "Dear Sister Irene," the block letters said, "I am doing well here and have time for reading and relaxing. The Manor is delightful. My doctor here is an excellent, intelligent man who has time for me, unlike my former doctor. If you have time, you might drop in on my father, who worries about me too much, I think, and explain to him what my condition is. He doesn't seem to understand. I feel about this new life the way that boy, what's his name, in *Measure for Measure*, feels about the prospects of a different life; you remember what he says to his sister when she visits him in prison, how he is looking forward to an escape into another world. Perhaps you could *explain* this to my father and he would stop worrying." The letter ended with the father's name and address, in letters that were just a little too big. Sister Irene, walking slowly down the corridor as she read the letter, felt her eyes cloud over with tears. She was cold with fear, it was something she had never experienced before. She knew what Weinstein was trying to tell her, and the desperation of his attempt made it all the more pathetic; he did not deserve this, why did God allow him to suffer so?

She read through Claudio's speech to his sister, in *Measure for Measure*:

Ay, but to die, and go we know not where;
To lie in cold obstruction and to rot;
This sensible warm motion to become
A kneaded clod; and the delighted spirit
To bathe in fiery floods, or to reside
In thrilling region of thick-ribbed ice,
To be imprison'd in the viewless winds
And blown with restless violence round about
The pendent world; to be be worse than worst
Of those that lawless and incertain thought
Imagines howling! 'tis too horrible!
The weariest and most loathed worldly life
That age, ache, penury, and imprisonment
Can lay on nature is a paradise
To what we fear of death.

Sister Irene called the father's number that day. "Allen Weinstein residence, who may I say is calling?" a woman said, bored. "May I speak to Mr. Weinstein? It's urgent—about his son," Sister Irene said. There was a pause at the other end. "You want to talk to his mother, maybe?" the woman said. "His mother? Yes, his mother, then. Please. It's very important."

She talked with this strange, unsuspected woman, a disembodied voice that suggested absolutely no face, and insisted upon going over that afternoon. The woman was nervous, but Sister Irene, who was a university professor, after all, knew enough to hide her own nervousness. She kept waiting for the woman to say, "Yes, Allen has mentioned you . . ." but nothing happened.

She persuaded Sister Carlotta to ride over with her. This urgency of hers was something they were all amazed by. They hadn't suspected that the set of her gray eyes could change to this blurred, distracted alarm, this sense of mission that seemed to have come to her from nowhere. Sister Irene drove across the city in the late afternoon traffic, with the high whining noises from residential streets where trees were being sawed down in pieces. She understood now the secret, sweet wildness that Christ must have felt, giving himself for man, dying for the billions of men who would never know of him and never understand the sacrifice. For the first time she approached the realization of that great act. In her troubled mind the city traffic was jumbled and yet oddly coherent, an image of the world that was always out of joint with what was happening in it, its inner history struggling with its external spectacle. This sacrifice of Christ's, so mysterious and legendary now, almost lost in time—it was that by which Christ transcended both God and man at one moment, more than man because of his fate to do what no other man could do, and more than God because no god could suffer as he did. She felt a flicker of something close to madness.

She drove nervously, uncertainly, afraid of missing the street and afraid of finding it too, for while one part of her rushed forward to confront these people who had betrayed their son, another part of her would have liked nothing so much as to be waiting as usual for the summons to dinner, safe in her room. . . . When she found the street and turned onto it, she was in a state of breathless excitement. Here lawns were bright green and marred with only a few leaves, magically clean, and the houses were enormous and pompous, a mixture of styles: ranch houses, colonial houses, French country houses, white-bricked wonders with curving glass and clumps of birch trees somehow encircled by white concrete. Sister Irene stared as if she had blundered into another world. This was a kind of heaven, and she was too shabby for it.

The Weinsteins' house was the strangest one of all: it looked like a small Alpine lodge, with an inverted-V-shaped front entrance. Sister Irene drove up the black-topped driveway and let the car slow to a stop; she told Sister Carlotta she would not be long.

At the door she was met by Weinstein's mother, a small, nervous woman with hands like her son's. "Come in, come in," the woman said. She had once been beautiful, that was clear, but now in missing beauty she was not handsome or even attractive but looked ruined and perplexed, the misshapen swelling of her white-blond professionally set hair like a cap lifting up from her surprised face. "He'll be right in. Allen?" she called, "our visitor is here." They went into the living room. There was a grand piano at one end and an organ at the other. In between were scatterings of brilliant modern furniture in conventional groups, and several puffed-up white rugs on the polished floor. Sister Irene could not stop shivering.

"Professor, it's so strange, but let me say when the phone rang I had a feeling—I had a feeling," the woman said, with damp eyes. Sister Irene sat, and the woman hovered about her. "Should I call you Professor? We don't . . . you know . . . we don't understand the technicalities that go with—Allen, my son, wanted to go here to the Catholic school; I told my husband why not? Why fight? It's the thing these days, they do anything they want for knowledge. And he had to come home, you know. He couldn't take care of himself in New York, that was the beginning of the trouble. . . . Should I call you Professor?"

"You can call me Sister Irene."

"Sister Irene?" the woman said, touching her throat in awe, as if something intimate and unexpected had happened.

Then Weinstein's father appeared, hurrying. He took long, impatient strides. Sister Irene stared at him and in that instant doubted everything—he was in his fifties, a tall, sharply handsome man, heavy but not fat, holding his shoulders back with what looked like an effort, but holding them back just the same. He wore a dark suit and his face was flushed, as if he had run a long distance.

"Now," he said, coming to Sister Irene and with a precise wave of his hand motioning his wife off, "now, let's straighten this out. A lot of confusion over that kid, eh?" He pulled a chair over, scraping it across a rug and pulling one corner over, so that its brown underside was exposed.

"I came home early just for this, Libby phoned me. Sister, you got a letter from him, right?"

The wife looked at Sister Irene over her husband's head as if trying somehow to coach her, knowing that this man was so loud and impatient that no one could remember anything in his presence.

"A letter—yes—today—"

"He says what in it? You got the letter, eh? Can I see it?"

She gave it to him and wanted to explain, but he silenced her with a flick of his hand. He read through the letter so quickly that Sister Irene thought perhaps he was trying to impress her with his skill at reading. "So?" he said, raising his eyes, smiling, "so what is this? He's happy out there, he says. He doesn't communicate with us any more, but he writes to you and says he's happy—what's that? I mean, what the hell is that?"

"But he isn't happy. He wants to come home," Sister Irene said. It was so important that she make him understand that she could not trust her voice; goaded by this man, it might suddenly turn shrill, as his son's did. "Someone must read their letters before they're mailed, so he tried to tell me something by making an allusion to—"

"What?"

"—an allusion to a play, so that I would know. He may be thinking suicide, he must be very unhappy—"

She ran out of breath. Weinstein's mother had begun to cry, but the father was shaking his head jerkily back and forth. "Forgive me, Sister, but it's a lot of crap, he needs the hospital, he needs help—right? It costs me fifty a day out there, and they've got the best place in the state. I figure it's worth it. He needs help, that kid, what do I care if he's unhappy? He's unbalanced!" he said angrily. "You want us to get him out again? We argued with the judge for two hours to get him in, an acquaintance of mine. Look, he can't control himself—he was smashing things here, he was hysterical. They need help, lady, and you do something about it fast! You do something! We made up our minds to do something and we did it! This letter—what the hell is this letter? He never talked like that to us!"

"But he means the opposite of what he says—"

"Then he's crazy! I'm the first to admit it." He was perspiring, and his face had darkened. "I've got no pride left this late. He's a little bastard, you want to know? He calls me names, he's filthy, got a filthy mouth—that's being smart, huh? They give him a big scholarship for his filthy mouth? I went to college too, and I got out and knew something, and I for Christ's sake did something with it; my wife is an intelligent woman, a learned woman, would you guess she does book reviews for the little newspaper out here? Intelligent isn't crazy—crazy isn't intelligent. Maybe for you at the school he writes nice papers and gets an A, but out here, around the house, he can't control himself, and we got him committed!"

"But—"

"We're fixing him up, don't worry about it!" He turned to his wife. "Libby, get out of here, I mean it. I'm sorry, but get out of here, you're making a fool of yourself, go stand in the kitchen or something, you and the goddamn maid can cry on each other's shoulders. That one in the kitchen is nuts too, they're all nuts. Sister," he said, his voice lowering, "I thank you immensely for coming out here. This is wonderful, your interest in my son. And I see he admires you—that letter there. But what about that letter? If he did want to get out, which I don't admit—he was willing to be committed, in the end he said okay himself—if he wanted out I wouldn't do it. Why? So what if he wants to come back? The next day he wants something else, what then? He's a sick kid, and I'm the first to admit it."

Sister Irene felt that sickness spread to her. She stood. The room was so big it seemed it must be a public place; there had been nothing personal or private about their conversation. Weinstein's mother was standing by the fireplace, sobbing. The father jumped to his feet and wiped his forehead in a gesture that was meant to help Sister Irene on her way out. "God, what a day," he said, his eyes snatching at hers for understanding, "you know—one of those days all day long? Sister, I thank you a lot. There should be more people in the world who care about others, like you. I mean that."

On the way back to the convent, the man's words returned to her, and she could not get control of them; she could not even feel anger. She had been pressed down, forced back, what could she do? Weinstein might have been watching her somehow from a barred window, and he surely would have understood. The strange idea she had had on the way over, something about understanding Christ, came back to her now and sickened her. But the sickness was small. It could be contained.

About a month after her visit to his father, Weinstein himself showed up. He was dressed in a suit as before, even the necktie was the same. He came right into her office as if he had been pushed and could not stop.

"Sister," he said, and shook her hand. He must have seen fear in her because he smiled ironically. "Look, I'm released. I'm let out of the nut house. Can I sit down?"

He sat. Sister Irene was breathing quickly, as if in the presence of an enemy who does not know he is an enemy.

"So, they finally let me out. I heard what you did. You talked with him, that was all I wanted. You're the only one who gave a damn. Because you're a humanist and a religious person, you respect . . . the individual. Listen," he said, whispering, "it was hell out there! Hell Birchcrest Manor! All fixed up with fancy chairs and *Life* magazines lying around—and what do they do to you? They locked me up, they gave me shock treatments! Shock treatments, how do you like that, it's discredited by everybody now— they're crazy out there themselves, sadists. They locked me up, they gave me hypodermic shots, they didn't treat me like a human being! Do you know what that is," Weinstein demanded savagely, "not to be treated like a human being? They made me an animal—for fifty dollars a day! Dirty filthy swine! Now I'm an outpatient because I stopped swearing at them. I found somebody's bobby pin, and when I wanted to scream I pressed it under my fingernail and it stopped me—the screaming went inside and not out—so they gave me good reports, those sick bastards. Now I'm an outpatient and I can walk along the street and breathe in the same filthy exhaust from the buses like all you normal people! Christ," he said, and threw himself back against the chair.

Sister Irene stared at him. She wantd to take his hand, to make some gesture that would close the aching distance between them. "Mr. Weinstein—"

"Call me Allen!" he said sharply.

"I'm very sorry—I'm terribly sorry—"

"My own parents committed me, but of course they didn't know what it was like. It was hell," he said thickly, "and there isn't any hell except what other people do to you. The psychiatrist out there, the main shrink, he hates Jews too, some of us were positive of that, and he's got a bigger nose than I do, a real beak." He made a noise of disgust. "A dirty bastard, a sick, dirty, pathetic bastard—all of them. Anyway, I'm getting out of here, and I came to ask you a favor."

"What do you mean?"

"I'm getting out. I'm leaving. I'm going up to Canada and lose myself. I'll get a job. I'll forget everything. I'll kill myself maybe—what's the difference? Look, can you lend me some money?"

"Money?"

"Just a little! I have to get to the border, I'm going to take a bus."

"But I don't have any money—"

"No money?" He stared at her. "You mean—you don't have any? Sure you have some!"

She stared at him as if he had asked her to do something

obscene. Everything was splotched and uncertain before her eyes.

"You must . . . you must go back," she said, "you're making a—"

"I'll pay it back. Look, I'll pay it back, can you go to where you live or something and get it? I'm in a hurry. My friends are sons of bitches: one of them pretended he didn't see me yesterday—I stood right in the middle of the sidewalk and yelled at him, I called him some appropriate names! So he didn't see me, huh? You're the only one who understands me, you understand me like a poet, you—"

"I can't help you, I'm sorry—I . . ."

He looked to one side of her and flashed his gaze back, as if he could control it. He seemed to be trying to clear his vision.

"You have the soul of a poet," he whispered, "you're the only one. Everybody else is rotten! Can't you lend me some money, ten dollars maybe? I have three thousand in the bank, and I can't touch it! They take everything away from me, they make me into an animal. . . . You know I'm not an animal, don't you? Don't you?"

"Of course," Sister Irene whispered.

"You could get money. Help me. Give me your hand or something, touch me, help me—please. . . ." He reached for her hand and she drew back. He stared at her and his face seemed about to crumble, like a child's. "I want something from you, but I don't know what—I want something!" he cried. "Something real! I want you to look at me like I was a human being, is that too much to ask? I have a brain, I'm alive, I'm suffering—what does that mean? Does that mean nothing? I want something real and not this phony Christian love garbage—it's all in the books, it isn't personal—I want something real—look. . . ."

He tried to take her hand again, and this time she jerked away. She got to her feet. "Mr. Weinstein," she said, "please—"

"You! You nun!" he said scornfully, his mouth twisted

into a mock grin. "You nun! There's nothing under that ugly outfit, right? And you're not particularly smart even though you think you are; my father has more brains in his foot than you—"

He got to his feet and kicked the chair.

"You bitch!" he cried.

She shrank back against her desk as if she thought he might hit her, but he only ran out of the office.

Weinstein: the name was to become disembodied from the figure, as time went on. The semester passed; the autumn drizzle turned into snow, Sister Irene rode to school in the morning and left in the afternoon, four days a week, anonymous in her black winter cloak, quiet and stunned. University teaching was an anonymous task, each day dissociated from the rest, with no necessary sense of unity among the teachers: they came and went separately and might for a year just miss a colleague who left his office five minutes before they arrived, and it did not matter.

She heard of Weinstein's death, his suicide by drowning, from the English Department secretary, a handsome whitehaired woman who kept a transistor radio on her desk. Sister Irene was not surprised; she had been thinking of him as dead for months. "They identified him by some special television way they have now," the secretary said. "They're shipping the body back. It was up in Quebec. . . ."

Sister Irene could feel a part of herself drifting off, lured by the plains of white snow to the north, the quiet, the emptiness, the sweep of the Great Lakes up to the silence of Canada. But she called that part of herself back. She could only be one person in her lifetime. That was the ugly truth, she thought, that she could not really regret Weinstein's suffering and death; she had only one life and had already given it to someone else. He had come too late to her. Fifteen years ago, perhaps, but not now.

She was only one person, she thought, walking down the corridor in a dream. Was she safe in this single person, or was she trapped? She had only one identity. She could make only one choice. What she had done or hadn't done was the result of that choice, and how was she guilty? If she could have felt guilt, she thought, she might at least have been able to feel something.

BERNARD MALAMUD

Black Is
My Favorite Color

Charity Sweetness sits in the toilet eating her two hard-boiled eggs while I'm having my ham sandwich and coffee in the kitchen. That's how it goes only don't get the idea of ghettoes. If there's a ghetto I'm the one that's in it. She's my cleaning woman from Father Divine and comes in once a week to my small three-room apartment on my day off from the liquor store. "Peace," she says to me, "Father reached on down and took me right up in Heaven." She's a small person with a flat body, frizzy hair, and a quiet face that the light shines out of, and Mama had such eyes before she died. The first time Charity Sweetness came in to clean, a little more than a year and a half, I made the mistake to ask her to sit down at the kitchen table with me and eat her lunch. I was still feeling not so hot after Ornita left but I'm the kind of a man—Nat Lime, forty-four, a bachelor with a daily growing bald spot on the back of my head, and I could lose frankly fifteen pounds—who enjoys company so long as he has it. So she cooked up her two hard-boiled eggs and sat down and took a small bite out of one of them. But after a minute she stopped chewing and she got up and carried the eggs in a cup into the bathroom, and since then she eats there. I said to her more than once, "Okay, Charity

Sweetness, so have it your way, eat the eggs in the kitchen by yourself and I'll eat when you're done," but she smiles absentminded, and eats in the toilet. It's my fate with colored people.

Although black is still my favorite color you wouldn't know it from my luck except in short quantities even though I do all right in the liquor store business in Harlem, on Eighth Avenue between 110th and 111th. I speak with respect. A large part of my life I've had dealings with Negro people, most on a business basis but sometimes for friendly reasons with genuine feeling on both sides. I'm drawn to them. At this time of my life I should have one or two good colored friends but the fault isn't necessarily mine. If they knew what was in my heart towards them, but how can you tell that to anybody nowadays? I've tried more than once but the language of the heart either is a dead language or else nobody understands it the way you speak it. Very few. What I'm saying is, personally for me there's only one human color and that's the color of blood. I like a black person if not because he's black, then because I'm white. It comes to the same thing. If I wasn't white my first choice would be black. I'm satisfied to be white because I have no other choice. Anyway, I got an eye for color. I appreciate. Who wants everybody to be the same? Maybe it's like kind of a talent. Nat Lime might be a liquor dealer in Harlem, but once in the jungle in New Guinea in the Second War, I got the idea when I shot at a running Jap and missed him, that I had some kind of a talent, though maybe it's the kind where you have a marvelous idea now and then but in the end what do they come to? After all, it's a strange world.

Where Charity Sweetness eats her eggs makes me think about Buster Wilson when we were both boys in the Williamsburg section of Brooklyn. There was this long block of run-down dirty frame houses in the middle of a not-so-hot white neighborhood full of pushcarts. The Negro houses looked to me like they had been born and died there, dead not long after the beginning of the world. I lived on the next street. My father was a cutter with arthritis in both hands, big red knuckles and swollen fingers so he didn't cut, and my mother was the one who went to work. She sold paper bags from a second-hand pushcart in Ellery Street. We didn't starve but nobody ate chicken unless we were sick or the chicken was. This was my first acquaintance with a lot of black people and I used to poke around on their poor block. I think I thought, brother, if there can be like this, what can't there be? I mean I caught an early idea what life was about. Anyway I met Buster Wilson there. He used to play marbles by himself. I sat on the curb across the street, watching him shoot one marble lefty and the other one righty. The hand that won picked up the marbles. It wasn't so much of a game but he didn't ask me to come over. My idea was to be friendly, only he never encouraged, he discouraged. Why did I pick him out for a friend? Maybe because I had no others then, we were new in the neighborhood, from Manhattan. Also I liked his type. Buster did everything alone. He was a skinny kid and his brothers' clothes hung on him like worn-out potato sacks. He was a beanpole boy, about twelve, and I was ten. His arms and legs were burnt-out matchsticks. He always wore a brown wool sweater, one arm half unraveled, the other went down to the wrist. His long and narrow head had a white part cut straight in the short woolly hair, maybe with a ruler there, by his father, a barber, but too drunk to stay a barber. In those days though I had little myself I was old enough to know who was better off, and the whole block of colored houses made me feel bad in the daylight. But I went there as much as I could because the street was full of life. In the night it looked different, it's hard to tell a cripple in the dark. Sometimes I was afraid to walk by the houses when they were dark and quiet. I was afraid there were people looking at me that I couldn't see. I liked it better when they had parties at night and everybody had a good time. The musicians played their banjos and saxophones and the houses shook with the music and laughing. The young girls, with their pretty dresses and ribbons in their hair, caught me in my throat when I saw them through the windows.

But with the parties came drinking and fights. Sundays were bad days after the Saturday night parties. I remember once that Buster's father, also long and loose, always wearing a dirty gray Homburg hat, chased another black man in the street with a half-inch chisel. The other one, maybe five feet high, lost his shoe and when they wrestled on the ground he was already bleeding through his suit, a thick red blood smearing the sidewalk. I was frightened by the blood and wanted to pour it back in the man who was bleeding from the chisel. On another time Buster's father was playing a crap game with two big bouncy red dice, in the back of an alley between two middle houses. Then about six men started fist-fighting there, and they ran out of the alley and hit each other in the street. The neighbors, including children, came out and watched, everybody afraid but nobody moving to do anything. I saw the same thing near my store in Harlem, years later, a big crowd watching two men in the street, their breaths hanging in the air on a winter night, murdering each other with switch knives, but nobody moved to call a cop. I didn't either. Anyway, I was just a young kid but I still remember how the cops drove up in a police paddy wagon and broke up the fight by hitting everybody they could hit with big nightsticks. This was in the days before La Guardia. Most of the fighters were knocked out cold, only one or two got away. Buster's father started to run back in his house but a cop ran after him and cracked him on his Homburg hat with a club, right on the front porch. Then the Negro men were lifted up by the cops, one at the arms and the other at the feet, and they heaved them in the paddy wagon. Buster's father hit the back of the wagon and fell, with his nose spouting very red blood, on top of three other men. I personally couldn't stand it, I was scared of the human race so I ran home, but I remember Buster watching without any expression in his eyes. I stole an extra fifteen cents from my mother's pocketbook and I ran back and asked Buster if he wanted to go to the movies. I would pay. He said yes. This was the first time he talked to me.

So we went more than once to the movies. But we never got to be friends. Maybe because it was a one-way prop-osition—from me to him. Which includes my invitations to go with me, my (poor mother's) movie money, Hershey choco-late bars, watermelon slices, even my best Nick Carter and Merriwell books that I spent hours picking up in the junk shops, and that he never gave me back. Once he let me go in his house to get a match so we could smoke some butts we found, but it smelled so heavy, so impossible, I died till I got out of there. What I saw in the way of furniture I won't mention—the best was falling apart in pieces. Maybe we went to the movies all together five or six matinees that spring and in the summertime, but when the shows were over he usually walked home by himself.

"Why don't you wait for me, Buster?" I said. "We're both going in the same direction."

But he was walking ahead and didn't hear me. Anyway he didn't answer.

One day when I wasn't expecting it he hit me in the teeth. I felt like crying but not because of the pain. I spit blood and said, "What did you hit me for? What did I do to you?"

"Because you a Jew bastard. Take your Jew movies and your Jew candy and shove them up your Jew ass."

And he ran away.

I thought to myself how was I to know he didn't like the movies. When I was a man I thought, you can't force it.

Years later, in the prime of my life, I met Mrs. Ornita Harris. She was standing by herself under an open umbrella at the bus stop, crosstown 110th, and I picked up her green glove that she had dropped on the wet sidewalk. It was in the end of November. Before I could ask her was it hers, she grabbed the glove out of my hand, closed her umbrella, and stepped in the bus. I got on right after her.

I was annoyed so I said, "If you'll pardon me, Miss, there's no law that you have to say thanks, but at least don't make a criminal out of me."

"Well, I'm sorry," she said, "but I don't like white men trying to do me favors."

I tipped my hat and that was that. In ten minutes I got off the bus but she was already gone.

Who expected to see her again but I did. She came into my store about a week later for a bottle of scotch.

"I would offer you a discount," I told her, "but I know you don't like a certain kind of a favor and I'm not looking for a slap in the face."

Then she recognized me and got a little embarrassed. "I'm sorry I misunderstood you that day."

"So mistakes happen."

The result was she took the discount. I gave her a dollar off.

She used to come in about every two weeks for a fifth of Haig and Haig. Sometimes I waited on her, sometimes my helpers, Jimmy or Mason, also colored, but I said to give the discount. They both looked at me but I had nothing to be ashamed. In the spring when she came in we used to talk once in a while. She was a slim woman, dark but not the most dark, about thirty years I would say, also well built, with a combination nice legs and a good-size bosom that I like. Her face was pretty, with big eyes and high cheek bones, but lips a little thick and nose a little broad. Sometimes she didn't feel like talking, she paid for the bottle, less discount, and walked out. Her eyes were tired and she didn't look to me like a happy woman.

I found out her husband was once a window cleaner on the big buildings, but one day his safety belt broke and he fell fifteen stories. After the funeral she got a job as a manicurist in a Times Square barber shop. I told her I was a bachelor and lived with my mother in a small three-room apartment on West Eighty-third near Broadway. My mother had cancer, and Ornita said she was very sorry.

One night in July we went out together. How that happened I'm still not so sure. I guess I asked her and she didn't say no. Where do you go out with a Negro woman? We went to the Village. We had a good dinner and walked in Washington Square Park. It was a hot night. Nobody was surprised when they saw us, nobody looked at us like we were against the law. If they looked maybe they saw my new lightweight suit that I bought yesterday and my shiny bald spot when we walked under a lamp, also how pretty she was for a man of my type. We went in a movie on West Eighth Street. I didn't want to go in but she said she had heard about the picture. We went in like strangers and we came out like strangers. I wondered what was in her mind and I thought to myself, whatever is in there its not a certain white man that I know. All night long we went together like we were chained. After the movie she wouldn't let me take her back to Harlem. When I put her in a taxi she asked me, "Why did we bother?"

For the steak, I wanted to say. Instead I said, "You're worth the bother."

"Thanks anyway."

Kiddo, I thought to myself after the taxi left, you just found out what's what, now the best thing is forget her.

It's easy to say. In August we went out the second time. That was the night she wore a purple dress and I thought to myself, my God, what colors. Who paints that picture paints a masterpiece. Everybody looked at us but I had pleasure. That night when she took off her dress it was in a furnished room I had the sense to rent a few days before. With my sick mother, I couldn't ask her to come to my apartment, and she didn't want me to go home with her where she lived with her brother's family on West 115th near Lenox Avenue. Under her purple dress she wore a black slip, and when she took that off she had white

underwear. When she took off the white underwear she
was black again. But I know where the next white was, if
you want to call it white. And that was the night I think I
fell in love with her, the first time in my life though I have
liked one or two nice girls I used to go with when I was a
boy. It was a serious proposition. I'm the kind of a man
when I think of love I'm thinking of marriage. I guess that's
why I am a bachelor.

That same week I had a holdup in my place, two big
men—both black—with revolvers. One got excited when I
rang open the cash register so he could take the money and
he hit me over the ear with his gun. I stayed in the hospital
a couple of weeks. Otherwise I was insured. Ornita came to
see me. She sat on a chair without talking much. Finally I
saw she was uncomfortable so I suggested she ought to go
home.

"I'm sorry it happened," she said.

"Don't talk like it's your fault."

When I got out of the hospital my mother was dead. She
was a wonderful person. My father died when I was
thirteen and all by herself she kept the family alive and
together. I sat shive for a week and remembered how she
sold paper bags on her pushcart. I remembered her life and
what she tried to teach me. Nathan, she said, if you ever
forget you are a Jew a goy will remind you. Mama, I say,
rest in peace on this subject. But if I do something you
don't like, remember, on earth it's harder than where you
are. Then when my week of mourning was finished, one
night I said, "Ornita, let's get married. We're both honest
people and if you love me like I love you it won't be such a
bad time. If you don't like New York I'll sell out here and
we'll move someplace else. Maybe to San Francisco where
nobody knows us. I was there for a week in the Second War
and I saw white and colored living together."

"Nat," she answered me, "I like you but I'd be afraid. My
husband woulda killed me."

"Your husband is dead."

"Not in my memory."

"In that case I'll wait."

"Do you know what it'd be like—I mean the life we could expect?"

"Ornita," I said, "I'm the kind of man, if he picks his own way of life he's satisfied."

"What about children? Were you looking forward to half-Jewish polka dots?"

"I was looking forward to children."

"I can't," she said.

Can't is can't. I saw she was afraid and the best thing was not to push. Sometimes when we met she was so nervous that whatever we did she couldn't enjoy it. At the same time I still thought I had a chance. We were together more and more. I got rid of my furnished room and she came to my apartment—I gave away Mama's bed and bought a new one. She stayed with me all day on Sundays. When she wasn't so nervous she was affectionate, and if I know what love is, I had it. We went out a couple of times a week, the same way—usually I met her in Times Square and sent her home in a taxi, but I talked more about marriage and she talked less against it. One night she told me she was still trying to convince herself but she was almost convinced. I took an inventory of my liquor stock so I could put the store up for sale.

Ornita knew what I was doing. One day she quit her job, the next she took it back. She also went away a week to visit her sister in Philadelphia for a little rest. She came back tired but said maybe. Maybe is maybe so I'll wait. The way she said it it was closer to yes. That was the winter two years ago. When she was in Philadelphia I called up a friend of mine from the Army, now a CPA, and told him I would appreciate an invitation for an evening. He knew why. His wife said yes right away. When Ornita came back we went there. The wife made a fine dinner. It wasn't a bad time and they told us to come again. Ornita had a few drinks. She looked relaxed, wonderful. Later, because of a twenty-four-hour taxi strike I had to take her home on the subway. When we got to the 116th Street station she told me to stay on the train, and she would walk the couple of blocks to her house. I didn't like a woman walking alone on the streets at that time of the night. She said she never had any trouble but I insisted nothing doing. I said I would walk to her stoop with her and when she went upstairs I would go back to the subway.

On the way there, on 115th in the middle of the block before Lenox, we were stopped by three men—maybe they were boys. One had a black hat with a half-inch brim, one a green cloth hat, and the third wore a black leather cap. The green hat was wearing a short coat and the other two had long ones. It was under a street light but the leather cap snapped a six-inch switchblade open in the light.

"What you doin' with this white son of a bitch?" he said to Ornita.

"I'm minding my own business," she answered him, "and I wish you would too."

"Boys," I said, "we're all brothers. I'm a reliable merchant in the neighborhood. This young lady is my dear friend. We don't want any trouble. Please let us pass."

"You talk like a Jew landlord," said the green hat. "Fifty a week for a single room."

"No charge fo' the rats," said the half-inch brim.

"Believe me, I'm no landlord. My store is Nathan's Liquors between Hundred Tenth and Eleventh. I also have two colored clerks, Mason and Jimmy, and they will tell you I pay good wages as well as I give discounts to certain customers."

"Shut your mouth, Jewboy," said the leather cap, and he moved the knife back and forth in front of my coat button. "No more black pussy for you."

"Speak with respect about this lady, please."

I got slapped on my mouth.

"That ain't no lady," said the long face in the half-inch brim, "that's black pussy. She deserve to have evvy bit of her hair shave off. How you like to have evvy bit of your hair shave off, black pussy?"

"Please leave me and this gentleman alone or I'm gonna scream long and loud. That's my house three doors down."

They slapped her. I never heard such a scream. Like her husband was falling fifteen stories.

I hit the one that slapped her and the next I knew I was laying in the gutter with a pain in my head. I thought, goodbye, Nat, they'll stab me for sure, but all they did was take my wallet and run in three different directions.

Ornita walked back with me to the subway and she wouldn't let me go home with her again.

"Just get home safely."

She looked terrible. Her face was gray and I still remembered her scream. It was a terrible winter night, very cold February, and it took me an hour and ten minutes to get home. I felt bad for leaving her but what could I do?

We had a date downtown the next night but she didn't show up, the first time.

In the morning I called her in her place of business.

"For God's sake, Ornita, if we got married and moved away we wouldn't have that kind of trouble that we had. We wouldn't come in that neighborhood any more."

"Yes, we would. I have family there and don't want to move anyplace else. The truth of it is I can't marry you, Nat. I got troubles enough of my own."

"I coulda sworn you love me."

"Maybe I do but I can't marry you."

"For God's sake, why?"

"I got enough trouble of my own."

I went that night in a cab to her brother's house to see her. He was a quiet man with a thin mustache. "She gone," he said, "left for a long visit to some close relatives in the South. She said to tell you she appreciate your intentions but didn't think it will work out."

"Thank you kindly," I said.

Don't ask me how I got home.

Once on Eighth Avenue, a couple of blocks from my store, I saw a blind man with a white cane tapping on the sidewalk. I figured we were going in the same direction so I took his arm.

"I can tell you're white," he said.

A heavy colored woman with a full shopping bag rushed after us.

"Never mind," she said, "I know where he live."

She pushed me with her shoulder and I hurt my leg on the fire hydrant.

That's how it is. I give my heart and they kick me in my teeth.

"Charity Sweetness—you hear me?—come out of that goddamn toilet!"

CYNTHIA OZICK

An Education

There are at least a couple of perfect moments in any life, and the one Una Meyer counted as second-best was a certain image of herself entering her college Latin class. It is a citified February morning. The classroom is in a great drab building, not really a skyscraper but high above the nearest church-tower, and the window looks out on the brick solemnity of an airshaft. A draft of worn cafeteria coffee slides by. Una is wearing a new long-sleeved dress with a patent-leather belt; the sleeves and the belt are somehow liberating and declare her fate to her. Besides, she is the only one in the class who can tell the difference between synecdoche and metonymy. One is the-part-for-the-whole, the other is the-sign-for-the-thing. Her body is a series of exquisitely strung bones. Her face has that double plainness of innocence and ordinariness. Her brain is deliciously loaded with Horace—wit, satire, immortality—and even more deliciously with Catullus—sparrows and lovers and a thousand kisses, and yet again a thousand, which no mean and jinxing spy shall ever see. Una has kissed no one but her parents, but she is an intellectual and the heiress of all the scholars who ever lived. The instructor's name is

Mr. Collie. He is Roger Ascham resurrected. He is violent
with Mr. Organski, who never prepares the lesson and can't
manage case-endings. Mr. Collie is terribly strict and
terribly exacting. Everything must be rendered precisely.
When he turns his back, Mr. Organski spits in the air. The
class shudders with indifference. "You're late," says Mr.
Collie in open joy. He never tolerates lateness in anyone
else, but he can't conceal his delight at seeing Una in the
doorway at last. He teaches only Una. "*Tell* Mr. Organski,
won't you, *why* he may not use the accusative case with the
verb I've just taken the great trouble to conjugate for him
on the blackboard? *Oblige* him, Miss Meyer, won't you?"
Mr. Organski patiently wipes the excess spit from his
mouth. He is a foreigner and a veteran; he is a year older
than Mr. Collie and has a mistress, which would disgust
Mr. Collie if he knew. In spite of everything Mr. Organski
does not hate Una, who is now hiking up her eyeglasses by
pushing on the nosepiece. He pities her because she is so
skinny; she reminds him of a refugee survivor. "Well it
takes the genitive," Una says, and thinks: If only the
universe would stay as it is this moment! Only a tiny
handful of very obscure verbs—who can remember them?—
take the genitive. Una is of the elect who can remember.
And she is dazzled—how poignantly she senses her stu-
pendous and glorious fate! How tenderly she contemplates
her mind!

That is the sort of girl Una Meyer was at eighteen.

At twenty-four she hadn't improved. By then she had a
master's degree in Classics and most of a Ph.D.—the only
thing left was to write the damn dissertation. Her subject
was certain Etruscan findings in southern Turkey. Their
remarkable interest lay in the oddity that all the goddesses
seemed to be left-handed. Una, who was right-handed, felt
she must be present at the dig—she was waiting for her
Fulbright to come through. No one doubted it would, but
all the same Una was positive she had deteriorated. It was

summer. Her dissertation adviser and his wife Betty and
sons Bruce and Brian had rented a cottage on Martha's
Vineyard. The younger teachers had taken a house on Fire
Island; no one had invited Una. The department office was
empty most of the day, and a pneumatic drill in the street
below roared and rattled the paper clips in the desk-drawers,
so Una took to spending her afternoons in the college
cafeteria. In six years the coffee had aged a bit—you could
tell by the brittle staleness meandering through the cigarette smells—but never Una. She still thought of herself as
likely to be damaged by caffeine, and she said she hated
lipstick because it was savagery to paint oneself brighter
than one was born, but mainly she was against coal tar.

And that was how she came to notice Rosalie. Rosalie was
one of those serious blue-eyed fat girls, very short-fingered,
who seem to have arrived out of their mothers' wombs with
ten years' experience at social work. She wore her hair
wrapped in a skimpy braid around her big head, which
counted against her, but she was reading *Coming of Age in
Samoa* in paperback, a good point in a place where all the
other girls were either paring or comparing—nails or
engagement rings as the case might be. It wasn't the
engaged girls that made Una feel she had declined—what
she felt for *them* was scorn. She was sure they would all
marry nightgown salesmen or accountants from the School
of Business Administration; not one of them would ever get
to Turkey to study left-handed Etruscan goddesses. But all
the same she was depressed. Her life struck her as very
ordinary—nowadays practically everyone she was acquainted
with could tell the difference between synecdoche and
metonymy (that was what came of being a graduate
student), but the sad thing was it no longer seemed important. That was her trouble: the importance of everything
had fallen. And more than that, she had a frightening ·
secret—she was afraid she really didn't care enough about
her dissertation subject. And she was afraid she would get

dysentery in Turkey, even though she had already promised her mother to boil everything. She almost wished
she was stupid and fit only to be engaged, so that she wouldn't
have to win a Fulbright.

Rosalie, meanwhile, had come to page 95, and was
gulping a lemonade without looking; when the straw gar-
gled loudly she knew she had attained the end of her
nourishment, and let go. The straw, though bitten, was a
clean yellow. Una, whom the sight of lipstick on straws
offended, decided Rosalie might be interesting to talk to.

"You realize Margaret Mead's a waste of time," she
began. "There aren't any *standards* in cultural anthropology"—this was just to start the argument off—"that's
what's wrong with it."

Rosalie showed no surprise at being addressed that way,
out of the blue. "That's the idea," she said. "That's the way
it's supposed to be. Cultural relativity. Whatever is, is.
What's wrong in New York can be right in Zanzibar."

"I don't go for that," Una said. "That sounds pretty
depraved. Take murder. Murder's wrong in any culture. I
believe in the perfectibility of man."

"So do I," Rosalie said.

"Then your position isn't really logical, is it? I mean if
you believe in the perfectibility of man you have to believe
in that very standard of perfection all peoples aspire to."

"Nobody's perfect," Rosalie said, going sour.

"I disagree with that."

"Well, name somebody who is."

"That has nothing to do with it," Una said in her most
earnest style, "just because I personally don't know anybody doesn't mean they don't exist."

"They *can't* exist."

"They might if they wanted to. They exist in theory. I'm
a Platonist," Una explained.

"I'm a *bezbozhnik*," Rosalie said. "That's Russian for
atheist."

Una was overwhelmed. "Do you know Russian?"

"I have this pregnant friend who was studying it last year."

"Say something else."

"*Tovarichka*, I don't know anything else, I only know the names those two call me."

"Two?" Una picked up. She was very good at picking up small points and turning them into jokes. "You have *two* pregnant friends who speak Russian?"

"One's the husband."

"Oh," Una said, because nothing bored her more than married couples. "How come you go around with people that old?"

"*She's* twenty-three and *he's* twenty-two."

Una was impressed, not to say horrified. "That's younger than *I* am. I mean that's *very* young to cage yourself up like that. I suppose they never had a chance to get any real education or anything?"

"Mary's a lawyer and Clement—well, if you're that way about Margaret Mead I won't tell you about Clement."

"Tell!" Una said.

"Clement *studied* with Margaret Mead and got his master's in anthropology at Columbia, but then he suddenly got interested in religion—mysticism, really—and now he commutes to the Union Theological Seminary. They had to move up to Connecticut so Mary can start on her J.S.D. at Yale Law School right after the baby comes. Actually"—Rosalie's stumpy forefinger scratched at *Coming of Age in Samoa*—"this is Clement's book. He lent it to me about two months ago, but I haven't seen either of them for ages—I'm going up there this weekend and I wouldn't dare turn up without it. They're *wild* on people who borrow books and don't give them back. They've got this little card catalogue they keep, just like a library, and when you return a book they ask you *questions* about it, just to make sure you didn't borrow it for nothing."

"So you're boning up!" Una concluded. She realized she

was jealous. The part about the card catalogue thrilled her. "They sound marvelous. I mean they sound really wonderful and delightful."

"They're very nice," Rosalie agreed coldly.

"What's their name? In case they get famous some day." Una always took note of potential celebrity as a sort of investment, the way some people collect art. "Their last name, I mean."

"Chimes. Like what a bell does."

"Chimes. That's beautiful."

"It was legally changed from Chaims."

"But isn't that Jewish?" Una asked. "I thought you said Union Theological Sem—"

"They're emancipated. I'm bringing them a four-pound ham. You should hear Clement on 'Heidegger and the Holocaust.' "

"Heidegger and the *what?*"

"The Holy Ghost," Rosalie said. "Clement's awfully witty."

2

The really perfect moment—the one that came just when Una had decided there were no new revelations to be had in the tired old world, and the one she promised herself she would remember forever and ever—happened on the shore of the State of Connecticut at half-past four in the afternoon. Now it is the very core of August. The sky is a speckless white cheek. Yards away the water fizzes up like soda-pop against a cozy rock in the shape of a sleeping old dog. A live young dog skids maniacally between the nibble-marks the tide has bitten into the sand. The dog's owners, a couple in their fifties, are packing up to go home. They stop for one last catch of a ball—it zooms over poor Spot's jaws, but in a second Clement has dropped *King Lear* and hypnotizes the

ball: it seems to wait in air for him to rise and pluck it from
the lip of the sun. "Good *boy*," says the man, "damn good
catch. Give 'er here." Back and forth goes the ball between
Clement and the stranger. The stranger's wife compliments
Clement: "You got a good build, sonny," she says, "only
you ruin your looks with that hairy stuff. I got a picksher of
my father, he wore one of them handlebars fifty years back.
What's a young kid like you want with that? Take my
advice, shave it off, sonny." Clement returns to the blanket
grinning—how forbearing he is with his inferiors! How
graceful! He is a thick-thighed middle-sized young man
who looks like the early Mark Twain; he is even beginning
crinkles around his eyes, and he is egalitarian with kings
and serfs. Una has been in Connecticut only an hour, but
he is as comradely toward her as though they had been
friends since spherical trigonometry. Mary is a bit cooler.
There has been the smallest misunderstanding: the Chimeses
were honestly under the impression that Rosalie said on the
phone she was bringing a Turk. Mary expected a woman in
purdah, and here is only bony Una in a bathing suit. The
Chimeses have had Indians, Chinese, Malayans, Chileans,
Arabs (especially these: on the Israeli question they are
pro-Arab); they have not yet had any Turks. Una is a
disappointment, but since she doesn't know it, she continues
in her rapture without a fault. They go back to reading the
play aloud. There are only three copies; Mary and Una
share one. Una scarcely dares to peek at Mary, her voice is
so dramatic, but she sees a little of her teeth, which are
very large and unabashed, perfect teeth unlike anyone
else's; cavities in Mary's teeth are inconceivable. The baby
she is harboring under her smock is also very large and
unabashed, and Mary, to accommodate its arc, leans down
hard on one elbow, like a mermaid. Mary is beautiful. Her
nose is ideally made and her eyes have broad skeptical lids
that close as slowly as garret shutters. Amazingly, a child's
laugh leaps from her mouth. Una is embarrassed when her
own turn comes, but then she is relieved—Rosalie doesn't

act well at all. Rosalie plays Goneril, Una is Regan, Clement is Cordelia, Mary is King Lear. "I prithee, daughter, do not make me mad," Mary says to Rosalie, "thou art a boil, a plague-sore, an embossed carbuncle," and they all four screech with hilarity. Mary's giggle runs higher and lasts longer than anyone's. "Mary went to a special drama school when she was ten," Clement explains. "Clement sings," Mary informs Una. "We ought to do a play with songs. He's got this marvelous baritone but you have to beg him." "Next time we'll do the *Beggar's Opera*," Clement teases. A little wind comes flying over them, raising a veil of sand. "Time to go home, you'll be cold, bunny," Clement tells Mary. He stretches across fat Rosalie to kiss the pink heel of Mary's foot, and in the very next moment, when they all slap their Shakespeares down and tussle with the pockets in the sand as they scramble up, a brilliance is revealed to Una. All the world's gold occupies the sky. The cooling sun drops a notch lower. They head for the iron staircase that leads to the Chimeses' seaside apartment, and Una carries in her ribs a swelling secret. Her whole long-ago sense of illimitable possibility is restored to her. It is as though she has just swallowed Beauty. A charm of ecstasy has her in thrall. She has fallen in love with the Chimeses, the two of them together. Oh, the two of them together!

They were perfect. Everything about them was perfect. Una had never before seen so enchanting an apartment: it was exactly right, just what you would expect of a pair of intellectual lovers. Instead of pictures on the walls, there were two brightly crude huge rectangles of tapestry, with abstract designs in them. Clement had sewn them. On the inside of the bathroom door, where vain people stupidly hang mirrors, Mary had painted a Mexican-style mural, with overtones of Dali. And all along the walls, in the kitchen and the bedroom and the living room and even in the little connecting corridor, were rows and rows of bookshelves nailed together very serviceably by Clement. Clement could build a bookcase, Mary said, in two hours flat. Meanwhile Rosalie was in the kitchen checking on the ham, which they had left cooking all afternoon.

"Is it done?" Mary asked from the bathroom.

"I'd guess another fifteen minutes," Rosalie said.

"Then I'm going to shower. You're next, Rosalie. Then Una. Then Clement."

Una went prowling among the books. Regiments of treasure marched by. The Chimeses had the entire original New York edition of Henry James. They had Jones's life of Freud. They had Christmas Humphreys on Buddhism, *Memoirs of Hecate County*, four feet of Balzac, a volume of Sappho translated into Mandarin on the facing pages, and a whole windowsill's length of advanced mathematics. There were several histories of England and plenty of Fichte and Schelling. There was half a wall of French.

Between a copy of *Das Kapital* and a pale handbook called "How to Become an Expert Electrician for Your Own Home Purposes in Just Thirty Minutes," Una discovered the card catalogue Rosalie had told her about. It was in a narrow green file box from Woolworth's. "What a fabulous idea," Una said, flipping through the cards. She adored anything alphabetical.

"We've only just started on our record collection. We've got about a thousand records and we're going to catalogue the whole shebang," Clement said.

The bathroom door clattered. "Your turn!" Mary yelled— Una had never known anyone to bathe so quickly. Out came Mary wrapped in a Chinese bathrobe, with her long dark hair pinned up. She smelled like a piney wood.

Rosalie said she didn't see the necessity of showering, she hadn't been on the beach an hour.

"You haven't improved a bit," Mary complained. "We *always* used to have to coax Rosalie to take baths."

"In our other apartment," Clement said.

"*My* apartment," Rosalie growled from under the shower. Like Mary, she kept the door open.

"Rosalie was paying a lot less rent than we were, so we

moved in with her," Mary said. "Up to two months ago we were all living together."

"Rosalie's a pretty good cook," Clement said, "but *we* taught her how to do a salad. She used to cut things up piecemeal. First the lettuce, then the cucumbers—"

"Cucumber rinds have no nutritional value whatso*ever*," Mary announced, "but we keep them on for cosmetic purposes. Poor Rosalie, after we came up here she was left all alone with her chunks of piecemeal lettuce."

"Her clumsy tomato-halves," Clement said, "her big pitted black ripe olives."

"Poor Rosalie," Rosalie called. "She was left all alone with the hole in the closet door."

"We put the loudspeaker for our hi-fi in it," Clement told Una.

"They always cut holes in closet doors," Rosalie called.

Una, who was very law-abiding, was privately awed at such a glamorous affront to landlords' rights. But when Rosalie came out of the shower Una hurried in after her, so that the Chimeses wouldn't think she was one of those girls who had to be coaxed to bathe.

After supper Clement asked Una what she would like to hear, and Una, a musical nitwit, timidly said *The Mikado*. "Is that all right for you?" she wondered.

"Oh, we like everything," Clement said. "Bach, jazz, blues—"

"What you want to remember about the Chimeses," Rosalie instructed, "is that they're Renaissance men, they're nothing if not well-rounded."

"Especially me," said Mary. She tossed out one of her childlike giggles and suddenly sat down on the floor in frog-position and puffed very fast, like a locomotive, while Clement counted up to fifty. "That's for painless childbirth. You anticipate the contractions," he said, and put on *The Mikado*. Mary's legs rolled in the air. "Listen, bunny, Una said she's going to help organize the record catalogue."

Una flushed. She didn't remember saying it, but she *had*

thought it—it was exactly what she hoped they would ask her to do. It was wonderful that Clement had guessed.

"Not me," said Rosalie, and spread herself on the sofa. Una decided Rosalie was terrifically lazy and not very sociable, and to show the Chimeses *she* wasn't at all like that, she squatted right down on the floor next to Mary and prepared for business. Mary gave Una a pile of index cards and her own fountain pen, and Clement took the records out of their folders and read out the date of issuance, the Köchel number, and all sorts of complicated-sounding musical information Una had never before encountered.

"We're going to index by cross-reference," Mary said. "Composer's name by alphabet, name of piece by order of composition, and then a list of our personal record-numbers by order of date of purchase. That way we'll know whether they're scratchy because of being worn or because of difficulties in the system itself."

Una hardly understood a word, but she went on gamely making notes, until Clement finally discovered she was no good for anything but alphabetizing.

"You could use her for your bibliographical index, she'd be fine for that," Mary suggested. "Do you know John Livingston Lowes's *The Road to Xanadu*? Well, Clement's doing something like that. He's working on the sources of Paul Tillich's thought."

Una said that must be pretty interesting, but unless you were a mind-reader how could you find them out?

"I'm researching all the books he's ever read. It's a very intricate problem. I'm in constant correspondence with him."

"You mean he sends you *letters?*" Una cried. "Paul *Tillich*, the philosopher?"

"No, he communicates by carrier-pigeon. And it's Paul Tillich the president of the carpenters' union," Clement said. "My God, girl, you need educating."

"Especially in library science," Rosalie sneered from the sofa.

But Una was stirred. "That's really *doing* something. It's thinking about the world. I mean it's really scholarship!"

"Don't you like what you're doing?" Clement asked.

"I don't. Oh, I don't. I'm sick to death of Latin and Greek and I don't give a damn about the Etruscan Aphrodite and I'm scared silly about getting a Turkish disease," she burst out. "Oh, I envy you two, I really do. You have a passion and you go right ahead with it, you're doing exactly what you want to do, you're right in the middle of being alive."

Mary said gravely, "You should never do what you don't want to do. You should never go against your own nature."

"It's the same as going against God," Clement said.

Rosalie tumbled off the sofa. "Oh God. If we're on God again I'm going home."

"I feel," Clement said, "that the teleological impulse in the universe definitely includes man."

Rosalie turned up the Lord High Executioner's volume.

"The thing is," Mary said, "if you're going after your Ph.D. only for fashionable reasons or prestige reasons you should give it up."

"I've got these fabulous recommendations," Una said morosely. "I'm probably going to *get* the damn Fulbright."

"You should give it up," Mary insisted.

Una had never considered this. It was logical, but it didn't occur to her that anyone ever took logic seriously enough to live by it. "I'd have to do something else instead. I don't know what I'd do," she argued.

"Find somebody and get married." This was Rosalie, that traitor. She was no different from all those other girls who came down to the cafeteria to show off their new rings. Probably she wished she had one herself, but she was too fat, and no one would so much as blink at her. The only reason Rosalie didn't wear lipstick was that Mary didn't. The only reason Una had been attracted to Rosalie in the first place was that Rosalie had been reading Clement's book. What a fake! What a hypocrite! Rosalie was a toad in Chimeses' clothing. Una felt the strictest contempt for herself—she had let that sly girl take her in. She was astonished that the Chimeses could ever have endured living with Rosalie, she was so ordinary. She wondered that they hadn't dropped her long ago. It only proved how incredibly superior they were. They always looked for the right motives not to do a thing.

"Marriage is exactly *not* the point," Clement snapped. Una could see he was just as impatient with Rosalie as she was, but he smothered his disgust in philosophy. "It's not a question of externals, it's a question of internals. Going to Turkey is an external solution. Getting married is an external solution. But the problem *of* the Self requires a solution *for* the Self, you can see that, can't you?"

Una wasn't sure. "But I wouldn't know what to *do*," she wailed.

"In an existential dilemma it isn't action that's called for, it's *in*action. Nonaction. Stasis. Don't think about what you ought to do, think about what you ought *not* to do. —Come on, Rosalie, cut out the noise, lower that damn thing down. What I mean," Clement said, "is stop looking at the world in terms of your own self-gratification. It's God's world, not yours."

"God knows it's not mine," Rosalie said. She reduced Nanki-Poo's song to the size of an ant's—she seemed good-natured enough, but really she had no mind of her own: she did whatever anyone told her to do. "If I owned the world Clement would've cut a hole in it by now."

Una was shocked. Here was a fresh view! And it was true, it was true, she was too proud, she had always thought of her own gratification. Clement was so clever he could look right through her. But all the same she was a little flattered—she had never before been in an existential dilemma. "I've always been very careerist," she admitted. "I guess the thing I've cared about most is getting some sort of recognition."

"You won't get it in Turkey," Mary warned, but her voice was now very kind.

"You'll get buried same as those left-handed Etruscans," Clement said.

This made Una laugh. Oh, they were perfect!

"Take my advice," Rosalie said. "Get your degree and be a teacher."

"Rosalie means be like Rosalie," Clement said.

"There's worse," Rosalie said.

"I'll give it up," Una said, but the momentousness of this was somehow lost, because Mary suddenly clapped the knot of her piled-up hair and shrieked "Breakfast! Clement, what'll we do for breakfast? There's not a scrap."

"I'll bicycle out to the market in the morning."

"Oh, I'll go," Una offered, charmed at the picture of herself pedaling groceries in the basket before her. It would almost make her one of them. "I'm a very early riser."

"There's not a scrap of cash either," Mary said ruefully. "Clement's scholarship money comes quarterly, and my scholarship money comes every month, but it doesn't start till the term starts. We were *counting* on Rosalie's bringing the ham, but I spent the last penny on tonight's baked beans."

"It wasn't your fault, bunny. And it wasn't the beans that did it, it was the wine I bought day before yesterday. Hell with budgets anyhow—come on, let's have the wine!"

"Here's to Una Meyer," Clement sing-songed, and Una glowed, because it was plain her cataclysmic avowal hadn't been overlooked after all. "Drink to Una on the Brink."

"Of disaster," Rosalie purred.

"Of Selfhood," Clement declared, and Una was nearly embarrassed with the pleasure of her importance. The wine was a rosé and seemed to blush for her. Mary poured it out in pretty little goblets, which she explained were the product of a brand-new African glass industry, and not only helped to make a budding economy viable, but were much cheaper than they looked. All at once the four of them were having a party. They switched off the record-player, and

Clement, after only two or three pleas from Mary, sang a comic version of an old-time movie version of "The Road to Mandalay." He sounded exactly like a witty Nelson Eddy. Then he took down his guitar from its special hook next to the towel-rack in the bathroom and they all joined in on "On Top of Old Smoky," "Once I Wore My Apron Low," "Jimmy Crack Corn," "When I Was a Bachelor," and a lot of others, and by the time Clement carried in the folding cot for Una and Mary covered the sofa pillow with a clean pillowcase for Rosalie, Una was happier than she had ever been in her life, until a wonderful thing happened. It touched her so much she almost wept with sentiment. When all the lights were off and everyone was very still, Clement and Mary came softly out of their bedroom in their pajamas, and, one by one, they kissed Una and Rosalie as though they had been their own dear children.

"Goodnight," Mary whispered.

"Goodnight," Una whispered back.

"Goodnight," Clement said.

"Goodnight," Rosalie said, but even in the dark, without seeing the sarcastic bulge of her neck, Una thought Rosalie sounded stubbornly unmoved.

"Rosalie honey," Clement said tenderly, "can you lend us five for breakfast?"

"All I've got's my trainfare back," Rosalie said in the most complacent tone imaginable. Una was certain Rosalie was lying for her own malicious ends, whatever they could be.

"Oh, let *me*, please," she cried, sitting upright very fast. "Listen, Clement, where do you keep your bikes? I'll get everything the minute I'm up."

"We wouldn't think of it," Mary said in her steadfast way. "It isn't just breakfast, you know, it's practically the whole week till Clement's check comes."

No one was whispering now.

"Oh, *please*," Una said. "I'd really like to, honest. I mean before today you didn't know me from a hole in the wall—"

"In the door," Rosalie crowed.

"—and you gave me all this marvelous hospitality and everything. It's only right."

"Well," Clement said—he seemed very stern, almost like a father—"if you really want to. Only don't forget the eggs."

"Oh, I won't," Una promised, and could hardly fall asleep waiting for the next day of living in the Chimeses' aura to begin.

3

Early in the fall the Chimeses moved into New Haven proper, which was a relief for everyone, but for no one more than Una, who hadn't really minded nights on the sofa until they had had to put the crib right up against her feet. There was no other place for it. The Chimeses' seaside bedroom, though it had a romantic view of the waves, was only a cubicle with a window—there wasn't even a cranny with a dresser in it, much less a crib. In New Haven they found a downtown tenement that was cheap and by comparison almost spacious. In the new flat there were three bedrooms: one for the Chimeses, one was a study for Mary, and the one farthest from this, to keep the noise at a distance, was the baby's. Clement bought a second-hand screen and put it between Una's bed and the crib—"to give the infant its privacy," he joked.

The birth itself had been remarkable—all the nurses agreed the hospital had never had anyone to match Mary. She was over and done with it in an hour, and with hardly any fuss. Mary attributed this to having learned how to deal with the contractions, and Clement, who had turned more ebullient than ever, laughed and said Mary had practiced with can't, won't, and ain't.

The baby, of course, was magnificent. It was unusually beautiful for a small infant and had long limbs. Mary had all

along been indifferent to its sex, but Clement claimed he
needed to free himself of potential incest-fantasies by
releasing them into reality: he had wanted a girl from the
start. Mary, Una, and Clement argued about names for
days, and finally compromised on Christina, after the
heroine of *The Princess Casamassima*. Christina, as a combination of two perfections, was exactly what Una had
expected, and she looked at her as on some sacred object
which she was not allowed to touch too often. But soon
Mary decided that she had to spend more and more time in
the law library, so she let Una wheel Christina around and
around the streets near the university for a couple of hours
a day.

Una had the time for it now: Clement had made up his
mind not to finish his bibliographical index. His correspondence had waned, and to Una's surprise it turned out
that the letters weren't really from Tillich, but from his
secretary. Clement said this was just like all theologians:
their whole approach was evasive, you could see it right in
their titles. *The Courage to Be*, Clement said, was a very
ambiguous book, and if the *product* was that ambiguous,
you could hardly follow up the sources, could you? He told
Una he would have dropped the project as futile long ago if
she hadn't taken such an interest in the way he went about
it. In the beginning he spent hours typing involved letters
on this or that point to obscure academics with names like
Knoll or Creed, but after a while he discovered he could
think better if he dictated and Una typed. Anyhow he was
always having to run off and help Mary with the baby, or
else he had to stop in the middle of a sentence to carry a big
bundle of diapers to the laundromat. Gradually Una could
complete his abandoned phrases without him. She got so
good at this that the two of them had a little conspiracy:
Una worked out the letters in Clement's style, all on her
own, and Clement signed them. He often praised her, and
said she could follow up leads even better than he could.
Now and then he told her she wrote very well for a

nonwriter, and at those moments Una felt that maybe she wasn't an imposition on the Chimeses after all.

She worried about this a lot, even though they let her pay a good chunk of the rent—she had begged them so poignantly they couldn't refuse her. At first she had tried not to get in their way, and reminded them several times a day that if they regretted their invitation they shouldn't hesitate a wink in withdrawing it. She still couldn't believe that they actually *wanted* her to live with them. They were always comparing her to Rosalie and reminding themselves what a nasty temper Rosalie sometimes had. Rosalie used to like to sleep to the last minute, when she realized perfectly well that they *depended* on her for breakfast—at that time they'd both had very tough schedules, much tougher than that sluggard Rosalie's, and if they missed breakfast they wouldn't eat again until supper. They had a lot of other Rosalie stories, all terrible. Una determined to be as unlike Rosalie as possible—for instance, she took to preparing breakfast every day, even though Mary and Clement were both shocked at her zeal and told her it wasn't in the least bit necessary. But Mary observed that if Una was going to be up anyway, she might as well give Christina her seven o'clock bottle, which would mean Una's getting up only fifteen minutes earlier than she had to to make the breakfast. Sometimes it was three-quarters-of-an-hour earlier, but Una didn't mind—whenever she lifted Christina she felt she was holding treasure. She knew Christina would turn out to be extraordinary.

Besides, she wanted to be as useful as possible, considering how Clement was sweating to get her some sort of subfellowship from the seminary. It was only fair, he said, now that she was doing practically half his work, even though it was the superficial half. He took the train to New York three days a week, and every time he returned it was with a solemn anger. "They're trying to get me to believe their budget's closed," he would say. Or, "Damn them, they don't realize the caliber of what I'm *doing*. They say they don't give money for research assistants to anyone lower than associate professor. That's a lot of baloney. Don't worry about it, Una, we'll get something for you." Una said it was all right—so far she still had some money in the bank account her grandmother had started for her: every year on Una's birthday or on holidays her grandmother had put in seventy-five dollars. Mary said it was a shame Una's grandmother was dead. "People don't *need* grandmothers any more," Clement said, "they've got fellowships nowadays." "If Una were getting her Fulbright money right now, it would help," Mary said in a voice a little more pinched than her usual one. "If Una were getting her Fulbright money right now," Clement noted, "she'd be in Turkey, and where would *we* be?—Look, I'll beat them down somehow, don't you worry about the moolah, Una."

Whenever the Chimeses mentioned her lost Fulbright—it *seemed* often, but it wasn't really—Una felt guilty. Just as she feared, she had won the thing, and her adviser came back from Martha's Vineyard with his wife and boys and flew into a fury. He called Una a fool and a shirker for saying she'd pass up a prize like that, and for what? It was only an honor and not life, Una said. He asked whether the real point wasn't that she was going off to be married like all of them. He said he was against women in universities anyhow; they couldn't be trusted to get on with their proper affairs. Her real trouble, he told her, was she didn't have the guts to settle down to hard work. Sometimes Una wondered whether any of this was true. She was busy with domestic details—washing up, making the beds, tending the baby (of course it wasn't *just* a baby), exactly like a married person. And even though helping Clement on top of all the rest wore her out, still that sort of thing didn't count as *work*, since she didn't really understand what it was he was getting at. Clement had explained that he couldn't take the time to show her the basic insight of his project, it was too complex for a philosophical novice, and without it she couldn't hope to get near the nerve of his idea. That was why, he reminded her, she mustn't expect more than a pittance of the sum he was demanding for her from the seminary.

But one day Clement stomped off the train and said he was never going back. They had suspended him.

"But why?" Una exclaimed. The first thought she had was that Clement had finally gone too far on her behalf. "Is it on account of badgering them all the time? The money I mean," she said in her shame.

"Don't be silly, it has nothing to do with you, why should it?"

"Haven't you noticed, Una?" Mary said. She wasn't a bit upset. "Clement's been losing his faith. He's been intellectualizing about it too much—that's always the first sign."

"I finally had to speak up in Systematic Dogmatics," Clement said modestly. "I told old Hodges today I didn't think he or any of them actually knew what the Gnostics were *after*. Well, he let on about it to the Dean, and the Dean called me in and asked whether I was really on the road to Damascus. 'The fact is,' I said, 'I don't feel the present ministry's coming to grips with the problem of the *Trinity*, sir.' And you know what the old baboon answers? 'Suppose we respect those feelings for a year or two, Mr. Chimes. If you're not at home with the Gnostics by then maybe you'd be better off among the *a*gnostics.' Very funny. I resigned then and there."

"And about time," Mary said.

"How humiliating!" Una cried. "How awful!" But Clement was wearing a hurt look, and immediately she understood she had made a mistake. She was sure he was offended.

"You think too much about status. Society may look up to the ministry, but what I've gotten out of all this is that I don't look up to society."

"You can't stand still in this world," Mary put in. "You have to shed your old skin every now and then."

Una was abashed. She realized that living with the Chimeses hadn't profited her an iota. She was as uneducated as ever. She still jumped to false conclusions, and she still needed instruction in life-values.

"Not that Clement wasn't *perfectly* right to leave," Una said quickly. It came out almost abject, and she could see Mary's teeth shine into forgiveness. Mary was so good! She was practically a saint. Just when you thought she was going to be terrifyingly severe, she turned around and gave you another chance to restore yourself to ordinary common sense.

"Fact is," Clement said, "I could never *be* part of the Establishment in any form. It's just something I've been avoiding coming face to face with. Actually I'm an anarchist."

"Now watch it," Mary said, giggling. "Una'll think you're secretly manufacturing bombs in the bathroom." The reason this was funny was that no place could have been less secret than the bathroom; Clement had taken off the door to make a desk for Mary's study.

"Let 'er think so, it's just what I intend to do."

"Make a *bomb?*" Una squealed, though she didn't feel like it. Sometimes she acted straight man just to please them.

"Exactly. A bomb called *Social Cancer.*"

"Oh, a book," Una said, since she knew Clement expected her to sound relieved. All the same she was really impressed.

"I intend to pillory the whole society from top to bottom in blank verse. It'll be an exposé of the rich and the poor, the common man and the intelligentsia—and a work of art besides. There hasn't been anything like it since Alexander Pope wrote *The Dunciad,*" Clement pointed out, "and Pope wasn't that comprehensive in his conception."

That night they celebrated Clement's new book, which he was going to start writing early the next morning. They wheeled Christina to the park and right in front of her carriage built a fire out of Clement's bibliographical index. Clement and Mary threw notebook after notebook into the

fire, and Una was sad, because there were so many months
of toil in them. She saw her own handwriting curl up and
char—all the notes she had taken for Clement on Buber
and Niebuhr and Bultmann and Karl Jaspers and Kierkegaard.
She had read all those difficult philosophers for nothing.

"It's not as though you haven't been through this sort of
thing yourself—you're always forgetting that," Mary said.
Mary was uncanny. She always knew when Una's thoughts
were limping off in the wrong direction. "You have to learn
how to dispense with the past, even if outsiders say it shows
personal instability. Remember the night we all drank to
you? You were great that time about letting the Fulbright
go," Mary said, "you were really one of us that night." Una
was stunned. Mary had never before given her such a
compliment. Mary was not indiscriminate with compliments
at all.

"That was different," Una objected—inside herself she
was wondering whether she should dare to take Mary's
praise as a sign of moral improvement, but at the same time
she was afraid Mary suspected her of thinking Clement
unstable. If so, it was a shameful calumny, and Mary
wanted Una to know it. "I wasn't *burning* anything," Una
said feebly.

"Yes you were," said witty Clement: "your ships behind
you!" He had hardly ever seemed more cheerful; it had
happened all at once, and it was plain even to Una that he
was glad to be rid of all that long theological drudgery,
which had been worthless all the time, though of course it
was only Una who hadn't realized it. At lunch the next day
he was delightful; he joked right through his coffee and
enunciated "Excoriate the corrupt republic" at Christina in
a comical falsetto until she screamed. "You're taking her
out, aren't you, Una? Brat can raise the dead."

"Mary said not until three o'clock." —Mary had gone off
to the library at ten that morning. She was preparing a
paper on the Jurisprudence of Domestic Relations. For an
epigraph it had a quotation from Rousseau urging the

mothers of France to nurse their own babies, but that was the only part Una could fathom; the rest of it was a forest of alien footnotes. "Christina might be catching cold," Una said. "She sneezed a couple of times, so Mary thought she ought to stay in most of the day." Una privately believed Mary was mistaken whenever she argued there was no inborn maternal instinct—Mary herself seemed to exemplify it admirably. She always knew exactly the right thing to do about Christina.

"Oh, what's the difference," Clement said. "She needs airing, doesn't she? Una, I'll *tell* you what you show, what you show is the definite effects of overprotectiveness in conjunction with a mother-fixation—it's a lot healthier for Christina to get a cold than a fixation, isn't it?" He waited for Una to appreciate this sally. "Take her out now, there's a honey. Can't hear myself cerebrate with all the racket."

It was true that Christina was still screaming, but Una couldn't help thinking she had been perfectly behaved before Clement had frightened her—Christina was far too young to understand Clement's humor. She went to fetch Christina's little woolen cap and booties.

"Besides," Clement said, following Una into Christina's room, "I haven't got much time. I figure I can just about get *into* the first chapter before six."

"You haven't begun it?" Una said.

"Oh, I've *begun* it, I just haven't put it down on paper yet."

"But I thought you'd already gotten to work on it," Una said, a little discomposed. "Wouldn't you be well into it by now?" Clement had locked himself up in Mary's study all morning, and Una had taken special pains to woo Christina's silence. She had played hushing games with her for three hours, and was heavy with weariness afterward. Christina woke so early nowadays that Una never really got enough sleep.

"I didn't say I didn't get to work on it," Clement gave out in his most complicated tone, the one that only pretended to pretend annoyance, but all the while was genuinely annoyed. "I said I just hadn't committed it to paper yet. Actually, Una honey, the trouble with you is you don't understand the most fundamental thing about the Muse. As per tradition, she has to be *invoked*, you silly," but he was so fresh-faced and wide awake that Una had the strangest idea. She hardly dared to articulate it, even to herself, but what she secretly wondered was whether Clement hadn't just gone back to sleep after breakfast. Not that she minded, of course.

"I know," she said, "Creation is a Many-Staged Process."

Clement warmed to her at once after that. She was quoting one of his own mottoes, which he had painted on the kitchen canisters. Instead of FLOUR he had put "Self-Discipline is Achievement," and instead of SUGAR (but the wet paint had dripped off the brush into the canister and they had to replace the whole five pounds), "Art is Love." The line about Creation was on the teabag can.

"But look," Una said, to make it up to Clement for seeming to criticize his working-habits (not that she meant to, but for the moment she *had* forgotten about the Muse), "you don't have to quit at six. I mean can't you work right through supper if you feel like it? Mary wouldn't mind, she'd just as soon eat in the commons anyhow. I can make you a sandwich—there's some baloney, I think—and you can have supper in the study. You don't have to *stop*."

Clement smiled at her so luminously that Una was sure she had set everything to rights again. "Well, to tell the truth, Una honey," he began, "you're still just a little bit obtuse, now aren't you? Is it your grandmother's shade that's going to pay for the baloney in my sandwich? Does it reach you what the condition of the writer is vis-à-vis a society economically structured against him?"

Christina's yells grew louder and her wriggles more unwieldy as Una tried to get the bootie on her foot. Her miniature arch was aristocratically high, but Una was too shocked by Clement's words to admire it. Still, his smile continued so brilliant that she thought the whole affair must be one of his jokes—he was right about how obtuse she was.

"Tell you what," Clement offered, "I'll put you straight on something. You want to hear the real reason I got bounced from the seminary? Lo, the greed of Una Meyer. You pushed just a little bit too far—not that I ever let on about it. But you know what they accused me of? Of trying to fatten up my scholarship *by unscrupulous methods*. I never told you that, and I wouldn't be mentioning it now if you weren't so thick—"

"Oh, Clement!" Una burst out. "I had no idea. I'm so ashamed! I was afraid it was my fault, but you said—"

"Never mind," Clement said. "Don't worry about it. I think I've got a good book in me, maybe even a great one if I can get to finish it, and by hook or crook I'm *going* to finish it. Hook: I refer to the hooks they sell at the hardware counter in Woolworth's. Crook: I refer to the management of same—they're tight-fisted enough, they pay like thieves."

"Clement, what do you *mean?*"

"It's not exactly a man's job, but for a philosopher it'll have to do. At least it's evenings—six to ten. I can write all day before I have to go, and what with Mary's law school money I guess we'll manage. Now listen, Una," he said, "I'll be candid with you. This house is a complex working hive. There isn't room for parasites. Visualize, if you will, the salt-shaker."

"Work or Die," Una said with a drying mouth. "You're going to work in the *five* and *ten?*"

"Spinoza was a lens-grinder. Don't be so appalled. Lincoln split logs. Clement Chimes will sell hooks, locks, bolts, and all manner of chains, some of them metaphysically displayed around his neck."

"Oh, Clement! It sounds awful! What's Mary say?"

"She says A, the work is beneath Clement, a view to which Clement heartily accedes, and B, we need the cash.

That being the hard case, will you now please remove the fire-siren from the premises so I can get *something* done?"

"Clement," Una said—meditatively she buttoned up Christina's sweater—"if it takes you practically the whole day to get started—"

"To invoke the Muse," Clement corrected.

"—and you only *really* begin about two or maybe three and you have to leave about five-thirty to get to the Woolworth's by six—"

"Congratulations. You're getting the point," Clement said. "Education is slowly setting in."

"—it means you'll have only about two hours or so to do any work at all."

"Insufficient and unfortunate," Clement agreed.

"But what about *Social Cancer?*"

" 'Twill suffer remissions," Clement said.

That evening, at great inconvenience to Mary, who had to rush home from the library to feed Christina and put her to bed, Una started her new job at the hardware counter in Woolworth's, and sold hooks, locks, bolts, and all manner of chains.

4

One afternoon Una was wheeling Christina along her usual route in the streets around Yale, when she decided to try a block she had never walked on before. It led her through the campus and past some of the old buildings. The day was cold and she pushed the carriage stolidly, without looking ahead of her, until she finally pushed it right into the briefcase of a young man hurrying across the path. The bag fell open and an assortment of medical instruments lay scattered on the ground.

"Well, look who it is," said the young man in an ugly

accent. He bent to retrieve his stethoscope. "Aunt? Babysitter? Unwed mother? None of the above?"

The voice was familiar. It was Mr. Organski.

"What are you doing in New Haven?" Una yelped.

"Being diligent at my Latin, as usual."

"You were terrible in Latin, you didn't go *on* with it!"

"I couldn t help it, they name diseases in it."

"Oh, you're a doctor," Una said, laughing and picking up a pair of clamps. From inside the carriage came a small sneeze.

"If I pass. So far I'm a pompous medical student. And you? Settled in New Haven? Married, I see."

Una frowned. "This is my friends' baby."

"Aha. A spinster doing a good turn. You prefer a career?"

"Well," Una said uncomfortably.

"I understand. In that case not another word. Classified information. You're a scientist with the government? They use the labs around here, I've heard. A cyclotronist perhaps. A supersonistician. In short you're not permitted to describe your work."

"It's hardware," Una muttered.

"Just as I thought. Missiles. The classicist who thinks up the tags? Titan. Nike. Mars. Don't tell me your latest, I couldn't bear the responsibility of knowing. What's the baby's tag?"

"Christina."

"Unworthy of a warhead, better return her to the pad. Take her home anyhow. Christina has a cold."

"She has this cough. Sometimes her eyes run." Una admitted.

"Your friends are dangerous madmen, why do they let her out?"

"Well, she's awfully noisy—"

"A common disease of babyhood—*infanta clamorata*—which passes with the onset of confinement in a school building—*kindergartenia absentia*."

"—and her father's writing a book."

"Aha. A question of immortality. Christina shows symptoms of mortality, however. Look, I think I'm going your way. Where are you going?"

Mr. Organski walked her home, but Una didn't invite him in. She explained she couldn't—Clement was working.

"And the female parent?"

"Studying jurisprudence."

"A remarkable family."

"It is," Una said fervently.

"They've taken you in? How fortunate for you," said Mr. Organski.

"I know," Una said.

"Yet your good fortune increases. You were born under a lucky star. This family of geniuses has taken you in but I, Organski, a failure at conjugation, am going to take you out. To the movies Saturday night, what do you say? Say thank you."

"I can't," Una said. "Clement and Mary are going. We decided on it days ago—they're so busy they hardly ever get out, I just couldn't spoil it for them."

"Aha," said Mr. Organski. "Call me Boris. We'll arrange something else immediately."

"What about your mistress?"

"My mistress?"

"You had one."

"Didn't I just say I was a failure at conjugation? I disown and disavow all previous alliances, without promising not to look forward to others more successful. Now listen carefully. When are Clement and Mary going to have the pleasure of meeting me?"

"Well, they're both home at night, but they're usually working—"

"This will be a medical visit. About Christina."

Una said humbly, "I'm the one who takes care of her mostly. If she's sick it's really my fault."

"Fine. Then you should be present at my lecture. Time, tomorrow night. Place, the crowded apartment of Clement and Mary and Christina and Una."

"My job is at night," Una demurred.

"Aha. Night maneuvers of the hardware. Top secret. Don't tell me anything. If the government has to hide its rocket failures under cover of darkness I don't want to share in its humiliation."

"It's *Woolworth's*," Una said in exasperation.

"Thank God, an ordinary Latinist after all. *Tedium Woolworthiae*, a harmless temporary state. I offer you a consolation. I suggest, in view of my having solemnly disowned and disavowed my previous conduct, that you undertake to shape my present conduct. Praise your stars. I'm asking you to become my current mistress."

Una giggled. It sounded just like Mary's giggle.

"I assume you lend a hand in paying your friends' rent?" Mr. Organski said. "Come and pay mine. My apartment is far less crowded."

5

The Chimeses didn't like Boris at all. In the first place, he didn't think Christina was perfect. He implied, in fact, that she was much worse than perfect. He said she was malnourished and needed liquid vitamins and her left lung wasn't clear. He said he would have to come often until he was confident she was improving. He asked to see where she slept.

"The room is too small," he insisted. "And when you put a screen around the crib like that, how do you expect the poor baby to breathe?"

"The screen is to give Una privacy," Mary said viciously.

"Take it out"

"I don't see how one thin little piece of plastic could make any difference," Clement said.

"Never mind the screen. I'm talking about the bed. Take out the bed."

"It's Una's."

"Well, all *right*," Mary said. "Una can sleep on the couch again. After all, she used to."

"Maybe you'd better ask her if she minds," Boris said.

"She won't mind."

"She never minds anything."

Boris said, "That sort of person can be an awful bore."

"As a matter of fact she is," Mary said. "She's the most obsequious person I've ever known."

Boris gave a labial croak that was meant to sound sympathetic. "Impedes intimacies, I would guess."

"You're a bit on the patronizing side, aren't you?" said Mary.

"As a matter of fact," Clement said, "she does. Always underfoot."

"She's only so-so with Christina, lets her howl."

"An impediment indeed," Boris said in his medical-student style, very grand. "I suppose she cooks?"

"If you call it that. Slices baloney. Opens cans."

"An adult should never sleep near a child," Boris said firmly. "She never gave it a thought. Is her intelligence low? I'm thinking of the kind of job she has—small metallic objects and so forth."

"Not particularly low," Clement said. "Though I wouldn't call Una *imag*inative, bunny, would you? The thing is she won a Fulbright once."

"Incredible."

"Passed it up. It was stupid, she would've seen Turkey on it."

"Mmm," Boris said, "interesting. A neighboring land. I myself am originally from Bulgaria. Of course she's too thin. She has very small breasts."

That night, when Una returned from the hardware counter—it was a whole hour later than usual—the Chimeses waylaid her in the living room and began to speak to her very sternly.

"You're not seeing the point. Listen, Una honey," Clement said, "that man is out for no good. He came sneaking around here when he knew you were out—"

"On purpose," Mary said. "Behind your back."

"Don't confuse the issue, bunny. That's the least of it. The point is he came to try to set us against you, Una. That's the point."

"It was plain as day that's what he was out for," Mary told Una. "I can't think what his motives could be."

"No motive," Clement said. "The world is full of jealous people like that. They can't bear seeing close relationships, they just have to wreck them."

"He's even trying to turn Christina against you," Mary said. "A *baby*, imagine. He thinks you contaminate her. He says you have to sleep somewhere else, for health reasons."

"There wasn't an item he didn't criticize. He just wouldn't be satisfied until he got us to say nasty things about you. Not that he managed it."

"It's written all over his face what he is," Mary said.

"He even insulted your *looks*," Clement said. "He's one of these belittlers, I know that kind. Medical types tend to think they're little gods. He said you didn't have the sense to deal with sickness. As if anybody's sick."

"If he keeps it up he'll frighten you off, Una, you'll be scared to go *near* Christina."

"He's pretty damn self-important, that guy. He's just looking to assert some so-called authority."

"Keep away from him," Mary advised.

Una thought it was odd that they were talking about Boris, whom they had only just met, exactly the way they always talked about Rosalie. "But I left him only ten minutes ago."

"Boris?" the Chimeses chimed together.

"When I came out of the Woolworth's there he was at the door."

"Waiting for you? He must've gone over right from here."

"He never said a word. Sly," Mary observed.

"We went to this place," Una explained, "for coffee. *He* had coffee, " she amended; "I had cocoa."

"You see? You see?" Mary said.

"She doesn't see," Clement said. "Una honey, *look* at it, it's right under your nose. He's trying to wreck things. Like Rosalie. Didn't Rosalie tell you not to move in with us? Didn't she? You can't deny it, we *knew* it, it would be just like her. You've never been sorry you came in halfies with us, have you?"

"Gosh no," Una said gratefully, but the truth was she felt a little muddled. It was after midnight; she had sold four Phillips screwdrivers, three combination locks and an ordinary padlock, two cans of furniture polish, a wad of picture-wire, a tube of automobile touch-up, a bicycle chain, a pair of bicycle clips, a dozen boxes of thumbtacks, and one doorknob. She longed for bed.

"Stop," Mary said. "Not in there. You're not supposed to use up any more of Christina's oxygen."

"Oh," said Una, and sank down on the sofa. *Pang,* went the bad spring. Mary, whose figure was every bit as good now as before her pregnancy, had broken the spring while doing her Royal Canadian Women's Division Air Force Exercises on the sofa. She did them every evening, and was very diligent and disciplined about it; she followed them out of a book.

"You'd be dead wrong if you were sorry, Una, I mean that seriously. I'm being very sincere with you. The point is you're not the same person you used to be, is she, bunny?"

"She had these awfully conformist ideas, remember? Honest to god, Una, you were worse than Rosalie. Well, not *worse* really, but you acted just like Rosalie when we first knew her. Always mooning around us and toadying up. We couldn't *stand* it from her. I mean *there* was a type who had no individuality whatever. She didn't *believe* in individuality."

"And when we told her about it—you know, open and candid—she just got fresher and fresher. Don't look so upset, Una honey, *you're* not like that. She wasn't educable. The thing about you, Una, you've improved a lot because you're educable. You're on the brink of maturity, you could find yourself, your true métier, any day now—I mean, look at Mary, if you want an example—and all it would take to throw you off is for a guy like Organski to come along right about now and give you the business and tell you you ought to be one of these little housewife-types—"

"He didn't say anything like that," Una said slowly. Then, just as slowly, she yawned. She was really very tired. I nearly forgot. Here." She held out a package. "It's the liquid vitamins for Christina. Boris said they're awfully expensive if you have to buy them in the drugstore. He said when he left here he remembered where he could get a whole load of doctors' samples, you know, for free, and then he ran right over to the Woolworth's with them. That's what he met me for. To deliver them. I'm so collapsed I think I'll just sleep in my clothes. Could you shut the light off, please?"

Pang, went the spring, but Una didn't hear.

6

After that Boris took to meeting Una outside the Woolworth's every night. At first she was astonished to see him there, leaning against the display windows and reading one of his medical books, waiting for her to come out; but he appeared so regularly that after the second week she began to look for him almost hopefully. The other clerks laughed

and called out at him, as they passed, names like Totem
Pole and Cigar Store Indian, and asked if he thought the
place would fall in if he weren't around all the time to hold
it up, and Boris always bowed comically but heartily to the
fattest girls. That, he told Una, was a lesson to her: only fat
girls were worth paying attention to. His object, he
explained, was to fatten her up before he made her his
mistress.

They always went to the same sandwich shop and Boris
always bought her two thick sandwiches.

"Eat, don't talk," he said, and kept his head down among
anatomical drawings until she was done. "I don't call that
finished," he objected—that was if she left her crusts—and
then he ordered her a chocolate malted milk, sometimes
with an egg beaten into it. Meanwhile he studied and forgot
his coffee until it was too cold to drink. He never took her
home before midnight, but on the way—they always
walked, even on the stormiest nights—he made up for his
two hours' silence in the sandwich place by teasing without a
stop. "Now promise, tomorrow I want a weight report.
Without shoes, please, and in the nude, and on a reliable
scale, try the one in the drugstore. I once had a mistress
who was all skin and bones, like you, an experience I hope
never to repeat. The points of her elbows made pinholes
right through my best sheets. You should see those sheets
today. In time the holes expanded to the size of washbasins,
but you don't get to marvel at this phenomenon until I can
observe the effects of ten pounds more in the clavicle area.
A clavicle should not have such exaggerated visibility. The
skeletal structure of the human body is not for public
display except in the medical laboratory. My bedroom is
not *that* sort of laboratory, my dear," but by then they were
at the Chimeses' door.

"What'll I *tell* them?" Una whispered one night, in the
middle of only her first sandwich.

"Eat, don't talk," said Boris.

"Boris!"

"Five minutes more. Just be quiet, my sweet, until I've done my gall bladder and liver. —Finish your crusts, there's a dear."

"Boris, I've *already* told Clement and Mary an awful lie. I told them the hardware supervisor extended my time by one hour."

Boris looked up from his book and scratched an ear. It happened to be Una's.

"Well, it was only because they're mad that I'm getting home so late. I couldn't tell them it's for nothing. I *had* to lie."

"Aha," Boris said. "Thank you. I'm obliged to you. To Miss Meyer, Mr. Organski is nothing."

"Oh, Boris! Just *listen*. First I told them I was working this one hour overtime, and so then they wanted to know where the extra money was. Then I had to say *some*thing, so I said it was just plain overtime, and there wasn't any pay for it. And they didn't believe me! And now they want to know where I *go* after work. I don't know what to tell them, Boris."

"Naturally they haven't heard you're out with Organski? Naturally. 'I'm out with nothing' doesn't sound convincing."

"It's because I'm getting home too late, Boris. Really, couldn't we leave earlier? Couldn't we leave right now?"

"Before you've had your fortified malted milk? Never!"

"But it's ruining everything, I keep oversleeping. I overslept practically every morning this week and nobody got any breakfast, not even Christina, and later on she howled for hours, and Clement was so mad he couldn't do his chapter, and Mary said she was sick to her stomach in the library the whole day. She gets that way on an empty stomach. It's because I'm getting home too late, Boris."

"All right," Boris said. "We leave now. Immediately. Will that satisfy you? It interferes with my studying, of course—that goes without saying—but if it satisfies you to interfere with my studying let's go. Organski's entire career may go up

the flue, but Una Meyer must be satisfied. Mr. and Mr.
Chimes *told* me what a model of selfishness you are, I can't
say I haven't been warned. Up with you. Come! Leave your
crusts, please, we have no time for them. There will be no
beverage tonight, madam," he yelled to the waitress.

"Oh, Boris, stop!" Una wailed. "I don't know *what* to do,
honest I don't."

"Abandon fantasy. Tell Clement and Mary you're out with
your lover. Excuse me. Your *prospective* lover—I'm afraid
you're still several pounds short of realization of the fact,
my dear. If you expose our liaison, you see, it will perhaps
hint to them that you have an adumbration of a chimera of a
life of your own."

"Boris, that's not the *point*," Una said, refusing even to
smile.

"Aha. Clement's phrase exactly. You've mastered his into-
nation to the life, my dear. He spoke those very words to
me, in that very tone, this very evening."

"You've seen *Clement?*" Una exclaimed.

"Only by chance. I intended to see Christina and he
happened to be in the house. He was eating an apple at the
time and comfortably reading the funnies. He said the
funnies were not the point. Meanwhile I took a sampling of
the poor child's sputum."

"Oh. Then she's worse," Una said.

"Dr. Chichester's having a peep at her in the morning—
obviously a good man, he recognized Organski's gifts and
gave him an A. That was last term. This term Una Meyer
does not permit Organski to study. Oh, there won't be a
fee, don't look so wild-eyed. Actually there *is* something
wrong with your eyes, now that I observe them."

"What?" Una cried.

"They're half shut. Tell you what. Beginning tomorrow
night, instead of fattening you here, I'll fatten you privately,
in my own apartment. I have a little kitchen you'll find
perfectly adequate for slicing baloney in. While I study
you'll sleep. On one condition—that you avoid further

puncturing my sheets with a randomly protruding bone. After which I'll walk you home."

"That won't solve anything," Una said gloomily.

"Ungrateful girl. Think of the Chimeses' going without breakfast! You'll have your duty sleep, won't you?"

"But what'll I tell Clement and Mary?"

"You'll tell them," Boris said peacefully, "the simple truth. That you were innocently slumbering in the bed of your lover."

7

Boris was right about his sheets. They were terribly ragged. And his apartment was a calamity. The lease was handed on from one generation of students to another, year after year, and though everyone always left something behind, no one ever took anything away. The two rooms were full of useless objects, and the grease on the stove was as high as a finger. There was a television set that didn't work, a vacuum cleaner ditto, and, right in the middle of the tiny kitchen, a bureau stuffed with old underwear.

"My goodness," Una said, "hasn't this place ever been swept at all?"

"Long, long ago, my sweet, but only by the primeval Flood," Boris replied, and opened the refrigerator with a flourish. It was crammed with food.

"I feel awful," Una said. "I feel so depressed about the whole thing, Boris, it's horrible. Clement and Mary are just sick about it."

"Eat, don't talk," Boris said. He settled himself at his desk. It stood at the foot of his unmade bed. The lamp had a red shade and his face looked pink under it. Una suddenly noticed how, when he lowered his head, the bulb of Boris's nose made a shadow over his mouth. He had a long, attractive nose, a bit thick at the tip, and long, stiff nostrils that stared downwards like an extra pair of eyes. It was as though everything he said was uttered under surveillance.

"Itt, dunt tuck," Una mocked; she had begun not to mind his accent so much. "Do you have any olives?" It was a thirdhand taste; Una had acquired it from the Chimeses, who had acquired it from Rosalie.

"In the closet. No, not that one, look in the one with my raincoat. There's a jar in the right pocket."

"I bet you spent the whole afternoon in the supermarket," Una accused, "and then you say you never get any time to study. These are green. Don't you have any black?"

"It doesn't matter, the fat content is nearly the same. —Oleo your bread, my dear, always oleo your bread."

"You can't imagine the atmosphere over there, Boris. Everybody's so upset. Clement's stopped work on his book. He doesn't think he'll ever finish it now, he says he's lost the thread. Boris?"

"No, dear, no conversation, please, I'm on the spleen tonight. The spleen is a very complicated organ."

"Boris, how long will Christina have to stay in the hospital?"

"Till Chichester lets her out. I suppose you forgot your toothbrush?"

"I brought it," Una said dejectedly. "I'm positive it's my fault she got sick in the first place."

"You're not a microscopic organism, my sweet. It can be proved incontrovertibly by the presence of your thirty-two teeth. Brush them, dear, and go to sleep right away or you won't wake up on time to go home. It's my duty to inform you that you're still five pounds avoirdupois short of spending the night."

But when Una got into Boris's bed he left his desk and started kissing her. She was rather surprised, because she was pretty sure he couldn't have progressed very far into his spleen.

"My luck," Boris said with his little croak. "For a mistress I have to pick a reader of the expurgated versions.

Listen, my sweet, your Catullus was bowdlerized—the
villains suppressed everything profitable, especially the
best verbs. Now, hold the principal parts *so*," and he kissed
her once more. And then Una was surprised all over
again—it turned out she liked it. She liked it so much, in
fact, that Boris finally had to give it up. "I don't want to
keep you awake, my dear, or you won't be able to say you
slept in Organski's bed. Well, Una," he finished, "anyhow I
can tell you you're educable."

"That's what Clement and Mary always say," Una
boasted, but dolefully. "Poor Mary. If Christina has to stay
in the hospital for very long she won't get her thesis done
on time. Dr. Chichester told them they'd better *be* in the
hospital every day till the danger's over. Mary might even
lose her degree. It's awful, that little perfect angel, all of a
sudden such a fever and everything," and, rather earlier
than they had expected to, they walked home to the
Chimeses, in gloom over Christina.

When Una opened the door she saw a terrible sight.
Clement and Mary were at war. Mary's left temple was
bleeding. Clement's shirt was ripped across the back. Mary
was dashing from room to room, spitting at things, and
Clement ran after her. His shouts were violent and dirty.
Mary spat on the tapestries, she fled from bookcase to
bookcase, spitting on the shelves. She pulled down *The
Princess Casamassima* and began tearing out handfuls of
pages. Her hair fell down over her neck and her teeth
blazed with spittle. "Damn it all," Mary said, "damn it all. *I*
was away all day, *you* were the one who was always
home—" "Crap on you, you're supposed to be the goddamn
mother, aren't you?" "Derelict! Psychotic! Theologian!"
Mary screamed, and for a moment a subtleness crept across
her face. Then she whirled and seized a pile of records,
trying to smash them with her shoe, but they were plastic
and wouldn't break, so instead she hurled them in a black
rain at Clement. Clement rushed at her shins and threw
her over. They rolled and squirmed, pounding at one

another—Clement was weeping, and a grid of long bright scratches was slowly bubbling red on Mary's arm. "Great, tag *me* with the blame, that's just the point, where *were* you, left her to a fool, a nincompoop, that girl doesn't know her thumb from her bum, an idiot—" "That's right, that's right, you've hit it," Mary yelled, "I left her with an idiot, I left her with you!"

Una was too stupefied to speak. A fight! Clement and Mary! Perfection!

She slipped out the door and raced down the street. Boris was trudging under the lamplight a block ahead of her. She ran and ran and caught up with him at last.

"Boris! I want to go back with you."

"Go home, Una."

"Boris, they're killing each other—"

"Unlikely. I eavesdropped for a second or so before boredom set in. Then I left. Go home."

"I can't go back there, Boris, they've *never* been like that. Boris, I want to stay with you tonight."

"I'm in no mood to collect rent, Una, go home to your friends."

"Boris," Una pleaded, "aren't you my friend? Be my friend, I can't go back there! They're crazy, they're insane, they're *attacking* each other—"

"Each other, no. An attack, yes. An attack of guilt. Go home, Una, they'll be all right," Boris said sadly. "Let me have a look at you. No lipstick, a convenience. Why don't you ever wear any?"

"I don't know," Una said. "Mary doesn't either."

"Mary's teeth stick out, she looks better without it. You should wear it," he said critically. He drew her away from the light and kissed her under a tree. It was a new kind of kiss.

"It wasn't like that in bed before," Una said wonderingly.

"Go home," Boris groaned, but it was half an hour before he let her go.

The house was quiet. A lava of wreckage spread everywhere. The Chimeses were waiting.

"About time," Clement greeted her. "Good morning, good morning."

Mary lay on the sofa face down. "We *saw* you come in before. We both saw you."

"We saw you slink out," Clement said. His shin was swollen and his mustache was a ruin. "You came in and you slunk right out again. We saw the whole thing."

"Christina's in the hospital and all Una Meyer can find to do is neck all night with a Bulgarian," Mary rasped into the upholstery. She shifted and sat up, and the bad spring snapped like the note of a bassoon.

"I'll be frank with you," Clement said. "Open and candid. We've been talking you over, Una. We've analyzed exactly what you've done."

"We've analyzed what you are."

"An exploiter," Clement said.

"Exploiter," said Mary. "Manipulator."

"When we asked you to come in halfies with us it was for your sake. Build up your ego and so forth. The Sorcerer's Apprentice, it turned out." Clement scowled. "We never dreamed you'd take over."

"You took over everything."

"The whole damn house."

"The books."

"The john."

"The records."

"The refrigerator."

"The baby," Mary said. "You had her out in the middle of blizzards, you were always practically suffocating her trying to shut her up—"

"She was abused," Clement said. "We depended on you and you abused the kid. You abused our good faith. You took over, that's all."

Una stared at the floor. A hassock had burst in the battle

and there were peculiar cloud-bits stirring like little roaming mice.

"A matter of neglect," Mary said bitterly. "It began with Organski. After he started hanging around you could never keep your mind on anything. We told you he was no good."

"He's *good*," Una said. "If not for Boris nobody would ever've found out what was wrong with Christina, it would've been worse—"

"*Could* it be worse?" Mary asked.

"Never mind, bunny, don't try talking decency to her. He's set her against us, that's the point."

Una felt obscurely startled; she tasted salt. Then a wetness heated her nose, and she realized she had been crying all along.

"Isn't it a bit late for theatricals?" Mary said. "The least you can do is clean up the place. Clement's shirt's in little pieces."

"One thing you managed to do, my God, Rosalie at her worst never could. You even set the two of us against each *other*. Compared to you Rosalie was a goddamn saint."

Una put her arms behind her. "I know it's my fault. Boris said it wasn't. I mean about Christina. But it really is my fault, I know it is," and went on silently discharging tears.

"Maudlin!" Mary cried. "That's the worst thing about you, it's disgusting the way you like to go on like that, it's just masochism. She's so *humble* it's sickening, a born martyr, always got her neck stuck out for persecutors. Look, if you want somebody to make you suffer, go find your pal Boris."

"Boris is good," Una repeated stupidly.

"He's not serious," Clement said. "These medical types never are. I know what you want out of him, but forget it. He's no damn good, whatever you say. Mary and I spotted it the first time we set eyes on him, but you knew better. You never listened to anything. We used to think something could be done with you, you could be salvaged, but the material turned out to be weak. You're in shreds, Una. That man will never marry you."

"She'll get what she deserves from that man," Mary said.

"If he's as good as she thinks he'll give it to her good," Clement said; and because this was rather witty, Una saw him suddenly smile.

8

Early in the morning the Chimeses went to the hospital. Una couldn't go with them; they told her only the parents were allowed. She washed the breakfast dishes and scrubbed Mary's blood off the sofa and swept the living room and heaped together a pile of broken plunder. Then she tried to read a little. It seemed to her years had passed since she had read anything at all. No book could interest her. She mooned into the study, looking for Clement's manuscript.

There it was finally: under a mound of newspapers on the table he had made for Mary out of the bathroom door. The first page said

SOCIAL CANCER
A DIAGNOSIS IN VERSE
AND ANGER
By Clement Chimes, M.A.

There was no second page.

The day was long and tedious. Una could think of nothing worth doing. At six o'clock she would have to go back to the hardware counter, but there were hours before that. She walked out to Boris's, and of course he wasn't home.

A family of young cockroaches filed out of a crack

between two boards and ducked their tall antennae over the sill. Una wished she had a key. Then she wished she could slide under the door like the cockroaches. She squatted on the floor in front of Boris's apartment and waited for his classes to be done. It grew dark in the corridor, and cold. "Oh Lord, a visitation," Boris muttered when he found her, and they nuzzled their way into bed and kissed there all afternoon. Una was late for work, but she felt warm and almost plump; her lips and cheeks and breasts and arms felt warm and golden. Boris's key was in her pocket.

The next evening the hardware supervisor gave her a warning for two latenesses in a row; it was easy to get girls these days, he said.

The Chimeses scarcely spoke to her. Their mood was strange. In the mornings they seemed to float out to the hospital, not with anxiety, but as though anxiety was over. They couldn't tell Una much about Christina. She was better, they murmured—she was definitely better. Boris, who kept in touch with Dr. Chichester, said nothing. Una was encouraged. Everyone struck her as optimistic—more than that, almost happy. The Chimeses' relief was clear. Boris rolled her all over his bed, laughing. By the end of the week she was fired, but the Chimeses only looked docile when Una told them she would have no money toward the rent.

She talked and talked to Boris. She talked to him about the Chimeses' queer enchanted gratitude. Day after day they passed through the hospital waiting rooms like scheming honeymooners. Afterward the nurses told how their heads were always close. They were noticed because they were beautiful and because they lived on candy bars. Their vigil left them not haggard but fresh and radiant. Una remembered how Mary had once, and more than once, praised the science of soil chemistry: it had more to contribute to the fortunes of the underdeveloped nations than bloodless jurisprudence could. And it came to her how Clement often spoke of traveling to a country where all the inhabitants practiced a totally unfamiliar religion, and how he always ended by twitting Una for throwing away her chance at diving into Turkey and the Koran. All along Mary had been bored and Clement jealous. They were relieved. They were glad to be interrupted. Fate had marred their perfect dedication and they did not despair. A brilliance stirred them. They were ready for something new.

By the beginning of the Chimeses' second hospital week Boris and Una were lovers in earnest, and in the middle of that same week Christina died. The sight of the small box handed down into a small ditch made Una think of a dog burying a bone. The young rabbi wore a crumpled bow tie. At the graveside he celebrated all students and intellectuals who do not neglect the duty of procreation—plainly it was his first funeral, and after it the Chimeses sold their books and left New Haven, and Una never saw them again.

9

Sometimes she thought she read about them. A headline would say WOMAN JOINS PEACE CORPS TO GIVE HUSBAND SOME PEACE; it would be about a girl who went to Tanganyika while her husband sat home in the quiet to write a novel about corruption in the banking business, and Una would hunt down the column avidly to see the names, but it was always about someone else. Or she would hear of a couple adopted by an Indian tribe and living right on the reservation, teaching the elders Hochdeutsch and solid geometry—it wasn't Clement and Mary, though. Once she got wind of a young man who had left his wife, a beautiful and dark-haired agronomist working in Burma, to enter a Buddhist monastery, and she was positive this at last must be the Chimeses, repaired and reconverted by fresh educations. But when the story was finally printed in *Time*, the remarkable pair turned out to be Soviet citizens; they hailed from Pinsk.

"Forget about them," Boris said, but she never could. She was always expecting the Chimeses to jump out at her from a newspaper, already famous.

"I've got their *card* catalogue, haven't I? What if they want to reconstitute their library some day? They'll need it."

"They're no good," Boris said.

"That's what they used to say about you."

"Two rights don't make a wrong."

"Ha ha," Una sneered. "They *were* wrong in one thing. They swore you'd never marry me."

Boris sighed. "After all they had a point."

"No they didn't. They meant you'd never *want* to."

"I want to, Una," Boris said, and he asked her to marry him for the thousandth time. "Why not? Why not? I don't see why you won't say yes. Really, Una, what're you worrying about? Everything would be just the same as it is now."

"You're embarrassed," Una accused. "You're ashamed. Everybody knows about us and you can't stand it."

"That caps it. Now look. Let's go over it again, all right? *I'm* not the one who cares; the hospitals do. How do you think I'm going to get a decent internship anywhere? In a first-class clinic? Who's going to take me? Enough is enough. Let's get married, Una."

"Don't talk about everything being the same," Una said. "Everything's different already. *You're* not the same."

"Neither are you. You're a lot dumber than you used to be. And a bit of a shrew. You don't have a thought in your head any more. You fuss over grease, you fuss over dust—"

"I'm not as educated as you are," Una said meanly. "I gave up my education for the sake of the Phillips screwdriver and the Yale lock."

"I told you not to go back to that idiotic job."

"Who paid the bill to have the place fumigated? Who paid for the kitchen paint? And I notice you don't mind eating," Una said. "You're more interested in eating than you are in me anyhow. You always were. The only thing you ever liked about me was watching me eat."

"It's a lot less agonizing than watching you cook. Shrew," Boris said, "let's get married."

"No."

"Why the hell not? Finally and rationally, what've you got against it?"

"There's no education in it!" Una yelled.

"I don't want a mistress," Boris said, "I want a wife."

In the end—but this was years later, and how it came about, what letters were written, how often and how many, who introduced whom: all this was long forgotten—Boris did get a wife. When Una visited the Organskis ten years after their marriage, Boris was unrecognizable, except for the length of his nose; Una thought to herself that he looked like a long-nosed hippopotamus. His little boy, though only seven years old, seemed more like the medical student she remembered; he was arrogant and charming, and kept her laughing. Mrs. Organski was herself deliciously fat—but then she had always been fat, even in girlhood. She was newly widowed when Una got the idea that she would do nicely for Boris. Boris was now a psychiatrist. He had never stopped writing her his complicated, outrageous letters; he said he had finally come to understand that she was suffering from an ineradicable marriage-trauma. She had already been married vicariously; she had *lived* the Chimeses' marriage, she continued to believe in its perfection, and she was afraid she would fail to duplicate it. Now and again he offered to marry her in spite of everything.

Una finished her Ph.D. at a midwestern university; her old adviser and his wife and sons telegraphed an orchid. Her dissertation topic was "The Influence of the Greek Middle Voice on Latin Prosody," and it required no travel, foreign or internal. By a horrid coincidence she joined the faculty of a small college in Turkey, New York. All her colleagues were invincibly domesticated. They gave each other little teas and frequent dinner parties. Occasionally they invited some of the more intelligent teachers from the high school that bordered on the campus. One of these turned out to be a Mrs. Orenstein, who taught social studies. Una and Mrs. Orenstein fell into one another's arms, and left the party early to reminisce in privacy. Mrs. Orenstein chafed her short fingers and told how Mr. Orenstein, a popular phys. ed. teacher, had been killed six months before in a terrible accident in the gym. Demonstrating a belly grind, he slipped off the parallel bars. The rest of the night they talked about the Chimeses. Mrs. Orenstein had heard from someone that Clement had become a dentist; an accountant from someone else; but she didn't know whether either was true. There was a rumor that Mary was with the State Department; another that Mary had become a nun and Clement a pimp for the Argentinean consul's brother-in-law. What was definite was that they lived in Washington; maybe they lived in Washington; they were both teaching astronomy at UCLA; they had no children; they had six girls and a boy; Mary was in prison; Clement was dead.

Finally Mrs. Orenstein asked Una why she had never married. Una thought the question rude and deflected it: "If you ever want to get married again, Rosalie, I have just the person. He'd like everything about you. Clement and Mary always used to say you were a good cook anyhow."

"I hated them," Rosalie said. "I hate them right now when I think about them, don't you?"

"I don't know," Una said. "I used to, but Boris mixed me up about them years ago. Just before I met Boris I was really hating them. I was a rotten hypocrite in those days. Then the baby died and they blamed it on me, so I started feeling sorry for them. The more Boris showed them up for selfish and shallow and all that, and not awfully bright after all, the more I began to see that they *had* something

anyhow. I mean they kept themselves intact. They had
that."

Rosalie snorted. "Anybody could see right through
them."

"Well, what of it?" Una said. "It didn't matter. You could
see through them and they were wonderful all the same,
just *because* you could see through them. They were like a
bubble that never broke, you could look right through and
they kept on shining no matter what. They're the only
persons I've ever known who stayed the same from start
to finish."

"I don't follow any of that," Rosalie said. "Who's this
Boris?"

Una laughed furiously. "Rosalie, Rosalie, aren't you
listening? Boris is your second husband."

She waited a decade before she dared to visit them; she
was forty-two years old. She had trouble with her gums,
had lost some teeth, and wore movable bridges. "Has anybody ever heard anything about the Chimeses?" No one
had.

"Ding dong," said the new Organski daughter, and everyone smiled.

Oddly enough the visit was a success. She observed the
Organskis' marriage. They had a full and heavy table, and
served three desserts: first pudding, then fruit, then cake
and tea. The two children would plainly never turn out to
be extraordinary. Boris's accent was as bad as ever. Rosalie
let the dust build; she quarreled with all her cleaning
women. The house held no glory and no wars.

Rosalie asked Una to come again, and she accepted, but
only with her lips. Inwardly she refused. It wasn't that she
any longer resented imperfection, but it seemed to her
unendurable that her education should go on and on and
on.

RICHARD YATES

A Really Good Jazz Piano

Because of the midnight noise on both ends of the line there
was some confusion at Harry's New York Bar when the call
came through. All the bartender could tell at first was that it
was a long-distance call from Cannes, evidently from some
kind of nightclub, and the operator's frantic voice made it
sound like an emergency. Then at last, by plugging his free
ear and shouting questions into the phone, he learned that
it was only Ken Platt, calling up to have an aimless chat
with his friend Carson Wyler, and this made him shake his
head in exasperation as he set the phone on the bar beside
Carson's glass of Pernod.

"Here," he said. "It's for you, for God's sake. It's your
buddy." Like a number of other Paris bartenders he knew
them both pretty well: Carson was the handsome one, the
one with the slim, witty face and the English-sounding
accent; Ken was the fat one who laughed all the time and
tagged along. They were both three years out of Yale and
trying to get all the fun they could out of living in Europe.

"Carson?" said Ken's eager voice, vibrating painfully in
the receiver. "This is Ken—I knew I'd find you there.
Listen, when you coming down, anyway?"

Carson puckered his well-shaped brow at the phone.

"You know when I'm coming down," he said. "I wired you, I'm coming down Saturday. What's the matter with you?"

"Hell, nothing's the matter with me—maybe a little drunk, is all. No, but listen, what I really called up about, there's a man here named Sid plays a really good jazz piano, and I want you to hear him. He's a friend of mine. Listen, wait a minute, I'll get the phone over close so you can hear. Listen to this, now. Wait a minute."

There were some blurred scraping sounds and the sound of Ken laughing and somebody else laughing, and then the piano came through. It sounded tinny in the telephone, but Carson could tell it was good. It was "Sweet Lorraine," done in a rich traditional style with nothing commercial about it, and this surprised him, for Ken was ordinarily a poor judge of music. After a minute he handed the phone to a stranger he had been drinking with, a farm machinery salesman from Philadelphia. "Listen to this," he said. "This is first-rate."

The farm machinery salesman held his ear to the phone with a puzzled look. "What is it?"

" 'Sweet Lorraine.' "

"No, but I mean what's the deal? Where's it coming from?"

"Cannes. Somebody Ken turned up down there. You've met Ken, haven't you?"

"No, I haven't," the salesman said, frowning into the phone. "Here, it's stopped now and somebody's talking. You better take it."

"Hello? Hello?" Ken's voice was saying. "Carson?"

"Yes, Ken. I'm right here."

"Where'd you go? Who was that other guy?"

"That was a gentleman from Philadelphia named—" he looked up questioningly.

"Baldinger," said the salesman, straightening his coat.

"Named Mr. Baldinger. He's here at the bar with me."

"Oh. Well listen, how'd you like Sid's playing?"

"Fine, Ken. Tell him I said it was first-rate."

"You want to talk to him? He's right here, wait a minute."

There were some more obscure sounds and then a deep middle-aged voice said, "Hello there."

"How do you do, Sid. My name's Carson Wyler, and I enjoyed your playing very much."

"Well," the voice said. "Thank you, thank you a lot. I appreciate it." It could have been either a colored or a white man's voice, but Carson assumed he was colored, mostly from the slight edge of self-consciousness or pride in the way Ken had said, "He's a friend of mine."

"I'm coming down to Cannes this weekend, Sid," Carson said, "and I'll be looking forward to—"

But Sid had evidently given back the phone, for Ken's voice cut in. "Carson?"

"What?"

"Listen, what time you coming Saturday? I mean what train and everything?" They had originally planned to go to Cannes together, but Carson had become involved with a girl in Paris, and Ken had gone on alone, with the understanding that Carson would join him in a week. Now it had been nearly a month.

"I don't know the exact train," Carson said, with some impatience. "It doesn't matter, does it? I'll see you at the hotel sometime Saturday."

"Okay. Oh and wait, listen, the other reason I called, I want to sponsor Sid here for the IBF, okay?"

"Right. Good idea. Put him back on." And while he was waiting he got out his fountain pen and asked the bartender for the IBF membership book.

"Hello again," Sid's voice said. "What's this I'm supposed to be joining here?"

"The IBF," Carson said. "That stands for International Bar Flies, something they started here at Harry's back in—I don't know. Long time ago. Kind of a club."

"Very good," Sid said, chuckling.

"Now what it amounts to is this," Carson began, and

even the bartender, for whom the IBF was a bore and a nuisance, had to smile with pleasure at the serious, painstaking way he told about it—how each member received a lapel button bearing the insignia of a fly, together with a printed booklet that contained the club rules and a listing of all other IBF bars in the world; how the cardinal rule was that when two members met they were expected to greet one another by brushing the fingers of their right hands on each other's shoulders and saying, "*Bzz-z-z, bzz-z-z!*"

This was one of Carson's special talents, the ability to find and convey an unashamed enjoyment in trivial things. Many people could not have described the IBF to a jazz musician without breaking off in an apologetic laugh to explain that it was, of course, a sort of sad little game for lonely tourists, a square's thing really, and that its very lack of sophistication was what made it fun; Carson told it straight. In much the same way he had once made it fashionable among some of the more literary undergraduates at Yale to spend Sunday mornings respectfully absorbed in the funny papers of the *New York Mirror*; more recently the same trait had rapidly endeared him to many chance acquaintances, notably to his current girl, the young Swedish art student for whom he had stayed in Paris. "You have beautiful taste in everything," she had told him on their first memorable night together. "You have a truly educated, truly original mind."

"Got that?" he said into the phone, and paused to sip his Pernod. "Right. Now if you'll give me your full name and address, Sid, I'll get everything organized on this end." Sid spelled it out and Carson lettered it carefully into the membership book, with his own name and Ken's as co-sponsors, while Mr. Baldinger watched. When they were finished Ken's voice came back to say a reluctant goodbye, and they hung up.

"That must've been a pretty expensive telephone call," Mr. Baldinger said, impressed.

"You're right," Carson said. "I guess it was."

"What's the deal on this membership book, anyway? All this barfly business?"

"Oh, aren't you a member, Mr. Baldinger? I thought you were a member. Here, I'll sponsor you, if you like."

Mr. Baldinger got what he later described as an enormous kick out of it: far into the early morning he was still sidling up to everyone at the bar, one after another, and buzzing them.

Carson didn't get to Cannes on Saturday, for it took him longer than he'd planned to conclude his affair with the Swedish girl. He had expected a tearful scene, or at least a brave exchange of tender promises and smiles, but instead she was surprisingly casual about his leaving—even abstracted, as if already concentrating on her next truly educated, truly original mind—and this forced him into several uneasy delays that accomplished nothing except to fill her with impatience and him with a sense of being dispossessed. He didn't get to Cannes until the following Tuesday afternoon, after further telephone talks with Ken, and then, when he eased himself onto the station platform, stiff and sour with hangover, he was damned if he knew why he'd come at all. The sun assaulted him, burning deep into his gritty scalp and raising a quick sweat inside his rumpled suit; it struck blinding glints off the chromework of parked cars and motor scooters and made sickly blue vapors of exhaust rise up against pink buildings; it played garishly among the swarm of tourists who jostled him, showing him all their pores, all the tension of their store-new sports clothes, their clutched suitcases and slung cameras, all the anxiety of their smiling, shouting mouths. Cannes would be like any other resort town in the world, all hurry and disappointment, and why hadn't he stayed where he belonged, in a high cool room with a long-legged girl? Why the hell had he let himself be coaxed and wheedled into coming here?

But then he saw Ken's happy face bobbing in the crowd—"Carson!"—and there he came, running in his overgrown fat boy's thigh-chafing way, clumsy with welcome. "Taxi's over here, take your bag—boy, do you look beat! Get you a shower and a drink first, okay? How the hell are you?"

And riding light on the taxi cushions as they swung onto the Croisette, with its spectacular blaze of blue and gold and its blood-quickening rush of sea air, Carson began to relax. Look at the girls! There were acres of them; and besides, it was good to be with old Ken again. It was easy to see, now, that the thing in Paris could only have gotten worse if he'd stayed. He had left just in time.

Ken couldn't stop talking. Pacing in and out of the bathroom while Carson took his shower, jingling a pocketful of coins, he talked in the laughing, full-throated joy of a man who had gone for weeks without hearing his own voice. The truth was that Ken never really had a good time away from Carson. They were each other's best friends, but it had never been an equal friendship, and they both knew it. At Yale Ken would probably have been left out of everything if it hadn't been for his status as Carson's dull but inseparable companion, and this was a pattern that nothing in Europe had changed. What *was* it about Ken that put people off? Carson had pondered this question for years. Was it just that he was fat and physically awkward, or that he could be strident and silly in his eagerness to be liked? But weren't these essentially likable qualities? No, Carson guessed the closest he could come to a real explanation was the fact that when Ken smiled his upper lip slid back to reveal a small moist inner lip that trembled against his gum. Many people with this kind of mouth may find it no great handicap—Carson was willing to admit that—but it did seem to be the thing everyone remembered most vividly about Ken Platt, whatever more substantial-sounding reasons one might give for avoiding him; in any case it was what Carson himself was always most aware of, in moments of irritation. Right now, for example, in the simple business of trying to dry himself and comb his hair and put on fresh clothes, this wide, moving, double-lipped smile kept getting in the way. It was everywhere, blocking his reach for the towel rack, hovering too close over his jumbled suitcase, swimming in the mirror to eclipse the tying of his tie, until Carson had to clamp his jaws tight to keep from yelling, "All *right*, Ken—shut *up* now!"

But a few minutes later they were able to compose themselves in the shaded silence of the hotel bar. The bartender was peeling a lemon, neatly pinching and pulling back a strip of its bright flesh between thumb and knife blade, and the fine citric smell of it, combining with the scent of gin in the faint smoke of crushed ice, gave flavor to a full restoration of their ease. A couple of cold martinis drowned the last of Carson's pique, and by the time they were out of the place and swinging down the sidewalk on their way to dinner he felt strong again with a sense of the old camaraderie, the familiar, buoyant wealth of Ken's admiration. It was a feeling touched with sadness, too, for Ken would soon have to go back to the States. His father in Denver, the author of sarcastic weekly letters on business stationery, was holding open a junior partnership for him, and Ken, having long since completed the Sorbonne courses that were his ostensible reason for coming to France, had no further excuse for staying. Carson, luckier in this as in everything else, had no need of an excuse: he had an adequate private income and no family ties; he could afford to browse around Europe for years, if he felt like it, looking for things that pleased him.

"You're still white as a sheet," he told Ken across their restaurant table. "Haven't you been going to the beach?"

"Sure." Ken looked quickly at his plate. "I've been to the beach a few times. The weather hasn't been too good for it lately, is all."

But Carson guessed the real reason, that Ken was embarrassed to display his body, so he changed the subject. "Oh, by the way," he said. "I brought along the IBF stuff, for that piano player friend of yours."

"Oh, swell." Ken looked up in genuine relief. "I'll take you over there soon as we're finished eating, okay?" And as if to hurry this prospect along he forked a dripping load of salad into his mouth and tore off too big a bite of bread to chew with it, using the remaining stump of bread to mop at the oil and vinegar in his plate. "You'll like him, Carson," he said soberly around his chewing. "He's a great guy. I really admire him a lot." He swallowed with effort and hurried on: "I mean hell, with talent like that he could go back to the States tomorrow and make a fortune, but he likes it here. One thing, of course, he's got a girl here, this really lovely French girl, and I guess he couldn't very well take her back with him—no, but really, it's more than that. People accept him here. As an artist, I mean, as well as a man. Nobody condescends to him, nobody tries to interfere with his music, and that's all he wants out of life. Oh, I mean he doesn't tell you all this—probably be a bore if he did—it's just a thing you sense about him. Comes out in everything he says, his whole mental attitude." He popped the soaked bread into his mouth and chewed it with authority. "I mean the guy's got *authentic* integrity," he said. "Wonderful thing."

"Did sound like a damn good piano," Carson said, reaching for the wine bottle, "what little I heard of it."

"Wait'll you really hear it, though. Wait'll he really gets going."

They both enjoyed the fact that this was Ken's discovery. Always before it had been Carson who led the way, who found the girls and learned the idioms and knew how best to spend each hour; it was Carson who had tracked down all the really colorful places in Paris where you never saw Americans, and who then, just when Ken was learning to find places of his own, had paradoxically made Harry's Bar become the most colorful place of all. Through all this, Ken had been glad enough to follow, shaking his grateful head in wonderment; but it was no small thing to have turned up an incorruptible jazz talent in the back streets of a foreign city, all alone. It proved that Ken's dependence could be less than total after all, and this reflected credit on them both.

The place where Sid played was more of an expensive bar than a nightclub, a small carpeted basement several streets back from the sea. It was still early, and they found him having a drink alone at the bar.

"Well," he said when he saw Ken. "Hello there." He was stocky and well-tailored, a very dark Negro with a pleasant smile full of strong white teeth.

"Sid, I'd like you to meet Carson Wyler. You talked to him on the phone that time, remember?"

"Oh yes," Sid said, shaking hands. "Oh yes. Very pleased to meet you, Carson. What're you gentlemen drinking?"

They made a little ceremony of buttoning the IBF insignia into the lapel of Sid's tan gabardine, of buzzing his shoulder and offering the shoulders of their own identical seersucker jackets to be buzzed in turn. "Well, this is fine," Sid said, chuckling and leafing through the booklet. "Very good." Then he put the booklet in his pocket, finished his drink and slid off the barstool. "And now if you'll excuse me, I got to go to work."

"Not much of an audience yet," Ken said.

Sid shrugged. "Place like this, I'd just as soon have it that way. You get a big crowd, you always get some square asking for 'Deep in the Heart of Texas,' or some damn thing."

Ken laughed and winked at Carson, and they both turned to watch Sid take his place at the piano, which stood on a low spotlighted dais across the room. He fingered the keys idly for a while to make stray phrases and chords, a craftsman fondling his tools, and then he settled down. The compelling beat emerged, and out of it the climb and waver of the melody, an arrangement of "Baby, Won't You Please Come Home."

They stayed for hours, listening to Sid play and buying him drinks whenever he took a break, to the obvious envy of other customers. Sid's girl came in, tall and brown-haired,

with a bright, startled-looking face that was almost beautiful, and Ken introduced her with a small uncontrollable
flourish: "This is Jaqueline." She whispered something
about not speaking English very well, and when it was time
for Sid's next break—the place was filling up now and there
was considerable applause when he finished—the four of
them took a table together.

Ken let Carson do most of the talking now; he was more
than content just to sit there, smiling around this tableful of
friends with all the serenity of a well-fed young priest. It
was the happiest evening of his life in Europe, to a degree
that even Carson would never have guessed. In the space of
a few hours it filled all the emptiness of his past month, the
time that had begun with Carson's saying "*Go*, then. Can't
you go to Cannes by yourself?" It atoned for all the hot
miles walked up and down the Croisette on blistered feet to
peek like a fool at girls who lay incredibly near naked in the
sand; for the cramped, boring bus rides to Nice and Monte
Carlo and St. Paul-de-Vence; for the day he had paid a
sinister druggist three times too much for a pair of sunglasses
only to find, on catching sight of his own image in the gleam
of a passing shop window, that they made him look like a
great blind fish; for the terrible daily, nightly sense of being
young and rich and free on the Riviera—the Riviera!—and
of having nothing to do. Once in the first week he had gone
with a prostitute whose canny smile, whose shrill insistence
on a high price and whose facial flicker of distaste at the
sight of his body had frightened him into an agony of
impotence; most other nights he had gotten drunk or sick
from bar to bar, afraid of prostitutes and of rebuffs from
other girls, afraid even of striking up conversations with
men lest they mistake him for a fairy. He had spent a
whole afternoon in the French equivalent of a dime store,
feigning a shopper's interest in padlocks and shaving cream
and cheap tin toys, moving through the bright stale air of
the place with a throatful of longing for home. Five nights
in a row he had hidden himself in the protective darkness of

American movies, just as he'd done years ago in Denver to get away from boys who called him Lard-Ass Platt, and after the last of these entertainments, back in the hotel with the taste of chocolate creams still cloying his mouth, he had cried himself to sleep. But all this was dissolving now under the fine reckless grace of Sid's piano, under the spell of Carson's intelligent smile and the way Carson raised his hands to clap each time the music stopped.

Sometime after midnight, when everyone but Sid had drunk too much, Carson asked him how long he had been away from the States. "Since the war," he said. "I came over in the Army and I never did go back."

Ken, coated with a film of sweat and happiness, thrust his glass high in the air for a toast. "And by God, here's hoping you never have to, Sid."

"Why is that, 'have to'?" Jaqueline said. Her face looked harsh and sober in the dim light. "Why do you say that?"

Ken blinked at her. "Well, I just mean—you know—that he never has to sell out, or anything. He never would, of course."

"What does this mean, 'sell out'?" There was an uneasy silence until Sid laughed in his deep, rumbling way. "Take it easy, honey," he said, and turned to Ken. "We don't look at it that way, you see. Matter of fact, I'm working on angles all the time to get back to the States, make some money there. We both feel that way about it."

"Well, but you're doing all right here, aren't you?" Ken said, almost pleading with him. "You're making enough money and everything, aren't you?"

Sid smiled patiently. "I don't mean a job like this, though, you see. I mean real money."

"You know who is Murray Diamond?" Jaqueline inquired, holding her eyebrows high. "The owner of nightclubs in Las Vegas?"

But Sid was shaking his head and laughing. "Honey, wait a minute—I keep telling you, that's nothing to count on. Murray Diamond happened to be in here the other night, you see," he explained. "Didn't have much time, but he said he'd try to drop around again some night this week. Be a big break for me. 'Course, like I say, that's nothing to count on."

"Well but *Jesus*, Sid—" Ken shook his head in bafflement; then, letting his face tighten into a look of outrage, he thumped the table with a bouncing fist. "Why prostitute yourself?" he demanded. "I mean damn it, you *know* they'll make you prostitute yourself in the States!"

Sid was smiling, but his eyes had narrowed slightly. "I guess it's all in the way you look at it," he said.

And the worst part of it, for Ken, was that Carson came so quickly to his rescue. "Oh, I'm sure Ken doesn't mean that the way it *sounds*," he said, and while Ken was babbling quick apologies of his own ("No, of course not, all I meant was—*you* know. . . .") he went on to say other things, light, nimble things that only Carson could say, until the awkwardness was gone. When the time came to say goodnight there were handshakes and smiles and promises to see each other soon.

But the minute they were out on the street, Carson turned on Ken. "Why did you have to get so damned sophomoric about that? Couldn't you see how embarrassing it was?"

"I know," Ken said, hurrying to keep pace with Carson's long legs, "I know. But hell, I *was* disappointed in him, Carson. The point is I never heard him *talk* like that before." What he omitted here, of course, was that he had never really heard him talk at all, except in the one shy conversation that had led to the calling-up of Harry's Bar that other night, after which Ken had fled back to the hotel in fear of overstaying his welcome.

"Well, but even so," Carson said. "Don't you think it's the man's own business what he wants to do with his life?"

"Okay," Ken said, "*okay*. I *told* him I was sorry, didn't I?" He felt so humble now that it took him some minutes to realize that, in a sense, he hadn't come off too badly. After

all, Carson's only triumph tonight had been that of the
diplomat, the soother of feelings; it was he, Ken, who had
done the more dramatic thing. Sophomoric or not, impul-
sive or not, wasn't there a certain dignity in having spoken
his mind that way? Now, licking his lips and glancing at
Carson's profile as they walked, he squared his shoulders
and tried to make his walk less of a waddle and more of a
headlong, manly stride. "It's just that I can't help how I
feel, that's all," he said with conviction. "When I'm
disappointed in a person I show it, that's all."

"All right. Let's forget it."

And Ken was almost sure, though he hardly dared
believe it, that he could detect a grudging respect in
Carson's voice.

Everything went wrong the next day. The fading light of
afternoon found the two of them slumped and staring in a
bleak workingman's café near the railroad station, barely
speaking to each other. It was a day that had started out
unusually well, too—that was the trouble.

They had slept till noon and gone to the beach after
lunch, for Ken didn't mind the beach when he wasn't alone,
and before long they had picked up two American girls in
the easy, graceful way that Carson always managed such
things. One minute the girls were sullen strangers, wiping
scented oil on their bodies and looking as if any intrusion
would mean a call for the police, the next minute they were
weak with laughter at the things Carson was saying, moving
aside their bottles and their zippered blue TWA satchels to
make room for unexpected guests. There was a tall one for
Carson with long firm thighs, intelligent eyes and a way of
tossing back her hair that gave her a look of real beauty, and
a small one for Ken—a cute, freckled good sport of a girl
whose every cheerful glance and gesture showed she was
used to taking second best. Ken, bellying deep into the sand
with his chin on two stacked fists, smiling up very close to
her warm legs, felt almost none of the conversational

tension that normally hampered him at times like this.
Even when Carson and the tall girl got up to run splashing
into the water he was able to hold her interest: she said
several times that the Sorbonne "must have been fascinating,"
and she sympathized with his having to go back to Denver,
though she said it was "probably the best thing."

"And your friend's just going to stay over here indefinite-
ly, then?" she asked. "Is it really true what he said? I mean
that he isn't studying or working or anything? Just sort of
floating around?"

"Well—yeah, that's right." Ken tried a squinty smile like
Carson's own. "Why?"

"It's interesting, that's all. I don't think I've ever met a
person like that before."

That was when Ken began to realize what the laughter
and the scanty French bathing suits had disguised about
these girls, that they were girls of a kind neither he nor
Carson had dealt with for a long time—suburban, middle-class
girls who had dutifully won their parents' blessing for this
guided tour; girls who said "golly Moses," whose campus-shop
clothes and hockey-field strides would have instantly
betrayed them on the street. They were the very kind of
girls who had gathered at the punch bowl to murmur
"Ugh!" at the way he looked in his first tuxedo, whose
ignorant, maddeningly bland little stares of rejection had
poisoned all his aching years in Denver and New Haven.
They were squares. And the remarkable thing was that he
felt so good. Rolling his weight to one elbow, clutching up
slow, hot handfuls of sand and emptying them, again and
again, he found his flow of words coming quick and smooth:

". . . no, really, there's a lot to see in Paris; shame you
couldn't spend more time there; actually most of the places
I like best are more or less off the beaten track; of course I
was lucky in having a fairly good grasp of the language, and
then I met so many congenial. . . ."

He was holding his own; he was making out. He hardly
even noticed when Carson and the tall girl came trotting

back from their swim, as lithe and handsome as a couple in a travel poster, to drop beside them in a bustle of towels and cigarettes and shuddering jokes about how cold the water was. His only mounting worry was that Carson, who must by now have made his own discovery about these girls, would decide they weren't worth bothering with. But a single glance at Carson's subtly smiling, talking face reassured him: sitting tense at the tall girl's feet while she stood to towel her back in a way that made her breasts sway delightfully, Carson was plainly determined to follow through. "Look," he said. "Why don't we all have dinner together? Then afterwards we might—"

Both girls began chattering their regrets: they were afraid not, thanks anyway, they were meeting friends at the hotel for dinner and actually ought to be starting back now, much as they hated to—"God, look at the time!" And they really did sound sorry, so sorry that Ken, gathering all his courage, reached out and held the warm, fine-boned hand that swung at the small girl's thigh as the four of them plodded back toward the bathhouses. She even squeezed his heavy fingers, and smiled at him.

"Some other night, then?" Carson was saying. "Before you leave?"

"Well, actually," the tall girl said, "our evenings do seem to be pretty well booked up. Probably run into you on the beach again though. It's been fun."

"God damn little snot-nosed New Rochelle bitch," Carson said when they were alone in the men's bathhouse.

"Sh-h-h! Keep your *voice* down, Carson. They can *hear* you in there."

"Oh, don't be an idiot." Carson flung his trunks on the duckboards with a sandy slap. "I hope they do hear me—what the hell's the matter with you?" He looked at Ken as if he hated him. "Pair of God damn teasing little professional virgins. *Christ*, why didn't I stay in Paris?"

And now here they were, Carson glowering, Ken sulking at the sunset through flyspecked windows while a pushing, garlic-smelling bunch of laborers laughed and shouted over the pinball machine. They went on drinking until long past the dinner hour; then they ate a late, unpleasant meal together in a restaurant where the wine was corky and there was too much grease on the fried potatoes. When the messy plates were cleared away Carson lit a cigarette. "What do you want to do tonight?" he said.

There was a faint shine of grease around Ken's mouth and cheeks. "I don't know," he said. "Lot of good places to go, I guess."

"I suppose it would offend your artistic sensibilities to go and hear Sid's piano again?"

Ken gave him a weak, rather testy smile. "You still harping on that?" he said. "Sure I'd like to go."

"Even though he may prostitute himself?"

"Why don't you lay off that, Carson?"

They could hear the piano from the street, even before they walked into the square of light that poured up from the doorway of Sid's place. On the stairs the sound of it grew stronger and richer, mixed now with the sound of a man's hoarse singing, but only when they were down in the room, squinting through the blue smoke, did they realize the singer was Sid himself. Eyes half closed, head turned to smile along his shoulder into the crowd, he was singing as he swayed and worked at the keys.

Man, she got a pair of eyes. . . .

The blue spotlight struck winking stars in the moisture of his teeth and the faint thread of sweat that striped his temple.

I mean they're brighter than the summer skies
And when you see them you gunna realize
Just why I love my sweet Lorraine. . . .

"Damn place is packed," Carson said. There were no vacancies at the bar, but they stood uncertainly near it for a while, watching Sid perform, until Carson found that one of the girls on the barstools directly behind him was Jaqueline. "Oh," he said. "Hi. Pretty good crowd tonight."

She smiled and nodded and then craned past him to watch Sid.

"I didn't know he sang too," Carson said. "This something new?"

Her smile gave way to an impatient little frown and she put a forefinger against her lips. Rebuffed, he turned back and moved heavily from one foot to the other. Then he nudged Ken. "You want to go or stay? If you want to stay let's at least sit down."

"*Sh-h-h!*" Several people turned in their chairs to frown at him. "*Sh-h-h!*"

"Come on, then," he said, and he led Ken sidling and stumbling through the ranks of listeners to the only vacant table in the room, a small one down in front, too close to the music and wet with spilled drink, that had been pushed aside to make room for larger parties. Settled there, they could see now that Sid wasn't looking into the crowd at large. He was singing directly to a bored-looking couple in evening clothes who sat a few tables away, a silver-blonde girl who could have been a movie starlet and a small, chubby bald man with a deep tan, a man so obviously Murray Diamond that a casting director might have sent him here to play the part. Sometimes Sid's large eyes would stray to other parts of the room or to the smoke-hung ceiling, but they seemed to come into focus only when he looked at these two people. Even when the song ended and the piano took off alone on a long, intricate variation, even then he kept glancing up to see if they were watching. When he finished, to a small thunderclap of applause, the bald man lifted his face, closed it around an amber cigarette holder and clapped his hands a few times.

"Very nice, Sam," he said.

"My name's Sid, Mr. Diamond," Sid said, "but I thank you a lot just the same. Glad y'enjoyed it, sir." He was leaning back, grinning along his shoulder while his fingers toyed with the keys. "Anything special you'd like to hear, Mr. Diamond? Something old-time? Some more of that real old Dixieland? Maybe a little boogie, maybe something a little on the sweet side, what we call a commercial number? Got all kind of tunes here, waitin' to be played."

"Anything at all, uh, Sid," Murray Diamond said, and then the blonde leaned close and whispered something in his ear. "How about 'Stardust,' there, Sid?" he said. "Can you play 'Stardust'?"

"Well, now, Mr. Diamond. If I couldn't play 'Stardust' I don't guess I'd be in business very long, France or any other country." His grin turned into a deep false laugh and his hands slid into the opening chords of the song.

That was when Carson made his first friendly gesture in hours, sending a warm blush of gratitude into Ken's face. He hitched his chair up close to Ken's and began to speak in a voice so soft that no one could have accused him of making a disturbance. "You know something?" he said. "This is disgusting. My God, *I* don't care if he wants to go to Las Vegas. I don't even care if he wants to suck *around* for it. This is something else. This is something that turns my stomach." He paused, frowning at the floor, and Ken watched the small wormlike vein moving in his temple. "Putting on this phony accent," Carson said. "All this big phony Uncle Remus routine." And then he went into a little popeyed, head-tossing, hissing parody of Sid. "Yassuh, Mr. Dahmon' suh. Wudg'all lak t'heah, Mr. Dahmon' suh? Got awl *kine* a toons heah, jes' waitin' to be played, and yok, yok, yok, and shet ma mouf!" He finished his drink and set the glass down hard. "You know damn well he doesn't have to talk that way. You know damn well he's a perfectly bright, educated guy. My God, on the phone I couldn't even tell he was colored."

"Well, yeah," Ken said. "It is sort of depressing."

"Depressing? It's degrading." Carson curled his lip. "It's degenerate."

"I know," Ken said. "I guess that may be partly what I meant about prostituting himself."

"You were certainly right, then. This is damn near enough to make you lose faith in the Negro race."

Being told he was right was always a tonic to Ken, and it was uncommonly bracing after a day like this. He knocked back his drink, straightened his spine and wiped the light mustache of sweat from his upper lip, pressing his mouth into a soft frown to show that his faith, too, in the Negro race was badly shaken. "Boy," he said. "I sure had him figured wrong."

"No," Carson assured him, "you couldn't have known."

"Listen, let's go, then, Carson. The hell with him." And Ken's mind was already full of plans: they would stroll in the cool of the Croisette for a long, serious talk on the meaning of integrity, on how rare it was and how easily counterfeited, how its pursuit was the only struggle worthy of a man's life, until all the discord of the day was erased.

But Carson moved his chair back, smiling and frowning at the same time. "Go?" he said. "What's the matter with you? Don't you want to stay and watch the spectacle? I do. Doesn't it hold a certain horrible fascination for you?" He held up his glass and signaled for two more cognacs.

"Stardust" came to a graceful conclusion and Sid stood up, bathed in applause, to take his break. He loomed directly over their table as he came forward and stepped down off the dais, his big face shining with sweat; he brushed past them, looking toward Diamond's table, and paused there to say, "Thank you, sir," though Diamond hadn't spoken to him, before he made his way back to the bar.

"I suppose he thinks he didn't see us," Carson said.

"Probably just as well," Ken said. "I wouldn't know what to say to him."

"Wouldn't you? I think I would."

The room was stifling, and Ken's cognac had taken on a faintly repellent look and smell in his hand. He loosened his collar and tie with moist fingers. "Come on, Carson," he said. "Let's get out of here. Let's get some air."

Carson ignored him, watching what went on at the bar. Sid drank something Jaqueline offered and then disappeared into the men's room. When he came out a few minutes later, his face dried and composed, Carson turned back and studied his glass. "Here he comes. I think we're going to get the big hello, now, for Diamond's benefit. Watch."

An instant later Sid's fingers brushed the cloth of Carson's shoulder. "*Bzz-z-z, bzz-z-z!*" he said. "How're you tonight?"

Very slowly, Carson turned his head. With heavy eyelids he met Sid's smile for a split second, the way a man might look at a waiter who had accidentally touched him. Then he turned back to his drink.

"Oh-oh," Sid said. "Maybe I didn't do that right. Maybe I got the wrong shoulder here. I'm not too familiar with the rules and regulations yet." Murray Diamond and the blonde were watching, and Sid winked at them, thumbing out the IBF button in his lapel as he moved in sidling steps around the back of Carson's chair. "This here's a club we belong to, Mr. Diamond," he said. "Barflies club. Only trouble is, I'm not very familiar with the rules and regulations yet." He held the attention of nearly everyone in the room as he touched Carson's other shoulder. "*Bzz-z-z, bzz-z-z!*" This time Carson winced and drew his jacket away, glancing at Ken with a perplexed little shrug as if to say, Do you know what this man wants?

Ken didn't know whether to giggle or vomit; both desires were suddenly strong in him, though his face held straight. For a long time afterwards he would remember how the swabbed black plastic of the table looked between his two unmoving hands, how it seemed the only steady surface in the world.

"Say," Sid said, backing away toward the piano with a glazed smile. "What *is* this here? Some kinda conspiracy here?"

Carson allowed a heavy silence to develop. Then with an air of sudden, mild remembrance, seeming to say, Oh yes, of course, he rose and walked over to Sid, who backed up confusedly into the spotlight. Facing him, he extended one limp finger and touched him on the shoulder. "Buzz," he said. "Does that take care of it?" He turned and walked back to his seat.

Ken prayed for someone to laugh—anyone—but no one did. There was no movement in the room but the dying of Sid's smile as he looked at Carson and at Ken, the slow fleshy enclosing of his teeth and the widening of his eyes.

Murray Diamond looked at them too, briefly—a tough, tan little face—then he cleared his throat and said, "How about 'Hold Me,' there, Sid? Can you play 'Hold Me'?" And Sid sat down and began to play, looking at nothing.

With dignity, Carson nodded for the check and laid the right number of thousand- and hundred-franc notes on the saucer. It seemed to take him no time at all to get out of the place, sliding expertly between the tables and out to the stairs, but it took Ken much longer. Lurching, swaying in the smoke like a great imprisoned bear, he was caught and held by Jaqueline's eyes even before he had cleared the last of the tables. They stared relentlessly at the flabby quaver of his smile, they drilled into his back and sent him falling upstairs. And as soon as the sobering night air hit him, as soon as he saw Carson's erect white suit retreating several doors away, he knew what he wanted to do. He wanted to run up and hit him with all his strength between the shoulder blades, one great chopping blow that would drop him to the street, and then he would hit him again, or kick him—yes, kick him—and he'd say, God damn you! God damn you, Carson! The words were already in his mouth and he was ready to swing when Carson stopped and turned to face him under a streetlamp.

"What's the trouble, Ken?" he said. "Don't you think that was funny?"

It wasn't what he said that mattered—for a minute it seemed that nothing Carson said would ever matter again—it was that his face was stricken with the uncannily familiar look of his own heart, the very face he himself, Lard-Ass Platt, had shown all his life to others: haunted and vulnerable and terribly dependent, trying to smile, a look that said Please don't leave me alone.

Ken hung his head, either in mercy or shame. "Hell, I don't know, Carson," he said. "Let's forget it. Let's get some coffee somewhere."

"Right." And they were together again. The only problem now was that they had started out in the wrong direction: in order to get to the Croisette they would have to walk back past the lighted doorway of Sid's place. It was like walking through fire, but they did it quickly and with what anyone would have said was perfect composure, heads up, eyes front, so that the piano only came up loud for a second or two before it diminished and died behind them under the rhythm of their heels.

JOHN UPDIKE

Separating

The day was fair. Brilliant. All that June the weather had
mocked the Maples' internal misery with solid sunlight—
golden shafts and cascades of green in which their conversations had wormed unseeing, their sad murmuring selves
the only stain in Nature. Usually by this time of the year
they had acquired tans; but when they met their elder
daughter's plane on her return from a year in England they
were almost as pale as she, though Judith was too dazzled
by the sunny opulent jumble of her native land to notice.
They did not spoil her homecoming by telling her immediately. Wait a few days, let her recover from jet lag, had
been one of their formulations, in that string of gray
dialogues—over coffee, over cocktails, over Cointreau—that
had shaped the strategy of their dissolution, while the earth
performed its annual stunt of renewal unnoticed beyond
their closed windows. Richard had thought to leave at
Easter; Joan had insisted they wait until the four children
were at last assembled, with all exams passed and ceremo-
nies attended, and the bauble of summer to console them.
So he had drudged away, in love, in dread, repairing
screens, getting the mowers sharpened, rolling and patching
their new tennis court.

The court, clay, had come through its first winter pitted and windswept bare of redcoat. Years ago the Maples had observed how often, among their friends, divorce followed a dramatic home improvement, as if the marriage were making one last twitchy effort to live; their own worst crisis had come amid the plaster dust and exposed plumbing of a kitchen renovation. Yet, a summer ago, as canary-yellow bulldozers gaily churned a grassy, daisy-dotted knoll into a muddy plateau, and a crew of pigtailed young men raked and tamped clay into a plane, this transformation did not strike them as ominous, but festive in its impudence; their marriage could rend the earth for fun. The next spring, waking each day at dawn to a sliding sensation as if the bed were being tipped, Richard found the barren tennis court, its net and tapes still rolled in the barn, an environment congruous with his mood of purposeful desolation, and the crumbling of handfuls of clay into cracks and holes (dogs had frolicked on the court in a thaw; rivulets had evolved trenches) an activity suitably elemental and interminable. In his sealed heart he hoped the day would never come.

Now it was here. A Friday. Judith was reacclimated; all four children were assembled, before jobs and camps and visits again scattered them. Joan thought they should be told one by one. Richard was for making an announcement at the table. She said, "I think just making an announcement is a cop-out. They'll start quarreling and playing to each other instead of focussing. They're each individuals, you know, not just some corporate obstacle to your freedom."

"O.K., O.K. I agree." Joan's plan was exact. That evening, they were giving Judith a belated welcome-home dinner, of lobster and champagne. Then, the party over, they, the two of them, who nineteen years before would push her in a baby carriage along Tenth Street to Washington Square, were to walk her out of the house, to the bridge across the salt creek, and tell her, swearing her to secrecy. Then Richard Jr., who was going directly from work to a rock concert in Boston, would be told, either late when he returned on the train or early Saturday morning before he went off to his job; he was seventeen and employed as one of a golf-course maintenance crew. Then the two younger children, John and Margaret, could, as the morning wore on, be informed.

"Mopped up, as it were," Richard said.

"Do you have any better plan? That leaves you the rest of Saturday to answer any questions, pack, and make your wonderful departure."

"No," he said, meaning he had no better plan, and agreed to hers, though it had an edge of false order, a plea for control in the semblance of its achievement, like Joan's long chore lists and financial accountings and, in the days when he first knew her, her too copious lecture notes. Her plan turned one hurdle for him into four—four knife-sharp walls, each with a sheer blind drop on the other side.

All spring he had been morbidly conscious of insides and outsides, of barriers and partitions. He and Joan stood as a thin barrier between the children and the truth. Each moment was a partition, with the past on one side and the future on the other, a future containing this unthinkable *now*. Beyond four knifelike walls a new life for him waited vaguely. His skull cupped a secret, a white face, a face both frightened and soothing, both strange and known, that he wanted to shield from tears, which he felt all about him, solid as the sunlight. So haunted, he had become obsessed with battening down the house against his absence, replacing screens and sash cords, hinges and latches—a Houdini making things snug before his escape.

The lock. He had still to replace a lock on one of the doors of the screened porch. The task, like most such, proved more difficult than he had imagined. The old lock, aluminum frozen by corrosion, had been deliberately rendered obsolete by manufacturers. Three hardware stores had nothing that even approximately matched the mortised hole its removal (surprisingly easy) left. Another hole had to be gouged, with bits too small and saws too big, and the old hole fitted with a block of wood—the chisels dull, the saw rusty, his fingers thick with lack of sleep. The sun poured down, beyond the porch, on a world of neglect. The bushes already needed pruning, the windward side of the house was shedding flakes of paint, rain would get in when he was gone, insects, rot, death. His family, all those he would lose, filtered through the edges of his awareness as he struggled with screw holes, splinters, opaque instructions, minutiae of metal.

Judith sat on the porch, a princess returned from exile. She regaled them with stories of fuel shortages, of bomb scares in the Underground, of Pakistani workmen loudly lusting after her as she walked past on her way to dance school. Joan came and went, in and out of the house, calmer than she should have been, praising his struggles with the lock as if this were one more and not the last of their chain of shared chores. The younger of his sons, John, now at fifteen suddenly, unwittingly handsome, for a few minutes held the rickety screen door while his father clumsily hammered and chiselled, each blow a kind of sob in Richard's ears. His younger daughter, having been at a slumber party, slept on the porch hammock through all the noise—heavy and pink, trusting and forsaken. Time, like the sunlight, continued relentlessly; the sunlight slowly slanted. Today was one of the longest days. The lock clicked, worked. He was through. He had a drink; he drank it on the porch, listening to his daughter. "It was so sweet," she was saying, "during the worst of it, how all the butcher's and bakery shops kept open by candlelight. They're all so plucky and cute. From the papers, things sounded so much worse here—people shooting people in gas lines, and everybody freezing."

Richard asked her, "Do you still want to live in England forever?" *Forever:* the concept, now a reality upon him, pressed and scratched at the back of his throat.

"No," Judith confessed, turning her oval face to him, its

eyes still childishly far apart, but the lips set as over something succulent and satisfactory. "I was anxious to come home. I'm an American." She was a woman. They had raised her; he and Joan had endured together to raise her, alone of the four. The others had still some raising left in them. Yet it was the thought of telling Judith—the image of her, their first baby, walking between them arm in arm to the bridge—that broke him. The partition between himself and the tears broke. Richard sat down to the celebratory meal with the back of his throat aching; the champagne, the lobster seemed phases of sunshine; he saw them and tasted them through tears. He blinked, swallowed, croakily joked about hay fever. The tears would not stop leaking through; they came not through a hole that could be plugged but through a permeable spot in a membrane, steadily, purely, endlessly, fruitfully. They became, his tears, a shield for himself against these others—their faces, the fact of their assembly, a last time as innocents, at a table where he sat the last time as head. Tears dropped from his nose as he broke the lobster's back; salt flavored his champagne as he sipped it; the raw clench at the back of his throat was delicious. He could not help himself.

His children tried to ignore his tears. Judith, on his right, lit a cigarette, gazed upward in the direction of her too energetic, too sophisticated exhalation; on her other side, John earnestly bent his face to the extraction of the last morsels—legs, tail segments—from the scarlet corpse. Joan, at the opposite end of the table, glanced at him surprised, her reproach displaced by a quick grimace, of forgiveness, or of salute to his superior gift of strategy. Between them, Margaret, no longer called Bean, thirteen and large for her age, gazed from the other side of his pane of tears as if into a shopwindow at something she coveted—at her father, a crystalline heap of splinters and memories. It was not she, however, but John who, in the kitchen, as they cleared the plates and carapaces away, asked Joan the question: *"Why is Daddy crying?"*

Richard heard the question but not the murmured answer. Then he heard Bean cry, "Oh, no-oh!"—the faintly dramatized exclamation of one who had long expected it.

John returned to the table carrying a bowl of salad. He nodded tersely at his father and his lips shaped the conspiratorial words "She told."

"Told what?" Richard asked aloud, insanely.

The boy sat down as if to rebuke his father's distraction with the example of his own good manners and said quietly, "The separation."

Joan and Margaret returned; the child, in Richard's twisted vision, seemed diminished in size, and relieved, relieved to have had the boogeyman at last proved real. He called out to her—the distances at the table had grown immense—"You knew, you always knew," but the clenching at the back of his throat prevented him from making sense of it. From afar he heard Joan talking, levelly, sensibly, reciting what they had prepared: it was a separation for the summer, an experiment. She and Daddy both agreed it would be good for them; they needed space and time to think; they liked each other but did not make each other happy enough, somehow.

Judith, imitating her mother's factual tone, but in her youth off-key, too cool, said, "I think it's silly. You should either live together or get divorced."

Richard's crying, like a wave that has crested and crashed, had become tumultuous; but it was overtopped by another tumult, for John, who had been so reserved, now grew larger and larger at the table. Perhaps his younger sister's being credited with knowing set him off. "Why didn't you *tell* us?" he asked, in a large round voice quite unlike his own. "You should have *told* us you weren't getting along."

Richard was startled into attempting to force words through his tears. "We *do* get along, that's the trouble, so it doesn't show even to us—" "That we do not love each other" was the rest of the sentence; he couldn't finish it.

Joan finished for him, in her style. "And we've always, *especially*, loved our children."

John was not mollified. "What do you care about *us*?" he boomed. "We're just little things you *had*." His sisters' laughing forced a laugh from him, which he turned hard and parodistic: "Ha ha *ha*." Richard and Joan realized simultaneously that the child was drunk, on Judith's home-coming champagne. Feeling bound to keep the center of the stage, John took a cigarette from Judith's pack, poked it into his mouth, let it hang from his lower lip, and squinted like a gangster.

"You're not little things we had," Richard called to him. "You're the whole point. But you're grown. Or almost."

The boy was lighting matches. Instead of holding them to his cigarette (for they had never seen him smoke; being "good" had been his way of setting himself apart), he held them to his mother's face, closer and closer, for her to blow out. Then he lit the whole folder—a hiss and then a torch, held against his mother's face. Prismed by his tears, the flame filled Richard's vision; he didn't know how it was extinguished. He heard Margaret say, "Oh stop showing off," and saw John, in response, break the cigarette in two and put the halves entirely into his mouth and chew, sticking out his tongue to display the shreds to his sister.

Joan talked to him, reasoning—a fountain of reason, unintelligible. "Talked about it for years . . . our children must help us . . . Daddy and I both want . . ." As the boy listened, he carefully wadded a paper napkin into the leaves of his salad, fashioned a ball of paper and lettuce, and popped it into his mouth, looking around the table for the expected laughter. None came. Judith said, "Be mature," and dismissed a plume of smoke.

Richard got up from this stifling table and led the boy outside. Though the house was in twilight, the outdoors still brimmed with light, the long waste light of high summer. Both laughing, he supervised John's spitting out the lettuce and paper and tobacco into the pachysandra. He took him by the hand—a square gritty hand, but for its softness a man's. Yet, it held on. They ran together up into the field, past the tennis court. The raw banking left by the bulldozers was dotted with daisies. Past the court and a flat stretch where they used to play family baseball stood a soft green rise glorious in the sun, each weed and species of grass distinct as illumination on parchment. "I'm sorry, so sorry," Richard cried. "You were the only one who ever tried to help me with all the goddam jobs around this place."

Sobbing, safe within his tears and the champagne, John explained, "It's not just the separation, it's the whole crummy year, I *hate* that school, you can't make any friends, the history teacher's a scud."

They sat on the crest of the rise, shaking and warm from their tears but easier in their voices, and Richard tried to focus on the child's sad year—the weekdays long with homework, the weekends spent in his room with model airplanes, while his parents murmured down below, nursing their separation. How selfish, how blind, Richard thought; his eyes felt scoured. He told his son, "We'll think about getting you transferred. Life's too short to be miserable."

They had said what they could, but did not want the moment to heal, and talked on, about the school, about the tennis court, whether it would ever again be as good as it had been that first summer. They walked to inspect it and pressed a few more tapes more firmly down. A little stiltedly, perhaps trying to make too much of the moment, to prolong it, Richard led the boy to the spot in the field where the view was best, of the metallic blue river, the emerald marsh, the scattered islands velvet with shadow in the low light, the white bits of beach far away. "See," he said. "It goes on being beautiful. It'll be here tomorrow."

"I know," John answered, impatiently. The moment had closed.

Back in the house, the others had opened some white

wine, the champagne being drunk, and still sat at the table, the three females, gossiping. Where Joan sat had become the head. She turned, showing him a tearless face, and asked, "All right?"

"We're fine," he said, resenting it, though relieved, that the party went on without him.

In bed she explained, "I couldn't cry I guess because I cried so much all spring. It really wasn't fair. It's your idea, and you made it look as though I was kicking you out."

"I'm sorry," he said. "I couldn't stop. I wanted to but couldn't."

"You *didn't* want to. You loved it. You were having your way, making a general announcement."

"I love having it over," he admitted. "God, those kids were great. So brave and funny. John, returned to the house, had settled to a model airplane in his room, and kept shouting down to them, "I'm O.K. No sweat." "And the way," Richard went on, cozy in his relief, "they never questioned the reasons we gave. No thought of a third person. Not even Judith."

"That *was* touching," Joan said.

He gave her a hug. "You were great too. Thank you." Guiltily, he realized he did not feel separated.

"You still have Dickie to do," she told him. These words set before him a black mountain in the darkness; its cold breath, its near weight affected his chest. Of the four children Dickie was most nearly his conscience. Joan did not need to add, "That's one piece of your dirty work I won't do for you."

"I know. I'll do it. You go to sleep."

Within minutes, her breathing slowed, became oblivious and deep. It was quarter to midnight. Dickie's train from the concert would come in at one-fourteen. Richard set the alarm for one. He had slept atrociously for weeks. But whenever he closed his lids some glimpse of the last hours scorched them—Judith exhaling toward the ceiling in a kind of aversion, Bean's mute staring, the sunstruck growth of the field where he and John had rested. The mountain before him moved closer, moved within him; he was huge, momentous. The ache at the back of his throat felt stale. His wife slept as if slain beside him. When, exasperated by his hot lids, his crowded heart, he rose from bed and dressed, she awoke enough to turn over. He told her then, "If I could undo it all, I would."

"Where would you begin?" she asked. There was no place. Giving him courage, she was always giving him courage. He put on shoes without socks in the dark. The children were breathing in their rooms, the downstairs was hollow. In their confusion they had left lights burning. He turned off all but one, the kitchen overhead. The car started. He had hoped it wouldn't. He met only moonlight on the road; it seemed a diaphanous companion, flickering in the leaves along the roadside, haunting his rearview mirror like a pursuer, melting under his headlights. The center of town, not quite deserted, was eerie at this hour. A young cop in uniform kept company with a gang of T-shirted kids on the steps of the bank. Across from the railroad station, several bars kept open. Customers, mostly young, passed in and out of the warm night, savoring summer's novelty. Voices shouted from cars as they passed; an immense conversation seemed in progress. Richard parked and in his weariness put his head on the passenger seat, out of the commotion and wheeling lights. It was as when, in the movies, an assassin grimly carries his mission through the jostle of a carnival—except the movies cannot show the precipitous, palpable slope you cling to within. You cannot climb back down; you can only fall. The synthetic fabric of the car seat, warmed by his cheek, confided to him an ancient, distant scent of vanilla.

A train whistle caused him to lift his head. It was on time; he had hoped it would be late. The slender drawgates descended. The bell of approach tingled happily. The great metal body, horizontally fluted, rocked to a stop, and sleepy teen-agers disembarked, his son among them. Dickie did not show surprise that his father was meeting him at this terrible hour. He sauntered to the car with two friends, both taller than he. He said "Hi" to his father and took the passenger's seat with an exhausted promptness that expressed gratitude. The friends got into the back, and Richard was grateful; a few more minutes' postponement would be won by driving them home.

He asked, "How was the concert?"

"Groovy," one boy said from the back seat.

"It bit," the other said.

"It was O.K.," Dickie said, moderate by nature, so reasonable that in his childhood the unreason of the world had given him headaches, stomach aches, nausea. When the second friend had been dropped off at his dark house, the boy blurted, "Dad, my eyes are killing me with hay fever! I'm out there cutting that mothering grass all day!"

"Do we still have those drops?"

"They didn't do any good last summer."

"They might this." Richard swung a U-turn on the empty street. The drive home took a few minutes. The mountain was here, in his throat. "Richard," he said, and felt the boy, slumped and rubbing his eyes, go tense at his tone, "I didn't come to meet you just to make your life easier. I came because your mother and I have some news for you, and you're a hard man to get ahold of these days. It's sad news."

"That's O.K." The reassurance came out soft, but quick, as if released from the tip of a spring.

Richard had feared that his tears would return and choke him, but the boy's manliness set an example, and his voice issued forth steady and dry. "It's sad news, but it needn't be tragic news, at least for you. It should have no practical effect on your life, though it's bound to have an emotional effect. You'll work at your job, and go back to school in

September. Your mother and I are really proud of what you're making of your life; we don't want that to change at all."

"Yeah," the boy said lightly, on the intake of his breath, holding himself up. They turned the corner; the church they went to loomed like a gutted fort. The home of the woman Richard hoped to marry stood across the green. Her bedroom light burned.

"Your mother and I," he said, "have decided to separate. For the summer. Nothing legal, no divorce yet. We want to see how it feels. For some years now, we haven't been doing enough for each other, making each other as happy as we should be. Have you sensed that?"

"No," the boy said. It was an honest, unemotional answer: true or false in a quiz.

Glad for a factual basis, Richard pursued, even garrulously, the details. His apartment across town, his utter accessibility, the split vacation arrangements, the advantages to the children, the added mobility and variety of the summer. Dickie listened, absorbing. "Do the others know?"

Richard described how they had been told.

"How did they take it?"

"The girls pretty calmly. John flipped out; he shouted and ate a cigarette and made a salad out of his napkin and told us how much he hated school."

His brother chuckled. "He did?"

"Yeah. The school issue was more upsetting for him than Mom and me. He seemed to feel better for having exploded."

"He did?" The repetition was the first sign that he was stunned.

"Yes. Dickie, I want to tell you something. This last hour, waiting for your train to get in, has been about the worst of my life. I hate this. *Hate* it. My father would have died before doing it to me." He felt immensely lighter, saying this. He had dumped the mountain on the boy. They were home. Moving swiftly as a shadow, Dickie was out of the car, through the bright kitchen. Richard called after him, "Want a glass of milk or anything?"

"No thanks."

"Want us to call the course tomorrow and say you're too sick to work?"

"No, that's all right." The answer was faint, delivered at the door to his room; Richard listened for the slam of a tantrum. The door closed normally. The sound was sickening.

Joan had sunk into that first deep trough of sleep and was slow to awake. Richard had to repeat, "I told him."

"What did he say?"

"Nothing much. Could you go say good night to him? Please."

She left their room, without putting on a bathrobe. He sluggishly changed back into his pajamas and walked down the hall. Dickie was already in bed, Joan was sitting beside him, and the boy's bedside clock radio was murmuring music. When she stood, an inexplicable light—the moon?— outlined her body through the nightie. Richard sat on the warm place she had indented on the child's narrow mattress. He asked him, "Do you want the radio on like that?"

"It always is."

"Doesn't it keep you awake? It would me."

"No."

"Are you sleepy?"

"Yeah."

"Good. Sure you want to get up and go to work? You've had a big night."

"I want to."

Away at school this winter he had learned for the first time that you can go short of sleep and live. As an infant he had slept with an immobile, sweating intensity that had alarmed his babysitters. As the children aged, he became the first to go to bed, earlier for a time than his younger brother and sister. Even now, he would go slack in the middle of a television show, his sprawled legs hairy and brown. "O.K. Good boy. Dickie, listen. I love you so much, I never knew how much until now. No matter how this works out, I'll always be with you. Really."

Richard bent to kiss an averted face but his son, sinewy, turned and with wet cheeks embraced him and gave him a kiss, on the lips, passionate as a woman's. In his father's ear he moaned one word, the crucial, intelligent word: *"Why?"*

Why. It was a whistle of wind in a crack, a knife thrust, a window thrown open on emptiness. The white face was gone, the darkness was featureless. Richard had forgotten why.

ABOUT THE AUTHORS

DONALD BARTHELME was born in Philadelphia in 1931, grew up in Texas, and lives now in Greenwich Village. He has worked as a newspaper reporter, museum director, editor, teacher, and public relations director for a university, and he served in the army in Korea and Japan. Now he makes his living as a writer, displaying a unique gift for social satire regularly in *The New Yorker*. He has published two novels, *Snow White* (1967) and *The Dead Father* (1975), and several collections of short pieces: *Come Back, Dr. Caligari* (1964), *Unspeakable Practices, Unnatural Acts* (1968), *City Life* (1970), *Sadness* (1972), *Guilty Pleasures* (1974), and *Great Days* (1979). His children's book, *The Slightly Irregular Fire Engine or The Hithering Thithering Djinn* received a National Book Award in 1972. Wrote Richard Todd in *The Atlantic*, "If [Barthelme] addresses himself mainly to sufferers of contemporary spiritual malaise, he is particularly merciless on the language that is used to describe that illness. . . ." Says Anatole Broyard, "Where Kafka erected a castle to house his anxieties, Barthelme has opened a boutique. The reduction in scale is not Barthelme's fault. Nobody builds castles anymore . . ."

ANN BEATTIE writes, "I was once the editor of the literary magazine at American University. I didn't write very well. I left American University and went to graduate school at the University of Connecticut, where I studied literature and didn't enjoy it very much, but where I met J. D. O'Hara, who taught me how to write a lot better." She taught at Connecticut for four years, and started sending stories out. *The Atlantic* bought one. After twenty or so rejections, *The New Yorker* did too, then bought several more. In 1976 her first two books were published simultaneously: *Chilly Scenes of Winter*, a novel, and *Distortions*, a collection of stories. Writing of the novel in *The New York Times Book Review*, J. D. O'Hara said: "Beattie renews for us the commonplaces . . . of the life of quiet desperation." "Wanda's" has some of the slightly offbeat quality of the early Eudora Welty stories. Another collection of stories, *Secrets and Surprises*, was published in 1978.

DORIS BETTS was born in 1932 and brought up in North Carolina's Piedmont country, and teaches in the English department at the Chapel Hill campus of the University of North Carolina. She has published three novels, *Tall Houses in Winter* (1957), *The Scarlet Thread* (1964), and *The River to Pickle Beach* (1972), and three short-story collections, *The Gentle Insurrection* (1954), *The Astronomer and Other Stories* (1966), and *Beasts of the Southern Wild and Other Stories* (1973), a finalist for the National Book Award. She was little known until *The River to Pickle Beach* was published and received more than the usual amount of hoopla. Jonathan Yardley wrote at the time that Doris Betts "is a tough, wise, and compassionate writer . . . with a firm hold on what we in the South call 'home truths.' "

ROSELLEN BROWN, who has moved around a lot, lived in Mississippi in the mid-sixties when she taught in a black college and started writing. Out of the Mississippi years came her first book, *Some Deaths in the Delta and Other Poems* (1970). In the late sixties she lived in Brooklyn, the setting for the loosely connected stories in *Street Games* (1974), from which "I Am Not Luis Beech-Nut" is reprinted. She was living in New Hampshire when her first novel, *The Autobiography of My Mother* (1964), was published. Another novel, *Tender Mercies*, was published in 1978. She writes, "Began announcing at age 8 or 9 that I was going to be a writer and, only semi-liberated, always added that it seemed to be a good career for a woman because I could do it 'at home and still manage marriage and children. Was entirely too smug about that at 9, but it *is* what I'm doing."

BRUCE JAY FRIEDMAN was born in New York City in 1930, a Jewish boy whose education at the predominantly non-Jewish University of Missouri provided material for the black humor of *Far from the City of Class and Other Stories* (1963). *Time* described his first book, *Stern* (1962), as "a strange, touching little first novel . . . about being Jewish in a lawn-proud suburb of mid-century, middle-class America." In his second novel, *A Mother's Kisses* (1964), he took on Mother Love. Writing from what one critic called "the frazzled deeps of his being," Friedman produced another short-story collection, *Black Angels* (1966), two successful stage plays, *Scuba Duba* (1967) and *Steambath* (1970), and screenplays. In the sixties his hero was commonly a *schlemiel* trying to live out the bourgeois-American Jewish dream. In *About Harry Towns* (1974), the hero has become a middle-aged screenwriter hooked on cocaine, suffering a broken marriage, and not yet quite accustomed to poolside sessions at the Beverly Hills hotel. His book of wry sketches, *The Lonely Guy's Book of Life*, was published in 1978.

ERNEST J. GAINES was born on a Louisiana plantation in 1933, spent part of his childhood working in the fields, and moved with his family to Vallejo, California, at the age of fifteen. After two years in the army, he received a B.A. from San Francisco State, then studied creative writing at Stanford University. His second novel, *Of Love and Dust* (1967), was a tense story about the power struggle between a white overseer and a black man who is sent to work on his plantation while awaiting trial for murder. The editors of *Dark Symphony*, an anthology of black writing in which his work appears, wrote: "Gaines, who thinks that the artist is the only free man left in the world, has so far been concerned in his fiction (usually about rural Louisiana) with individuals determined, often heroically, . . . to maintain their codes of conduct among debasing or confusing forces" or to face the consequences of changing with the times. The collection *Bloodline* (1968) contains five stories about the rural South, including "The Sky Is Gray" (reprinted here) and a fine short novel, *A Long Day in November*. In the novel *The Autobiography of Miss Jane Pittman* (1971), Gaines tried to capture the black experience in America; its dramatization on television with Cicely Tyson in the lead role brought Gaines national recognition.

BERNARD MALAMUD, born in Brooklyn in 1914, has combined a writing career with life as a teacher. His fiction deals with urban Jews, a natural symbol for his favorite theme: redemption through suffering. Malamud's style ranges from stark realism to an imaginative, even dreamlike symbolism, sometimes tragic, sometimes comic, often both. His novels include *The Natural* (1952), *The Assistant* (1957), *A New Life* (1961), *The Fixer* (1966), *The Tenants* (1971), and *Dubin's Lives* (1979). His short stories have been collected in *The Magic Barrel* (1958), *Idiots First* (1963), *Pictures of Fidelman* (1969), and *Rembrandt's Hat* (1973). He received a National Book Award for *The Magic Barrel*, and *The Fixer* won both the National Book Award and the Pulitzer Prize.

JOYCE CAROL OATES, born in Lockport, New York, in 1938, has, like Malamud, combined college teaching with a prolific writing career. Wrote Calvin Bedient in *The New York Times Book Review*, "Oates is a potent myth-maker in the drab guise of a social naturalist. . . . The focus of her myth—like that of Emily Bronte and Lawrence—is the greed, the overreaching, the 'experimental' excitement, in human relationships. . . . Her fiction [is] striking in its relentless and subtle pursuit of psychological observation . . . cautiously original in technique, and boldly indifferent to formal intentness . . . propelled forward by successive new impetuses, in the jagged rhythm of life." Her novels include *With Shuddering Fall* (1964), *A Garden of Earthly Delights* (1967), *Expensive People* (1968), *Them* (winner of the National Book Award in 1970), *Wonderland* (1971), *Do With Me What You Will* (1973), and *Son of the Morning* (1978). Story collections include *By the North Gate* (1963), *Upon the Sweeping Flood* (1966), *The Wheel of Love and Other Stories* (1970), and *Marriages and Infidelities* (1972). She also writes poetry and criticism.

FLANNERY O'CONNOR (1925–1964) was born and lived her life in Georgia, where her Catholic family had lived for generations. She saw her duty as a Catholic writer to reveal unsparingly those distortions of modern life which we have come to view as natural ("my subject in fiction is the action of grace in territory held largely by the devil") and, as Alfred Kazin observed, she saw the South as a metaphor for the Fall of Man. She had a sharp ear for the rhythms of rural dialect and a deadly eye for the quirks of human behavior. She saw Ruby Turpin in "Revelation" as "one of those country women . . . who just sort of springs to life; you can't hold them down or shut their mouths," but told a friend not to mistake Ruby for "just an evil Glad Annie." In her lifetime she published two short novels, *The Violent Bear It Away* (1960) and *Wise Blood* (1962), and two collections of short stories, *A Good Man Is Hard to Find* (1955) and *Everything That Rises Must Converge* (1965). After her death at the age of thirty-nine from a long and painful illness, lupus erythematosus, her collected stories (*The Complete Stories*) were published in 1971. A collection of her letters, *The Habit of Being*, was published in 1979.

CYNTHIA OZICK was born in New York City in 1928, studied at New York University and Ohio State University, and has taught literature courses at several universities. She has published one novel, *Trust* (1966), and two collections of short fiction: *The Pagan Rabbi and Other Stories* (1971) and *Bloodshed and Three Novellas* (1976). She has also written poetry, essays, criticism, and translations, and has made many public appearances to encourage a Jewish literature with meaningful ties to the Jewish past and Jewish languages. A *Newsweek* reviewer noted that one of the major themes of her stories is "living fraudulently, whether by ignorance or design," which she treats as both comic and sad

PETER TAYLOR was born in Tennessee in 1919, taught for several years at the University of North Carolina at Chapel Hill, and teaches now at the University of Virginia. He has written several plays and one novel, *A Woman of Means* (1950), but is known chiefly for his short stories, fine character studies which often portray "familiar" (family) relationships among Tennessee's middle class, and the pain and loneliness attending radical changes in Southern culture. Writes James Penney Smith: "His 'acceptable' subject matter, his quiet style, his indirection and understatement are profoundly unlike the sensationalism, contortion, and richly suggestive language of some of his fellow Southerners. His people are not grotesque, his action is not violent, his language is not flamboyant. Mr. Taylor's strongest impact comes through the quiet revelation of the unconscious complexity of human motivation, and his knowledge of the limited vision which determines our simplest actions." His stories have been collected in *A Long Fourth and Other Stories* (1948), *The Widows of Thornton* (1954), *Happy Families Are All Alike* (1959), *Miss Leonora When Last Seen and Fifteen Other Stories* (1963), *The Collected Stories of Peter Taylor* (1969), and *In the Miro District and Other Stories* (1977).

JOHN UPDIKE was born in 1932 in Shillington, Pennsylvania, the "Olinger" of many of his stories. He attended Harvard (graduating *summa cum laude*) because he wanted to draw cartoons for the *Lampoon* and eventually for *The New Yorker*. Instead he has become one of *The New Yorker*'s most famous writers, a stylistic virtuoso who, as Richard Locke put it, writes about "the inner surface of banal experiences." "My subject," he told Jane Howard in 1966, "is the American Protestant small-town middle class. I like middles. It is in middles that extremes clash, where ambiguity restlessly rules. . . . There's a 'yes-but' quality about my writing that evades entirely pleasing anybody. It seems to me that critics get increasingly querulous and impatient for madder music and stronger wine, when what we need is a greater respect for reality, its secrecy, its music." He has written ten novels, includ- ing *Rabbit, Run* (1960), *Of the Farm* (1965), *Couples* (1968), *Rabbit Redux* (1971), *A Month of Sundays* (1975), *The Poorhouse Fair* (1977), and *The Coup* (1978). He has also published verse, parodies, reviews, children's books, a play, and six collections of stories: *The Same Door* (1959), *Pigeon Feathers* (1962), *The Music School* (1966), *Bech: A Book* (1970), *Museums and Women* (1972), and *Too Far to Go: The Maples Stories* (1979), in which "Separating" is reprinted. He received the National Book Award for his novel *The Centaur* (1963).

RICHARD YATES was born in Yonkers, New York, in 1926, and has spent much of his life in and around New York City, except for time spent in Europe in the early 1950s, when he wrote the story reprinted here. Yates served in the infantry in World War II, and to support his fiction writing has worked at various jobs: journal- ism, publicity, ghostwriting, and writing for television, the movies, and industrial and technical publications. He has published five novels: *Revolutionary Road* (1961), *A Special Providence* (1969), *Disturbing the Peace* (1975), *Easter Parade* (1976), and *A Good School* (1978). One collection of short stories, *Eleven Kinds of Loneliness*, came out in 1962, and he is at work on a collection of stories and novellas.

PAT McNEES, who worked several years as an editor in book publishing, retired to write free-lance (for *New York* and other magazines) when her daughter was born. She began editing short-story anthologies because they could be done from New York City sandboxes. Her two previous collections are *Contemporary Latin American Short Stories* (1974) and *Friday's Child* (1977).

TRENT BATSON, who is married to Pat McNees, is director of the American Studies program at Gallaudet College, a school for the deaf. He and Eugene Bergman edited the collection *The Deaf Experience* (1976).